Joseph Teller was born and raised in New York City. After graduating from law school, he spent three years working undercover for the Federal Bureau of Narcotics. For the next thirty-five years he was a criminal defence lawyer. Not too long ago he decided to "run from the law" and began writing fiction. *The Tenth Case*, his first novel for MIRA Books, will be followed by further Jaywalker titles.

THE TENTH CASE

Joseph Teller

MIRA

*MIRA is a registered trademark of Harlequin Enterprises Limited,
used under licence.*

*Published in Great Britain 2009.
MIRA Books, Eton House, 18-24 Paradise Road,
Richmond, Surrey, TW9 1SR*

© Joseph Teller 2008

ISBN 978 0 7783 0308 4

58-0809

*MIRA's policy is to use papers that are natural, renewable and
recyclable products and made from wood grown in sustainable
forests. The logging and manufacturing processes conform to the
legal environmental regulations of the country of origin.*

*Printed and bound in Spain
by Litografia Rosés S.A., Barcelona*

It struck me on my latest birthday that I've now reached the same age at which my father left this life, much too soon. He was a physician who specialised in obstetrics, a five-foot-tall "baby doctor" in more ways than one. He was revered by his staff and colleagues, and absolutely adored by his patients. To this day, I run into people who, upon learning that his last name and mine are not mere coincidence, scream with delight, "Oh, my God. He delivered my children!" or occasionally "He delivered me!"

Not that my father was without faults, by any means. He was a driven over-achiever in everything he did, which meant getting the best grades in school, baiting a fishhook just so and running out a grounder on the baseball diamond at full speed. He was a true perfectionist, an early-day obsessive-compulsive.

He was, in a word, a Jaywalker.

ACKNOWLEDGEMENTS

I am indebted to my editor Leslie Wainger and executive editor Margaret O'Neill Marbury, as well as assistant editor Adam Wilson, for their faith in me and their excitement over my alter ego, Jaywalker. I am grateful to my literary agent and friend Bob Diforio for having been smart enough to put us together.

My wife, Sandy, deserves credit for nearly gagging when I told her about a terrific idea I had for a book, and making me trash it and write this one instead.

And to my friends and former colleagues down at 100 Centre Street, many of whom I still hear from, I thank you for the camaraderie you showed me in the trenches, and for the stories you shared with me over the years, some of which may even have crept into these pages.

1

A SPONTANEOUS ACT OF GRATITUDE

"We turn now to the issue of what constitutes an appropriate punishment for your various infractions," said the judge in the middle, the gray-haired one whose name Jaywalker always had trouble remembering. "Disbarment certainly occurred to us, and would no doubt be fully deserved, were it not for your long years of service to the bar, your quite obvious devotion to your clients, as well as your considerable legal skills, reflected in your current string of, what was it you told us? Ten consecutive acquittals?"

"Eleven, actually," said Jaywalker.

"Eleven. Very impressive. That said, a substantial period of suspension is still in order. A very substantial period. Your transgressions are simply too numerous, and too serious, to warrant anything less. Bringing in a lookalike for a defendant in order to confuse a witness, for example. Impersonating a judge to trick a police officer into turning over his notes. Breaking into the evidence room in order to have your own chemist analyze some narcotics. Referring to a judge, *on the record,* as—and I shall paraphrase here—*a small portion of excrement.* And finally, though by no means least of all, receiving, shall we say, a 'sexual favor' from a client in the stairwell of the courthouse—"

"It wasn't a sexual favor, Your Honor."

"Please don't interrupt me."

"Sorry, sir."

"And you can deny it all you want, but my colleagues and I have been forced to watch the videotape from the surveillance camera several times through—complete, I might add, with what appears to be you *moaning*. Now I don't know what *you* would call it, but—"

"It was nothing but a spontaneous act of gratitude, Your Honor, from an overly appreciative client. She'd just been acquitted of a trumped-up prostitution charge. And if only there'd been a sound track, you'd know I wasn't moaning at all. I was saying, *'No! No! No!'*"

Actually, there was some truth to that.

"Are you a married man, Mr. Jaywalker?"

"I'm a widower, sir. As a matter of fact, I'd been distraught over my wife's death."

"I see." That seemed to give the judge pause, though only briefly. "When did she die?"

"It was a Thursday. June ninth, I believe."

"This year?"

"Uh, no, sir."

"Last year?"

"No."

There was an awkward silence.

"This *millennium?*"

"Not exactly."

"I see," said the judge.

Sternbridge, that was his name. Should have been easy enough for Jaywalker to have remembered.

"The court," Sternbridge was saying now, "hereby suspends you from the practice of law for a period of three years, following which you shall be required to reapply to the Committee on Character and Fitness." He raised his gavel. But Jaywalker, who'd been to an auction or two with his late wife, back in the previous millennium, beat him to it just before he could bring the thing down.

"If it please the court?"

Sternbridge peered at him over his reading glasses, momentarily disarmed by Jaywalker's rare lapse into courtspeak. Jaywalker took that as an invitation to continue.

"In spite of the fact that I knew this day of reckoning was coming, Your Honor, I find I still have a number of pending cases. Many involve clients in extremely precarious situations. These are people who've put their lives in my hands. While I'm fully prepared to accept the court's punishment, I beg you to let me see these matters through to completion. Please, *please,* don't take out your dissatisfaction with me on these helpless people. Add a year to my suspension, if you like. Add two. But let me finish helping them."

The three judges mumbled to each other, then swiveled around on their chairs and huddled, their black-robed backs to the courtroom. When they swung back a minute later, it was the one on the right, the woman named Ellerbee, who addressed Jaywalker.

"You will be permitted to complete five cases," she said. "Provide us with a list of those you choose to retain by the end of court business tomorrow, complete with a docket or indictment number, the judge to which each case is assigned, and the next scheduled court date. The remainder of your clients will be reassigned to other counsel. As for the five cases you'll be keeping, you'll be required to appear before us the first Friday of every month, so that you can give us a detailed progress report on your efforts to dispose of them."

Dispose of them. Didn't she understand that these weren't diapers or toilet paper or plastic razors? They were *people.*

"Understood?" Judge Ellerbee was asking him.

"Understood," said Jaywalker. "And—"

"What?"

"Thank you."

* * *

That night, working in his cramped, poorly lit office well past midnight, Jaywalker did his best to pare the list down. But it was like having to choose which people to throw out of a life raft. How could he abandon a fourteen-year-old kid who'd trusted him enough to accept a year-long commitment to a residential drug program? Or an illegal alien facing deportation to the Sudan for the unforgivable crime of selling ladies' handbags with an expired vendor's permit? Or a homeless woman fighting for the right to visit her two small children in a shelter once a month? How did he tell a former gang member that the lawyer it had taken him two years to open up to and confide in was suddenly going to be replaced by a name chosen at random off a computer-generated list? How would he write to a completely innocent inmate doing fifteen-to-life in Sing Sing to say that he wouldn't be getting an attorney's visit any longer, come the first Saturday of the month? Or a retarded janitor's helper that his next lawyer might not be willing to hold his hand and squeeze it tightly each time they stood before the judge, so the poor man wouldn't have to shake uncontrollably and wet his pants in front of a courtroom of laughing strangers?

In the end, with a great deal of difficulty, Jaywalker managed to get the list down to a pretty manageable seventeen names. He printed it out and submitted it to the judges the following afternoon, along with a lengthy apology that it was the best he could possibly do, followed by a fervent appeal to their understanding. A week later, a letter arrived from the court, informing him that the court had trimmed the list down to ten, and warning him not to drag out any of the cases unnecessarily.

2

JAYWALKER

His name wasn't really Jaywalker, of course. Once it had been Harrison J. Walker. But he hated Harrison, which had struck him as overly pretentious and WASPy, for as long as he could remember being aware of such things. And he hated *Harry* even more, associating it with a bald head, a potbelly and the stub of a day-old cigar. So, long ago, he'd taken to calling himself Jay Walker, and somewhere along the line someone had blurred that into Jaywalker. Which had been all right with him; the truth was, he'd never had the patience to stand on a curb waiting for a light without a pair of eyes of its own to tell him whether it was safe to cross or not, or the discipline to walk from midblock to corner to midblock again, all in order to end up directly across from where he'd started out in the first place. He answered his office phone (his soon-to-be *former* office phone) "Jaywalker," responded unthinkingly to "Mr. Jaywalker," and when asked on some form or other to supply a *surname* or a *given name* (for the life of him, he'd never been able to figure out which was which), he simply wrote "Jaywalker" in both blanks, resulting in a small but not insignificant portion of his mail arriving addressed to "Mr. Jaywalker Jaywalker." It was sort of like being Major Major, he decided, or Woolly Woolly. Names, he'd come to believe, were vastly overrated.

His office wasn't really an office at all. What it was, was a room in a suite of offices that surrounded a center hallway, which in turn served as a combination conference room, library and lunchroom. The arrangement, which was repeated throughout the building and a dozen others in the area, enabled sole practitioners such as himself to practice on a shoestring. For five hundred dollars the first of the month, he got a place to put a desk, a couple of chairs, a secondhand couch, a clothes tree, and some cardboard boxes that he liked to think of as portable file cabinets. On top of the desk went his phone, his answering machine, his computer, various piles of paper and faded photos of his departed wife and semi-estranged daughter. For no extra charge, he got the use of not only the aforementioned conference/library/lunchroom, but a modest waiting room, a receptionist, a copier and a fax machine, all circa 1995, except for the receptionist, who was considerably older.

There was no restroom in the suite, only a MEN'S and a WOMEN'S down the hall and past the elevator bank. On nights when Jaywalker ended up sleeping on the sofa—and since there was nobody back at his apartment to go home to, those nights were more than occasional, especially when he was in the midst of a trial—the men's room was where he brushed his teeth, washed his face and shaved. It was only the absence of a shower, in fact, that forced him to go home as often as he did.

Jaywalker's suitemates (a word he'd grown especially fond of, ever since the spellcheck feature on his computer had tried to correct it to *sodomites*) included two P.I. lawyers (the initials standing for *personal injury,* a considerably more polite designation than the also-used A.C. for *ambulance chaser*); an immigration practitioner named Herman Greenberg, who, in a stroke of marketing genius, had had his business cards printed on green card stock,

forever earning himself the aka Herman Greencard; a bank-
ruptcy specialist known in-house as "Fuck-the-Creditors"
Feinblatt; an older guy who did nothing but chain-smoke,
cough, read the *Law Journal* and handle real estate clos-
ings; and a woman who didn't seem to do much of anything
at all but wait for her next Big Case to walk through the
door, her last Big Case having walked out the door fifteen
years ago.

Jaywalker was the only criminal defense lawyer in the
suite. For one reason or another, criminal defense lawyers
have always been pretty much solo practitioners, and those
who've attempted to organize them into groups or associa-
tions, or even gather them under a single roof, have tended
to come away from the experience feeling as though
they've been trying to line up snakes single file.

But flying solo had always suited Jaywalker just fine.
He'd spent two years at the Legal Aid Society, where he'd
found quite enough collegiality, and nearly enough
bedmates, to last him a lifetime. There he'd also learned
how to try a case—or, more precisely, how *not* to.

Once he'd cut the cord and gone out into private
practice, Jaywalker had gradually retaught himself. Over
the next twenty years, he earned a reputation as a renegade
among renegades. It was almost as though he was determined to give new meaning to the term *unorthodox.* He
broke every rule in the book, defied all the axioms ever
preached about how to try a case, and in the process
managed to infuriate at least a score of seasoned prosecutors and otherwise unflappable judges. But he also built a
record unlike anything ever seen outside Hollywood or
television land. In a business where district attorneys'
offices routinely boasted of conviction rates of anywhere
from sixty-five to ninety-five percent, and where many
defense lawyers heard the words *Not guilty* only at an arraignment, Jaywalker achieved an acquittal rate of just
over ninety percent.

How did he do it?

If asked, he probably couldn't have explained it nearly as well as he did it. But those who watched him work on a regular basis—and there was a large and growing number who did—invariably pointed to a single phenomenon. By the time a Jaywalker jury retired to deliberate on a case, they'd come to understand, *truly* understand, that it wasn't their job to figure out whether or not the defendant had committed the crime. Rather, it was their job to figure out whether, based upon the evidence produced in the courtroom, or the *lack* of such evidence, the prosecution had succeeded in *proving* that the defendant had committed the crime, and whether it had done so beyond all reasonable doubt.

The difference proved to be staggering.

By the time he stood before the three judges who would deliver his punishment, Jaywalker had become something of a legend in his own time at 100 Centre Street. But his success hadn't come without a price. For one thing, he drove himself relentlessly, demanding of himself that he come into court not only better prepared than his adversary but *ten* times better prepared, *fifty* times better prepared. He slept almost not at all when he was on trial, and when he did, it was with pen and paper within reach, so that he could jot down random thoughts in the dark and try to decipher them come morning. He planned for every conceivable contingency, agonized over every detail, and organized with the fanaticism of the obsessive-compulsive he was. Walking out of the courthouse after yet another acquittal, he would look upward and utter thanks to a god he didn't believe in, followed by a prayer that he might never have to go through the ordeal another time.

But, of course, there always was another time.

His remarkable record, even as it earned him the admiration of his colleagues in the criminal defense bar, also created a problem for them, in much the same way that the acquittal of a former football star and minor celebrity, three thousand miles away and a decade earlier, had created a problem for them. "If he can do it," their clients demanded to know, "why can't you?" It was perhaps no surprise, therefore, that many of those who'd attended Jaywalker's punishment hearing, almost all of whom admired him on a professional level, liked him personally and in most respects truly wished him well, also secretly rejoiced at the thought of being rid of him, if only for a while.

But even to the most relieved of them, three years had seemed like a rather stiff suspension for blowing off a few rules and succumbing to something that didn't sound so different, when you got right down to it.

All of that had been back in September.

It had taken Jaywalker until the following June, and the ninth first-Friday-of-the-month appearance before the three-judge panel, to report that he'd succeeded in *disposing of* virtually all of his remaining clients.

The fourteen-year-old kid in the drug program was now fifteen, drug-free and in aftercare. The Sudanese handbag salesman had been granted permanent residence status, thanks to a little help from Herman Greencard. The homeless woman had an apartment of her own, a job and custody of her two children. The former gang member had relapsed, jumped bail and fled to southern California, from where he sent Jaywalker postcards picturing scantily-clad (or nonclad) sunbathers. The Sing Sing inmate's appeal had been heard, and a decision was expected shortly. The pants-wetter's case had been dismissed. A drunk driver had pleaded guilty to operating a motor vehicle while impaired. A minor drug dealer had settled for a sentence of probation. And a three-card-monte player had been acquitted once Jaywalker had convinced a jury that the man's skill in conning his victims was so consummate that it completely negated the "game of chance" element required by the language of the statute.

Nine months, nine cases, nine clients, nine pretty good results.

Leaving exactly one.

Samara Moss.

3

SAMARA

Her name was Samara Moss, and she was a gold digger. At least that had been the universal consensus of the tabloids, ever since she'd set her sights on Barrington Tannenbaum. That had been nine years earlier, when Tannenbaum had been sixty-one. He'd made his fortune buying and selling oil and gas leases, than made it multiply several times over in the shipping business. Among the things he'd shipped were munitions, body armor and jet fighter planes. He had a short list of clients, but most of them had titles like "Sultan" or "His Excellency" before their names. Tannenbaum's net worth had once been estimated at somewhere in the range of ten to twenty billion dollars.

Samara's net worth, at the time she married Tannenbaum, had been somewhere in the range of ten to twenty dollars.

She'd grown up in a third-rate trailer park in Indiana, where she'd become so accustomed to hearing the phrase *trailer trash* that she no longer considered it an insult, much the way ghetto blacks think little of calling each other *nigger*. She was raised by a single mother who alternately waited tables, bartended and lap-danced at night, leaving Sam—as everyone had called her for as long as she could remember—in the care of a string of boyfriends. Some of those boyfriends ignored her; others taught her how to drink beer, curse and do drugs. By the time she was ten, Sam could roll a perfect joint, using either gummed or ungummed paper. At twelve, she was smoking the joints she rolled. To hear Sam tell it, several of those same boy-friends molested her on occasion, although the extent is unknown and the certainty remains unestablished to this day. Two things are clear, though. She was pretty enough to make her junior high school cheerleading squad at age twelve (no mean feat), and undisciplined enough to be kicked off it two months later.

She ran away from home the day after her fourteenth birthday, landing first in Ely, Nevada, then in Reno and finally in Las Vegas, with dreams of becoming a showgirl and eventually a Hollywood star. She became, instead, a cocktail waitress and sometime prostitute, though she would have been quick to deny the latter description, insisting that she went to bed only with nice men to whom she was attracted. Who was she to complain when some of them chose to express their admiration in the form of gifts, including the occasional monetary one?

It was in Las Vegas that Barrington Tannenbaum spied her, in the cocktail lounge at Caesars Palace, at three o'clock one Sunday morning. Barry was newly divorced at the time, a three-time loser at love. Although he was absurdly rich, he was also lonely, bored and as much in need of a project as Samara was in need of a sugar daddy. And one thing about Barry Tannenbaum—if you listened to his business associates or bitter rivals, most of whom counted themselves in both columns—was that once he got involved in a project, he never did so halfheartedly. From the moment he and Samara met, he was as determined to save her as she appeared determined to snare him. If it wasn't quite a match made in heaven, it certainly had an otherworldly ring to it.

It has been said that we are doomed to repeat our mistakes, and recent history had amply demonstrated that

Barry Tannenbaum was the marrying kind. The truth is that for all of his new money, Barry was an old-fashioned sort of guy. He'd grown up in an age when, if you loved the girl, you married her, had kids and lived happily ever after—even if *ever after* was something of a relative term. It's therefore not all that surprising that, in spite of his dismal track record, Barry felt compelled to make an honest woman of Sam, in the most old-fashioned sense of the expression. Eight months to the day after he'd first set eyes on her in the neon glow of Caesars Palace, he married her. By that time, he was sixty-two.

Samara was still not quite nineteen.

If the tabloids had had fun with the forty-two years and fifteen billion dollars that separated the couple, they weren't the only ones. It seems that gold diggers tend to arouse feelings of ambivalence in most of us. The hooker-turned-heroine played by Julia Roberts in *Pretty Woman* earns our unabashed cheers when she lands the wealthy Richard Gere character, but only because the script took care to make it clear that she didn't set out to do so from the start. Anna Nicole Smith, the Playmate of the Year and self-described "blond bombshell" who at twenty-six married an eighty-nine-year-old Texas billionaire, won considerably less public support. Still, there was an audible "You go, girl!" sentiment expressed by many when it appeared that Anna Nicole's stepson—himself old enough to be her grandfather—might have overreached in manipulating her out of his father's will. In a poll taken as the case headed toward the Supreme Court (polls having pretty much been established as the operative method of governance by the dawn of the twenty-first century), nearly forty percent of Americans with an opinion on the matter responded that Smith deserved all or most of the $474 million she sued for when her husband happened to die a year into their marriage.

Chances are Samara wouldn't have fared as well in the court of public opinion. For one thing, there was the fact that she lived with Tannenbaum for only the first of their eight years of marriage, quickly setting up residence in a town house just off Park Avenue, which she'd persuaded Barry to buy her because she'd never had a place of her own. The price tag had been $4.5 million. Small change, to be sure. But a wee bit unseemly, perhaps.

For another thing, there were the affairs Samara carried on, some with discretion, but others with an openness that bordered on outright flaunting. Not an issue of the *National Enquirer* hit the stands without an account of SAM'S LATEST FLING, more often than not accompanied by a photo of the cheating couple entering or exiting some trendy club, complete with an overabundance of calf or cleavage.

And finally, there was the small but not-to-be-over-looked detail of Samara's having taken an eight-inch steak knife and plunged it into her husband's chest, "piercing the left ventricle of his heart and causing his death," as recounted by the New York County District Attorney, and followed up in short order with a murder indictment handed down by a grand jury of Samara's peers.

Which was right about where Jaywalker had come in.

4

A SLIGHT MISCALCULATION

Not that Jaywalker was a total stranger to Samara Moss by any means. They'd met six years earlier, when she'd shown up at his office, delivered there by her chauffeur. Or Barry Tannenbaum's chauffeur, to be more precise. The thing was, Samara wasn't driving herself anywhere right then. Two weeks earlier she'd borrowed one of Barry's favorite toys, a $400,000 Lamborghini. And *borrowed* might be a stretch, seeing as she'd simply found the keys one evening, gone down to the twelve-car garage beneath Barry's Scarsdale mansion and taken off for Manhattan. She'd made it all the way to Park Avenue and 66th Street, when she realized she was a bit too far downtown and attempted a U-turn. Normally, one would execute that maneuver between the raised islands that separate the avenue's southbound lanes from its northbound ones. Samara, however, had attempted it mid-island, a slight miscalculation. The result had been a one-car, $400,000 accident, and an arrest for driving while intoxicated, reckless driving, refusal to submit to a blood-alcohol test, driving without a license, and a little-known and seldom-used Administrative Code violation entitled "Failure to Yield to a Stationary Object."

To woefully understate the fact, Barry had been mightily

pissed off. He'd posted Samara's bail, then assigned his chauffeur the task of finding her a criminal lawyer who was good enough to keep her off death row, but not so good that she'd walk away scot-free. The chauffeur spent a couple of days asking around. The name that kept coming up, it seems, was Jaywalker's.

They'd talked for an hour and a half, with Jaywalker almost literally unable to take his eyes off her the entire time. He was already widowed back then, and over the course of his life he'd seen a dozen prettier women up close, and slept with half of them (not that he hadn't tried with the remaining half). But there was something captivating about Samara, something—he would decide later—absolutely arresting. She was small, not only of height and build, but of facial feature. Her hair was dark and straight, whether naturally or with help. Only her lower lip was standard issue, making it too large by far for the rest of her face and giving her a perpetual pout. But it was her eyes that held him most. They were so dark that he would have had to call them black. They had a slightly glassy look to them, suggesting that she might have been wearing contacts too long, or was on the verge of crying. And they seemed totally impenetrable, taking in everything while letting out absolutely nothing.

The things she said made little or no sense. She'd taken the car because she'd felt like it. She'd drunk a large glass of Scotch before she'd set out because she'd been nervous about working the Lamborghini's standard transmission, which was something of a mystery to her. No, she had no driver's license, never had. She'd meant to end up at 72nd Street but had kept going past it by mistake. She'd been trying to downshift and turn left when the median island suddenly rose up in front of her and hit her head-on. She was sorry about the accident, but not overly so. "Barry has lots of cars," she explained.

Jaywalker told her that given her lack of a previous

record, he was all but certain he could keep her out of jail. What he didn't tell her was that no judge with eyeballs was going to send her to Rikers Island. No male judge, anyway. That said, there were going to be some pretty stiff fines to pay. That was okay, she said. "Barry has lots of money, too."

"Will you take my case, then?" she asked.

"Yes," he said.

She stood up to leave. She couldn't have been more than five-three, he guessed, and she was wearing serious heels.

"We have to talk about my fee," said Jaywalker.

"Talk to Robert," she said, waving vaguely in the direction of the waiting room. "I'm not allowed to deal with money matters."

Robert was summoned. He was actually wearing a uniform, complete with a chauffeur's cap. He reminded Jaywalker of those limo drivers who met people at airports, holding stenciled signs against their chests. He produced a check from an inner pocket and sat down across from Jaywalker, in the seat Samara had vacated. Jaywalker could see that the check was signed, but that the dollar amount had been left blank. Robert picked up a pen from the top of the desk—there were a half dozen of them strewn around, a few of which worked—and looked at Jaywalker expectantly.

"I'll need a retainer to start work—"

Robert held up a hand. "If it's all right," he said, "Mr. Tannenbaum prefers to pay the full amount in advance."

Jaywalker shrugged. In his business, which was dealing with criminals, you tried to get a half or a third up front, knowing that collecting the balance would be a process similar to dental extraction. If you were lucky, you got twenty percent. Paying the full amount in advance didn't happen.

Jaywalker stroked his chin as though in deep concentration. In fact, he was fighting hard to recover from his shock and come up with a fair number. He drew a complete blank.

"If there's no trial…" he began, trying to buy time.

"No ifs," said Robert. "Give me the bottom line. I don't want to have to go through this next time, and the time after that."

"Fair enough," said Jaywalker, before lapsing back into chin-stroking. His normal fee for a drunk driving case was $2,500, with another $2,500 due if the case couldn't be worked out with a guilty plea and had to go to trial. He'd gotten more once or twice, but only where there'd been some complicating factor, such as a prior DWI conviction, or the fact that the case was outside of the city and meant travel time.

Still, there was the Lamborghini factor, the chauffeur, and that comment that was still reverberating in his ears: "Barry has lots of money."

Fuck it, he decided. *Why not go for it?*

"The total fee," he said, in as steady a voice as he could muster, "will be ten thousand dollars."

"No way," said Robert.

"Excuse me?" Jaywalker said, feigning surprise, but knowing immediately that he'd blown it. Greed will get you every time.

"Mr. Tannenbaum will never go for it," he heard Robert saying. "Not in a million years. Anything less than thirty-five grand and he'll think he's getting second-rate service." He proceeded to fill out the amount in the blank space.

Two hours after they'd left, Jaywalker was still pulling the check out of his pocket every fifteen minutes to stare at it, counting the zeroes one by one to make sure it said what he thought it did.

Thirty-five thousand dollars.

He'd gotten less on murder cases.

A lot less.

The matter had been resolved with what Jaywalker liked to think of as mixed results. Samara ended up pleading guilty to driving while impaired and operating a motor vehicle without a license. She entered her plea on her third court appearance, Jaywalker having obtained two earlier postponements for no reason other than fear of being disbarred for life for charging a fee that worked out to something in the neighborhood of $17,500 an hour.

Grand larceny, by any measure.

Samara paid—or rather, Robert paid on her behalf—a fine of $350, plus another hundred or so in court costs. She was compelled to take a one-day safe-driving course (no doubt she elected Lamborghini Navigation 101) and attend a three-hour substance abuse seminar, and was prohibited from applying for a learner's permit or driver's license for a period of eighteen months.

That was the good news.

The bad news, at least so far as Jaywalker was concerned, was that his infatuation with Samara never progressed beyond the staring point. Robert was always around. And the truth was, as even Jaywalker would have had to admit in his more reflective moments, had Robert not been around, things would have been no different. Not once did Samara ever indicate that she was the least bit interested in anything from Jaywalker besides legal representation. When the case ended and he went to embrace her (something he'd done with men and women, killers and rapists, he rationalized), she turned her head at the very last second, so that his kiss landed dryly on her cheek.

"Stay out of trouble," he told her.

"I will," she promised.

5

RIKERS ISLAND

Promises being what they are, they occasionally go unkept.

Six years later, Jaywalker had been looking over the front page of the *New York Times* Metropolitan section when he spotted an item well below the center fold. Apparently the *Times* considered the news fit to print, but only barely.

WIFE HELD IN KILLING OF WEALTHY FINANCIER

it said. He might have read no farther, having little empathy for financiers on the best of days, let alone wealthy financiers. In fact, he was trying to figure out if the phrase was redundant when his eyes, drifting down the fine print, came to rest on the name Samara Moss Tannenbaum, and stopped right there. It was as though he were suddenly seeing her again, sitting across his office desk, utterly powerless to take his eyes off her, just as now he was powerless to take them off her printed name.

He forced himself to blink, once, then twice, just so he could look away. Then he lowered himself into his chair—

the same chair he'd sat in six years earlier, behind the same desk—and, folding the paper in half, began to read.

A 26-year-old woman was arrested early this morning in connection with the death of her husband, a financier described by *Forbes* magazine as having a net worth in excess of ten billion dollars.

According to a source close to the investigation, who insisted upon anonymity because he is unauthorized to speak publicly for the police department, Samara Moss Tannenbaum was accused of stabbing her husband, Barrington Tannenbaum, 70, once in the chest. The wound was deep enough to perforate the victim's heart and cause him to bleed to death, said the source.

(Continued on page 36)

Jaywalker unfolded the paper and thumbed his way through the section until he found page 36. He spread it open in front of him, fully intending to read the balance of the article. But it would turn out to be hours before he did. What stopped him was a pair of photographs, typical black-and-white newspaper portraits arranged side by side. The one to the left was of a slight balding man in a business suit and tie who, Jaywalker knew, had to be the victim. But he never so much as read the caption beneath it. It was the other photo, the one to the right, that captured him. Staring directly at him was Samara Tannenbaum, her eyes narrowly set and black as coals, her lower lip curled into what either was or could easily have been mistaken for a pout. Jaywalker would stare at the photograph for what seemed like hours, as utterly unable to look away as he had been the day she'd first walked into his office six years earlier.

For two full days he thought of no one and nothing else. He thought about her lying in bed at night. He

dreamed about her. He awoke thinking about her. He had
to beg a judge for an adjournment of a trial long scheduled to begin, feigning conjunctivitis when the real
problem was concentration. He ate little, slept less and
lost six pounds.

Just before two o'clock in the afternoon of the third day,
as he was getting ready to go back to court for a sentencing on a marijuana case, the phone rang. Jaywalker was
going to let the answering machine get it, but at the last
moment he decided to pick up.

"Jaywalker," he said.

"Samara," said a recorded female voice, followed by a
male one, "is calling collect from a correctional facility. If
you wish to accept the charges, please press one now."

Jaywalker pressed one.

He met with her the following day, at the Women's
House of Detention on Rikers Island. *Met with* being something of a stretch, since their conversation was in actuality
conducted through a five-inch circular hole cut out of the
center of a wire-reinforced, bulletproof pane of glass.

"You look terrible," he told her.

"Thanks."

It was true, in a way, the same way Natalie Wood might
have looked terrible after four days in jail, or a young
Elizabeth Taylor. Samara's hair was a tangle of knots (so
much for its being naturally straight), her eyes were puffy
and bloodshot and her skin had an artificial, fluorescent
cast to it. She was wearing an orange jumpsuit that had to
be three sizes too big for her. Yet once again, Jaywalker
found it impossible to take his eyes off her.

"I didn't do it," she said.

He nodded. Earlier that morning, he had phoned the
lawyer who'd been assigned to stand up for her at her first
court appearance. They'd talked for ten minutes, long
enough for Jaywalker to learn that the charge was murder,

that the detectives had executed a search warrant at Samara's town house and come up with a veritable shitload of evidence, including a knife with what looked like dried blood on it, and that Samara was so far denying her guilt.

That was okay. A lot of Jaywalker's clients claimed they were innocent early on in the game. It was only after they'd gotten to know him for a while that they dared to trust him with the truth. He understood that, and knew that it was part of his job to gain that trust. Also that it was a process, one that didn't always come easily. Sometimes it didn't come at all. When that happened, Jaywalker considered the failure his, not his client's.

With Samara, he was pretty sure, the trust and the truth would come. But not now, not here. Not through reinforced bulletproof glass, with a corrections officer seated fifteen feet away and, Jaywalker had to assume, a microphone hidden somewhere even closer. So every time Samara started talking about the case, he steered her away from it, assuring her that she'd have plenty of time to tell her story.

The truth was, Jaywalker was there not to win the case at that point but just to *get* it. In that sense, he knew, he was no better than the P.I. lawyers in his suite, the ambulance chasers. They made hospital calls and home visits in order to sign up clients before the competition beat them to it. He was doing the same thing. The only difference was that it wasn't some bedside he was visiting. That and the fact that his client had arrived here not by ambulance, but chained to the seat of a Department of Corrections bus.

"Will you take my case?"

It was the exact same question she'd asked him six years ago. There wasn't much he'd forgotten about her over that time, he realized. He gave her the same answer now that he'd given her then.

"Yes."

She smiled.

"About the fee," he said.

He hated that part. But it was what he did for a living, after all, how he paid his bills. And he was already in trouble with the disciplinary committee, with the very real possibility of a lengthy suspension looming on the horizon. Jaywalker was no stranger to pro bono work, having done his share and then some over the years. But with unemployment in his future, now was no time to be handing out freebies. Not on a murder case, anyway, especially one where the defendant was claiming to be innocent and might well insist on going to trial.

"I'll be worth a zillion dollars," said Samara, "once Barry's estate gets prorated."

He didn't bother correcting her word choice. Still, he knew that it would be months, probably years, before there would be a distribution of assets. Moreover, if Samara were to be convicted of killing her husband, the law would bar her from inheriting a cent. He didn't tell her that, either, of course. Instead, he simply asked, "And in the meantime?"

She shrugged a little-girl shrug.

"Should I get in touch with Robert?" Jaywalker asked her.

"Robert's gone," she said. "Barry discovered he was stealing."

"Is there a new Robert?"

"There's a new chauffeur, although…" Her voice trailed off. "But," she suddenly brightened, "I have a bank account of my own now, sort of."

The "sort of" struck Jaywalker as a strange qualifier, but at least it represented progress. He remembered the twenty-year-old who hadn't been permitted to deal with money matters.

"With how much in it?"

Another shrug. "I don't know. A couple hundred—"

"That's it?"

"—thousand."

"Oh."

He got the name of the bank and explained that he would bring her papers to sign to withdraw enough for a retainer. Then he described what would be happening over the next week or two, how the evidence against her would be presented to a grand jury, and how she would almost certainly be indicted. He told her that she had a right to testify before the grand jury, but that in her case it would be a very bad idea.

"Why?"

"The D.A. knows much more about the facts than we do at this point," he explained. "You'd end up getting indicted anyway, and then they'd have your testimony to use against you at trial." When she looked at him quizzically, he said, "Trust me."

"Okay," she said.

He was grateful for that. What he didn't want to have to tell her at this point was that if she went into the grand jury and denied having had anything to do with Barry's death, it would make it hard to claim self-defense later on, or argue that she hadn't been mentally responsible at the time, or that she'd killed her husband while under the influence of extreme emotional disturbance. Those were all defenses, complete or partial, that Jaywalker wanted to keep open, *needed* to keep open.

Finally he told her the most important part. "Keep your mouth shut. This place is crawling with snitches. Yours is a newspaper case. That means every woman in this place knows what you're here for. Anything you tell one of them becomes her ticket to cut a deal on her own case and get her out of here. Understand?"

"Yup."

"Promise me you'll shut up?"

"I promise," she said, drawing a thumb and index finger across her mouth in an exaggerated zipping motion.

"Good," said Jaywalker.

It was only once he was outside the visitors' gate, heading for the bus that would take him back to Manhattan, that Jaywalker recalled that in terms of promises kept, Samara was so far 0 for 1.

By the time Jaywalker made it back to Manhattan, it was too late to go to Samara's bank to find out what he'd need to do to get money out of her account. He knew he could phone them and ask to speak to the manager or somebody in the legal department, but he'd learned from past experiences that such matters were better handled in person. He had been told often enough that he had an honest face and a disarming way about him that he'd come to accept that there must be something to it. Juries believed him; judges trusted him; even tight-assed prosecutors tended to open up to him. The truth was, he was a bit of a con man. "Show me a good criminal defense lawyer," he'd told friends more than once, "and I'll show you a master manipulator." Then he would hasten to defend the skill, pointing out that establishing his own credibility and trustworthiness was not only his stock-in-trade, but was often absolutely critical to getting an innocent defendant off.

He talked less about the guilty ones he also got off, but he didn't lose sleep over them. He believed passionately in the system that entitled the accused—*any* accused, no matter how despicable the individual, how heinous the crime, or how overwhelming the proof against him—to one person in his corner who would fight as hard and as well as he possibly could for him. That left it to the city's thirty thousand cops, two thousand prosecutors and five hundred judges (the great majority of whom were former prosecutors, tough-on-crime politicians, or both) to fight just as hard and just as well to put the guy away forever. That made for pretty fair odds, as far as Jaywalker was concerned, and if he succeeded in overcoming them—as he'd been doing on a pretty regular basis lately—he felt no need to apologize. It all came down to a simple choice, he'd realized long ago. You fought like hell, trying your hardest to win—yes, *win*—or you regarded it as nothing but a job, and you simply went through the motions. Jaywalker knew a lot of lawyers who did just that. When they lost—and they lost every bit as often as Jaywalker won—they shrugged it off and said things like, "The scumbag was guilty," "The idiot self-destructed on the witness stand," or "Justice was done." Jaywalker had a term for them. He called them whores.

Tolerance had never been one of his virtues.

He phoned Tom Burke, the assistant D.A. who was prosecuting Samara Tannenbaum. He'd seen Burke's name in the *Times* article, and had confirmed that it was his case during the conversation he'd had with the lawyer who'd handled Samara's initial court appearance.

"Burke," said a deep voice.

"Why don't you pick on somebody your own size?" Jaywalker asked.

"Who is this?"

"What's the matter, doesn't the old man spring for caller ID?"

"Are you kidding?"

"I never kid."

"Jaywalker?"

"Very good."

Jaywalker liked Burke. They'd had a couple of cases together in the past, though none of them had ended up going to trial. Burke was no legal scholar, but he was a hardworking, straight-shooting, seat-of-the-pants lawyer.

"How the fuck are you?" he asked.

"Not bad," said Jaywalker.

"Let me guess. Samara Tannenbaum?"

"Bingo."

"Why am I not surprised?" Then, "Oh, yeah. You represented her on that DWI thing."

"I see you've been doing your homework."

"You assigned?" Burke asked.

"No," said Jaywalker. "I weaned myself off the public tit some time ago, just in time to miss the rate hike." It was the truth. Fresh out of Legal Aid, Jaywalker had been happy to take all the court-appointed cases he could get, even at twenty-five dollars an hour for out-of-court work and forty an hour for in-court. He'd been putting his daughter through law school at the time, and needed every cent to do it. Once she'd graduated and had found a job, he'd stopped taking assignments, except for an occasional favor to a judge, or when New York briefly restored the death penalty. A few years ago, under pressure from a lawsuit, they'd finally gotten around to raising the rates to seventy-five an hour, in-court and out. But Jaywalker hadn't been tempted. By that time he had enough private work to keep him busy, and his expenses were low enough that he didn't need the extra money. Getting rich had never been high on his list of priorities.

"If you don't mind my asking," said Burke, "who's retained you?"

"Samara. Or at least she's in the process."

"It's not going to work."

"Oh?"

"I've gotten an order freezing all of Barry Tannen-baum's assets," said Burke. "Including a bank account in Samara's name."

"Shit," was all Jaywalker could think to say.

Tom Burke had only been doing his job, of course. He'd been able to trace the deposits to Samara's account and demonstrate to a judge that every dollar—and there were currently nearly two hundred thousand of them—had come from her husband. Under the law, if Samara were to be convicted of killing him, she would lose her right to the money, as well as to any other of Barry's assets. Next, Burke had informed the judge that he'd already presented his case to a grand jury, which had voted a "true bill." That meant an indictment, which amounted to an official finding of probable cause that Samara had in fact committed a crime resulting in Barry's death. Based upon that, the judge, a pretty reasonable woman named Carolyn Berman, had had little choice but to freeze all of Barry Tannenbaum's assets, the bank account included.

Even if Burke and Berman had only been doing their jobs, the result certainly added up to a major headache for Jaywalker. The good news was that he could now skip going to the bank. But that consolation was more than offset by the fact that instead he had to spend two days drawing up papers so that he and Burke could go before the judge and argue about the fairness of the ruling.

They did that on a Friday afternoon, convening at Part 30, on the 11th floor of 100 Centre Street, the Criminal Court Building. Jaywalker's home court, as he liked to think of it.

"The defendant has a constitutional right to the counsel of her choice," he argued.

"True enough," Burke conceded, "but it's a limited right. When you're indigent and can't afford a lawyer, the court assigns you one. Only you don't get to choose who it is."

"But she's *not* indigent, and she *can* afford a lawyer," Jaywalker pointed out. "At least she could have, until you two decided that instead of her paying for counsel, the taxpayers should get stuck footing the bill."

It was a fairly sleazy argument, he knew, but there were a half-dozen reporters taking notes in the front row of the courtroom, and Jaywalker knew that the judge didn't want to wake up tomorrow morning to headlines like JUDGE RULES TAXPAYERS SHOULD PAY FOR BILLION-AIRESS'S DEFENSE.

In the end, Judge Berman hammered out a compromise of sorts, as judges generally try to do. She authorized a limited invasion of the bank account for legal fees and necessary related expenses. But she set Jaywalker's fee at the same seventy-five dollars an hour that it would have been had Samara been indigent and eligible for assigned counsel.

Great, thought Jaywalker. *Here I got paid thirty-five grand to cop her out on a DWI, and now I'm going to be earning ditch-digger wages for trying a murder case.*

"Thank you," was what he actually said to Judge Berman.

With that he walked over to the clerk of the court and filled out a notice of appearance, formally declaring that he was the new attorney for Samara Moss Tannenbaum. And was handed a 45-pound cardboard box by Tom Burke, containing copies of the evidence against his client. So far.

Nothing like a little weekend reading.

6

A LITTLE WEEKEND READING

It turned out to be a horror story.

Jaywalker began his reading that night, lying in bed. The cardboard box Burke had given him contained police reports, diagrams and photographs of the crime scene, the search warrant for Samara's town house, a "return," or list of items seized there, a typewritten summary of what Samara had said to the detective who first questioned her, requests for scientific tests to be conducted on various bits of physical evidence, and a bunch of other paperwork.

It was a lot more than the prosecution was required to turn over at this early stage of the proceedings. A lot of assistants would have stonewalled, waiting for the defense to make a written demand to produce, followed up with formal motion papers and a judge's order. Tom Burke didn't play games like that, a fact that Jaywalker was grateful for.

At least until he began reading.

From the police reports, Jaywalker learned that when Barry Tannenbaum hadn't shown up at his office one morning and his secretary had been unable to reach him either at his mansion in Scarsdale or his penthouse apartment on Central Park South, she'd called 9-1-1. The Scarsdale police had kicked in the door, searched the mansion, and found nobody there and nothing out of order. The

NYPD had been luckier, if you chose to look at it that way. Let into the apartment by the building superintendent, they'd found Barry lying facedown on his kitchen floor, in what the crime scene technician described as "a pool of dried blood." If the terminology was slightly oxymoronic, the meaning was clear enough.

There'd been no weapon present, and none found in the garbage, which hadn't been picked up yet, on the rooftop, or in the vicinity of the building. Officers went so far as to check nearby trash cans and storm drains, with, in police-speak, "negative results."

There was no sign of forced entry, and no indication from the security company that protected the apartment that any alarms had gone off. The apartment was dusted for fingerprints, and a number of latent prints were lifted or photographed. Blood, hair and fiber samples were collected.

The medical examiner's office was summoned, and the Chief Medical Officer himself, not all that averse to publicity, responded. On gross examination of the body, he found a single deep puncture wound to the chest, just left of the midline and in the area of the heart. There appeared to be no other wounds, and no signs of a struggle. The M.E. took a rectal temperature of the body. Based on the amount of heat it had lost, as well as the progression of lividity and rigor mortis, he was able to make a preliminary estimate that death had occurred the previous evening, sometime between six o'clock and midnight.

The building was canvassed to determine if anyone had heard or seen anything unusual the night before. Only one person reported that she had, a woman in her late seventies or early eighties, living alone in the adjoining penthouse apartment. She'd heard a loud argument between a man and a woman, shortly after watching *Wheel of Fortune.* She recognized both voices. The man's was Barry Tannenbaum, whom she knew well. The woman's, she was just as certain, was his wife, known to her as Sam.

According to *TV Guide, Wheel of Fortune* had aired that evening at seven-thirty Eastern Standard Time, and had ended at eight.

The doorman who'd been on duty the previous evening was located and called in. He distinctly recalled that Barry Tannenbaum had had a guest over for dinner. As he did with every non-tenant, the doorman had entered the guest's name in the logbook upon arrival and again upon departure. Although in this particular case he hadn't required her to sign herself in. The reason, he explained, was that he knew her personally.

Her name was Samara Tannenbaum.

At that point a pair of detectives had been dispatched to Samara's town house. They had to buzz her from the downstairs intercom and phone her unlisted number repeatedly for a full fifteen minutes before she finally cracked the door open, leaving the security chain in place. They told her they wanted to come in and ask her a few questions.

"About what?" she asked.

"Your husband," they said.

"Why don't you ask him yourselves?"

The two detectives exchanged glances. Then one of them said, "Please, it'll only take a few minutes."

At that point Samara unchained the door and "did knowingly and voluntarily grant them consent to affect entry of the premises." Jaywalker would go to his grave in awe over how cops abused the English language. It was as though, in order to receive their guns and shields, they were first required to surrender their ability to spell correctly, to follow the most basic rules of grammar, and to write anything even remotely resembling a simple sentence.

Samara had seemed nervous, they would later write in their report. Her hair "appeared unkept," her clothes were "dishelved," and she "did proceed to light, puff and distinguish" a number of cigarettes.

They asked her when she'd last seen her husband.

"About a week ago," she replied.

"Are you certain?"

"Am I certain I saw him a week ago?"

"No, ma'am. Are you certain you haven't seen him since?"

"Why?" she asked. Jaywalker could picture her nervously lighting, puffing and "distinguishing" a cigarette at that point. "What's this all about?"

"It's just routine," they assured her. "We only got a few more questions."

"Well, if you don't want to tell me what this is about," Samara told them, "you can just routine yourselves right out the door."

Again the detectives exchanged glances. "We have people who place you at your husband's apartment last night," said one of them.

"So what?"

"So we'd like to know if it's true, that's all."

"So what if it is?"

"Is it?"

Samara seemed to think for a moment before answering. Then she said, "Yeah, sure. We had dinner together."

"At a restaurant, or at your husband's apartment?"

"His apartment."

"Did he cook?"

"Barry? Cook?" She laughed. "The man couldn't boil water. He told me the first thing he did when he bought the apartment was to have the stove ripped out to make room for a bigger table."

"What did you eat?"

"Chinks."

Being detectives, they didn't have to ask her what she meant. Besides, the crime scene guys had found half-empty containers of Chinese takeout on the counter and in the garbage, when they'd been looking for a weapon.

"Are we done here?" she asked. "Or maybe you'd like to know how many steamed dumplings I ate."

"Did you have a fight?" they asked.

"No."

"We've got people who tell us they heard a fight."

"So? Big deal. We always fight."

"Who hit who first?"

"Nobody hit nobody."

Jaywalker wondered if maybe Samara might not have made a pretty good cop.

"So what kind of a fight was it?"

"A word fight. An argument, I believe they call it."

"About what?"

"Who the fuck remembers? Stupid stuff. He started it."

"Then what happened?"

"I don't know. I told him he could go fuck himself, and I left. Now maybe you'd like to tell me what this is all about?"

"Sure. It's about your husband's murder."

"Barry? Murdered? You're shitting me."

They said they weren't shitting her.

"Wait a minute," she said, the light finally going on. "You think I killed Barry?"

They said nothing.

"I want a lawyer," said Samara.

The magic word having been uttered, the interview was effectively over. Nonetheless, the detectives weren't quite done. "Would it be okay if we had a quick look around?" they asked her.

"You got a warrant?"

"We can get one," they said. "Or you can save us all a lot of time and trouble."

She looked them in the eye and said, "I ain't saving you shit."

With that, they "did handcuff her, pat her down, administrated her Miranda rights, exited the premises, and transported her to the precinct for fingerprinting, processing and mug shooting."

God bless.

Whatever time and trouble it had cost them, that afternoon the detectives did indeed apply for and obtain a search warrant for Samara's town house, aimed at finding "a weapon or other instrument, as well as other physical evidence relating directly or indirectly to the murder of Barrington Tannenbaum."

Apparently Tom Burke had taken over the writing.

The warrant was executed the same evening. The return listed more than two dozen items that had been seized. It was hard at that point for Jaywalker to appreciate the significance of most of them, but at least three were pretty easy to understand.

6. One silver-handled, steel-bladed steak knife, 9 inches long overall, with a sharply pointed tip and a blade 5 inches long by three-quarters of an inch wide by one-sixteenth of an inch thick, on which there appears to be a dried, dark-red stain.

9. One blue towel, with an irregular dark-red stain measuring approximately 1" x 3".

17. One ladies' blouse, size S, with a dark-red splatter pattern on the front, approximately 3" in diameter.

If the nature of the items was troubling to Jaywalker, the location where they'd been discovered was just as damning. All three had been found rolled up together and wedged behind the toilet tank of a top-floor guest bathroom.

Those items, along with a number of others removed from the crime scene, were currently being tested for the presence of DNA. Fingerprint comparisons were awaited. In addition, a full autopsy had been conducted on Barry's body, and a report was expected in a few weeks, as well as serology and toxicology findings. Hair and fiber analyses were being done, too.

Yet as bad as things looked for Samara at the moment, Jaywalker had every confidence that given a little time, they would look a lot worse.

He turned off the light and lay on his back in the darkness. Samara Tannenbaum's face appeared at the foot of his bed, her eyes darker even than the room, her lower lip pouting.

"I didn't do it," she said.

Right.

7

Monday was Samara's "One-eighty-eighty" day, a reference to the section of the Criminal Procedure Law that entitles a defendant to be released unless the prosecution has obtained an indictment or is ready to go forward with a preliminary hearing. A lot of defendants do get released: complaining witnesses disappear, cops screw up and assistant D.A.s occasionally get overextended, and have to pick and choose which cases to treat as priorities and which to let slide. Some defendants are lucky enough to slip into the cracks that are inevitable in a system that processes many thousands of cases a year.

Barry Tannenbaum having disappeared in the most literal sense imaginable, the complaining witness in Samara's case was now The People of the State of New York, and they weren't going anywhere. As far as Jaywalker knew, no cops had screwed up, so long as spelling and grammar didn't count. Tom Burke was certainly treating the case as his top priority, if not his career-maker. Given all that, the chances of Samara's case slipping into some crack, necessitating her release from jail, were absolutely zero.

Jaywalker explained all this to her before they went before the judge, during a five-minute conversation in the "feeder pen" adjoining the courtroom. The term, no doubt, had come from the fact that the small lockup "feeds" defendants into the courtroom, one by one. But every time he heard it, Jaywalker couldn't help but picture bait fish being served up to frenzied sharks, or small rodents to ravenous wolves.

"After the court appearance," he told Samara, "we'll sit down in the counsel visit room and talk as much as we need. Okay?"

She nodded, looking appropriately worried.

He described what would happen when they appeared before the judge: in a word, nothing. Once an indictment was announced, the only remaining bit of business would be the setting of an adjourned date.

"Can you make a bail application?" Samara asked.

Apparently she'd been getting some jailhouse advice, a commodity never in short supply on Rikers Island. Inmates devour every word of it, never pausing to notice that the dispensers of the advice have one thing in common: every last one of them is still sitting in jail.

"I can," he told her, "but it'll only be denied. You're going to have to wait until we get to Supreme Court."

"They say that can take years."

"Different Supreme Court," said Jaywalker, not helped all that much by a system in which some Einsteins had gotten together and decided to call the lowest felony court in the city *supreme*. But Jaywalker spared Samara the explanation. What he did tell her was that asking for bail was not only pointless, but might actually hurt their chances later on. Bail was almost never granted in murder cases, and on the rare occasion when it was, it was usually set prohibitively high. In this case, that wouldn't take much. With her bank account frozen and no other assets to her name, even were a modest bail to be set, Samara had nothing to post it with. So while there might come a time when it made sense to ask for bail, it certainly wasn't now.

Finally, Jaywalker warned Samara that the press

would be in the courtroom. The American public, denied a throne by the founding fathers, makes do with celebrity and wealth in lieu of royalty. How else to explain such curious heroes as Bill Gates, Jack Welch or Paris Hilton? Barry Tannenbaum had been rich. If not quite Bill Gates rich, certainly Donald Trump rich. He'd married a reformed hooker (some commentators, inclined to reserve judgment, preferred the term "former hooker"), forty-two years his junior. Now she'd stabbed him to death.

The press would definitely be in the courtroom.

"Your appearance, please, counselor," said the bridgeman, once the case had been called.

As always, Jaywalker was tempted to say, "Five-eleven, a hundred and seventy pounds, graying hair…" Instead, he controlled himself, stating his name and office address for the court reporter to take down.

True to form, Tom Burke announced that he'd obtained an indictment against Samara. The judge set a date for arraignment in Supreme Court.

And that was it.

Anyone expecting to find the twelfth-floor counsel visit area to be the functional equivalent of a private hospital room would have been seriously disappointed. But Jaywalker had been there a thousand times before and knew better. The area was laid out more like a ward or, if you wanted to be extremely charitable about it, a semiprivate room.

After being ushered through the middle one of three steel-barred outer doors, he entered the lawyers' area, a row of bolted-down chairs that extended to the far wall on either side. Each chair had a small writing surface in front of it, with wooden partitions rising on either side. Above the writing surfaces was a metal-screened window. If one squinted sufficiently, he could see that on the other side of the screen was another writing surface, and behind it another bolted-down chair, facing his own.

The inmates were led in through the other doors, one side for men and one for women. That way, segregation was maintained for the three groups—lawyers, male prisoners and female prisoners. Someone had apparently decided that it was safe to permit lawyers of both sexes to mingle.

The arrangement was an imperfect one, because unless you talked in a whisper with your client or resorted to sign language, you ran the risk of being overheard by lawyers on either side of you, and inmates on either side of your client. Still, it was better than talking over some staticky telephone hookup, or through a hole in reinforced glass, so Jaywalker wasn't about to complain.

You picked your battles.

He spent the better part of twenty minutes reviewing his file on Samara's case, already two inches thick. He knew it would take a while for them to bring her up from the fourth-floor feeder pen.

When she came in and took her seat across from him, he was struck again by how tiny she seemed, and how vulnerable. He'd stood alongside her in the courtroom half an hour ago, but his attention had been focused elsewhere then—on the judge, the prosecutor, the court reporter, even the media. Now he had only Samara to look at, and what he saw was a young woman on the verge of tears. He wondered if he'd missed that downstairs, when he'd been all business.

"Are you okay?" he asked her.

"No, I'm not okay," she said, using the heels of her hands to blot her eyes. So much for the verge of tears.

"I'm sorry," he said. He meant it, both about her obvious distress and the fact that his dumb question had triggered her meltdown.

She took a deep breath, fighting to compose herself. "Listen," she said, "you've got to get me out of here."

"I'll do my best," Jaywalker promised. It was only half a lie. He would certainly do his best, that much was true. The lie part was that even his best wouldn't be enough to get her out of jail. But he knew she wasn't ready to hear that, not yet. "We need to talk about the case," he told her instead, "so we can figure out our best chance of getting you out." His father, long dead, had been a doctor, the old-fashioned kind. He'd never told his patients that they had a bellyful of inoperable cancer and were going to die from it. He told them they had "suspicious cells," and that the radiation or chemotherapy he was sending them for was simply a "precautionary measure." That was what *he* was doing with Samara now, he recognized. There were times when being a criminal defense lawyer turned you into something you weren't in a hurry to write home about, he'd realized some years ago, before gradually coming to terms with the fact. Sometimes you donned the white hat and rode the white horse. But there were other times, times when, without quite breaking the rules, you bent them a little and adapted them to the situation. In the long run, you did what you had to do. Did he blame his father for having lied to his patients? He certainly had at the time, back when he was young and idealistic and had all the answers. Now, battle-tested and closing in on fifty himself, he knew enough to look at things a little differently.

"What do you want to hear?" Samara was asking him.

"Everything."

"From the beginning?"

"From the beginning."

8

PRAIRIE CREEK

"I was born in Indiana," Samara said. "Prairie Creek. Nice name for a town, huh?"

Jaywalker nodded.

"It was a shithole."

He made a written note on the yellow legal pad in front of him. It didn't say *Indiana*, though, or *Prairie Creek*. CLEAN UP HER MOUTH, it said.

"I never knew my father," she said. "I grew up with my mother in a trailer, an old rusty thing set up on cinder blocks. My mom, well, she worked her ass off, I'll say that much for her."

"Is she still alive?"

That got a shrug, telling him that Samara either didn't know or didn't much care.

"I think she also *sold* her ass off, though I don't know for sure. She was pretty, prettier'n me."

Jaywalker tried picturing *prettier than Samara,* but didn't know where to start.

"She wasn't home much. Always working or whatever." Leaving the *whatever* to hang in the air for a few beats. "I remember being left with babysitters a lot. Guys, mostly."

"How did that go?"

Another shrug. "I learned a lot."

"Like what?"

"How to do shots of beer. How to roll joints."

"Anything else?"

Samara broke off eye contact, looked downward. She tried to shrug again, but this attempt didn't come off with the same *Who-the-fuck-cares?* as the two previous ones. It seemed to Jaywalker that her lower lip was pouting more than ever, but maybe it was only the tilt of her head.

"Is it important?" she asked him.

"It might be."

She seemed to ponder that for a moment before looking up again. When she did, Jaywalker locked eyes with her. *Trust me,* he told her, without speaking the words out loud.

"Yeah," she said, cocking her head slightly, but not looking away. "I learned how to give hand jobs and blow jobs, and how to thigh fuck."

"Thigh fuck?" A new one for Jaywalker. He underlined CLEAN UP HER MOUTH, then underlined it a second time.

"Yeah, you know. Letting the guy stick it in between my legs. All the way up there, but not inside. I was too small for inside. Then, with my legs tight around the guy, I'd let him fuck away until—"

"Okay," said Jaywalker, pretty much getting the picture.

"Get me out and I'll show you." Smiling now.

"How'd you do in school?" he asked her.

She laughed, whether at his abrupt change of subject or at the thought of her academic career. "How do drunk, stoned, fucked-up kids usually do?" she asked.

He took it as an answer.

"How far did you go?"

"I stuck around till the day after my fourteenth birthday. I wanted to see if I got any good presents." Apparently she hadn't. "I caught a bus to Terre Haute, then hitchhiked my way west, to Nevada. I wanted to be a showgirl or an actress, something like that. But you know what they told me? Too short. *Too short.* Now if I'd'a been too fat, or too thin, or too something-else-like-that, I could'a done something about it. But *too short?* What the fuck was I supposed to do about *that?*"

"So?"

"So I tended bar and waited tables, mostly."

"Mostly?"

"And supplemented my income every now and then."

"By doing what?"

"By doing what I would have done anyway. Only thing I did was when a guy wanted to give me something after, I took it."

"And that *something* included money?"

"Sometimes."

"Ever get arrested? Other than this and that DWI thing?" Her criminal record printout showed nothing else, but Jaywalker knew that there might be out-of-state cases, or arrests that hadn't led to convictions that often wouldn't show up.

"No."

"Are you absolutely sure?"

A pause, then, "Maybe there was this one time in Reno for *attempted soliciting*. It was pure bullshit. I was standing in front of a club, smoking a cigarette. Some vice cop decided that meant I had to be hooking."

Underneath CLEAN UP HER MOUTH, Jaywalker wrote WORK ON GETTING HER TO TELL THE TRUTH, and underlined it three times. "What happened to the case?" he asked.

"It was dismissed."

"How much of a fine did you pay?"

"Fifty dollars."

When a case was dismissed, there was no fine to pay. Jaywalker added an exclamation point to his latest reminder.

"Other arrests?"

"No."

"Absolutely sure?"

"Yes!" she snapped. Then, "Sorry."

"How did you meet Barry?"

She'd been working for tips off a phony driver's license in Vegas, serving drinks to the rollers in one of the lounges in Caesars Palace. She was eighteen at the time. "It was like three o'clock in the morning, going into Sunday, and the crowd was beginning to thin out. I see this guy staring at me, I mean *really* staring. I bring him a drink, a Diet Coke. He tells me I'm the most beautiful thing he's ever seen. Not the most beautiful *person,* the most beautiful *thing.* Shit, I should'a known right then. But being eighteen and dumb, I think it's pure poetry. Know what I mean?"

Jaywalker nodded. He'd come up with worse lines in his day, though not by all that much.

"I go up to his room after I get off, and we talk. *Talk.* For like five hours I'm carrying on a conversation with a man who's been to college, knows about politics and world affairs and wine and all sorts of other stuff. But he wants to know about *me.* Where I grew up, what it was like, why I ran away, what my hopes and dreams are. Hopes and dreams. And I'm telling him shit I wouldn't tell my best friend, if I had one. Like I'm opening my heart to him.

"Eleven o'clock comes, and he's got to go to a meeting. Asks me if he can kiss me. I say, 'Sure.' With that he touches me, *barely* touches me, with both hands on the sides of my face, and gives me the gentlest kiss in the world. No tongue, no open mouth, no grabbing. I gotta tell you, I felt like Madonna."

Jaywalker was pretty sure he knew which one she was referring to.

"Anyway, he leaves, goes back to New York. But he keeps calling me, like every day, and sending me flowers. Next he asks me to come east to visit him. I tell him right, like I've got money for a bus ticket. He tells me that won't be necessary, he'll send one of his planes to get me. *One of his planes.* So I go to New York, and we get married eight months later."

To Jaywalker, the segue seemed natural enough.

The fact that the marriage had survived for eight years was hardly testimony to its success. The place Samara had persuaded Barry to buy her before the first year was over was the four-story brownstone in the lower Seventies, between Park and Lexington. The city's inflated real estate had driven up the asking price to close to five million dollars, but if Barry complained, it was to deaf ears. "He used to tip that much in a year," according to Samara.

Within a few months she had basically set up residence in the town house. She continued to appear in public with Barry but made no secret of the fact that theirs had become an "open marriage," a throwback phrase from an earlier generation. Still, there was no talk of divorce. Barry had been there and done that three times already, and apparently had no taste for a fourth go-round.

"But according to your statement to the police," Jaywalker pointed out, "you admitted having fights, the two of you."

"That was their word," said Samara. *"Fights."*

"And your word?"

"Arguments."

"What did you argue about?"

"You name it, we argued about it. Money, sex, my driving, my clothes, my drinking, my language. Whatever couples argue about, I guess."

A corrections officer came into the lawyers' section of the room and asked for everyone's attention. "Anyone who wants to make the one o'clock bus back," he announced, "wind it up. You got ezzackly five minutes."

Jaywalker looked at Samara. If she missed the one o'clock, it meant she'd be stuck in the building till after five, which could mean not getting back to Rikers before ten or eleven, and having to settle for a bologna or cheese sandwich instead of what passed for a hot meal. But Samara gave one of her patented shrugs. Jaywalker took it as a good sign that she was willing to make personal sacrifices in order to finish telling him her story.

He should have known better.

There was a lot of rustling in the room as other inmates rose to leave, and other lawyers gathered their papers and snapped their briefcases shut.

"Tell me about the month or so before Barry's death," he said.

"What about it?"

"What was going on? Any new arguments? Anything out of the ordinary?"

Samara seemed to think back for a moment. "Not really," she said. "Barry was sick, and—"

"Sick?"

"He had the *flu*." The way she spat out the word suggested that she'd had little sympathy for him. "He thought I should be around more. You know, to take care of him. I told him that's what doctors are for, and hospitals. I mean, it's not like he couldn't afford it. Still, I did see a little more of him than usual."

"Where?"

"His place, mostly. Mine, once or twice. Out, a couple of times. I don't know."

"And how did the two of you get along on those occasions?"

Two shrugs.

"What does that mean?" Jaywalker asked.

"We got along the same as always," she said. "When we were apart, fine. When we were together, Barry always found a way to pick a fight."

"A fight?"

"An argument. Jesus, you're as bad as the cops."

"Sorry," said Jaywalker. "Tell me about the evening

before you found out Barry had been killed. Your statement says you first denied seeing him, then admitted you'd gone to his place. Is that true?"

"Is what true?"

Objection sustained. Jaywalker gave Samara a smile, then broke it down to a series of single questions. "Did you go there?" he asked.

"Yes."

"Did you deny it to the detectives at first?"

"Yes."

"Why?"

"I didn't think it was any of their goddamned business."

That was a pretty good answer, actually, if you took away the *goddamned* part. If believed, it showed that Samara hadn't known about Barry's murder. *If believed.* He made a note of it on his yellow pad.

"What caused you to change your story," he asked, "and admit you'd been there?"

"They said they already knew. The old bat next door heard us arguing."

"Were you?"

"Yeah."

"What about?"

"Who remembers? Barry was still pissed off that I'd walked out of some opera a few nights earlier, leaving him sitting there. Maybe that was it."

"Why had you done that?"

"Why? *Why?* Have you ever sat through five hours of some three-hundred-pound woman wearing a helmet, sweating like a pig and singing in German? Next to someone with the flu?"

"No," Jaywalker had to admit.

"Try it sometime."

"Tell me everything you remember about that last evening at Barry's," said Jaywalker. "What prompted you to go there in the first place?"

"Barry asked me to," Samara said. "Otherwise I wouldn't have. He said he wanted to talk to me about something, but it turned out to be some bullshit, something about how much I'd spent at Bloomingdale's or something like that. Who remembers?"

"What else?"

"Nothing much. He'd ordered Chinese food, and we ate. I ate, anyway. He said he couldn't taste anything, on account of being all clogged up, so he barely touched it. I remember that, 'cause I asked him if he was poisoning me."

Jaywalker raised an eyebrow.

"It was a joke," said Samara. "You know, like if I pour us each a glass of wine and tell you to drink up, but meanwhile I don't touch mine?"

"What did Barry say to that?"

"He laughed. *He* knew it was a joke."

"What else happened?"

"I don't know," Samara said. "He asked me if I wanted to make love. It was his expression for fucking. I said no, I didn't want to catch whatever he had, thank you very much. I said I was tired and was leaving. He said, 'Just like the other night at the opera?' And that did it. I told him what he could with his fucking opera, and he told me I was a dumb something-or-other, and we went at it pretty good."

"But just words?"

"Yeah, just words. Loud ones, but just words."

"And then?"

"And then I left."

"That's it?"

"That's it."

"What time was it?"

"Who knows?" said Samara. "Eight? Eight-thirty?"

"Where'd you go?"

"Home."

"Straight home?"

"Yeah."

"How?"

"Cab."

Jaywalker made a note to subpoena the Taxi and Limousine Commission records, see if they could come up with the cabdriver. If they found him and he remembered the fare, he might be able to remember whether Samara had seemed agitated or acted normally.

"Did anyone see you?" he asked. "Other than the doorman and the cabby?"

"Not that I know of."

"What did you do when you got home?"

"You really want to know?"

Jaywalker nodded. His guess would've been that she'd run a load of laundry and taken a shower. You stabbed somebody in the heart, chances were you were going to get some blood on you.

"I really *need* to know," he said.

"Fine," she said, her eyes never leaving his. "I jerked off."

Okay, not exactly what he'd expected to hear. Then again, the literature was full of accounts of serial killers describing how their crimes aroused them sexually and prompted them to masturbate, either right there at the scene or at home, shortly afterward. True, all of them were men, as far as Jaywalker could recall. But, hey, this was the twenty-first century, and having long held himself out as a supporter of equal rights for women, who was he to renege now?

"Do you have any idea," he asked Samara, "who killed your husband?"

"No."

"Can you think of anyone who might've wanted him out of the way?" As soon as he'd said the words, he regretted them. They sounded like something out of an old black-and-white movie from the forties.

"You don't make billions of dollars," said Samara, "without making enemies along the way."

Come to think of it, *she* belonged in an old black-and-white movie from the forties.

"I only know one thing," she added.

"What's that?"

"I didn't do it. You gotta believe me."

"I do," Jaywalker lied.

9

NICKY LEGS

That had been ten months ago, that first sit-down in which Samara had protested her innocence and Jaywalker had mumbled his "I do" with all the conviction of a shotgun groom. It had been two weeks before his appearance before the judges of the disciplinary committee, when he'd learned of his three-year suspension and begged to be permitted to complete work on his pending cases. He'd countered their offer to let him "dispose of" five with a list of seventeen, which they'd then pared down to ten.

Now, in June, with nine of those ten *disposed of,* Jaywalker found himself in the strangest of all positions, a criminal defense lawyer with only one criminal left to defend.

Why had he included Samara Tannenbaum in his must-keep list, when her case was barely two weeks old at that point and he had dozens of others in which he'd invested far more time, effort and emotion? To put it into the vernacular of modern mallspeak, it had been a no-brainer. First off, Samara's was a murder case. Jaywalker had once heard a colleague refer to a murder charge as nothing but an assault case in which you knew the complainant wasn't going to show up in court to testify against your client. Either the lawyer was joking, or he was a total jerk. Murder was like no other crime. There were longer trials, to be sure, and more complicated ones, and ones with lots more witnesses and paper and hearings and tape recordings and exhibits. There were crimes that carried equally severe sentences. Arson, for example, or kidnapping, or selling a couple of ounces of heroin or cocaine. Still, murder stood apart. Judges knew that, juries knew that and Jaywalker knew that. A life had been taken, the most important of the holy commandments had been broken, and the passion play that followed was almost biblical in its proportions. If for no other reason than that it was a murder charge, Samara's case deserved to be on Jaywalker's short list.

But there'd been other reasons, too.

By holding on to the case, Jaywalker knew that he would be able to keep the wolf from the door for as long as possible. With Samara insisting on her innocence, however ludicrously, came the promise of months of investigation, motions and preparation, followed by a trial and then, if she was convicted, a sentencing. If he strung it all out, it might even be long enough for his final act. He was tired, Jaywalker was. Twenty years of defending criminals might not seem like much to an outsider, but to Jaywalker, it had felt like an eternity. The thing about it was, you were always fighting. You fought prosecutors, cops and witnesses. You fought judges. You fought court officers and corrections officers. You fought your own clients, and your clients' family and friends. And if you had your own family and friends—which Jaywalker, perhaps tellingly, had precious few of—you got around to fighting them, too, sooner or later.

There'd been a time when he'd laughed at the word *burnout*. Like when his daughter had called from college two months into her freshman year to report that she was burned out from all the stress and needed plane fare to come home over Thanksgiving. He'd sent her a check, of course, but he'd had a good laugh at her complaint. Now, after twenty years of almost ceaseless fighting, Jaywalker knew there was indeed such a thing as burnout.

If he played his cards right, he figured, he could ride this hand for a year or more, maybe even two or three, before they began his actual suspension. That would be enough. No reapplying, no promises to the Character and Fitness Committee to behave himself better next time around. They could pull his ticket and do whatever they wanted to with it at that point. He'd get a job, write a book, drive a cab, go on welfare, get food stamps, rob a bank. Whatever. So simply in terms of forestalling the inevitable for as long as possible, Samara's case, coupled with her denial of her guilt, was an ideal one.

But if Jaywalker really wanted to be honest with himself, he knew there was more to it even than that. There was Samara herself.

From the moment he'd first seen her six years ago, when she'd come in on that drunk driving charge, he'd been swallowed whole by her dark eyes and pouting lower lip. Even as he'd fought to play the mature, steady defender to her reckless, impulsive child, from the beginning it had been she who'd owned him. Owned him in the sense that, try as he might, he could never take his eyes off her when he was in her presence. He'd dreamed of her at night and fantasized about her by day. Sexual fantasies, to be sure. But life-altering ones, as well. In one of his darker reveries, it had been the sudden, unexplained death of Samara's older husband that had driven her headlong into Jaywalker's comforting arms. So real and so elaborate had that particular scenario been that years later, when he first heard that Samara had been arrested for Barry's murder, Jaywalker had been forced to wonder if he himself weren't somehow complicit in the crime.

So the reasons were many why he'd hung on to her case, even at seventy-five dollars an hour. And now, as June gave way to July, it was all he had left, the only thing that stood between practicing his craft and being put out to pasture. And it represented his one last grand chance to overcome the impossible odds, slay the dragon, and win the dark-haired, dark-eyed princess of his dreams.

Why impossible odds?

Because in the ten months since he'd first sat down across from Samara in the counsel room to hear her say she hadn't killed her husband, things had indeed gone as Jaywalker had suspected they would—from bad to worse to downright dreadful.

The progression had begun almost immediately. From the twelfth-floor counsel visit room, Jaywalker had ridden the elevator down to the seventh floor, where he'd paid a visit to Tom Burke.

"Hey, Jay. Howyadoon?"

A lot of people called him Jay. Not having a first name kind of limited their options.

"Okay, I guess," said Jaywalker. "I've just spent the last three hours with Samara Tannenbaum." It was true. After Samara's denial of her guilt and his own assurance that he believed her, they'd talked for another hour and a half. If he'd been impressed with her willingness to miss the one o'clock bus back to Rikers, he was somewhat troubled by her evident need to keep the meeting going as long as possible.

"From what I hear," said Burke, "people have paid good money to spend thirty minutes with her. But I'll say this. She sure is good to look at."

"That she is," Jaywalker agreed.

"It's a shame she's a cold-blooded killer."

Jaywalker said nothing. He was there to listen and, hopefully, to learn a thing or two, not to posture about his client's innocence. Particularly when he himself was having trouble buying it.

"Did you read the stuff I gave you Friday?" Burke asked him.

"Yeah. And I appreciate your generosity." Jaywalker

wasn't being facetious. They both knew Burke had handed over much more than the law required at such an early stage of the proceedings.

"Hey," said Burke. "I got nothing to hide on this one. In my office, it's what we call a slam dunk."

"Why?"

"*Why?* I've got witnesses who put her there and have her arguing with the deceased at the time of death. I've got her false exculpatory statements, first that she wasn't there, then that they didn't fight. I've got the murder weapon hidden in her home. And I've got ten bucks that says that little dark-red stain on it is going to turn out to be a perfect DNA match with Barry's blood."

"No," said Jaywalker. "I didn't mean, *Why is it a slam dunk?* I meant, *Why did she do it?*"

Burke gave an exaggerated shrug. Jaywalker decided he could use a lesson or two on the art from Samara. "Hey," said Burke, "why do seventy percent of murders happen? Two people who know each other get into an argument about some trivial piece of bullshit. They start swearing and calling each other names. Maybe they've been drinking, or smoking something. One thing leads to another. If there happens to be a gun around, or a knife…" He extended his arms, elbows bent slightly, palms turned upward, as if to say that in such situations, murder was all but inevitable, a part of the human condition.

"That's it?"

"What are you looking for?" Burke asked. "A motive?"

"God forbid," said Jaywalker. The prosecution was never required to come up with a motive; the most they were ever asked to prove was intent. They taught you the difference in law school. You shot or stabbed or clubbed someone to death with the *intent* to kill them. Whether your *motive* behind that intent happened to be greed, say, as opposed to revenge or sadism, didn't matter.

Only it *did* matter, Jaywalker knew. Because if a crime

didn't make sense to him, it might not make sense to a jury, either.

"Tell you what," said Burke, reading Jaywalker's mind. "Give me two weeks, I bet I'll have a motive for you. Want to go double or nothing on that ten bucks?"

"Sure," said Jaywalker. "You're on."

It was less than two weeks later that Jaywalker found himself standing before the three disciplinary committee judges. So if now he needed yet another reason to include Samara's name on his list, he had it: he had twenty bucks riding on the outcome.

With Samara indicted but yet to appear in Supreme Court for her arraignment, the case fell into a legal limbo of sorts. In terms of formal proceedings, nothing would happen for the time being. No written motions could be filed yet, no hearings could be asked for, no plea could even be entered. Before any of those things could take place, the case would first have to travel from the fourth floor of 100 Centre Street to the eleventh. In real time, such a journey might be expected to take two minutes, three if the elevators were out of order, a fairly regular occurrence. But in courthouse time, it took three weeks.

"Sorry, counselor," the lower court judge would always say. "If I give you an earlier date, the papers won't make it upstairs in time."

"Give 'em to me," Jaywalker had pleaded over the years. "I'll have 'em up there before you can unzip your robe." But all it ever got him were unamused stares and even longer adjournments. To paraphrase an old saying, judges don't get mad, they get even.

That said, the fact that Samara's case was stalled in traffic for the next three weeks didn't mean it was time for Jaywalker to sit on his hands or catch up on old issues of *The New Yorker.* Quite the opposite.

Perhaps the single most overlooked job of the criminal

defense lawyer—overlooked by not only the general public but by too many defense lawyers themselves—is investigation. To far too many lawyers, investigation meant reading the reports turned over by the prosecution and, in the rare case that the defendant screamed loudly enough and often enough that he had an alibi, going through the motions of checking it out.

In Samara's case, Jaywalker had read, reread and all but memorized every word in the materials supplied by Tom Burke. He'd picked his client's brain and probed the recesses of her memory for a solid three hours, more time than a lot of lawyers spent talking with their clients over the life of a case. As far as any alibi defense was concerned, he'd ruled that out in the first five minutes. Samara, after initially lying to the detectives, now freely admitted that she'd been at Barry's apartment right around the time of his murder and had gone straight home from there, spending the rest of the evening alone.

Still, one of the first things Jaywalker did was to subpoena the records for both her home phone and her cell. There'd been a time when all you could get were records of outgoing long distance calls. Nowadays, with everything done by computer, there was a record of every call. MUDDs and LUDDs, they called them, for Multiple Usage Direct Dialed and Local Usage Direct Dialed. Who knew what might turn up? Suppose she'd phoned Barry right after getting home and had since forgotten that she'd done so. If he'd picked up, that fact would show up on her records, proving that he'd been alive, or at least that someone who was alive had been there. Either way, it would mean that Samara was innocent.

Innocent.

Funny word, thought Jaywalker. To him, it had an almost religious mystique. For in criminal law, the word all but disappeared. You pleaded *guilty* or *not guilty,* and the jury was instructed to decide if your guilt had been proven or not, and told to return a verdict of guilty or not guilty. The only time the words *innocent* or *innocence* were even uttered during the course of a trial occurred when the judge charged the jury to remember that in the eyes of the law, the defendant was presumed innocent. After that, it was all about guilty or not guilty; rarely was the word *innocent* ever heard again.

Which was just as well, particularly in Samara's case. For despite her insistence that she hadn't done it, Jaywalker knew it was just a matter of the passage of time and the building up of trust until she told him otherwise. Murder cases fell into two categories, he'd come to understand. There were the *whodunnits* and the *whyithappeneds*. If the evidence demonstrating that your client was the killer was shaky, you turned the trial into a whodunnit, raising what was sometimes referred to as the *SODDI* defense, for *Some Other Dude Did It.* On the other hand, if the evidence that your client did it was overwhelming, you looked around for things like self-defense, insanity or extreme emotional disturbance. In other words, you conceded that it was your client who committed the act that resulted in the victim's death, and focused instead on the circumstances, particularly the defendant's state of mind at the time of the incident.

What you never did was try to cover all bases. You didn't tell the jury, "My client didn't do it. And if he did, it was self-defense. And if it wasn't self-defense, he was insane." There was a name for lawyers who hedged their bets like that.

Losers.

Jaywalker was confident that Samara's case was going to turn into a *whyithappened.* When, sooner or later, she got around to admitting that she'd killed Barry, they would talk about the why. Her husband had done something to provoke her, no doubt. Perhaps he'd tormented her or threatened her, or come at her with something that, in her

desire to conceal her presence at his apartment, she'd
hidden or taken with her. Whatever it was, there had to be
a reason. Samara wasn't a cold-blooded killer, Jaywalker
was pretty sure. Something had happened that night, something significant enough to cause her to pick up a knife and
plunge it into her husband's chest. Getting Samara to let
go of the truth might prove to be a slow and painful process,
but it would happen.

Only it hadn't happened yet. Which meant that, for the
time being at least, Jaywalker had to proceed as though his
client were, well, *innocent.* As though indeed, some other
dude (or dame) had done it. In other words, it was time for
some investigation.

One of the things that set Jaywalker apart from his colleagues was that he did a lot of his own investigation. He
came by it naturally enough. Before he'd passed the bar
and landed his first lawyering job with Legal Aid, he'd put
in four years as an undercover agent with the DEA, the
Drug Enforcement Administration. There they'd taught
him how to bug a room, tap a phone, pick a lock, lift a print,
tail a car, run a license plate and locate the subscriber of
an unlisted phone number. He'd learned how to shoot a
gun, too, and, for that matter, how to break a nose, crush
a larynx and deliver a knee to the balls with astonishing ef-
ficiency, though those particular skills had pretty much
atrophied over the years. Most of all, he'd learned how to
pass, how to blend in. How to wear the clothes, walk the
walk and talk the talk of the street like one who'd grown
up on it. So once he'd made the move from apprehender
to defender, whenever a case called for some investigation—and to Jaywalker's thinking, *all* cases called for investigation—he liked nothing better than to assign the task
to himself.

There were times, however, when that didn't work.
Chief among them was when it was reasonable to believe
that somewhere down the line, Jaywalker the lawyer might

have to call Jaywalker the investigator to testify at trial. Woody Allen had actually given it a pretty good try in *Take the Money and Run,* alternately posing questions from the lectern and then racing to the witness stand to answer them. But it was pulling stunts just like that that had landed Jaywalker in hot water with the disciplinary committee, and he knew this was a particularly inopportune time to stage a retrospective of his antics. He decided that the investigation needed at the moment in Samara's case might indeed become the subject of trial testimony. It was, therefore, time to call someone else.

Unlike a few big earners he knew, Jaywalker didn't have his own private in-house investigator. Instead he had to rely on a handful of independents, from whom he cherry-picked, depending on the particular circumstances of the case at hand. If he wanted a Spanish-speaking investigator, for example, he reached out to Esteban Morales. If the assignment was in Harlem or Bed-Stuy, he'd call on Leroy "Big Cat" Lyons. If accounting expertise was required, there was Morty Slutsky, a CPA. If a woman's touch was indicated, Maggie McGuire had spent eight years as a rape crisis counselor.

But Jaywalker passed over all those names now, settling instead on Nicolo LeGrosso. LeGrosso, better known as "Nicky Legs," was a retired NYPD detective who'd put in his papers the day he had his "25 and 50," twenty-five years on the job and fifty years on the planet. "The job's changed," he'd told Jaywalker more than once. "In the old days, nobody messed with the Man. They might not'a liked you, but they left you alone. Nowadays, you walk down the block, they'd just as soon put a bullet in your ass as say hello to you."

Even at fifty-five, LeGrosso still had cop written all over him. His hair had grayed over the years, and his gut had grown, but there was no mistaking the instant impression that beneath his sports jacket, which he continued to wear on the hottest days of July, was a snub-nosed Smith & Wesson .38 detective special. None of the fancy new 14-round, 9 mm semiautomatic Glocks for Nicky Legs. If the revolver had been good enough for him and his brother, and his father before them, it was good enough for him still.

It was precisely because of LeGrosso's old-school looks and ways that Jaywalker reached out to him now. At this stage, Samara's case called for the reinterviewing of witnesses at Barry Tannenbaum's building, specifically the old woman in the adjoining apartment, and the doorman who'd seen Samara come and go the evening of the murder. Witnesses tended to get annoyed at having to repeat their stories over and over, Jaywalker knew. Still, they got less annoyed if the questioner presented himself as a father figure and one of the good guys. LeGrosso had a way of flashing his shield and announcing "Private detective" with so much emphasis on the second word that people tended to miss the *private* part altogether, even swore later on that they thought they'd been talking to a cop. And when called to testify in court, LeGrosso's demeanor was indistinguishable from that of real detectives, a quality that put him on equal footing with the prosecution's witnesses.

But there was even more. Twenty years on the job had taught LeGrosso how to deal with both government agencies and private companies. If there were two things he was universally known for, at least in the universe of New York City law enforcement, they were foul cigars and an uncanny ability to navigate the bowels of the most impenetrable bureaucracy.

If it was Jaywalker's theory that someone other than Samara had killed Barry Tannenbaum—and for the moment that had to be his theory, for lack of another—he needed a list of likely suspects. Samara had hinted in her statement to the police that Barry had made enemies on the way to amassing his fortune. Jaywalker wanted to know who those enemies were and if any of their grudges might have survived to the time of Barry's death, might even have figured in it.

Did he hope to solve the crime that way? Hardly. He was still pretty certain that it had been Samara herself who'd plunged the knife into her husband's chest, and almost as certain that over time she'd get around to admitting it and explaining why.

But suppose she didn't.

Some defendants never learned to trust their lawyers with their guilt, fearful that as soon as their secret had been shared, the passion would go out of their lawyer as surely as air goes out of a punctured balloon. And who could really blame them for feeling that way, given the fact that, as a group, lawyers had managed to earn themselves the reputation of being little more than suits filled with hot air?

Jaywalker liked to think that he was different, and that one of the things that made him different was that his clients learned to trust that he would fight as hard for them if he knew they'd committed the crime as he would if he believed they hadn't. But Samara might turn out to be one of the few who clung to her claim of innocence to the end. Should that turn out to be the case, finding Barry's enemies might not solve the crime, but it might be enough to cast doubt on Samara's guilt. And in a system that required the prosecution to prove her guilt beyond a reasonable doubt, that could mean the ball game.

He dialed Nicky Legs's number.

That same night, Jaywalker got a phone call from Samara. So far as he knew, he was the only criminal defense lawyer on the face of the earth who regularly gave out his home number to his clients. But he regarded it as nothing more than a necessary corollary of his also being the only lawyer who didn't own a cell phone. He hated the things, hated everything about them, and swore he'd go to his grave before he'd buy one. So what were his clients supposed to do when they desperately needed to reach him once he'd left his office? Talk to his answering machine?

"You're there," she said.

"I'm here." It seemed obvious enough, but he let it go. "What time is it?" he asked instead. He'd fallen asleep on the sofa, no doubt aided by a tumbler half full of Kahlúa.

"Five of ten," she said. "Listen, I need to see you. Can you have me brought over tomorrow for another visit?"

"I just saw you today," he reminded her. "For three hours. Besides, it's too late. I have to let them know by three o'clock."

"Shit," she said. "How about the day after?"

"Okay, sure."

They talked for another minute before he heard a C.O. telling her to wind it up. Evidently ten o'clock was cutoff time for the phones.

He got up from the sofa and tried to straighten up, but his back was having none of it; an ancient tennis injury saw to that. A lot of juniors on the tour got hurt, blowing out shoulders, elbows or knees on a fairly regular basis. Leave it to Jaywalker to have been different. In a moment of exhilaration following a straight-set upset of a highly ranked opponent, he'd made the mistake of jumping over the net in celebration. Most of him had cleared it, but the heel of his right sneaker had caught the very top of the tape. The result was an extremely red face (both literally and figuratively), three cracked vertebrae, and the sudden end to a promising career.

Maybe Samara was ready to trust him with the real story of Barry's death. That would be helpful. He jotted down a note to order her over for a counsel visit the day after tomorrow. Then he drained the last sip of Kahlúa from his tumbler. It was an absurd choice of drink, and he knew it, but he was way past apologizing for it. After his wife's death, he'd been completely unable to sleep, spending the hours twisting and turning, rearranging the covers, flipping the pillows, and reaching out for the warm body that was no longer his to find. The pills they prescribed for him left him feeling thick and groggy during the daytime, and unable to get any work done. Never much of a drinker, he gave it a try out of pure desperation and discovered that a glass of Scotch in the evening would buy him a couple hours of fitful sleep. Only thing was, it was like downing paregoric, or cod-liver oil. He tried bourbon, gin and vodka. He tried wine, beer, even hard cider. But everything tasted bitter and medicinal. Finally he followed his sweet tooth toward brandy, Amaretto and Grand Marnier, and found them drinkable, but barely. Then he came across an old, nearly empty bottle of Kahlúa in the very back of the bar cabinet. His wife had brought it back from Mexico and used it on special occasions, in place of sugar, to sweeten her coffee. Jaywalker took a swallow directly from the bottle and winced. It was almost like drinking maple syrup. But a sip or two later, he decided that once he got past the initial sweetness, he actually liked the taste of it.

Big mistake.

Huge mistake.

Still, he decided, there were probably worse things than being a nighttime alcoholic. He no longer drove, having long ago traded in his car and its $300-a-month reserved underground parking spot for a lifetime's worth of bus and subway MetroCards. He drank alone and only at home, so as not to make a fool of himself in public. And if he was gradually destroying his liver from the alcohol and wrecking his pancreas from the sugar, well, there were probably worse ways to die, too. You could amass a fortune, for example, only to end up with the business end of a steak knife in your heart.

He turned off the light and lay back down on the sofa. The good news was that he wouldn't have to make the bed in the morning.

10

"So what's up?"

"Nothing much," said Samara.

It was two days later, and they were sitting, as before, across from one another in the twelfth-floor counsel visit room. Samara looked tired, more tired than even the four-o'clock wake-up call should have made her look. Her hair was stringy, dark semicircles had begun to appear beneath her eyes, and her skin had taken on even more of that artificial fluorescent hue to it. Yet with all that, and the added distortion of the metal screen that separated the two of them, Jaywalker still couldn't pry his eyes off of her.

"You wanted to see me," he said. "You made it sound important."

"I can't stand it over there," she said. "All you do is sit around all day and listen to women cursing and screaming and fighting. From wakeup till lights-out, I spend every minute trying to keep from being beaten up or stabbed or worse."

He didn't need to ask her about *worse*.

"So I'd rather you have me pulled out every day and brought over here. If you don't mind."

It was Jaywalker's turn to shrug. "I don't mind," he said. "Except this Friday won't work."

She cocked her head, as though to ask why.

"I've got a little date with the disciplinary committee judges. It seems they want to take away my license to practice for a while."

Her eyes widened in panic. "But who's going to—"

"Don't worry," he said. "I'm pretty sure they'll let me finish up my pending cases."

"What did you do?"

"Oh, a lot of things."

"Like what?"

He smiled. "Want to know the best one?" he asked her, not quite sure why he was going there, but sure he was.

She nodded through the screen, and leaned forward conspiratorially. He guessed that if you spent your days listening to cursing and screaming and fighting, and trying to keep from being beaten up, stabbed or worse, a little naughty-lawyer gossip was a welcome change.

"It seems," he said, "that they've got a witness who says I, uh, got a blow job on the fifth-floor stairway landing."

"Hah!" she erupted with nothing less than glee.

It was the first time he'd heard her laugh out loud, or even seen her break out in a real smile. It barely mattered that her mirth had come at his expense; it was worth it.

"Did you?" she wanted to know.

"Well, it depends on what you mean by *did.*" Hey, if it had worked in the White House, why not in the Big House?

They spoke for a little over an hour, long enough for her to miss the one o'clock bus. They talked about a lot of things, including the meaning of *did,* his long-dead wife, and her recently dead husband. But not once did she come close to admitting that she'd killed Barry. Nor did he press her on the subject. Sometimes these things took time, he knew.

Before Jaywalker left, Samara made him promise to order her over for the following day, and for every day the next week. "And good luck on Friday," she added, "you stud, you."

He whistled his way back to the office that afternoon and the whole way home that evening, mercifully drowned out by the roar of the Number 3 train.

You stud, you.

"When can you get me out of here?" Samara asked him the following afternoon. "I don't know if I can make it through the next three days, stuck over there."

"You'll make it," he said. For a smart man, he was fully capable of saying truly stupid things. "It'll be another two weeks before I can even ask for bail, and..." He let his voice trail off, hoping she'd missed the *and*.

"And what?" Apparently not.

He explained to her that once they got to Supreme Court, they would have three chances to make a bail application, and that strategically it was essential that they pick the right one. There would be the judge in the arraignment part, the judge they would be sent to in the trial part, and—if he felt that both of those were disinclined to set bail—as a last resort, there were the judges of the Appellate Division. What he didn't have the heart to tell her was how poor their chances were, no matter which door they picked.

So she asked him, damn her.

"It's a long shot," was the most he was willing to tell her. The thing was, she looked so *fragile.* Her hair was better today, but the shadows beneath her eyes were darker than they'd been the day before, and her skin had even more of that pasty, fluorescent cast to it.

"I need you to promise me something," she said. Even through the wire mesh, he could tell she was looking at him intently.

Anything, he wanted to say. Instead, he simply stared back at her, waiting to hear what impossible demand she was going to make of him.

"I need you to get me out of here," she said in a steady

voice. "I don't care how. I'll do whatever I have to on my end, and I'll do it well. I'll have a heart attack, or a stroke. I'll go into an epileptic seizure. I don't care what it takes, I'll do it. Do you understand what I'm saying?"

"Yes, but—"

"No *buts,*" she said. "Promise me you'll think about it and come up with a plan." Her voice didn't rise at the end of the sentence. It wasn't a question so much as a demand.

As he replayed her words in his mind, he rationalized that technically, all she was really asking was that he think about it and try to come up with something. That much he could promise her, so he had. And with any other client, it would have ended right there and been forgotten. But Samara Tannenbaum wasn't any other client, and in the weeks that followed, Jaywalker would obsess over what she'd said and how she'd said it. There were defendants you knew almost instinctively not to trust. If you made a suggestion to them about the best way to phrase something on the witness stand, and they followed it and it didn't come out right, they would think nothing of saying, "My lawyer told me to say it that way." But there were other clients, too, clients you could count on to go down in flames before they would ever give you up. By telling Jaywalker that she'd do whatever it might take on her end, Samara Tannenbaum had announced that she was from that second, stand-up group as surely as she could have. What was more, she'd displayed an almost uncanny ability to locate and push the right button. Begging a lonely widower closing in on fifty to do whatever he could to fulfill his half of the bargain was sheer genius on her part. Could she possibly know the magnitude of the effect she had on him? Did she already comprehend, as he was only now beginning to, the lengths to which he would go to please her?

He suspected she did.

The realization sent an unexpected chill up the length

of his back, causing him to shudder. And for the first time, he could suddenly picture Samara lifting that knife in her small clenched fist and sliding it between her husband's ribs.

Friday came, and with it Jaywalker's appearance before the disciplinary committee judges, their imposition of the three-year suspension, and his plea that they allow him to complete his pending cases. At the end of the following week he had ten cases remaining on his calendar.

Including, of course, the one numbered Indictment 1846/05 and entitled *The People of the State of New York versus Samara Tannenbaum.*

Even with suspension looming and Jaywalker working hard to please the three-judge panel by *disposing of* as many of his remaining cases as possible, he still managed to find time each day to spend an hour locked up across from Samara in the twelfth-floor counsel visit room, and to remember each afternoon to request that she be brought back over again the following day.

Each day she asked him if he'd come up with any ideas to get her out, and each day she reaffirmed her willingness to do whatever it would take on her end. Each day he told her he was thinking about it, working on it, and that he'd come up with some ideas that he was playing around with in his mind. At the beginning of the week, these were lies, meant simply to placate her and put her off. But as the week wore on, Jaywalker found that his assurances were beginning to take on a life of their own, and he spent his evenings trying to concoct some scheme or plan that might just convince some judge to set bail. And by week's end, he'd actually come up with the seeds of an idea, however preliminary and far-fetched.

In the meantime, the case against Samara continued to mount.

* * *

On Monday, Nicolo LeGrosso had called to tell Jaywalker that he'd succeeded in interviewing both Barry Tannenbaum's next-door neighbor and the doorman who'd been on duty the evening of the murder. Both of them reiterated the accounts they'd given the detectives. The neighbor was as certain as she could be that it had been Barry and his wife "Sam" she'd heard arguing, and that after Sam had left there'd been no more voices. And although the doorman no longer had the logbook to show LeGrosso (the NYPD detectives having taken it), he was absolutely positive that Mr. Tannenbaum's only guest that evening had been his wife.

Nicky also reported that he'd struck out on trying to identify and interview the cabby who'd driven Samara home from Barry's the night of the murder. His subpoena to the Taxi and Limousine Commission had come back "no record." Either Samara had lied about taking a cab directly back to her place, or the cabby had taken her off the meter, pocketing the fare for himself. Other than Samara's word, there was no way of knowing.

On Wednesday, Tom Burke had phoned. "You owe me ten bucks," he announced.

"What for?" Jaywalker had forgotten what they'd bet on, but he was pretty sure from Burke's smug tone that it was Samara who was going to turn out to be the big loser.

"The knife," said Burke. "The one found behind the toilet tank at her place?"

"Right."

"Preliminary DNA tests show it's got Barry's blood on it. Ditto the blouse and the towel."

"You got the report already?"

"Not yet," said Burke. "They're way backed up over there. I got a phone call this morning, though, and I thought you'd like to know."

"Thanks," said Jaywalker. "You've made my day."

"Come on, don't tell me you're surprised."

"No, I'm not surprised."

"And, Jay?"

"Yeah?"

"Sorry about the suspension thing."

"Thanks, Tom. I'll be okay."

"They going to let you wind down your cases?"

"Seems like it. Some of them, anyway."

"Jay?"

"Yeah?"

"Keep this one, if you can. God knows she's going to need you."

Burke had called again the following day. "I still don't have the DNA report," he said. "But they phoned to tell me they've quantified the odds of its being anyone else's blood on the stuff besides Barry's."

"I can hardly wait," said Jaywalker. In the old days, back when all they could do was type blood by group, such as A Positive, AB Negative or O Positive, the best they could typically tell you was that fifty or sixty percent of the population could be excluded as suspects. Then, with the advent of HLA testing, the figure jumped, reaching the nineties. But DNA was a different story altogether. Now the numbers suddenly lifted off and soared into the stratosphere. And it was those numbers, typically described as "astronomical," that had completely revolutionized the science of identification.

"You ready?" asked Burke.

"Sure. Lay it on me."

"The odds that it's *not* Barry's blood are precisely one in twelve billion, six hundred and fifty-two million, one hundred and eighty-nine thousand, four hundred and twelve."

Although Burke had read off the numbers deliberately enough for Jaywalker to copy them down, he hadn't both-

ered. He knew his DNA, and as soon as he'd heard the
twelve billion part, it had been enough for him.

There weren't that many people on the planet.

By Friday Jaywalker had been told that he could keep
enough cases to know that Samara's would be among them.
He broke the news to her through the wire mesh of the
twelfth-floor counsel visit room.

"That's terrific," she said. "Have you come up with a
plan to get me out?"

"Let me ask you a question first."

"Okay."

"Remember that stuff they say they found behind the
toilet tank at your place?" He was careful to include the
words "they say." Omitting them would have told her that
he was willing to accept the detectives' version as true.

"Yes," she said. "The knife, the blouse and..."

"The towel."

"Right. What about them?"

"You told me you didn't know anything about them,
right?"

"Right."

"Are you absolutely sure?"

"Yes," she said. "Why?"

"They've found Barry's blood on them."

Shrug time.

"Who could have put them there?" he asked.

"I don't know. Whoever killed Barry and wanted to
make it look like I did it?"

"From the time you got home after leaving Barry's,
until the police showed up and arrested you, was there
anyone else in your place, besides you? Think carefully."

She seemed to do just that for a moment. What Jaywalker had no way of knowing was whether she was
genuinely trying to reach back three weeks earlier and
remember. Or had it suddenly dawned on her what a

terrible trap she'd put herself into? Half of him expected her to break down right then and there and confess. The other half, knowing Samara, knew better.

Liars tended to stick to their lies, however absurdly. Years ago, after he'd informed a client that a full set of his prints had been found on a demand note left behind at a bank robbery, the man had looked Jaywalker squarely in the eye and said, "Hey, what can I tell you? Somebody must be using my fingerprints."

"No," said Samara. "No one else was there."

"So how could those things have gotten there?"

"I have no idea," said Samara, this time without hesitation. "I guess the cops must've put them there."

Somebody must be using my fingerprints.

"So, have you come up with a plan?" she pressed.

"Sort of," said Jaywalker, amazed that she could recover quickly enough to change the subject without missing a beat.

She leaned forward.

"Not now," he said, looking around. "Not here." Although his words and glances were meant to convey that there were too many eyes and ears nearby, the truth was that Jaywalker's *sort of* plan suddenly seemed foolish and unworkable. On top of that, Samara's cavalier attitude, in the face of a truly damning piece of evidence, upset him more than he was willing to admit. If she wasn't willing to level with him and trust him with the truth, how could he possibly become a co-conspirator in a scheme to get her bailed out on false pretenses?

"When?" she asked him.

"Monday," he said. "We're due in court for your arraignment. We'll talk then."

She sat back in her chair, crossed her arms in front of her breasts and pouted, but it was only a little pout. Monday was only three days away, after all, and even in the world that Samara Tannenbaum inhabited, where there was no past and no future, and everything was about imminent peril and instant gratification, three days was evidently something she could handle.

11

DID YOU SAY BAIL?

"Samara Tannenbaum," read the clerk, "you have been indicted for the crime of murder, and other crimes. How do you plead, guilty or not guilty?"

"Not guilty," said Samara.

This was the moment when Jaywalker would normally ask the judge for bail. But they were in front of Carolyn Berman again. She was the one who'd frozen Samara's bank account last month, then modified it only to the extent of allowing her to retain counsel at the rate of seventy-five dollars an hour. Besides, she was a woman, and experience had taught Jaywalker that, as a rule, women judges were tougher on women defendants than male judges were. It was a rule that took on even more meaning when the defendant happened to be not only a woman, but a young, pretty woman, and one of immense privilege.

So Jaywalker said nothing.

He liked saying nothing, another fact that set him apart from every other lawyer he knew. He especially liked saying nothing at a time like this, when the media were assembled in the audience behind him—the print reporters, the gossip columnists, the entertainment-show beauties and the sketch artists peering over their pads in their bifocals. Afterward, outside the courtroom, when they would follow him, train their floodlights on him and poke their microphones in his face, he would elaborate on saying nothing and tell them, "No comment."

"Part 51," said the clerk. "Judge Sobel."

At last they'd caught a break of sorts. Matthew Sobel was a gentle person, a judge who wore his robe with modesty, and treated lawyers and defendants with respect. While he was no "Cut-'em-loose" Bruce Wright, or Murray "Why-are-you-bringing-me-this-piece-of-shit-case?" Mogel from the old days, you could count on getting a fair trial in front of him, and ending up with a reasonable sentence even if you lost. What's more, he was open-minded on the issue of bail. And he was a man.

"Judge Sobel asks that you pick a Tuesday," said Judge Berman.

"How's tomorrow?" Jaywalker asked.

"Too soon."

Again that old problem of papers having to make their way from one courtroom to another, in this case from the eleventh floor all the way up to the thirteenth.

"A week from tomorrow?"

"Fine," said Judge Berman. "Next case."

Afterward Jaywalker met with Samara. This time, however, they enjoyed the semiprivacy of a holding pen, a close cousin of a feeder pen. Since Samara was the only woman who'd been brought down for court so far that morning, she had the pen to herself, and they spoke through the bars, close enough to touch—a fact that Jaywalker was acutely aware of.

After hearing the conditions of his suspension, the weekend had rejuvenated him somewhat. It had also given him a chance to get over his annoyance at Samara's apparent lack of concern over Barry's blood having been found on the items hidden in her town house. He leaned forward against the bars and spoke to her in hushed tones. She, the better part of a foot shorter than he, listened intently, her face turned upward, her eyes meeting his, her lips silently mouthing his words as if to commit them to memory.

They spoke for twenty minutes like that, until a corrections officer interrupted them to explain that he had to bring Samara back upstairs, so they could use the holding pen for an "obso," a mental case, someone who had to be segregated from the general population and kept under observation.

Riding down the elevator and walking out into the mid-morning daylight, all Jaywalker could think of was Lynne Stewart, the lawyer who'd made news by getting caught on tape and sent off to federal prison for things she'd said to her client during a jailhouse visit.

What am I doing? he asked himself.

Talk about an obso.

A week went by. Jaywalker managed to *dispose of* the first case on his list of ten and dutifully reported the fact to the disciplinary committee judge monitoring his progress. Outdoors, there was a noticeable chill in the air each morning, prompting him to put away his two summer suits for warmer ones, and the October evenings seemed to settle in earlier and earlier with each passing day. At home alone in his apartment, Jaywalker found he was filling his tumbler of Kahlúa a little fuller each night, and draining it a little more quickly.

A copy of the DNA report arrived in the mail from Tom Burke, confirming the fact that the blood found on the knife, the blouse and the towel found in Samara Tannenbaum's town house had indeed been her late husband's, to a certainty factor of 12,652,189,412 to 1.

Samara continued to be brought over from Rikers Island each morning and returned each evening. In between her bus trips, Jaywalker saw her each day in the twelfth-floor counsel visit room. They talked very little about her case, even less about her chances of being granted bail on her next appearance. But he could see she was doing her homework, holding up her end of the bargain. The shadows beneath her eyes had darkened and widened into deep hollows. Her hair had taken on an unwashed, dead quality. Her lips had dried and cracked, and the lower one had shrunk visibly, until it was now almost normal in size.

She was, in a word, *wasting,* wasting away before his eyes, like some third-world refugee from a famine or a plague.

"Perfect," he told her.

They made their first appearance before Judge Sobel the following Tuesday. The media was barely in evidence this time. Jaywalker's strategy of keeping their courtroom sessions as brief as possible and saying nothing quotable afterward had evidently had its desired effect. And by delaying his arrival to the late afternoon, daring those who'd showed up early to wait around all day, he'd managed to thin their ranks even more.

A judge's courage tends to grow, Jaywalker had learned, in inverse proportion to the size of his audience. Fill a courtroom with spectators and press, and even the best judge, even a Matthew Sobel, will posture and play to them, however subtly and even unconsciously. Wait until the end of the day, when the rows of benches have emptied, and your chances of getting what you need for your client multiply almost exponentially.

"Is your client all right?"

Those were literally the first words out of the judge's mouth, upon seeing Samara brought into the courtroom.

"No," said Jaywalker. "Actually, she's not."

Samara was permitted to sit at the defense table, facing the judge. Sobel had no doubt seen photographs of her; everyone had. But the photographs unfailingly depicted a stunningly beautiful woman, a diminutive version of the trophy wife in every respect except for her hair, which was dark and straight, instead of the expected bimbo blond.

The woman Judge Sobel was staring at now looked like an advanced-stage AIDS patient who'd survived a train wreck. In addition to the wasted look she'd developed over the month of her incarceration, she sported a gash across her forehead and a black left eye, noticeable not so much because of its discoloration, which blended almost seamlessly into the dark hollow beneath it, but because the eye itself was swollen nearly shut and tearing visibly. Tufts of her hair appeared to have been pulled out, and she reached for the side of her head repeatedly, a gesture that only served to draw attention to the large white bandage that covered her hand.

"Is this in honor of Halloween?" Tom Burke asked, perhaps in the hope that a bit of levity might break the silence that had enveloped the courtroom.

Jaywalker turned in Burke's direction, fixing him with a hard stare but saying nothing, choosing instead to let the remark twist in the air.

Judge Sobel finally found his voice. "Come up," he motioned the lawyers, "and tell me what's going on."

At the bench, with the court reporter taking down every word but the spectators unable to hear, Jaywalker spoke softly. "Not surprisingly," he explained, "my client immediately became a target on Rikers Island. She's white, she's rich, she's small and she's pretty. *Was* pretty, at least. Anyway, she tried to be a trooper, putting up with the harassment as long as she could. The breaking point came when she was sexually assaulted. That's when she finally reached out for help. The problem was, she didn't know whom to reach out *to*. Instead of calling me or asking to see a captain, she phoned the corrections commission."

"Those clowns?" said Burke.

It was true. The commissioners belonged to an oversight group, separate and apart from the corrections department, and were loathed as meddlers by everyone in the prison hierarchy.

"How was she supposed to know?" asked Jaywalker. "Anyway, they began investigating. I've got one of the commissioners here in court, if you want verification. They interviewed officers, lieutenants, even a captain or two. Or at least tried to. Needless to say, that only made things worse. Now my client gets attacked by inmates on an hourly basis, and the C.O.s not only look the other way, they write her up for instigating. She's been put in an impossible position."

"She's put herself in it," said Burke.

Sobel ignored the remark. "Okay," he said, "the first thing she needs is medical attention."

"With all due respect," said Jaywalker, sensing his opening, "the first thing she needs is to get out of there."

"Maybe my office could get her transferred to Bedford Hills," said Burke. "Or a federal prison."

"There's a problem with that," said Sobel. "As soon as I do it with one, I set a precedent. Next thing you know, we'll have busloads of inmates showing up with self-inflicted wounds, looking to get transferred out."

Jaywalker bit down on the inside of his cheek, willing any thoughts of self-inflicted wounds to evaporate from the judge's mind. "Is there any chance you'd consider some kind of bail?" he asked. "I'm afraid that if she doesn't get out, we're going to have another death on our hands."

"Did you say *bail?*" yelped Burke. For someone who should have seen where this was going, he seemed incredulous. "This is a *murder* case."

Sobel held up his hand, but Jaywalker decided it wasn't meant for him. "Look," he said, "she's not going anywhere. Take her passport, strap an ankle bracelet on her, lock her up in her house."

"This is a *murder* case," Burke repeated. "I've got a *DNA match.* You can't go and set *bail.*"

It was the wrong thing to say.

Turning to Burke, Judge Sobel spoke as calmly as ever.

But it was clear from his words that he hadn't particularly cared for being told what he could and couldn't do. "Tell me," he said. "If this were any other kind of case, would we be arguing that this defendant presents a particularly significant flight risk?"

Burke hesitated for just a moment. Jaywalker could imagine the struggle going on within him. A less honest prosecutor would have immediately answered "Yes" without blinking. Burke was trapped by his own decency. "The point is," he said, trying to address the question without quite answering it, "the murder charge is what gives her the incentive to flee."

"That's a bit circular," Sobel observed, "isn't it? I mean, if the seriousness of the charge were the only consideration, judges would have to deny bail in all serious cases. But we don't. As a matter of fact, we set bail in murder cases from time to time, if the circumstances are unusual. I myself remember setting bail in a murder case of yours, Mr. Burke, as well as in one of Mr. Jaywalker's. And neither of those defendants fled, as I recall."

"But what are the unusual circumstances here, judge?" An edginess was beginning to appear in Burke's voice that sounded very much like the beginning of panic.

"Take a good look at the defendant for a moment, why don't you? Tell me that's not unusual."

Burke looked, said nothing.

Jaywalker didn't say anything, either. He'd long ago learned what most lawyers never do, to quit when you're ahead.

It took the better part of the week, what with getting Judge Berman's order modified once again, tracking down the title to Samara's town house, and dealing with the bank where her account was. Banks, it seems, like to dot all the *i*'s and cross all the *t*'s before coughing up a hundred thousand dollars. Then there was the matter of surrendering Samara's passport, and the necessity of getting her fitted with what one corrections official quaintly referred to as a "Martha Stewart bracelet, only in petite."

But that Friday afternoon, when Jaywalker walked out of the courthouse and into the early November chill, Samara Tannenbaum was at his side. This time the media were there in all their glory, video cameras running, still cameras clicking, furry microphones extended. Samara, who actually looked a bit better than she had three days earlier, forced a half smile but didn't speak. But Jaywalker, forsaking his usual silent treatment of the press, was positively expansive.

"Samara's going home to rest and recuperate," he told them. "We wish you all a very pleasant weekend."

12

TWENTY-FIVE MIL

In terms of trial preparation, the difference between having a client in jail and having one out on bail is all the difference in the world. Conversations that would otherwise have to be conducted in whispers through bars or wire mesh, or over antique telephones, can suddenly be held in normal tones, unimpeded by physical barriers. Documents that would have to be copied and mailed, or slid through security slits, can instead be studied shoulder to shoulder. Friendly witnesses can be approached as a unified team, rather than by a solitary stranger bearing a dubious letter of introduction scribbled on a square of jailhouse toilet paper.

The very act of getting a client out of jail also tends to win the trust of that client in a way that little else can, short of actually winning an acquittal. Especially when the charge is murder, and the odds against getting bail set had seemed almost as prohibitive as those that it was someone else's blood besides Barry's on the items found in Samara's town house.

It was Jaywalker's hope, and in fact his honest expectation, that he would be able to parlay that newly earned trust into getting Samara to level with him, to finally tell him the truth about what had happened the evening of Barry's death. While the terms of her release kept her largely confined to her home, they allowed her to travel to and from the courthouse, her lawyer's office and a short list of stores, so long as she phoned ahead to announce her intention, and received permission to come and go. The least infraction would land her back on Rikers Island, Judge Sobel had promised her. And should she attempt to remove the electronic monitoring device, or cut the bracelet that fastened it to her ankle, a signal would be automatically transmitted to the corrections department, and she could expect to be apprehended within thirty minutes. Still, it was a lot of freedom, compared to the conditions she'd lived under for the previous month.

There was yet another reason why Jaywalker held high hopes that Samara would come clean with him. They were co-conspirators now. Each of them had played a role in a scheme to obtain bail under what amounted to false pretenses. As was typical of his signature stunts, Jaywalker hadn't exactly broken the law, though he'd come about as close as he could without ever quite crossing the line. Nothing he'd said to Judge Sobel had been literally untrue. Samara had indeed become a target on Rikers Island. As much as Jaywalker hated playing the race card, the combination of his client's whiteness, her prettiness, her size and her notoriety had been too much for the other inmates to ignore. She'd been taunted, cursed at, spat at, shoved and slapped around. Even the business about a sexual assault had been true, though it had amounted to little more than a hallway groping. What's more, Samara *had* called the corrections commissioners. But she'd done so only because Jaywalker had instructed her to, knowing full well that the commission's investigation would have the precise negative repercussions that it turned out to.

For her part, Samara had accentuated her physical decline by starving herself of both food and sleep. Her daily visits to the courthouse allowed her to miss her two-a-week showers; while she made a concession to that deprivation when it came to deodorant, the absence of shampoo took a visible toll on her hair. As far as the shiner, the forehead gash and the bandaged hand were concerned, Jaywalker neither knew nor particularly wanted to know the details, but her rapid recovery from all three ailments strongly suggested they'd been greatly exaggerated, if not out-and-out self-inflicted.

So they were in this together, this soon-to-be-suspended lawyer and his malingering murderer of a client. And Jaywalker had every reason to hope that, just as it's said that there's honesty among thieves, so too would there be candor between conspirators.

He made his first stab at it in his office, five days after he'd walked Samara out of the courthouse. She was half sitting, half reclining on his sofa, an old thrift-shop thing that a lot of Naugas must have surrendered their hides to cover. He sat half a room away, by design safely ensconced behind the barrier of his desk. It wasn't Samara he was afraid of this time; it was he himself Jaywalker didn't trust.

"Listen, Samara," he said.

"I'm listening."

"I need you to talk to me."

"Once upon a time—"

"Stop," he said. "I know you're happy to be out, and I'm happy for you. But this is serious. I mean I need you to talk to me about the case."

"What about it?"

"Well, for starters, you were the only one at Barry's apartment that evening. The two of you have an argument, loud enough to be heard through the wall of a prewar building. After you leave, the apartment suddenly becomes quiet. Barry's body gets found the next day with a fatal stab wound to the heart. Along with a blouse and a towel, a knife is found hidden away in your place. All three have Barry's blood on them. Nobody but you had been there since his death. When questioned by the police, you lie about having been at Barry's, and about having argued."

"Looks bad, huh?"

"Yes, it looks bad." Jaywalker realized that, almost unconsciously, he'd gradually been lowering his volume as he'd progressed through his narrative, and at the same time he'd slowed his tempo. It was his sad voice, his voice of the inevitable. By using it, he'd been verbally putting his arms around Samara from across the room, hugging her to him as a father might hug a daughter, all the while calming her, patting her, stroking her softly. With the modulation of his voice, he'd been telling her that it was all right for her to let go of the awful burden that came with not being able to share some terrible secret. He'd been trying to make it seem that her *not* opening up to him would be infinitely worse, nothing less than a betrayal, in fact, a signal that he wasn't a trustworthy friend after all, just another lawyer better kept at arm's length.

Now he put it into words, offering her the key. Lowering his voice even further, he looked into her eyes and said the actual sentence that needed to be said. "It's okay to tell me."

Samara sat up straight. For a second Jaywalker's ego got the better of him, and he readied himself to hear her *mea culpa.*

"You know what?" Samara asked him.

"What?"

"*Fuck you,* that's what." Then she said it again, at least the *Fuck you* part, as though he needed to hear it more than once. Then she stood up, grabbed her jacket and said, "Can I use your phone? I've got to tell them I'm going home."

"Sit down, Samara."

The firmness of his own voice took Jaywalker by surprise. It seemed to make something of an impression on Samara, too. She didn't actually sit down, but she did at least look his way and engage him.

"I don't care *how* bad things look," she hissed. "You can't *possibly* know I killed Barry."

Given her choice of the word *know,* Jaywalker was about to agree on a technicality, when he realized Samara had merely taken a midsentence breath and had more to say.

"Because I didn't," she added. "So fuck you for making it sound like I did. You have no right."

"Sorry," he said, "but not only do I have the right, I have the obligation. It's my job. It's what you're paying me the big bucks for. Look, Samara, you may not enjoy looking at the evidence and seeing how strong it is, but sooner or later that's exactly what a jury's going to be asked to do. So we've got a choice. We can stick our heads in the sand and ignore it, or we can talk about what they're going to see when they look. Besides which, if you *didn't* kill Barry—and you're right, I can't possibly know if you did or you didn't—it's only by looking at the evidence that we're ever going to figure out a way to win this thing."

That seemed to help. At least she sat back down.

But there are victories, and there are victories. Though they talked for another hour, not once did Samara even come close to admitting that she'd killed her husband. She was evidently one of those people, he decided, who found denial the toughest addiction of all to break.

Outside the lone window to the office, the November darkness was already settling in, and Jaywalker decided it was time to call a halt to the meeting. Samara phoned the corrections department to tell them she was heading home, well in advance of her eight o'clock curfew. Jaywalker shared a cab uptown with her, stopping directly in front of her building. Opening the door to get out, she turned to him and asked, "Want to come in?"

"Uh, I don't think that would be, uh, the best, uh… Know what I mean?"

Smiling at his embarrassment, Samara turned away and got out. He watched her until she'd unlocked the door of her building and disappeared from view. Then he gave his own address to the cabdriver. The man, who looked Middle Eastern and according to the placard on the partition went by the name of Ali Bey Ali, responded with something that sounded like *Yoonorn*. Though Jaywalker couldn't quite make sense of it, he figured it might have been *New York*, so he said, "Yes, New York." It was only twenty blocks later that it came to him.

The man had said, "You moron."

With Samara firmly in denial, Jaywalker realized that, in contrast to the way things had proceeded in her DWI case six years earlier, this time there would be no quick guilty plea. He was in the case for the long haul. Which meant it was time to prepare written motions. He had long ago devised a computer template for the purpose, and the following day he pulled it up on his screen. His motions, like most everything else about him, differed markedly from those of his colleagues. Where theirs were lengthy and exhaustive, asking for all sorts of things they weren't entitled to, his were short and focused. Where theirs cited long strings of cases that were rarely if ever on point, his rarely contained a single citation. And where theirs were written in florid and redundant legalese, his were crafted in crisp, short sentences. He'd tried preaching his method to those who were willing to listen, but he'd won few converts. The more pages a set of motion papers ran to, the more hours its creator felt justified in billing for. In the end, as so often happened, other lawyers tended to make more money, while Jaywalker got better results.

As required by the statute, Jaywalker made a motion to have Samara's indictment dismissed. But knowing it would be denied, he wasted little time on it. Ditto when it came to discovery. Tom Burke had already given the defense far more than it was entitled to under the statutory timetable, and he could be counted on to continue doing so. When it came to the matter of suppression of evidence, however, Jaywalker slowed down. This was the important part of motion practice, he knew.

The constitutions of both the United States and the state of New York prohibit, among other things, conducting unreasonable searches and compelling a person to testify against himself. For many years, if a police officer violated either of those provisions—say by searching an individual's home with no good reason, or by beating a confession out of a suspect—the officer could be prosecuted, administratively punished, even sued for damages. But those things happened about as often as Martian landings. Beginning in the 1950s, the Supreme Court (the real one this time, not the one on the upper floors of 100 Centre Street) finally got around to realizing that if the prohibitions were to amount to anything in real life terms, the judges would have to come up with a more meaningful formula for discouraging police misconduct. What they came up with has come to be known as the exclusionary rule.

The exclusionary rule, surprisingly enough, means pretty much what it sounds like. It means that, in order to deter that unreasonable search or beating, the fruits of it will be excluded from trial, or suppressed. In a series of landmark cases, among them *Mapp v. Ohio* (search and seizure) and *Miranda v. Arizona* (confessions), the so-called Warren court added teeth to the exclusionary rule, by defining "unreasonable" and "involuntary" in broad terms. More recently, the so-called Rehnquist court did its level best to pull those teeth, but with no better than mixed results.

Written motion papers are the vehicle by which a defense lawyer seeks to trigger an evidentiary hearing, one in which witnesses testify, to determine whether something ought to be suppressed. If that something happens to be physical evidence, the lawyer must assert facts to support three things. First, he must demonstrate *illegality,* that an unreasonable search in fact occurred and led to the seizure of the evidence. Second, that there was *state action*, that it was some branch of law enforcement, whether federal, state or local, that conducted the unreasonable search. Third, that the defendant has the requisite *standing* to complain about the illegality, by being the person *aggrieved* by the violation of his reasonable expectation of privacy.

The knife, the blouse and the towel fit the bill nicely enough. There certainly had been a search, and if the affidavit in support of the search warrant recited less than probable cause to believe that Samara had committed some crime, then the seizure of the items was illegal. The detectives were employed by the NYPD, satisfying the state action requirement. And Samara was certainly the person aggrieved by any illegality, since it was her home that had been searched.

The requirements are similar, though slightly different, when it comes to confessions or admissions, which are partial confessions, elicited from suspects. In that case the issue changes from whether the search was reasonable or not to whether the statement was *voluntary* or not. First, there must have been a statement made; defendants who make no statements therefore get nowhere by insisting they were never read their Miranda rights. Second, there must once again have been state action; the statement must have been made in response to questioning by law enforcement personnel. A spontaneous utterance therefore fails the test, as does a confession made to a private person. Third, the questioning must have taken place in a custodial setting—at a point in time when the individual was under arrest or, at very least, under the impression that he wasn't free to leave. Finally, there must have been a failure on the part of the questioner to both advise the individual of his right not to answer, and to obtain from the individual a *knowing and intelligent waiver* of that right.

Samara's false exculpatory statements—first that she hadn't been at Barry's apartment that evening, and then that they hadn't argued—qualified as admissions. They were made to detectives, who were certainly law enforcement personnel. And never did those detectives read her her Miranda rights, or obtain a waiver of them from her. Once she asked for a lawyer, there would have been no point to their doing so, since the questioning was effectively terminated at that point. The stumbling block, Jaywalker knew, would be the custody issue. The detectives had been careful to question Samara before placing her under arrest. He would have to argue that their presence in her home, coupled with their overbearing demeanor, reasonably led her to believe that she wasn't free to leave or to kick them out.

It would be an uphill battle, to say the least.

When he was done, Jaywalker's motion papers ran to ten pages, longer than in most of his cases. Unhappy about the fact, he reminded himself that this was a murder case. And he took consolation from having seen lawyers bringing motions to the clerk's office in shopping carts.

That afternoon, Jaywalker got a call from Nicolo Le-Grosso.

"Howyadoon?" LeGrosso said.

"Okay," said Jaywalker. "Whadayagot for me?"

When Jaywalker's wife had been alive, she'd often complained about his chameleonlike habit of seamlessly lapsing into the speech pattern of whomever he was talking to, whether it happened to be a defendant, a witness, a cop or someone else accustomed to butchering the English language. "Speak like a lawyer," she'd scolded him. "You'll never win their respect by sounding like one of them." He'd tried to explain that it wasn't respect he was trying to win, only cases.

Now that his wife was dead, he still heard her voice every time he broke her admonition. But he couldn't help himself. Four years in law enforcement had done it to him, the same way four years in the military probably would have, or four years in a locker room. And the truth was, he wouldn't have changed even if he could have. It was one of the things that drew people to him, made them feel at ease with him. It's not such a long leap, after all, from "He sounds like one of us" to "He *is* one of us."

"I got *bobkiss,*" said Nicky, proving that Italians who try to talk Jewish shouldn't. "Got the LUDDs and MUDDs you subpoenaed on your girlfriend's phones."

"She's not my girlfriend."

"Yeah, right. I seen her picture. I give you one month before you're in the sack with her."

Jaywalker thought about protesting, but let the remark go. You never won an argument with Nicky, he'd learned. Besides, he made it a policy never to bet against himself. "Anything on the phone records?" he asked instead.

"Nah. A couple of calls that night, but nothing to Barry boy."

"How about finding out if Barry had any enemies?" Jaywalker asked him. "Any luck there?"

"You bet," said Nicky. "A shitload of 'em, actually. Gimme a couple days, I'll have a whole who's who for you."

"Good."

Maybe one of them would turn out to have had a reason to kill Barry. And even if Jaywalker couldn't prove that some enemy had been able to get into the apartment that evening to do it, at least it would be a start. Because up until now, with unrelenting consistency, everything continued to point in Samara's direction. Something needed to happen, and it needed to happen soon.

Something did.

But when it did, it was anything but what Jaywalker was hoping for.

Tom Burke phoned to announce that Jaywalker now owed him not ten but twenty bucks.

"What?" Jaywalker asked. He'd forgotten what their double-or-nothing had been riding on.

"Motive," said Burke.

Jaywalker, who'd been standing up when he answered the phone, slumped into his chair, already feeling as though he might lose his lunch. Not that losing a bag of pretzels and a bottle of Snapple iced tea would be the end of life as he knew it.

"Check this out," said Burke, with barely restrained glee. "A month before the murder—actually thirty-three days, if you want to get technical—your client takes out a life insurance policy on her husband. Costs her a pretty penny, too, like twenty-seven grand. Want to guess how much the policy was for?"

"A trillion dollars." Jaywalker always went for the ridiculous in such conversations. That way he could pretend to be unfazed when he heard the actual lesser amount.

"Close," said Burke. "Twenty-five mil."

"Shit," said Jaywalker, way beyond fazed.

13

GIVING UP

Looking back on the case afterward, Jaywalker would never fail to remember that phone call, in which Tom Burke had broken the news of the life insurance policy to him, as the moment he gave up on Samara Tannenbaum.

It had long been Jaywalker's belief that if you were to pull any ten criminal cases out of a hat, one of those ten could be won by the very worst of defense lawyers. A vital prosecution witness would die or disappear, the arresting officer would get indicted as part of a car-theft ring, or something else would happen, causing the case against the defendant to disintegrate in front of the jury. At the opposite end of the spectrum would be the tenth case, one that even the best of defense lawyers couldn't possibly win. The D.A. would not only have the proverbial smoking gun, but would be prepared to back it up with a videotape of the defendant committing the crime, a DNA match, fingerprints and a signed confession. In between those two extremes lay eight cases that were up for grabs. With prosecuting offices reporting conviction percentages anywhere from the mid-sixties all the way up to the high nineties, it followed that many defenders won none of the remaining eight—ever. Average lawyers won two, maybe three. It was only the exceptional lawyer who could win half.

Jaywalker won them all.

He knew, because he kept track.

He hadn't always done so. He'd begun after one particularly satisfying acquittal on a double-murder case, when it dawned on him that it made six in a row. Ever since, he'd kept tabs. Not on paper—that would have been far too vain. He kept tabs in his head, the way he'd secretly kept track of his batting average in Little League, comparing himself to Rod Carew or Wade Boggs, or whoever happened to be leading the major leagues at the time. In a business where most of his colleagues were struggling to win a third of their cases, Jaywalker's success rate topped ninety percent. It was the same success rate that the disciplinary committee had taken note of, even as they'd handed down his three-year suspension.

Now he'd learned that barely a month before her husband's murder, Samara had secretly bet twenty-seven thousand dollars on a thousand-to-one shot that Barry would be dead before the year was out. *Secretly,* because according to Burke, she'd taken out the policy on her own, authorizing in writing the payment of the premium from her own bank account, apparently without Barry's even knowing about it. And *before the year was out,* because it was a term policy, the term being six months, without so much as a standard renewability clause.

With that knowledge, Jaywalker had mentally taken Samara's case and moved it from the *up-for-grabs* stack over to the *can't-be-won* pile. It wasn't just the insurance policy itself, even with its pregnant timing and damning clauses. No, it was more than that. It was the way that Samara had hidden its existence from him, just as she'd hidden it from Barry. And the way that, when confronted about it, she continued to deny knowing anything about it. Jaywalker was forced to obtain from Burke one of the original duplicate application forms, so that he could have Samara examine her signature, her address, her date of birth, her Social Security number and her designation of herself as sole beneficiary.

"It sure looks like my writing," she admitted. "But maybe we should get one of those handwriting expert guys, just to make sure."

"Don't worry," Jaywalker told her. "Burke's already doing that."

He spent Thanksgiving at his daughter's, in New Jersey. Both she and her husband remarked about how tired he looked and asked him if it was the suspension that was getting him down.

"Not really," he said. "I was working too hard on a murder case, I guess."

"How'd it turn out?" his son-in-law asked.

"It's still going on."

Though they said nothing, he gathered from their stares that there'd been something strange about the way he'd said *I was working,* as though the case was indeed over.

November gave way to December, and Jaywalker turned his attention to other cases on his list of ten, by now down to seven. He rented a car and drove two hours up to Rhinebeck to visit his fourteen-year-old client in drug rehab, bringing a smile to the kid's face that lit up the whole rec room. He obtained an S visa for his Sudanese umbrella salesman, saving him from almost certain deportation. And he held the hand of his janitor's helper, making it three straight court appearances that the man hadn't wet his pants while standing in front of the judge.

As the holidays approached, business at 100 Centre Street slowed to a crawl, and Samara's case was adjourned into January. There were developments, none of which were particularly good. The only difference was that, having given up on her, Jaywalker no longer took them personally, no longer winced at each disappointment, no longer cringed at each setback. She'd murdered her husband; he now knew that for sure. Let her handle the pain herself. She deserved it, and then some.

Burke responded to Jaywalker's motions, and Judge Sobel ruled that the search warrant had been properly issued and executed. He ordered a hearing on the issue of whether Samara's false exculpatory statements to the detectives would be admissible at trial. But it hardly mattered, Jaywalker knew; Samara's lies were the least of the evidence against her.

Nicky Legs phoned to say that he'd narrowed Barry's enemy list down from eight to four. Out of the original eight, two had airtight alibis, one turned out to be a paraplegic, and another had died a few months before the murder. The four that were left included one of Barry's former lawyers, who'd left over an accusation of embezzlement; an accountant who'd wielded tremendous power over Barry's personal finances; the president of the co-op board, who wanted Barry to pay for water damage to his own apartment directly beneath Barry's, caused by a leak from an unauthorized washing machine; and the building's super, who'd sided with the president on the issue and had once been overheard calling Barry "a worthless Jew billionaire."

And Tom Burke called with the results of the handwriting analysis performed on the insurance policy application. An expert who'd compared the writing on the application with known exemplars of Samara's handwriting had found the two to be identical, to a certainty factor of ninety-nine percent. Not quite the astronomical numbers you got with DNA comparisons, to be sure, but good enough to amount to yet another body blow in an already one-sided fight.

A copy of the autopsy protocol arrived in the mail, along with the serology and toxicology reports. Jaywalker skimmed over the preliminaries—height, weight, clothing, old scars, general health, evidence of disease and stomach contents—and zeroed in on the important stuff. As suspected, Barry Tannenbaum had died of a single puncture wound to the left ventricle of his heart, inflicted by a blade at least five inches in length by about three-quarters of an inch wide, serrated on the cutting edge and smooth on the opposite edge. The case had been ruled a homicide and the official cause of death listed as "cardiac arrest following exsanguination." In plain English, that meant Barry had bled to death. Samples of blood, brain and liver had been taken at the post mortem examination and sent for laboratory analysis, which subsequently revealed the presence of a small amount—.03%—of ethanol and an indeterminate amount of Seconal, a fairly strong barbiturate. Apparently Barry had had a drink sometime that afternoon or evening, and he'd probably taken a sleeping pill sometime during the twenty-four hours preceding his death. Then again, maybe Samara had slipped something into his egg drop soup or his fried rice before stabbing him. It might explain the absence of any signs of a struggle.

As was his habit, Jaywalker dutifully reported each new discovery to Samara. He knew a lot of lawyers who kept things from their clients, the way a lot of doctors kept things from their patients. Jaywalker was a firm believer in sharing things. Sharing, he believed, was an essential building block in the construction of attorney-client trust, even if it had so far failed to inspire Samara to reciprocate. By telling his clients about every development, both the good ones and the bad, he sent them the message that he wasn't going to censor anything or slip a rose-colored filter over it. That way, when he broke some piece of news to them, they would know they were hearing it straight, and that it was really as good—or as bad—as he was making it out to be. Moreover, on an ethical level, he felt he had no right to withhold information from a client in the name of protectionism or paternalism. It wasn't his case he was working on, after all; it was the client's case.

But there was yet another reason behind Jaywalker's

sharing each new development with Samara. The news that kept coming in was so consistently bad that he figured that sooner or later the cumulative effect of it would have to overwhelm her resistance and force her to admit her guilt.

He figured wrong.

Every time he presented her with some new damning piece of evidence that Tom Burke or Nicky Legs had uncovered, she would deflect it, deny any role in it, or insist that she had no recollection of it. An extremely stubborn man himself, Jaywalker had to marvel at her intransigence, even as he despaired at her self-destructiveness.

At his daughter's insistence, Jaywalker spent Christmas Eve and the following day in New Jersey. But with New Year's Eve approaching, he begged out of making a return trip, citing a mild case of the flu. He dozed off in front of the television set well before midnight, spared Dick Clark and the dropping ball, an almost empty tumbler of Kahlúa by his side.

14

COURT DATES

Murder indictments tend to work their way through the court system more slowly than other cases. Perhaps it's the relative complexity of the proof involved, or the seriousness of the charge, or even the fact that there's no complaining witness around to give the D.A.'s office a nudge. Even the law recognizes that murder cases are different in terms of how quickly they must be brought to trial. Not only are murders exempted from the statute of limitations, which determines how long after the commission of a crime a defendant may be charged, but in New York murders are also excluded from the speedy trial law, which determines how soon after being charged a defendant must be brought to trial.

But as slowly and as deliberately as the average murder case proceeds, the pace drops to an absolute crawl if the defendant happens to be fortunate enough to be released on bail. Once a murder defendant is out of jail, his case moves to the very back of the line, behind misdemeanors, felonies, or ever newer murder cases involving defendants in jail. One thing about murder defendants who aren't in jail: they're in no hurry to get anything but another postponement.

By late winter it had begun to dawn on Jaywalker that being on the slow track with Samara was going to turn out to be a very mixed blessing. Back in September, when he'd first listed her case among those he desperately needed to keep, he'd done so because he recognized its potential to be a long-distance runner. (Okay, there was also the fact that his middle-aged testosterone troops were lobbying feverishly for its inclusion.) That potential had been enhanced twice since: first when she stubbornly and unreasonably insisted on her innocence, and again when they'd succeeded in getting her out on bail. The combination of those three ingredients—murder, stubbornness and bail—all but guaranteed that the case would far outlive all the others on his list. It would stretch to the limit what he'd come to think of as "the suspension of his suspension." It would carry him off into the twilight. It would be his swan song.

Which was a problem.

Because by now he knew full well that no matter what he did, he was going to lose Samara's trial. It had turned into a case that not even the best defense lawyer in the world, on his best day ever, could possibly win. It had become that tenth case at the far end of the spectrum.

Jaywalker would go out a loser.

Did the realization bother him, this man who liked to think of himself as totally without an ego? Who thought so little of his personal appearance that he'd been known to arrive in court in the mismatched jacket and pants of two altogether different suits, or to wear the same necktie for two weeks in a row? Who considered vanity the moral equivalent of any three other deadly sins combined? Who routinely broke more rules, conventions and mores in a month than most people did in a lifetime?

You bet it did.

Not because he loved winning so much. To Jaywalker, winning was great, but not just for its own sake, or even that of the client, who might or might not "deserve" to be acquitted in a perfect universe. No, winning at its essence was a means to achieve an end, an end that was far more important, that was nothing short of essential, in fact. An end that justified the twenty-two-hour days he put in during the course of a trial, the blotting out of everything else, be it sleep, food, health or human contact. An end that drove him, that absolutely *consumed* him. But an end that at the same time made him among the very best in the business, and by far the most burned out.

And what was that end?

Not losing.

If you or one close to you should ever suffer the misfortune of being accused of a crime, whether justly or unjustly, and find yourself shopping around for a lawyer, do yourself a favor. Don't look for the one with the best reputation or the most impressive client list, the biggest office or the finest suits, or the best hair or the smoothest speaking voice. Look for the one who hates to lose the most.

Look for a Jaywalker.

So yes, the thought of losing Samara's trial, still months away, was already plunging Jaywalker into depression. He could find it in his heart to forgive her for having killed her husband. He could forgive her for not getting rid of the murder weapon and her bloody blouse, and the towel she'd wrapped them in. He could forgive her for lying to the detectives. He could even forgive her for handing Tom Burke the perfect motive to put the icing on his cake. The one thing he couldn't forgive her for was insisting upon a trial that couldn't be won, and, in the process, taking him down in flames with her.

Week by week, winter grudgingly loosened its grip on the city. The days became noticeably longer, and the afternoons warmer. Jaywalker put away his threadbare overcoat, then his wrinkled trench coat, and finally the wool sweater vest he wore under his suit jacket.

One by one, he finished up the outstanding cases on his list. He found an apartment for the homeless mother and succeeded in reuniting her with her two small children. On

the basis of a DNA mismatch, he won the release of the Sing
Sing inmate who'd been wrongly imprisoned for the past
eight years for a murder committed by a police informer.
And he rented another car and drove up to Rhinebeck again,
so that he could cry his eyes out at the graduation from
rehab of his fourteen-year-old drug addict, who'd somehow
transformed himself into a fifteen-year-old young man.

By June he'd crossed off nine of the cases from the list of
ten that the disciplinary committee had allowed him to keep.
The only name that remained was Samara Tannenbaum's.

By that time, Jaywalker and Samara had become virtual
strangers. They checked in with each other by phone on a
fairly regular basis but saw each other only when the case
appeared in court, which, now that Samara was out on
bail, meant only once a month or so. On those occasions,
they greeted each other warmly enough, the way first
cousins might greet each other at family gatherings during
the holidays. Each time he saw her, Jaywalker was struck
anew by how terrific she looked, and he would think about
her for days afterward, even dream of her at night. But then
she would gradually fade from his thoughts and his dreams,
and he would lose her face, only to be surprised all over
again on the next of their court dates.

Court dates.

That was what he'd come to think of them as.

They would hug in the hallway upon recognizing one
another, and catch up on whatever was new in their lives,
which was never much—in Jaywalker's case because he
had no life to speak of, and in Samara's because her ankle
bracelet, curfew and other restrictions pretty much assured
that she didn't, either. Then they would sit side by side in
the courtroom, Jaywalker forsaking the "lawyers only"
front two rows for the general admissions section, waiting
for the case to be called. Sometimes he would purposely
delay signing them in, just so he could prolong the time he
would get to sit next to Samara. He would feel the touch

of her shoulder against his, smell the scent of whatever perfume she was wearing that day, and listen to the rise and fall of her breath. Once the case was called, they would walk together up the aisle to the defense table, where they stood as one for a minute or two, rarely longer, as the judge inquired about the progress of the case, looked at his calendar and announced the next of their court dates.

Court dates.

By mid-July it was clear to Jaywalker that Samara's case wouldn't go to trial until fall, at the very earliest. Like therapists, judges tend to take their vacations in August. So do prosecutors, defense lawyers, clerks, court officers, stenographers and even jurors. A handful of trials are held, but by and large they involve long-term detainees. Bail cases that make it through July almost always make it through August, as well. Samara's would be no exception; it was adjourned until right after Labor Day. This adjournment was slightly different from the previous ones, however. For the first time, in announcing the new date, Judge Sobel added the words "for hearing and trial."

But even that phrase was a misnomer, Jaywalker knew. All it meant was that there was nothing left but the hearing and the trial. There still remained other cases ahead of theirs, some older, some younger but involving jailed defendants. By Jaywalker's calculation, a September trial was unlikely, with October or November no better than even money. And once you got into December, there were the holidays looming, and you were safe until January.

With his law practice whittled down to a single case, it would have been vintage Jaywalker to throw all his considerable energy into preparing for it. He'd won trials in the past by walking into court not only better prepared than his adversary but *infinitely* better prepared. He would visit and revisit crime scenes, interview witnesses to the point of exhaustion, all but commit reports to memory, and organize his case file into subfiles and sub-subfiles that would enable him to locate the most obscure document on a moment's notice, without having to shuffle papers and fumble around for it.

Now, as summer stretched into fall, he did none of that. Instead he spent mornings sleeping in, and afternoons taking long walks by the river or sunning himself on a park bench. Evenings he propped himself in front of the TV, half watching a Yankee game or an old movie, a tumbler of Kahlúa on the table beside him.

And when winter came, the only concessions he made were to sleep in even later in the morning, to bundle up and walk more briskly in the afternoon, and to switch from baseball to football or basketball in the evening.

Just because he was going to have to lose the last trial of his career, that didn't mean he had to spend an entire year doing it.

Would he have kept it up, this totally uncharacteristic avoidance of responsibility? Would he have gone into trial no better prepared—and indeed, considerably *less* prepared—than the prosecution? Or would he have awakened on his own from his self-inflicted paralysis in time to pull himself together, put in the long hours that had become his trademark, and—even if he were destined to lose—try the case of his life, as he had every other time out?

The answer is, there's simply no way of knowing for sure. Because before Jaywalker could awake on his own, if ever he was going to, the phone woke him. It rang on a Thursday night in mid-December. He picked up on the sixth ring, or maybe the seventh. He'd been asleep at the time, so he had no way of knowing. And he'd disconnected his answering machine months earlier, shortly after his list of remaining cases had dwindled down to one.

He mumbled "Jaywalker" into the phone, his voice thick with Kahlúa and sleep. He found the remote and muted the TV set, half noticing that an old *M*A*S*H* episode was on. Hawkeye and Radar were planning some trick on Frank Burns.

"Are you awake?" It was a woman's voice, a vaguely familiar one. For an instant he thought it might be his wife. Then he remembered. His wife was dead. She'd died almost a dozen years ago.

"Sorta," he said. "Who is this?"

"Sam."

"What time is it?"

"Eleven," she said. "Five after eleven."

"Jesus."

"Jaywalker?"

"Yeah?"

"I need you to come over."

"Now?" he asked.

"Now."

"Why?"

"Because I've found something."

15

IN THE SPICE CABINET

Samara met his cab in front of her town house and ushered him in. She took his overcoat, a threadbare thing he'd owned forever, and hung it up in a closet, unnecessarily dignifying it, as far as Jaywalker was concerned. He would have preferred to toss it on a chair, or, better yet, to keep it on for warmth. What time had she said it was?

"You're freezing," she said. She left the room, and when she reappeared, she was carrying a wool blanket. Without so much as asking him, she pushed him down onto a chair, straddled him and wrapped the blanket around him, tucking the corners underneath him. She could be a real Nurse Ratched when she wanted to be.

He tried to tell her that, and to explain that he was fine without it, but a sudden lump in his throat kept the words from coming out. Once, when he and his wife had been hiking too late in the year in the Canadian Rockies, they'd made it back to their cabin in the early stages of hypothermia, shivering uncontrollably. They'd stripped off their clothes, pulled the blankets off the bed, swaddled themselves together in them, and spent the rest of the day laughing and loving themselves warm.

"I'm okay," he said, not because he was, but because he

needed to hear the sound of his own voice to bring him back from where he'd gone.

"You're not okay," she told him. "You're freezing. Keep it on. I don't want to be responsible when you get pneumonia and die."

Even as he succumbed and kept the blanket wrapped around him, he was aware that there was something about the way she'd said it that bothered him. Not the part about her ordering him around; that felt strangely comforting. No, it was the other part. Shouldn't she have said, *"if* you get pneumonia and die," rather than *"when"*? He decided it was a thought best kept to himself.

"Okay," he said. "Tell me what you found."

"Come," she said.

He and the blanket followed her up a flight of stairs and into a kitchen that looked spotless. Either Samara was an extremely neat housekeeper or a woman in the same mold as her late husband, who'd never cooked. He was pretty sure where he would lay his money on that one.

She walked past the stove and opened a narrow cabinet. Inside were little jars of herbs and spices, the expensive organic ones.

"Look," she said.

He looked. He saw basil, oregano, parsley, tarragon, cumin and a dozen others. "Look at what?" he asked. He found it hard to believe that she'd called him to come over in the middle of the night because she'd suddenly discovered she had spices.

"In the back row," she said.

He looked in the back row. There, among the little jars, was an amber-colored plastic container with a white top, the kind prescription drugs came in. He reached in and lifted it out by the ribbed top, being careful not to touch the smoother surface of the container itself. He read the label, saw that it was in Samara's name, had been prescribed by a Dr. Samuel Musgrove, and had been filled a year ago August. That would have been less than a month before Barry's murder. It was for Seconal, twenty-five pills. He held the bottle up to the light. Inside were three or four whole pills and a powder of ground-up ones. All told, the bottle was about a quarter of the way full. He guessed that at least half the pills had been removed.

It was, Jaywalker instantly knew, a piece of evidence every bit as incriminating as that twenty-five-million-dollar insurance policy Samara had taken out on Barry's life right around the same time and had since conveniently forgotten about. Only this time she'd dodged a bullet; in searching the house, the police somehow hadn't noticed the pills.

"Tell me about this," he said.

"There's nothing to tell," said Samara, punctuating her remark with one of her trademark shrugs. "I've never seen it before. I don't know anything about it."

Vintage Samara.

"So why were you in such a hurry to show it to me?"

"I was looking for the chocolate syrup," she said. "I had an urge for an ice cream sundae. And I saw this. I read the label and saw it was for Seconal. I remembered you said that was one of the things they found in Barry's blood."

"So you picked up the bottle?"

"No," she said. "I have no idea who ordered it, who picked it up, or who put it in there."

"No, no," said Jaywalker, uninterested in yet another of her absurd denials. "What I mean is, you picked it up in your hands *tonight,* before calling me."

She nodded.

So much for his careful handling of it. Now, he knew, it would have her fingerprints on it, even if she'd been smart enough to wipe them off more than a year ago. He wondered if the law imposed an obligation upon him to turn the bottle over to Tom Burke or to the court. He knew that as a so-called "officer of the court," whatever that was supposed to mean, he couldn't very well throw evidence away or destroy it; doing so would amount to obstruction of justice, or criminal tampering. But did he have to come forward with it, and in the process bury his own client even deeper than she was already buried? He decided not. Any law that required him to do that was a law he had no interest in obeying.

"I'll tell you what," he said to Samara. "Why don't we just forget tonight happened, make this whole thing our little secret?"

"You mean you're not going to do anything about it?"

"Do anything about what?"

"About the Seconal."

"Seconal? What Seconal?" And with that he walked over to her trash can. It was one of those fancy ones, all shiny chrome with a foot pedal that activated the lid. He gave the pedal a tap, then another one, figuring Samara might get the hint. After all, *she* wasn't an officer of the court.

"Don't you see?" said Samara. "Someone's *framing* me." So much for hints.

"Right," said Jaywalker. "A month before Barry's murder, someone goes and gets a prescription filled with your name on it. He takes half of it and slips it into Barry's coffee before stabbing him to death. Then he takes the trouble, and the risk, of sneaking in here, so he can hide the bottle in the back of your spice cabinet. And tonight, through the miracle of telekinesis, he's gotten you to put your fingerprints all over it. I'll tell you what, Samara."

"What?"

"I'm going home."

"You can't."

"Why not?"

"You're wearing a blanket."

"I don't care."

It took Jaywalker fifteen minutes just to get a cab to stop for him. Several empty ones slowed down before speeding up and passing him by. You could get away with almost anything in the city, but wearing a blanket for an outer garment was presumptive evidence that you were either broke or dangerous.

By the time he got home, he was shivering all over again. He turned the heat up and poured himself an inch of Kahlúa.

He must be dealing with a complete idiot in Samara, he decided. A beautiful one, to be sure, but an idiot all the same. Why else would she have called him and made him rush over in the middle of a winter night, just so he could see yet another devastating piece of evidence against her? Where did she get this insatiable need to punish herself? Was her guilt over what she'd done so enormous that it drove her to do everything she possibly could to guarantee that they would lock her up for the rest of her life? Did she really want to go to prison that much?

But she'd *hated* prison. She'd literally begged him to get her out of jail and all but offered her body to him in exchange. She'd made him bring her over for daily counsel visits on three hours of sleep. She'd gone without showers, starved herself, cut herself, pulled out tufts of her hair and blackened an eye. It sure didn't *seem* like she wanted to go back.

Why, then, this bizarre need to incriminate herself at every opportunity? Why show him the Seconal, instead of simply throwing it away?

There was simply no answer.

He drained the last of the Kahlúa, took off his shoes, turned off the light and lay down on the sofa. His clock, the one with the alarm that had gone unused for months now, glowed green in the dark, telling him that it was just after two in the morning. He was exhausted. He remembered how, when he couldn't fall asleep as a boy, his mother had told him it was because he was too tired to sleep. He'd had no idea what she'd meant, of course. Years later, when the concept finally made some sense to him, he'd told his wife about it, and it had become their private joke. Whenever they were lying in bed and he wanted to make love with her, instead of saying so, he would tell her he was too tired to sleep. And she'd laugh and roll toward him, and they'd make love. And afterward, almost always, he fell right asleep.

Where was she when he needed her?

Something was nagging at him, something he couldn't quite put his finger on. He tried to picture his wife, but the only image he could summon was of her lying in a hospital bed, wasting away. He tried reaching back over the years, tried conjuring up a younger woman, but all he could come up with was Samara.

"Why?" he asked himself, the sound of his own voice surprising him in the darkness. He had the sudden sensation that the room had filled with water, black impenetrable water, and he was floating on top of it. Why would she have done what she'd done tonight? There had to be an answer. But if there was, it was buried so deeply that he couldn't begin to fathom it. It was as though the answer lay beneath the water, way down at the bottom, beneath the ocean floor itself.

He was drowning, spinning slowly in a whirlpool of black water. He wasn't naked, as he was in most of his dreams. This time he was wearing nothing but a blanket. But it had become so waterlogged that it was dragging him down from its sheer weight. His shoulders were under now, then his neck, and finally his head. There was a gurgling sound, and bubbles were rising all around him. Some of them were getting underneath the blanket and filling it, inflating it like a parachute, lifting him back up toward the surface. He opened his mouth to gulp for air but swallowed only water. Choking, coughing, he clawed with his hands and strained to reach his head higher, broke the surface, took another gulp and somehow found air.

* * *

He was sitting up on his sofa, in the dark, choking and coughing. It seemed to happen whenever he fell asleep on his back instead of on his side. The saliva would collect in the back of his throat and try to get down his windpipe.

The clock read four-twenty. He'd been dreaming. About water, and about something gurgling up from the depths of the ocean.

Samara's showing him the bottle of Seconal had completely confounded him. Its presence did nothing but tie her all the more tightly to her husband's murder. The missing pills, together with the ones that had been ground up into a powder, were truly devastating pieces of evidence against her, and she had to have known that. Yet as much as she hated the thought of going back to prison, she'd woken him in the middle of the night just so she could show him what was bound to send her there. No matter how you looked at it, it made absolutely no sense at all.

Unless.

Unless she truly *was* innocent.

Unless somebody really *was* trying to frame her.

16

A DATE CERTAIN

Not that it made any more sense to him in the morning than it had the night before.

For one thing, how had the police managed to find the things hidden behind the toilet tank—the knife, the blouse and the towel—but miss the bottle of Seconal in the spice cabinet? Well, Jaywalker himself had missed it, hadn't he? Even after Samara had pointed him right to it. But he'd had plenty of excuses. He'd been tired, for one thing, and cold, for another. Besides, he was seriously out of practice. Back in his DEA days, he never would have missed it. Other than the refrigerator and the freezer, the spice cabinet was one of the first places he used to look. Dealers were always hiding stuff there, cramming their marijuana into the oregano jar, or stashing their heroin or cocaine into the flour canister. Not the sugar bowl, though; too many expensive and even deadly accidents happened that way.

But the cops who'd searched Samara's place had had excuses, too. They hadn't been looking for drugs. The information about the Seconal in Barry Tannenbaum's system hadn't come out until weeks later, after the autopsy had been done, and the serology and toxicology results had come in. They'd been looking for a knife, and you didn't hide a knife in between little bottles of spices. You hid it—well, you hid it behind an upstairs toilet tank, for example. It was a clever enough spot, but not so clever that it would have eluded the police during the course of a thorough search.

So that part of it made sense.

The only part that didn't was why Samara had been so eager to show him what she claimed she'd just found, and how she thought it proved that someone was framing her. Jaywalker wasn't ready to buy that, not by a long shot. Still, the incident had had its effect on him. Until last night, he'd succeeded in burying Samara's case. He'd ignored it, blocked it out of his thoughts, pretended it no longer existed. Why? Because he was so wrapped up with his own ego, and so afraid he was going to lose his last trial.

Shame on him.

No matter how guilty she might be, Samara Tannen-baum still deserved the best effort he could possibly give her. Wasn't that exactly what he'd preached his entire career, the pompous lecture he delivered whenever people asked him how he could represent people he knew were guilty? It was his job to go to war for them, he would in-sist, his solemn duty. No less so than if he knew they were innocent. That was what separated him from the hacks, the guys who were in it only for the money, the guys who went through the motions. If a lawyer pulled one punch or held back the tiniest bit because he thought—or even *knew*—that his client had committed the crime, he was worthless.

Samara deserved better.

Samara deserved nothing less than a warrior.

It was time for Jaywalker to stop sulking in his tent. It was time to drag his armor out of the back of his closet, dust it off and suit up. He had a trial date on a murder case. He might have a guilty client with a ton of evidence stacked against her, but that was no excuse, and now was no time to desert her.

He picked up the phone and punched in Nicolo Le-

Grosso's number but had to settle for the answering machine. "Nicky," he said after identifying himself, "I want you to get to work on Barry Tannenbaum's enemies. Concentrate on anyone who had access to Barry's apartment, and cross-reference that against any of them who might have had access to Samara's place, as well. I know it's a long shot, but it's the only shot we've got at the moment."

Then he called Samara and told her he was coming over.

"What time is it?" she asked groggily.

He laughed and hung up.

She met him at the door wearing nothing, so far as he could tell, but a short white bathrobe and her ankle bracelet. Yet he could see she'd found time to shower, wash her hair and put on her makeup. Samara's days of jailhouse deprivation were clearly behind her, at least for the time being.

Jaywalker extended the blanket she'd lent him the night before, the one he'd worn home like an idiot.

"It's not like you had to make a special trip," she said.

"I didn't. I came over because I want to talk some more."

She let him in, and he followed her as she climbed a flight of stairs, furtively peeking upward like a schoolboy. They ended up in a room he hadn't been in before. She walked to one of two facing club chairs and motioned for him to sit in the other. As she lowered herself and went to tuck her legs beneath her, the bottom of her robe came open, and he looked away, causing her to smile once again at his embarrassment.

"I'm sorry," he said.

"For looking? Or for *not* looking?"

"Neither," he said. "For last night."

"I'm the one who woke *you* up, remember?"

"I do," he said, "and now we're even. But I still owe you an apology."

She raised one eyebrow, a considerable talent in Jaywalker's book. As a boy, he'd spent an hour in front of a mirror one afternoon, trying unsuccessfully to master the art. He'd finally concluded it was a girls-only thing.

"What for?" she asked.

"For not taking your case seriously enough."

She seemed to think about that for a moment, then said, "Okay, apology accepted."

"So did you throw out the Seconal?"

"Of course not," she said. "I'm the one who knows I didn't put it there, remember?"

He smiled. She was good, he had to give her that much. She was also awfully good to look at, especially in her bathrobe. He stood up, figuring he might not be able to do so if he waited much longer. "Listen," he said, "I want to have a look around, see what else the cops might have missed when they were here."

They started on the top floor and worked their way down. The search took the better part of an hour, and though it turned up nothing as earthshaking as the Seconal, there were a couple of interesting finds. There was a copy of Samara and Barry's prenuptial agreement, for example, which basically would have left her without a dime if she'd divorced him. There was a drawer full of the skimpiest, sexiest underwear Jaywalker had ever set eyes on.

"Thongs," explained Samara, stretching the string of one. It was so thin it could have been dental floss. She smiled wickedly as he averted his eyes.

There was a freezer dedicated to nothing but quarts and quarts of ice cream, most of them in designer flavors like Kiwi Mango Moment. And in a kitchen drawer were half a dozen stainless steel steak knives with sharp tips and serrated cutting edges that, when compared to a photograph Jaywalker had pulled from his file and brought along, looked absolutely identical to the murder weapon, the one found behind the upstairs toilet tank, the one with Barry's blood on it.

He pulled out a second photo, one showing the bloodstained blouse. "What's the story with that?" he asked Samara.

"Mine," she acknowledged.

"Did you wear it that last evening you spent with Barry?"

She shrugged. "Who remembers?"

"Well, if you weren't wearing it, where would it have been?"

"In my dresser, I guess, or hanging up in my clothes closet."

"And this?" he asked, showing her the third and last photo, depicting the bloodstained towel.

"Looks like one of mine."

He let her talk him into staying for breakfast, or, more properly by that hour, brunch. She had French Vanilla with Ginger Root, topped with chocolate fudge sauce. Where she put the calories, he had no idea. He opted for the Double Dutch Chocolate, with a side of Mango Chutney Sorbet. They ate directly out of the containers, trading *oohs* and *aahs* with every shared spoonful. It was fun. It was the first time Jaywalker could remember having fun in…well, in a very long time.

He spent the next two weeks feverishly playing catch-up. He read, reread and re-reread every scrap of paper in his file, which by this time had grown into three large cardboard boxes. He drew maps and charts, and had photographs blown up and mounted. He organized everything into subfiles, making extra copies of documents that related to more than one witness, so that at trial he wouldn't have to rummage around for something he needed to put his finger on.

He made notes and outlines for cross-examination. He prepared questions for jury selection. He worked on an opening statement and on a summation. He prepared for the pretrial hearing. He wrote out requests for the judge to include in his charge to the jury.

He bugged Nicky Legs to redouble his efforts on investigating Barry Tannenbaum's enemies. And while between them they were able to come up with a handful who'd hated Barry enough to have wished him dead, including two or three who might have had keys to Barry's apartment, none of them had access to Samara's, and none seemed likely candidates to have taken their fantasies and translated them into deeds.

He took a couple of suits and a handful of shirts to the cleaners. He shined two pairs of shoes and coordinated them with matching belts. He even uncharacteristically picked out three or four ties, enough to stretch out over what he guessed would be a two- or three-week trial.

Mostly, he spent time with Samara. Convinced that it would be a must for her to take the stand and deny any involvement in Barry's death, he began preparing her for direct examination and running her through a series of mock cross-examinations. He would sit her on a straight-backed chair in his office—not in her home, where she might feel more at ease—and fire questions at her in his best Tom Burke impersonation, grilling her on her whereabouts the evening of the murder, her initial lies to the detectives, her extramarital affairs and her signature on the life insurance policy.

And she got good, if *good* can be defined as able to answer questions in such a way as to inflict as little damage to herself as possible. But good wasn't going to do the trick, Jaywalker knew. The evidence against her was so devastating that no matter what she said and how well she said it, it was going to take nothing short of a miracle to walk her out of court. But that was his job, Jaywalker knew. Doctors are expected to deliver babies, preachers to deliver sermons, newsboys to deliver papers. Criminal defense lawyers are expected to deliver miracles. Nothing more, nothing less. And Jaywalker had delivered so many of them over the past few years that even he had begun to wonder if he might not be able to walk on water. But walking on water could be a tricky proposition, he knew, and almost everyone who'd tried had sooner or later ended up soaking wet.

He also spent time with Samara because he'd grown to genuinely like her. She never hid from her checkered past, never denied having married for money, never apologized for having cheated on her husband. And there was something real about her, something honest in the way she responded to a question without first repeating the question aloud while she calculated the consequences of her answer. It was as though she had no agenda, no more interest in hiding the facts than she had in censoring her emotions. And despite Jaywalker's constant efforts to "clean up her mouth," as he put it, Samara continued to be every bit as quick with a bit of foul language as she was with a laugh. There seemed to be no guile to her. Her lower lip could curl into a pout in one moment, only to soften into a smile the next. For Jaywalker, that openness represented at once both a significant asset and a serious liability, depending upon how you chose to look at it. A juror could easily fall in love with Samara—as he himself realized he was doing, on some level—or just as easily come to loathe her, interpreting her unapologetic indifference as arrogance.

And never did she retreat one inch from her insistence on her innocence. Not when Jaywalker cornered her repeatedly during his mock cross-examinations, not when he confronted her with some new damning piece of evidence, not when he lied to her one day and told her that Tom Burke was willing to let her serve as little as four years if only she would plead guilty to manslaughter, not even when he proposed that she take a lie detector test. In fact, she readily agreed to the suggestion, and it was Jaywalker who vetoed the idea. Polygraph examinations, he'd learned long ago, were useful tools. But their value pretty much began and ended with finding out who was willing, or even eager, to take one and who was afraid to, a test Samara had passed. In terms of their actual scientific validity, well, he was fond of saying there was a reason polygraphs weren't admissible in court.

There were times when Samara's denials moved him close to the point of believing her. But then he would refocus on the evidence and on the two questions for which he had absolutely no answers: If Samara hadn't murdered Barry, who had? And how had they managed to leave things in such a way that everything pointed at her?

Having begun with her arrest two Augusts ago, Samara's case was now about to enter its third calendar year, a considerable span for a criminal case but not all that unusual for a murder prosecution involving a defendant out on bail. Yet when they went back to court in the second week of December, it was clear that Judge Sobel was under pressure to move the case to trial. Whether that pressure was the result of the simple passage of time, came from the urging of Tom Burke, or was a response to a renewed interest on the part of the media was unclear. Jaywalker secretly suspected that the disciplinary committee judges, their patience tested over the length of his suspended suspension, might have had a hand in it. But after sixteen months of delays, he was hardly in a position to complain.

"January fifth," said the judge, "for hearing and trial. And, counsel?"

"Yes?" said Jaywalker and Burke in unison.

"Clear your calendars, because that's a date certain."

It was how judges warned lawyers to set aside all other business and be ready to start without fail. If the admonition posed any sort of logistical problem for Burke, he offered no complaint. Assistant district attorneys are, in a very real sense, associates in a large law firm. When ordered to trial, they simply pass their other business on to other assistants, other associates in the firm. Jaywalker, all of whose other business had long ago been set aside or passed on, made a note of the date in his otherwise spotless pocket calendar and circled it.

"I can do that," he said.

With the trial less than a month away, Jaywalker really got down to business. He met half a dozen times with Nicky Legs, and together they interviewed several of the people on Barry Tannenbaum's enemies list. The co-op board president, a beady-eyed retired navy SEAL, readily admitted that he'd feuded with Barry but laughed at the suggestion that he'd murdered him. The building's super, an earnest-looking Puerto Rican, was shocked at the thought. "*Me? Kill Tannenbaum?* I no killer. I change lightbulbs, wash windows, fix locks, clean ovens. I no kill Tannenbaum."

But the two individuals who interested Jaywalker the most, Barry's accountant and his former lawyer, refused to be interviewed. "You want me to testify," said the lawyer, "you serve me with a subpoena. Otherwise, don't bother me." The accountant said pretty much the same thing, albeit more politely. "Whatever I have to say," he told Jaywalker, "I'd prefer to say in court," leading Jaywalker to suspect that the two might have talked the matter over together, and to wonder if Burke might be planning on calling one or both of them as witnesses.

He increased his sessions with Samara, both in frequency and duration, gradually polishing the rough edges off her. Her locker-room language gave way to an acceptable version of plain English. Her denials took on more plausibility. Her eye contact, never a problem, expanded to take in the imaginary jurors, as well as her questioner. But Jaywalker also knew when to quit. He didn't want her to come off as rehearsed. Memorizing a few key phrases was good, but not at the expense of spontaneity. By the end of the month, she was good enough that he called a halt to their sessions. It was a hard thing for him to do, but he knew it was time. Samara would be a good enough witness. Under different circumstances, she might even have been a great one. But the problem had never been her. From day one, the problem had always been the facts.

And two days before the year ended, when other New Yorkers were returning presents, recovering from over-eating and readying themselves for yet another round of parties, Jaywalker convinced Tom Burke to take him on a tour of Barry Tannenbaum's penthouse apartment. Jaywalker was surprised to see the yellow-and-black crime scene tape still in place. But Barry had lived alone and on the top floor, and evidently its presence hadn't bothered anyone enough to remove it. Now a detective who had accompanied them lifted the tape above their heads, broke the seal, unlocked the door and let them in.

It struck Jaywalker as a modest enough *pied-à-terre,* by billionaire standards. A thirty-foot living room, formal dining room, den, library, study, kitchen, pantry, three bedrooms, and four and a half bathrooms. And Samara had been right about the kitchen: there was no oven or range in sight, only a small microwave on the countertop. The room was at one end of the apartment, meaning it shared a common wall with the adjacent penthouse, no doubt kitchen-to-kitchen. The woman next door probably had a TV set in her kitchen, where she'd no doubt been when she'd heard Samara and Barry arguing the evening of his murder.

Jaywalker walked to the window. As did most of the windows, it faced north, providing a commanding view of Central Park. Off to the east and west were the roofs of other, lower buildings. You were high above everything else here. Whoever had murdered Barry hadn't had to worry about being seen doing it, not unless there'd been a Peeping Tom at work that night in a helicopter, with a Hubble-quality telescope trained on the penthouse windows.

On the quarry tile kitchen floor was the outline of a body, just like you saw on TV shows. A large area of tile, toward the midsection of the outline, was stained almost black. People tended to think of blood as red, Jaywalker knew. But dried, it darkened and became almost unrecognizably black. He'd discovered that the hard way. It had been after his wife's surgery, after the chemotherapy and the radiation, after the last of the time-buying transfusions. It had been after he'd signed her out of the hospital against medical advice and brought her home to die. Each morning there would be blackened clots on her pillowcase, a few more than the morning before. Each day he would throw the pillowcase away and replace it with a fresh one. Then, after a week, the stains began to be smaller, and he dared to hope for a miracle, one last remission. But the truth was, she'd simply been running out of blood.

"This is where it happened," said the detective.

"No shit," said Burke.

It did seem pretty obvious, but Jaywalker had long ago learned not to trust the obvious. "How do you know?" he asked.

"No other blood," said the detective.

"Unless the killer cleaned it up."

"Ever try getting blood outa this kinda tile?"

"No," said Jaywalker, who'd never tried to get blood out of any kind of tile, at least so far as he could recall. "And everything's exactly the way it was?"

"Yup. The first officer on the scene secured it right away. We haven't even let the maid in, or the real estate brokers in to get a look at it. And I've got to tell you, we could've made a bundle by giving one or two of 'em a sneak preview. Had to tell them sorry, no peeking until after the conviction."

"Suppose there *is* no conviction?"

The detective laughed politely, to let Jaywalker know that he'd gotten his joke. But when they left a few minutes later, he was back to all-business, locking the apartment door, replacing the broken seal with a new one and restringing the crime scene tape.

Jaywalker celebrated New Year's Eve home alone, having turned down an offer from Samara to come over. Some things didn't change, he guessed. He was still a moron. But the professional in him, or at least what was left of the professional in him, knew that no matter how much you wanted to, you didn't sleep with your client. Not till after the case was over, anyway. By which time, of course, it would be too late. Last he'd checked, they weren't allowing conjugal visits on Rikers Island.

He made it to midnight this time, draining the final drops from his last bottle of Kahlúa. There would be no place in his life for alcohol once the trial began, he knew. And as far as sleep was concerned, well, there would pretty much be no place for that, either.

17

PANEL ENTERING

"Calendar number one," read the clerk, "for trial. The People of the State of New York versus Samara Tannenbaum."

Once again they took their places at the defense table in the front of the courtroom. "Are The People ready?" asked Judge Sobel.

"Yes," said Tom Burke.

"The defendant?"

"Yes," said Jaywalker.

"Bring in the panel."

He'd done it a hundred times, two hundred. He knew the case now, forward, backward and inside out. He could have delivered his opening statement at a second's notice. Hell, he could have delivered his *summation,* if called upon to do so. He was as ready as any lawyer had ever been for any trial. Yet none of that kept the butterflies from making their presence known. They were beating their wings now, just beginning to flap wildly, rising somewhere between his stomach and his throat. They would quiet down soon enough. They always did, the way a prizefighter's nerves quieted down with the first punch, or a quarterback's with the first completion. But for the moment, they were all he could feel, the butterflies.

They'd barely been around the day before, when they'd had the suppression hearing. Of course, there'd been no jurors then, and the whole thing had lasted barely an hour. Burke had called a single witness, one of the two detectives who'd gone to Samara's town house the day after the murder. She'd invited them in, he testified, and answered their questions willingly. She'd denied having been at her husband's apartment the previous evening, and then, when told she'd been both seen and heard there, she'd changed her story. She'd denied that they'd argued, and then she'd admitted that, too, once they'd confronted her with the facts. At no time during the interview had Samara been in custody. It was only when she'd said she wanted to call a lawyer that the questioning had stopped and they'd arrested her. Subsequently, the detectives had applied for and obtained a search warrant for her home, and it had been during that search that they'd found the knife, the blouse and the towel, hidden behind the toilet tank of an upstairs bathroom.

Jaywalker had gone into the hearing knowing he had no chance of getting any evidence suppressed. But he'd wanted to put Burke through it anyway, to use it as discovery. On cross-examination, Jaywalker had asked the detective a dozen or so questions, nailing him down on a couple of things he wanted to use at trial and generally sizing him up as a witness. He'd called no witnesses of his own; there had been no reason to expose Samara to cross-examination. Better to save her for the trial, when he would be needing her, than to give Burke a crack at her now.

As expected, Judge Sobel had refused to suppress anything. Samara's statements had been noncustodial, he ruled, and therefore required no Miranda warnings. And since they'd been voluntarily made, they hadn't tainted the issuance of the search warrant.

They'd then had a Sandoval hearing, a misnomer, because it wasn't really a hearing at all—no witnesses were called—but a legal argument. Burke wanted to be able to bring out Samara's six-year-old drunk driving conviction if she were to take the stand at trial, on the theory that the jurors might feel it adversely affected her credibility. Jaywalker argued against it. The conviction had been for driving while impaired, he pointed out, which was only a traffic infraction. Unlike a conviction for perjury, fraud, or even larceny, it had little to do with credibility and everything to do with prejudicing the jury against Samara. The judge had agreed. Burke would be prohibited from asking about it, unless Samara were to testify that she'd never been arrested or convicted of anything. As for the Las Vegas arrest for attempted soliciting, or whatever the charge had been, Burke either didn't know about it or realized it was too old to ask about. Whichever was the case, Jaywalker wasn't about to bring it up.

"Anything else?" the judge had asked.

There'd been nothing else.

"Panel entering!" announced a court officer, and a hundred and twenty prospective jurors were ushered into the courtroom. They carried overcoats, hats, briefcases, tote bags, shopping bags, umbrellas, books, knitting, laptops, cell phones, lunch bags and whatever else they'd thought to bring with them to the courthouse that morning. They looked at the judge, at the lawyers, at the court officers, and at the American flag and the curious IN OD WE TRUST sign on the wall above it. But mostly they looked at Samara Tannenbaum. *Stared* at her, to be more precise. With jury selection looming, the media had recently rediscovered the case, and any of the prospective jurors who claimed over the next two days to know nothing about the defendant or the crime she stood accused of—and there would be a handful—were either brain-dead, living on another planet or flat-out lying.

Jaywalker, sitting next to the object of the stares, did his best to project an attitude of quiet confidence. Right now, as the prospective jurors took seats in the long rows of benches that made up the spectator section, he was speaking with his client, one hand on her shoulder, the way a father might speak with a daughter. *Look at me,* he was telling the jurors. *Look at how I trust her. I'm sitting right next to her, talking with her, touching her, making contact with her. There's nothing scary about her, no reason for me to be afraid of her. Or for you to be, either, for that matter.*

The touching was a big part of it, so much so that there was actually one judge in the system who'd gone so far as to prohibit it altogether. Jaywalker, who personally believed that the consensual touching of another adult was a form of expression protected by the First Amendment, had persisted in doing so, despite several mid-trial warnings. His behavior had cost him a contempt citation, a thousand-dollar fine and a one-night sleepover date at Rikers Island.

But he'd won the trial.

Judge Sobel didn't have a no-touching rule, and Tom Burke either hadn't noticed or was too confident of his case to worry about it. Even Jaywalker himself knew that it was going to take a lot more than touching Samara to get her off. In fact, jury selection itself posed a huge problem for him. Going into a trial, Jaywalker almost always had a preconceived notion as to what kind of jurors he wanted on that specific case. Because the process was a crapshoot—meaning you never really knew what you were getting with any particular individual—you were pretty much reduced to playing hunches and going with the odds. And going with the odds meant you followed stereotypes. Prosecutors invariably looked for establishment types— clean-shaven, Republican-voting, white businessmen who showed up wearing suits and ties, carrying leather attaché cases. Jaywalker sought out ethnic minorities drawn to teaching, social work and the humanities, people who would no more put on a necktie to do jury service than they would rent a tuxedo to watch a ball game on TV. He looked for those young enough to still be idealistic, or old enough to have learned how to forgive. Unemployed was good, a military background bad. Irish, Germans and Italians were to be avoided as tough on crime, blacks and Jews embraced as empathetic toward underdogs. Crime victims were suspect, while those who'd been accused of crimes were sought after. And so the guessing game went.

But beyond stereotypes, it was the nature of the case—and, even more so, the nature of the defendant—that dictated what type of juror Jaywalker wanted. If his client was African-American, he wanted blacks; if Hispanic, he wanted fellow Latinos. If the case was likely to turn on the word of police witnesses, he wanted jurors from Harlem who knew that cops stole and lied. People who viewed them as oppressors, in other words, rather than protectors. If it was sympathy he needed, he wanted women. But not just *any* women. No, he wanted women who took in HIV-positive foster children, looked after crack babies, volunteered at soup kitchens and read to the blind in their spare time.

Samara's case posed huge problems. The media had unfailingly portrayed her as a spoiled brat, a gold digger and a shameless adulteress. She was white and rich. Accused of plunging a knife into her husband's heart, she was hardly a candidate for sympathy. And the evidence would show that it hadn't been the police who'd lied this time around, but Samara herself who'd lied to *them*. Even her looks might work against her. Women of all ages, sizes, shapes and shades of color were likely to be jealous of Samara's prettiness and petiteness. Men, even as they might be dazzled by her beauty, could hardly be forgiven for identifying with her husband-victim.

Which left precious little room for the ideal juror. Unless, that was, Jaywalker happened to come across twelve equally pretty and petite gold diggers who'd had occasion to murder their husbands, either in real life or only in their fantasies.

As the clerk swore in the panel, Jaywalker looked

around the room to see which of the prospective jurors would choose to affirm, rather than take an oath that ended with the words "So help me, God." A prohibitive long shot in the trial, he was looking for anyone with the slightest anti-establishment bent. After all, it would take twelve jurors to convict Samara, but only one to hang the jury.

Every one of them took the oath.

The clerk spun a large wooden drum, the kind they used to use at bingo parlors, and pulled out a slip of paper. "Seat number one," she said, "Ronald Macauley, M-A-C-A-U-L-E-Y." A man rose from the back of the room and made his way to the jury box. He was white, fiftyish, wore a dark suit and tie, and carried a Coach attaché case. No good, Jaywalker thought. On a tear sheet of a homemade chart on the table in front of him, he wrote:

MR. MACAULEY
W
NG

The clerk repeated the process until the box had been filled, with twelve jurors taking up the regular seats and another six relegated to the chairs set aside for alternates. Jaywalker made notes for each of them. By the time the eighteenth was seated, he had two *OKs,* five question marks and eleven *NGs.*

As he'd expected, it was going to be a very long day.

Judge Sobel addressed the panel, speaking loudly enough so that not only those in the jury box could hear him but so could those back in the spectator section. He introduced the "parties," as he referred to them—Burke, Jaywalker and Samara—and had each of them stand in turn and face the rear of the room. Then he described the case, reading the indictment as part of it, and made some general remarks. Next he asked if there were any prospective jurors who felt they were unqualified to serve on the case.

A sea of raised hands responded. One by one, jurors approached the bench to explain why they couldn't possibly serve.

"I could never judge a fellow human being."

"I look at her, and I know she's guilty."

"I'm indispensable at work."

"I have plane tickets to Aruba this Friday."

"I have a cat I can't leave home alone all day."

"I have an unusually small bladder."

"No speak English."

One by one, the judge excused them. Then he individually questioned the eighteen sitting in the box, a number that included some who'd been there from the start and others who'd been added to replace casualties of the process. He inquired about their occupations, their places of birth and their family status, and whether they'd ever been the victim of a crime or been accused of having committed one. Each time a juror said something meaningful to Jaywalker's way of thinking, he made a note of it on the corresponding tear sheet, and from time to time he even changed his overall impression of a particular juror. A couple of original question marks soured into *NGs,* and several *NGs* became *NG!s.* But at the end there were still only two *OKs,* and neither of those had sprouted an *!*

A very long day indeed.

Tom Burke rose, and for the next half hour he asked questions of the potential jurors, some general, some addressed to a particular individual. Burke was a no-nonsense lawyer with a nice way about himself. He asked the jurors what organizations they belonged to or donated money to, what magazines they subscribed to or read on a regular basis, and what television programs they liked best. He asked for their assurances that they wouldn't be influenced by the defendant's prettiness, or by the fact that she was a woman. He asked them to promise that if he proved her guilt by the legal standard, they would return a verdict of guilty.

They promised.

Jaywalker's turn didn't come until after the lunch break. Lunch for everyone else, that was. Jaywalker, who never ate breakfast and skipped lunch when he was on trial, found a spot on a windowsill by the elevator bank, and spent the hour reviewing his notes and composing his questions. But the truth was, he'd pretty much known what he was going to ask for weeks now, for months. His approach to jury selection was radically different from just about every other lawyer he knew. As much as he was interested in what magazines a prospective juror read, he never asked. He had two reasons.

First, while it was comforting to know that a juror preferred *The New Yorker* to *Guns and Ammo,* the price of learning that piece of information was that the D.A. learned it, too, and would now use it to exercise one of his peremptory challenges against the liberal *New Yorker* reader. So the knowledge gained was illusory and, in the long run, worthless.

Second, there was simply no time for such nonsense. Samara Tannenbaum was on trial for murder. The sixteen jurors whom Jaywalker was about to question had walked into the courtroom figuring she was guilty, either for sure or probably. A couple of them had even been honest enough to say so, or smart enough to know that saying so would get them a ticket home. Jaywalker had exactly half an hour to change that perception and turn the trial into a ball game. That worked out to less than two minutes a juror. He'd be damned if he was going to spend one second of that time asking them about magazines.

Nor would he ask them for promises of fairness. If a juror was the kind of person who was inclined to be fair, no promise was necessary. And if the juror *wasn't* going to be fair, it logically followed that no promise he or she made could be trusted. And again, there was simply no time to waste on such nonsense.

"My name is Jaywalker," he told them, when finally it was his turn to get up and talk to them, "and I represent the defendant, Samara Tannenbaum." Standing behind her now, placing a hand on each of her shoulders. Just in case they'd missed it this morning.

Jaywalker's philosophy of jury selection, as radical as it was, was quite simple. It began with the proposition that, as the last of the three to ask questions—the judge having been the first and the prosecutor the second—he already knew enough about each of them to make an informed guess as to whether he wanted them or not. That, along with the fact that anything additional he might now learn would help his adversary as much as it would help him, meant that he almost never asked questions aimed at seeking more information. What he set out to do instead was condition them. Actually, a more precise way of putting it would have been to say he wanted to brainwash them. But that term, however apt, carried a decidedly negative, *Manchurian Candidate* connotation to it, even were one inclined to think of the process in its most thera-peutic definition.

> brain•wash ('brane ˌwosh), v., to cleanse the mind so as to
> rid it of prejudices and other preconceived notions that have
> no goddamned business in a criminal trial in the first place.

The methods Jaywalker employed were twofold. First, in the guise of asking information-seeking questions, he would proceed to reveal to the jurors the most damning evidence against his client. Then, purely to avoid drawing an objection, he would ask them if, having heard that, they could still be fair and impartial. Second, again posed in question form, he would repeatedly hammer into them the magic words upon which they were ultimately going to base their acquittal of the defendant: that the prosecution, and only the prosecution, bore the burden of proof, a burden that not only required them to prove that the defendant was guilty, but required them to prove it beyond all reasonable doubt. Over and over he would say those things, until the jurors could sense when the words were coming, knew them by heart and mouthed them along with him. They would take the words home with them at night, bring them back in the morning, and internalize them to the point that they were no longer just words but had become a refrain of sorts, a refrain that punctuated every line and every verse of the trial. A *mantra*.

And then Jaywalker would combine the two methods into one.

MR. JAYWALKER: Ms. Heywood, the evidence is going to show, not just beyond a reasonable doubt, but beyond *all* doubt, that when first confronted by the detectives, Samara Tannenbaum lied to them. Not only did she lie once, she lied twice. And she didn't just lie about silly stuff, but about stuff that turns out to look important. Hearing from me, her lawyer, that she lied like that, can you still give her a fair trial?

Now, it didn't matter a bit whether Ms. Heywood answered that she could or thought she could, or that she'd try her best, or that it depended on the rest of the evidence. The important thing was that by bringing out the fact that Samara had lied before Tom Burke could establish the fact through the testimony, Jaywalker was defusing the issue, taking all the drama out of it. And by getting the jurors—for they were all listening, not just Ms. Heywood—to commit to being fair in spite of Samara's having lied, he was in effect getting them to discount it. If Ms. Heywood had answered no, she couldn't be fair, then Jaywalker wouldn't even have to waste a peremptory challenge on her; he would get her excused for cause.

MR. JAYWALKER: And when I say, "give her a fair trial," Mr. Monroe, you understand what I mean by those words. I mean that you must hold the prosecution to their burden of proof, and require them, if they can, to not only prove that Samara is guilty, but to prove it *beyond* all reasonable doubt.

And by placing great vocal stress on the word *beyond,* no one—not Tom Burke, not even Judge Sobel—caught the fact that Jaywalker had quietly changed the word immediately following it from *a* to *all.* Not until the next day, at least, or the day after that. Not until it was too late, not until it had become part of the refrain, part of the jury's mantra. Not until Jaywalker's little sleight of hand had succeeded in raising the prosecution's burden of proof from "beyond *a* reasonable doubt" to "beyond *all* reasonable doubt."

Sound like a little thing?

Perhaps.

But experience had taught Jaywalker that it was precisely the kind of little thing that translated into the difference between winning and losing.

So he didn't just tell the prospective jurors about Samara's lies to the detectives. He also told them about her presence in Barry Tannenbaum's apartment shortly before the time of his death, about the items found hidden behind her toilet tank, about the overwhelming certainty that Barry's blood was present on them, even about the life insurance policy application with Samara's signature on it. And after each damning revelation, he asked the jurors if they still could give his client a fair trial and hold the prosecution to its burden of proving guilt beyond all reasonable doubt.

A few said no, they no longer could. Which was fine; they would be excused for cause.

But the vast majority said yes.

Jaywalker took a glance at his watch. He'd been on his feet for close to twenty-five minutes now. He had barely five minutes left. And he had a cardinal rule that he never broke. It was a rule that, like so much else he did, set him apart from just about all his colleagues. As early as the jury selection process, he made it a hard and fast policy to tell the jurors whether or not his client would take the stand.

MR. JAYWALKER: Mrs. O'Sullivan, you heard the judge tell you this morning that the burden of proof rests entirely upon the prosecution, that they're the ones who have to prove guilt, and have to prove it *beyond* all reasonable doubt. You also heard him tell you that the defense doesn't have to prove anything, doesn't have to *disprove* anything, doesn't have to call a single witness. That the defendant herself doesn't have to testify, and that if I elect to not put Samara on the stand, you may draw no inference from that whatsoever.

Nevertheless, I tell you right now that in this trial, Samara Tannenbaum *is* going to testify. She's going to take the stand, and she's going to tell you in her own words what she did the evening of her husband's death—and what she *didn't* do.

Now, I suspect that you may end up not liking Samara very much. She's done some things in her life that she's not particularly proud of. For example, she's slept around. She's accepted gifts, including money, in exchange for sex. She's gotten by on her looks. In fact, she'll tell you she married Barry Tannenbaum, in large part, for his money. After marrying him, she didn't live with him very long. And she cheated on him. What's more, unlike you and most of your fellow jurors, she hasn't worked for a number of years. She's what we sometimes call a gold digger.

But do you understand, Mrs. O'Sullivan, that this trial isn't about whether you end up liking Samara or not? That this trial is about one thing, and one thing only? That at the end of the day, this trial is about whether or not the prosecution, which continues to have the only burden of proof, *even when Samara takes the stand and tells her story,* can meet and exceed that burden of proof? And that that burden requires them to convince every last one of you that Samara is guilty of murder, and convince you of it *beyond* all reasonable doubt?

Mrs. O'Sullivan assured Jaywalker that she understood all that and could follow the judge's instructions. Jaywalker wasn't fooled for a minute. No red-faced, two-hundred-pound Irish-American housewife, the mother of eight children and the wife of a former cop now working as an armed security officer at a bank, could be counted on to give Samara Tannenbaum the time of day, let alone a fair trial. But it didn't matter. The important thing was that Jaywalker had effectively taken away Tom Burke's cross-examination of Samara. And he'd so lowered the jurors' expectations of her that no matter how she came across, she couldn't possibly seem as bad as he'd painted her.

He thanked the jurors and sat down.

The term *jury selection* is something of a misnomer. The lawyers don't really get to select the jurors they want. The process might better be called *jury rejection,* or *jury deselection.* The way it works is that jurors with admitted or identifiable biases get challenged for cause, or upon the consent of the opposing lawyers. There's no preset limit as to the number who can be removed in that way.

Once challenges for cause or consent have been made and ruled upon, the lawyers take turns exercising their peremptory challenges, of which they have a limited number. That number increases along with the severity of the charges, as defined by the maximum sentence allowable under the law. Thus, in a lowly petit larceny case, each lawyer is allotted only three peremptory challenges. In a robbery or burglary trial, the number rises either to ten or fifteen, depending upon the degree of the crime charged. Only in murder cases and other class A felonies do the lawyers get the full complement of twenty peremptory challenges.

Unlike challenges for cause, peremptory challenges may be exercised for any reason, or for no particular reason at all, so long as they're not motivated by a demonstrable attempt to exclude members of any particular race or other legally recognized minority.

Burke, as the prosecutor, had to go first. With two of the prospective jurors in the box having been removed for cause, he now used five of his peremptory challenges. Jaywalker, reviewing his notes, had concerns about almost all of the remaining eleven. But he also had a finite number of challenges, and he didn't want to fall seriously into a hole. That would give Burke too much of a hand in shaping the jury.

Some jurisdictions allow the jurors, once all have been selected, to vote on who becomes their foreperson, or spokesman. Others draw lots, or leave it to the judge to decide. In New York, the rule is simple: the first juror to be called, selected and sworn in automatically becomes the foreperson. Knowing this, Jaywalker now used his first two peremptory challenges on jurors who, unless challenged, would have fit the bill. That left a barely acceptable, though certainly not truly desirable, cabdriver as the foreman. Men, Jaywalker had decided some time ago, even if they might be inclined to identify more closely with Barry Tannenbaum, would at least react positively to Samara's looks.

Women, unless they themselves had just climbed out of the pages of a *Victoria's Secret* catalog, could hardly be expected to.

Jaywalker used six more of his challenges, leaving him with twelve to Burke's fifteen. The three jurors who hadn't been challenged were sworn in, including the cab-driver foreman. Then they were excused for the balance of the process.

Jaywalker checked his watch, saw it was almost four o'clock. They'd been at it most of the day and had three sworn jurors to show for it.

The clerk, going to her bingo drum, filled the box with eighteen new jurors, and the process started all over again, beginning with the judge's questions. And that was as far as they got that day.

"God, it takes *forever,*" complained Samara on the way out of the courtroom. "And talk about *boring.*"

Jaywalker agreed with her on both counts. Jury selection was time-consuming and repetitive, especially with his own insistence on hammering home the twin concepts of burden of proof and reasonable doubt. It was, as a result, by far the most neglected portion of the trial. But he knew that it was also one of the most critical. Approached properly, it presented a unique opportunity to condition jurors to be receptive to arguments they might otherwise reject out of hand. And handled skillfully, it could set the stage for winning all but the most difficult of trials.

What worried Jaywalker right now, as he rode the ancient elevator down to the ground floor, were those two little words in the caveat: *all but.*

They were back in court the following morning, with Tom Burke addressing the new group of prospective jurors, followed by Jaywalker. This time there were three challenges granted for cause. Burke used four of his peremptories, leaving him with eleven. Jaywalker used six of his twelve. The remaining five jurors were sworn in, bringing the number selected to eight.

On the third round, four were knocked off for cause. Burke peremptorily challenged six, Jaywalker five. But the numbers were still working against him. With one regular juror still to be picked, Burke had five challenges left to Jaywalker's one.

Jaywalker used his remaining challenge on the final round as best as he could, but Burke took advantage of the numbers to cherry-pick the twelfth juror, a retired marine colonel, muscles bulging beneath a skin-tight, mustard-colored turtleneck. Jaywalker had caught him looking at Samara at one point with nothing short of firing-squad contempt in his eyes.

From the remaining jurors, they picked six alternates who would hear the testimony but join in the deliberations only if one of the twelve regulars became incapacitated. It was almost five-thirty by the time they broke for the day.

But they had their jury.

Stanley Merkel, the cabdriver and foreman: white, balding, fortyish. Leona Sturdivant, a retired school administrator: white, prim, sixty-something. Vito Todesco, an importer-exporter: white, Italian-American, fiftyish. Shirley Johnson, a nurse's aide at a Catholic hospital: black, God-fearing, seventy. David Wong, an engineering student: Chinese-American, late twenties. Mary Ellen Tomlinson-Marchetti, an investment counselor: fortyish, white, Protestant, evidently married to an Italian-American. Leonard Schrier, a retired shopkeeper: white, late sixties, either a sympathetic Jew inclined to forgive Samara or a former storm trooper ready to herd her into the ovens. Carmelita Rosado, a kindergarten teacher: Hispanic, very quiet, thirtysomething. Ebrahim Singh, a speech therapist: Indian or Pakistani, fiftyish. Angelina Olivetti, an out-of-work actress waiting tables: white, Italian-American and cute. Theresa McGuire, a self-described homemaker: white,

Irish-American, ageless. George Stetson, the Colonel
Mustard whom Burke had settled on when Jaywalker ran
out of challenges: sixtyish, ramrod-straight, and very, very
white.

Six men, six women. Eight white, one black, one His-
panic, one Asian, one Middle Eastern. Six Catholics, two
Protestants, one likely Buddhist, and three question marks.
No one with anything more than a master's degree, if that.

Backed up by six alternates of assorted sizes, shapes,
colors and religious backgrounds, these were the jurors
who would ultimately decide Samara Tannenbaum's fate.
On a scale of ten, Jaywalker might have given them a
collective two or three, at very best. But the truth was, he
wasn't interested in who they'd been when they'd first
walked into the courtroom. He'd had his two minutes with
each of them since then—his chance to condition them, to
desensitize them to the worst Tom Burke could possibly
throw at them. And, yes, his chance to brainwash them. If
he'd failed, the fault was his, and no one else's.

Though the consequences would be Samara's.

18

TWO JOURNEYS

When he'd begun trying cases, more than twenty years ago, Jaywalker had been schooled in the Legal Aid Method. Whatever you did, they'd taught him, never commit to any single defense or trial strategy, lest something happen in the middle of the trial to turn you into a fool and your client into a convict. Keep your options open at all times. Play things close to the vest. Adopt a wait-and-see attitude. Avoid unnecessary risks.

The first way you put those guiding principles into action, they explained, was to refrain from making an opening statement. Or, if you absolutely insisted upon making one, you were to keep it short, general and non-committal. Talk, if talk you must, about maintaining an open mind, waiting until all the evidence was in before drawing any conclusions, and keeping your eyes and ears open, and your nose to the grindstone.

To Jaywalker's way of thinking, it made no sense at all. As far as he was concerned, about all you got by keeping your nose to the grindstone was a smaller nose.

Still, he'd given it a try. And what he'd gotten for being a good soldier were convictions. Not always, but a good half of the time out. "Fifty percent acquittals?" said his supervisor. "That's *fabulous!*"

Not to a perfectionist, it wasn't. Not to Jaywalker.

So over time he gradually abandoned the Legal Aid Method in favor of the Jaywalker Method. By the time he went out on his own two years later, he was committing to a particular trial strategy long before jury selection even began. He knew precisely what his defense would be, whether or not his client was going to testify, what he would say when he did, and how he would say it. And he told the jurors, at the very first opportunity.

He discovered that the opening statement, long avoided as nothing but a death trap by the mavens at Legal Aid, presented the perfect opportunity to shape the course of everything that followed. Why wait for a poorly educated, inarticulate defendant to haltingly tell his story from the witness stand, interrupted by questions, objections and rulings until it came out like some jerky, stop-and-go amateur home movie, when Jaywalker himself could present it to the jury in free-flowing, wide-screen, three-dimensional, stereophonic, living color?

Almost immediately, his acquittal rate jumped to seventy-five percent. And while he continued to work on perfecting the rest of his trial skills until that number would climb into the low nineties, never again would he miss an opportunity to open, and to open expansively.

Samara's case would be no different.

That said, months had gone by in which Jaywalker had had absolutely no clue what he could possibly say in his opening. The problem was a direct corollary of his certainty that not only was Samara guilty as charged, but that her case was all but unwinnable.

A lot of criminal defense lawyers—including Jaywalker himself in the early days of his career—went into such a trial hoping to somehow discover a defense in the testimony. A key prosecution witness would fail to materialize, perhaps, or recant his previous version of the facts. A cop would screw up, either in his paperwork, on the stand, or both. An inexperienced prosecutor would inadvertently leave something important out of his case. Manna would fall from the heavens.

But Jaywalker had come to learn that on overwhelming cases, there were always other witnesses who would show up, who *wouldn't* recant. That there would be other cops who *wouldn't* screw up. That Tom Burke was not only experienced, but talented and extremely thorough. And that manna rarely, if ever, fell from heaven. So going into the most daunting trials, along with bringing his own experience, talent and thoroughness, Jaywalker always brought something else with him. Always.

What he brought was a theory.

And he would share that theory with the jurors early on, so that even as the prosecutor's evidence came in and piled up and threatened to crush the defense table with its sheer weight, the jurors would at the very least have an alternative framework in which to consider that evidence.

There was another thing Jaywalker liked to do, and that was to concede things. If he was trying a possession of stolen property case, for example, he would readily concede that the property had in fact been stolen, that the defendant had indeed possessed it, and that it was even worth whatever dollar amount the prosecution's expert claimed it was. But, Jaywalker would argue, the defendant hadn't *known* it was stolen, and without that essential knowledge, he wasn't guilty. Making concessions not only narrowed the focus of the trial to something debatable, it carried the added benefit of earning both Jaywalker and his client credibility with the jury, so that when it came time to argue about whether or not the defendant had known of the theft, the jurors were open to the possibility that he hadn't. After all, he'd been so forthcoming and honest in admitting all those other things, didn't it follow that his one denial deserved deference?

Weeks ago, when Jaywalker had finally allowed himself

to at least consider the remote possibility that Samara
wasn't guilty, he'd been forced to come up with a theory
of defense. The lack of phone calls to or from Barry after
she'd gotten home had left her utterly without an alibi. Self-
defense wouldn't work, with Samara continuing to insist
she'd never stabbed Barry, not even to protect herself from
attack or abuse, whether real, threatened or merely imagined. And with Samara looking and sounding perfectly
normal and having no history of mental illness, insanity
was out of the question.

It had been the discovery of the Seconal, along with
Samara's insistence that she knew absolutely nothing about
it, that had ultimately provided Jaywalker with a theory.
Someone had framed Samara. Someone had murdered
Barry and then gone to great lengths to not only cover his
own tracks, but to plant evidence making it look as though
Samara had committed the crime. He'd been smart enough
to know that in looking to solve a murder, particularly one
without a robbery component, the police invariably focused
their suspicions on the husband or wife, boyfriend or girlfriend. And hadn't they done just that in Samara's case?

Sure, it was a long shot. But when you were down to
one shot, it didn't much matter how long or short it was.
You took it, and you hoped for the best.

Now it was time to tell the jurors about it.

For the first time since they'd been selected, the jurors
took their permanent seats, assigned to them in the order
in which they'd been chosen. They were sworn in once
again, this time as a body. The judge then spoke to them
for twenty minutes, explaining their function and his, and
outlining the course of the trial that was about to begin in
earnest. Then it was Tom Burke's turn to open. He spoke
for fifteen minutes, pretty much following the book that all
prosecutors seem to use. First he read the indictment, lingering an extra beat on the word *murder*. Then he com-

pared his opening statement to a table of contents, a guide to what he intended to prove through his witnesses and by his exhibits. Next he got down to specifics. He told the jurors about the discovery of Barry Tannenbaum's body; the next-door neighbor's account of having heard Barry and his wife "Sam" arguing; Samara's lies to the detectives; the finding of the bloodstained evidence in her town house; the DNA match of that evidence to a known sample of Barry's; and finally the *pièce de résistance,* the motive, the life insurance policy application, complete with Samara's signature. It was strong stuff, and Jaywalker couldn't help but notice that more than a single pair of jurors' eyes rolled upward as the list grew in length and weight. Finally Burke did what all prosecutors do.

"At the end of the evidence," he said, "the rules will provide me another opportunity to address you. And at that time I'll ask you to find the defendant guilty as charged, guilty of the murder of her husband, Barry Tannenbaum." Then he thanked them and sat down.

Under New York law, prosecutors are required to deliver opening statements; they're given no say in the matter. Defense lawyers get to choose. This apparent inequity is really no inequity at all. It's nothing but a logical extension of the rule that the prosecution bears the burden of proving guilt, while the defense bears no burden at all.

Judges routinely inquire of defense lawyers ahead of time whether they intend to open or not, and in this regard Judge Sobel had been no exception. Jaywalker, who'd been up all night going back over his opening, had known forever that he would open; he always opened. Nonetheless, when asked by the judge earlier that morning, before the jury had entered the courtroom, he'd answered, "It depends upon what Mr. Burke has to say in his remarks." It was a lie, to be sure, but a harmless one, meant to fool no one. And judging from the grins it brought from both the judge and Burke, it didn't.

Still, like everything Jaywalker did during the course of a trial, the lie had its purpose, and that purpose became clear now.

"Mr. Jaywalker," said the judge, "do you wish to make an opening statement on behalf of the defendant?"

For a second or two he just sat there, as though pondering the offer and trying to decide whether to take the judge up on it or not. Eighteen pairs of eyes peered at him from the jury box. Finally, he said, "Yes, I do," gathered some notes, decided not to use them after all, rose from his chair and walked to the front of the jury box.

"It is August," he tells them, starting off in a voice so soft that the jurors in the second row have to lean forward and cock their heads just to hear him. No introduction, no "Mr. Foreman, ladies and gentlemen," no "May it please the court." Just "It is August."

"Not this past August, but two Augusts ago. Samara Tannenbaum has been invited to her husband's apartment for dinner. If that sounds strange to you—and it sure sounds strange to me—the evidence will show that while the couple shared a home in Scarsdale, both Barry and Samara had their own separate places in the city. Theirs was not a perfect marriage, by any stretch of the imagination."

A couple of jurors smile, and there's even an audible chuckle. As Jaywalker's voice gradually rises, they no longer need to crane forward to hear him. Still, none of them have settled back into their seats. None of them are looking anywhere but into his eyes. Thirty seconds into his opening, and he has them.

"They eat Chinese takeout food. They argue about something foolish, as they almost always do. They raise their voices, call each other names. Sometime around eight o'clock, Samara, having had enough, gets up, says goodnight and leaves. There has been no fight, no struggle, no physical contact whatsoever. Absolutely no crime of any sort has been committed.

"Samara hails a cab and goes directly home. Tired, she goes to bed before ten. Without showering or bathing, without so much as washing her hands and face, in fact."

A juror in the first row picks up on the significance of that and nods thoughtfully. Jaywalker fights the impulse to include Samara's little detail about having "jerked off." He's decided that as credible as the addition might be, it's decidedly a double-edged sword.

"Later that same day, two detectives show up. Samara, who's never been overly fond of cops, lets them in anyway. When they begin asking her questions about her and her husband, but refuse to tell her what it's all about, she decides it's none of their business and barely gives them the time of day. In fact, she lies to them, telling them she hadn't been at Barry's the evening before. As soon as they tell her they know otherwise, she admits it. They ask her if she and Barry fought, and she says no. They spend a few minutes debating the difference between a fight and an argument. And then, just like that, they slap handcuffs on her and arrest her for murdering her husband."

If only it were so simple, thinks Jaywalker, *if only that's all there was to it.* But there's more, much more, and like it or not, he has to deal with it. So it's theory time.

"Members of the jury, you are about to embark on the journey of a lifetime. Nothing you've ever been through, in all your years, will have fully prepared you for it. And nothing you will ever experience over the rest of your lives will even come close to matching it. Put your hands firmly on the armrests of your seat, and hold on as tightly as you can. And make sure you use both hands. Because this isn't going to be just one journey, but two."

A few of them—not all, but a few—actually do as they're told, grip the armrests of their seats.

"Mr. Burke has ably and forcefully outlined the first

journey for you. His is a journey that's going to take you from one piece of evidence to the next, and then to the one after that. And each piece of that evidence, whether it comes to you in the form of a witness's testimony, some physical object or a sheet of paper, is going to point overwhelmingly to the guilt of Samara Tannenbaum. That's right, you heard me correctly. If you choose to take that first journey, and that first journey alone, you'll end up convinced that Samara's guilty. Because it'll all be there right in front of you, served up on a silver platter. Samara's presence at Barry's apartment shortly before the murder. Their voices raised in argument. Her initial lie to the detectives. A knife capable of having caused the fatal wound hidden away in her home, along with a blouse of hers and a towel, all three of them with Barry's blood on them. A month-old application for an insurance policy on Barry's life, with Samara's signature on it. The policy that was issued, worth twenty-five million dollars in the event of Barry's death. A perfect motive, if ever there was one.

"Jurors, you can confine yourselves to this one journey, the journey Mr. Burke has outlined for you. If you decide to do that, it'll take you no time at all to become convinced of Samara's guilt, and you'll come out of this trial thinking that this was the strongest case there ever was. And in a sense, you'll be right. *Strong?* The word doesn't begin to do it justice. Try *overwhelming. Airtight. Perfect.* So perfect, in fact, that it should scare the living daylights out of you and make you ask yourselves if things are ever, *ever,* so perfect in real life.

"Because, jurors, there's another journey you can take, if you're up to it. If you dare. A second journey through the very same evidence outlined by Mr. Burke. A second journey I beg you to take, *implore* you to take. This journey begins with a proposition, a proposition that flows from the rule of law that asks you, *requires you,* demands of you, that you presume Samara innocent. It's a proposition that, if you give it a chance, may explain why this case seems so incredibly strong, so utterly convincing, so absolutely perfect, when almost nothing ever is in this world we inhabit.

"And here—" dropping his voice again now, forcing them to lean forward once more "—is the proposition. Samara Tannenbaum is being framed."

The collective gasp is so audible that Jaywalker fears he's gone over the top and lost them. But there's no turning back. All he can do now is repeat himself, dig in, and hope that one or two of them will stay with him.

"That's right," he says, *"framed.* As you listen to the evidence, jurors, try not to be dazzled by it. Shield your eyes from the blinding light, protect yourselves from the blast of heat, and try to see through to the core of it, the essence, the part that truly makes sense. The damning items found in Samara's home, for example. Was that really where she would have hidden them, if indeed she'd murdered her husband? In a place where they were absolutely sure to be found? The life insurance policy. Did she really expect to collect twenty-five million dollars on a policy taken out a month before murdering her husband? Did she think nobody would notice? This woman who lives in the glare of publicity? Come on, she's smarter than that, and so are you. The clumsy, obvious lies to the detectives. Proof that Samara's a murderer? Or that she's simply someone who doesn't particularly like cops, especially cops who seem to be prying into the details of her marriage? The fact that she argued with her husband. Earthshaking? Or a pretty common thing? The list goes on and on. What you'll find is that every single piece of evidence against Samara has a flip side to it, if only you'll allow it to reveal itself.

"So, jurors, there's an easy way to look at this case, and a hard way. Mr. Burke makes it all sound easy. In fact, he's already told you that at the end of the trial he'll be asking you to convict Samara. He's told you that, as a matter of fact, before you've had a chance to hear one single word of testimony. Think about that for a minute. Me? I'm not asking you to acquit Samara. I have no right to do that at this point, not before you've heard the evidence. What I'm asking you to do instead—*all* I'm asking you to do, in fact—is to take both journeys, the obvious one and the not-so-obvious one, the easy one and the hard one. I'm asking you to listen with both ears, to watch with both eyes, and, if you detect something a little foul in the air, to smell with both nostrils.

"Who's framing Samara? I don't know. I wish I did, but I don't. Maybe the evidence will yield a clue or two. Maybe not. But remember this—I have no burden of proof in this trial. I don't have to identify the framer. Nor do you. At the end of the day, it will be enough if you walk back into this courtroom, look us squarely in the eye and tell us that, having taken both journeys through the evidence, you are unable to say that you are convinced that my client is guilty of murder, and that you are *certainly* unable to say you are convinced beyond all reasonable doubt."

He turned from them, walked back to the defense table and sat down. He'd spoken for almost half an hour. He had no idea if he had them or not. At very least, though, he'd presented them with a theory—a proposition, he'd called it—and none of them had laughed. That itself he counted as a victory of sorts.

The bad news, of course, was that the evidence was about to begin.

19

A GRUESOME DEATH

"The People call Stacy Harrington."

A lot of prosecutors like to start off with a bang, calling a key witness first. While this practice makes for exciting TV drama, it often accomplishes little more than confusing jurors.

Tom Burke was anything but a showman, and drama was the last thing he was interested in. In the choice of his leadoff first witness, he made it clear that it wasn't ratings he was after, but chronology and clarity.

Stacy Harrington, small, black and attractive, was employed as an executive assistant—a new title for the old job Jaywalker had grown up calling a secretary—in the offices of Tannenbaum International, Barry Tannenbaum's flagship company. She'd been among the first to notice Barry's lateness in showing up one August morning, a year and a half ago. And the thing about Barry, at least one of the many things about Barry, was that he was never late for anything.

| MR. BURKE: | What did you do, when he didn't show up? |
| MS. HARRINGTON: | I called his home, both homes. |

MR. BURKE: And?

MS. HARRINGTON: He didn't answer.

MR. BURKE: At either place?

MS. HARRINGTON: At either place.

MR. BURKE: What did you do then?

MS. HARRINGTON: I called the police.

MR. BURKE: Which police?

MS. HARRINGTON: The New York City police. It
                        was my understanding that
                        Barry, that Mr. Tannenbaum,
                        was staying in the city. And
                        that way was easier. I just di-
                        aled 9-1-1.

MR. BURKE: And what, if anything, did
                        the police tell you?

MS. HARRINGTON: They recognized the name.
                        They said they'd send some-
                        one over, and would contact
                        the Scarsdale police and
                        have them do the same up
                        there.

Jaywalker asked no questions of Ms. Harrington. His
rule of thumb was that less was better, and none was even
better than less. Too many cross-examiners insisted on
making a show of questioning every witness called by an

adversary. To Jaywalker, that made no sense at all. If a witness hadn't said anything to hurt his client, why disguise that fact by asking questions? Why not instead highlight it by shrugging and saying that you had no questions?

Burke called Anthony Mazzini. Mazzini was the superintendent of the building in which Barry Tannenbaum had a penthouse apartment. Around midday, two uniformed police officers had arrived at the building. They'd explained that Mr. Tannenbaum hadn't shown up for work that morning, and that people at his office were concerned for his welfare. After unsuccessfully trying to reach Tannenbaum by intercom and telephone, Mazzini had taken the officers up to the penthouse. There he'd rung the doorbell and knocked on the door, getting no response. Eventually he'd unlocked it with a passkey. The door hadn't been chained or bolted from the inside, and the alarm had been off. Mazzini had followed the officers inside.

MR. BURKE: Did you find anything unusual?

MR. MAZZINI: Unusual? Yeah, plenty.

There was a ripple of nervous laughter from the jury box.

MR. BURKE: What was it?

MR. MAZZINI: We found Mr. Tannenbaum laying on the kitchen floor in a mess of blood.

Once again, Jaywalker had no questions. Mazzini was actually on his short list of suspects, but he knew that now was no time to go after him. For one thing, the rules of evidence limited cross-examination to those topics covered in direct examination. If Jaywalker wanted to attack the super, he would have to call him later, during the defense case, and, if need be, have him declared a hostile witness. But even beyond that technical consideration, what was he going to do? Come right out and ask Mazzini if he'd murdered Barry and framed Samara?

Burke called Susan Connolly, one of the two "first officers" to arrive at the scene. Officer Connolly had quickly determined that Tannenbaum was dead, and had probably been dead for a number of hours. She and her partner had established a crime scene, prohibiting any unauthorized personnel from entering, and seeing to it that nothing was moved or otherwise disturbed. Then they'd called their precinct commander, who'd told them to wait there until the detectives arrived.

MR. BURKE: Which way was the body facing?

P.O. CONNOLLY: Excuse me?

MR. BURKE: Was the body lying faceup or facedown?

P.O. CONNOLLY: Facedown, mostly.

MR. BURKE: Did either you or your partner ever turn it over?

P.O. CONNOLLY: No, sir.

MR. BURKE: Thank you. No further questions.

At that point Jaywalker decided he might as well take a shot and see if he could raise some questions about the previous witness.

MR. JAYWALKER: What about Mr. Mazzini, the super? What did he do?

P.O. CONNOLLY: He didn't touch him, neither.

MR. JAYWALKER: No, not what he *didn't* do, what he *did* do.

P.O. CONNOLLY: When?

MR. JAYWALKER: The entire time he was in the apartment.

P.O. CONNOLLY: I don't know. Stood around, mostly. Looked around.

MR. JAYWALKER: Looked around in various rooms?

P.O. CONNOLLY: I guess so.

MR. JAYWALKER: You yourself stayed with the body, though. Right?

P.O. CONNOLLY: Right, once we'd secured the area and made sure that there was no one else in the apartment.

MR. JAYWALKER: I see. How long did it take before the detectives arrived?

P.O. CONNOLLY: *(Refers to memo book)* Twenty-five minutes.

MR. JAYWALKER: When they arrived at the apart-
                    ment, did they have much con-
                    versation with Mr. Mazzini?

P.O. CONNOLLY: Some. I wouldn't say much.

MR. JAYWALKER: So he was still there?

P.O. CONNOLLY: I'm not sure.

MR. JAYWALKER: Didn't you just tell us the detectives had some conversation with him when they
arrived at the apartment?

(No response)

MR. JAYWALKER: Was Mr. Mazzini still there?

P.O. CONNOLLY: Yes.

MR. JAYWALKER: So by that time, he'd been there
                    a good half an hour, right?

P.O. CONNOLLY: I guess so, right.

MR. JAYWALKER: Like you said, standing around,
                    looking around in various
                    rooms?

P.O. CONNOLLY: Right.

If it wasn't much, at least it was a start. It showed that
the super, who had a passkey, had also had full access to
the apartment the day after the murder. And that the integ-
rity of the crime scene had been compromised, a fact that
jurors raised on a diet of O.J. and *CSI* might find troubling.

Then again, what was Jaywalker really doing here? Hoping for the cops to screw up? Waiting for manna to fall from the heavens? It seemed so.

They broke for lunch.

That afternoon Burke led off with Detective Anne Maloney. Maloney was assigned to the Crime Scene Unit, a fact that immediately grabbed the attention of the jury. Having labored for years in almost total obscurity, CSU had almost overnight become the darlings of the department. The agent of change, of course, had been the television set. Programs like *CSI,* along with myriad spinoffs and competitors, had thrust the unit into the forefront of police work. These days, if you were to canvas a roomful of twelve- to fourteen-year-olds, you'd likely find that of all the careers the youngsters aspired to, crime scene technician outpolled its nearest competitor by a margin of twenty to thirty percentage points. Kids no longer wanted to be doctors, movie stars, shortstops, firemen or forest rangers; they wanted to be David Caruso or Marg Helgenberger. (Assuming, of course, that they couldn't be the next *Fantasia.*)

Detective Maloney was no American Idol. Plain and a bit on the stocky side, with a pageboy haircut straight out of the fifties, she was all business. She and fellow members of her unit had arrived at the scene at, as she put it, "fourteen forty-five hours." Translated for the jury, that was a quarter of three in the afternoon. She'd found that the apartment had been secured by two uniformed patrol officers, who'd established a crime scene, indicated by the presence of familiar yellow-and-black tape at the door to the apartment.

Inside, things had seemed quite orderly, with two exceptions, both in the kitchen. First, there were a half-dozen half-empty cartons of Chinese food spread out on the countertop. And then there was the floor. On it was a body, subsequently identified as that of Barry Tannenbaum.

MR. BURKE: Can you describe the condition
                    of the body for us?

DET. MALONEY: It was dead.

Her understatement drew a few nervous snickers from
the jury box.

MR. BURKE: I was actually hoping you could
                    give us a little more detail.

The snickers erupted into laughter. Burke had a nice
way of putting jurors at ease. That said, Jaywalker had no
doubt that he'd planted that little bit of comic relief, even
if he hadn't bothered telling his witness what he was doing.
Jaywalker knew that because, from time to time, he did the
same thing with his own witnesses.

DET. MALONEY: The body was lying facedown,
bent into a sort of fetal position. A significant amount
of dried blood was visible underneath it.

MR. BURKE: Did you check for a pulse, or
                    other vital signs?

DET. MALONEY: No. That had already been done,
                    with negative results.

MR. BURKE: Did there come a time when you
                    turned the body over?

DET. MALONEY: Yes. After photographing the
                    body in the exact position we
                    found it in, we turned it over.

MR. BURKE: And what, if anything, did you
                        observe at that time?

DET. MALONEY: We observed—

MR. JAYWALKER: Objection.

THE COURT: Yes, sustained. You can tell us
only what you yourself observed.

DET. MALONEY: I observed a large area of what
                        appeared to be a bloodstain on
                        the front of the victim's clothing.

At this point Burke walked to the prosecution table and
retrieved a large brown paper bag. Returning to the lectern,
he withdrew an item and handed it to one of the uniformed
court officers, who in turn placed it in front of the witness.

MR. BURKE: I show you what has been
marked People's One for identification, and ask you
if you recognize it.

DET. MALONEY: Yes, I do.

MR. BURKE: And what is it?

DET. MALONEY: It's a white cashmere sweater,
                        the outer garment Mr. Tannen-
                        baum was wearing.

MR. BURKE: How do you recognize it?

DET. MALONEY: From the large stain on the
front of it. Also, these are my initials, A.L.M. I wrote
them on the label that day, in ink.

Burke repeated the process with the inner garment, a long-sleeved beige turtleneck. The stain on it was even larger than the one on the sweater. Both stains were almost black in color, with only a suggestion of red around the edges.

After photographing and examining the body, Maloney had conducted a search of the apartment, finding nothing remarkable and nothing out of place. There'd been no signs of a forced break-in, and nothing to suggest a burglary. From the absence of bloodstains anywhere else in the apartment, she'd been able to conclude that the victim had been killed right where he'd fallen.

Maloney had taken a series of photographs, which Burke now entered into evidence. She'd made measurements and drawn a rough sketch, which she'd later enlarged into a poster-sized diagram, also received in evidence. She'd also dusted the apartment for fingerprints, paying particular attention to the Chinese food containers and the area around the doorknob to the entrance. She'd succeeded in lifting several latent prints, and she'd photographed several others. She'd also taken the fingerprints of the victim and the two uniformed officers, so their prints could be ruled out when comparisons would later be made.

Next, Burke had Maloney describe how she'd collected a number of hairs and fibers from the body and clothing of the victim. She'd retrieved each one with tweezers, inserted each into an individual plastic bag, and marked each bag with the specific location where the enclosed evidence had been found. Later, she'd catalogued the items and turned them over to the Criminal Identification Division for analysis.

Burke asked Maloney if her search of the apartment, or any of the areas surrounding it, had turned up anything in the way of a possible weapon. No, she replied. Along with other CSU members, she'd combed the hallway, the elevator bank, the trash area, the rooftop and even the air shafts and ground level beneath the apartment, all without finding a knife or similar instrument that might have been used in the murder.

Burke was finished with the witness, but before turning her over to Jaywalker for cross-examination, he asked Judge Sobel for permission to "publish" the diagram and the photographs. The judge agreed, and an easel containing the diagram was placed directly in front of the jury box, so that the jurors could see it. They leaned forward to look at it, but gave no sign that they were overly impressed with it.

The photographs were a different matter.

Prior to jury selection, Jaywalker had fought hard to keep them out. The worst of them showed Barry Tannenbaum, lying facedown and slightly curled up, in a puddle of what looked like very, very dark red paint. In one particular photo, the body had been turned over to reveal a large stain of the same color on the chest area of Barry's otherwise white cashmere sweater. Jaywalker had lost the fight, and although he'd made a point of describing the photos during jury selection and eliciting the jurors' assurances that they wouldn't be overwhelmed when they saw them, he now heard audible groans from the jury box. Death had a way of doing that, he knew. Especially gruesome death, recorded in glossy, 81/2 x 11" living color.

On cross-examination, Jaywalker asked Maloney if she'd fingerprinted Mr. Mazzini, as well.

DET. MALONEY: Who?

MR. JAYWALKER: Mr. Mazzini, the building superintendent.

DET. MALONEY: I didn't see any building superintendent.

MR. JAYWALKER: The officers didn't tell you

	he'd had the run of the apartment for half an hour?
MR. BURKE:	Objection to "run of the apartment."
THE COURT:	Sustained.
MR. JAYWALKER:	Did the officers tell you that the super had let them in?
DET. MALONEY:	Not that I recall.
MR. JAYWALKER:	And that he'd remained in the apartment for a good half an hour?
DET. MALONEY:	No.
MR. JAYWALKER:	During which time he'd walked from room to room?
DET. MALONEY:	No.
MR. JAYWALKER:	If you'd known those things, would you have fingerprinted the super, as well?
MR. BURKE:	Objection, calls for speculation.
THE COURT:	Sustained.

MR. JAYWALKER: Would it have been good police practice to fingerprint everyone who'd been in the apartment that day?

MR. BURKE: Objection.

THE COURT: Overruled.

DET. MALONEY: I guess so.

MR. JAYWALKER: You *guess so?* Or is the answer,
                     "Yes, it would have been"?

DET. MALONEY: Yes, it would have been.

It wasn't much, but it was as good a place as any to quit. When it came time for deliberations, juries often requested read-backs of various witnesses' testimony, and Jaywalker liked to end on a positive note whenever he could. He'd even toyed with the idea of asking Maloney if she'd bothered to fingerprint the co-op board president, or Barry Tannenbaum's accountant or his recently fired lawyer, knowing he would get a "Who?" from the witness. But he knew that line of questioning would also get him a series of objections from Burke and likely an adverse ruling from the judge, the combination of which would serve to dilute any gains the questions might earn him. Once again, less was more.

Next Burke called Roger Ramseyer, a detective assigned to the Criminal Investigation Division. Ramseyer had received a number of items brought in by Detective Maloney, including latent prints, hairs and fibers. He'd subsequently been supplied with fingerprint cards and sample hairs representing individuals who'd been known to have been in Barry Tannenbaum's apartment the day his body was discovered. He referred to the first group of items as "questioned" and the second group as "known." Burke took him carefully through each item.

With respect to the latent, or questioned, fingerprints found in the apartment, Ramseyer was able to make positive comparisons to the known prints of Barry Tannenbaum, Police Officer Susan Connolly and Samara Tannenbaum. Specifically, Samara's prints had been found on the interior doorknob to the apartment, as well as the exterior doorknob and lock plate, two of the Chinese food containers, and on two glasses, one empty, the other partially filled with water. Two hairs removed from Barry Tannenbaum's sweater proved to be of human origin and microscopically indistinguishable from known hair samples supplied by Samara. And one red silk thread, also lifted from Barry's sweater, was similarly indistinguishable from the red threads of a multicolored silk woman's blouse, separately delivered to Ramseyer by a different detective, two days later.

Jaywalker started to rise to object, but decided against it. The detective who'd brought the blouse in hadn't testified yet, so technically there'd been no proper foundation laid as to where the blouse had been found. But the judge would no doubt either take Ramseyer's testimony about the threads subject to later connection or make Burke recall his witness later on in his case. Either way, Jaywalker's victory would be short-lived, and in the long run it would only place more emphasis on the testimony. Better to let it in unchallenged. Trying to keep it out would only highlight it for the jury.

So, too, with the reliability of hair and fiber comparisons. Jaywalker had tried enough cases and done enough reading to know that the science behind such testimony was shaky, particularly when judged by DNA standards, or even against fingerprint research. But he had little interest in showing off, and none in disputing Ramseyer's conclusions. His defense, he'd already told the jury, was that his client was being framed. She'd been in Barry's apartment on the evening of his murder, and she was going to testify to as much. It was only to be expected that her fingerprints would be found there, on the food containers she ate from, the glass she drank from, and the doorknob she turned to let herself out. So, too, her hairs, and even a fiber from her clothing. Either those items had ended up on Barry's sweater naturally or they'd been planted there. No mileage was to be gained by arguing with Ramseyer that the scientific basis for his findings might be dubious.

So when Burke finished with the witness, Jaywalker had only a few questions for him.

MR. JAYWALKER: Detective Ramseyer, did you end up with any latent prints that you still would have to classify as "unknown"?

DET. RAMSEYER: Yes.

MR. JAYWALKER: How many?

DET. RAMSEYER: May I review my notes?

MR. JAYWALKER: By all means. In fact, why don't you turn to the top of page four of your report.

DET. RAMSEYER: Thank you. Yes, I was left with six unknown prints, corresponding to four individuals.

Jaywalker asked him the same question with respect to hairs and fibers. The detective answered that he'd been left with four unknown hairs, belonging to three individuals, and three unknown fibers, each one indistinguishable from the others.

MR. JAYWALKER: So you ended up knowing for a fact that at least four additional individuals left their fingerprints in the apartment. And three or four individuals, perhaps the same ones, perhaps not, left

human hairs or fibers on the victim's body or clothing. Is that correct?

DET. RAMSEYER: That's correct.

MR. JAYWALKER: And yet you have absolutely no
way of telling us who those
people were?

DET. RAMSEYER: Correct.

MR. JAYWALKER: Tell me, detective. Were you
ever supplied known finger-
prints, hairs or fibers corresponding to one Anthony
Mazzini?

DET. RAMSEYER: No, sir.

MR. JAYWALKER: Corresponding to one Alan
Manheim?

DET. RAMSEYER: No, sir.

MR. JAYWALKER: To one William Smythe?

DET. RAMSEYER: No.

MR. JAYWALKER: To one Kenneth Redding?

DET. RAMSEYER: No.

MR. JAYWALKER: Thank you.

It was after four-thirty, and Jaywalker guessed that
Judge Sobel would adjourn for the day. But Burke indi-

cated at the bench that he had a short witness he'd like to get in before they broke.

"Who is he?" the judge asked.

"She," said Burke. "The victim's sister."

"Body ID?" Jaywalker wanted to know.

Burke nodded.

"I'll stipulate," Jaywalker offered. He was ready to concede that it was in fact Barry Tannenbaum who'd been murdered, and the last thing he wanted was a sobbing relative on the stand, particularly at the end of the day.

"No, thanks," said Burke, who had the right to refuse Jaywalker's offer.

"Keep it brief," said the judge.

As soon as they'd returned to their tables, Burke called Loretta Tannenbaum Frasier. A stooped-over woman was led into the courtroom. By Jaywalker's estimate, she couldn't have been five feet tall, even in shoes. A short witness, indeed.

As soon as she'd been sworn in and had identified herself as the victim's sister, Jaywalker stood up, the judge's ruling notwithstanding. "We're quite willing to concede that it was indeed her bother who was murdered," he said. "If that's what calling this witness is all about."

"You may proceed, Mr. Burke," said Judge Sobel, as annoyed at Jaywalker's theatrics as Jaywalker was at Burke's.

With a shrug that would have done Samara proud, Jaywalker sat down. But he'd made his point. As early as jury selection, one of the things he'd warned the jurors about was that the prosecution might bring in a grieving family member to stir their sympathies. What's more, he would remind them of this stunt in his summation. But for the moment, all he could do was feel sorry for this poor little woman whose only brother had been stabbed to death.

Just as the jurors were no doubt doing.

Then again, had Jaywalker been in Tom Burke's shoes, he would have done the same thing. Hell, he would have brought in a dozen family members, each one of them sobbing more pitifully than the previous one.

To his credit, Burke got to the point with Mrs. Frasier and didn't overdo things. When Jaywalker indicated he had no cross-examination, they broke for the day.

They'd gotten through six witnesses, and Samara wasn't dead yet. But to Jaywalker, that was little comfort. Tom Burke was a good lawyer with a strong case, albeit a circumstantial one. He was putting it together brick by brick. If the first day's witnesses had only touched Samara tangentially, that was by design. Tomorrow would be another day, Jaywalker knew. The jurors would hear from the real witnesses, the detectives who'd investigated the bulk of the case. They would tell the jurors about Samara's lies, what they'd found hidden in her apartment—and her motive.

The worst, in other words, was yet to come.

20

A MASSIVE LOSS OF BLOOD

Jaywalker had left court Thursday afternoon expecting Tom Burke to begin the next day's session by calling one of the two detectives who'd "caught" the case and done the major investigative work on it. But Burke called Jaywalker at home that evening to let him know that the detective would be unavailable, and that as a result Burke would be reshuffling the order of his witnesses.

"Thanks for letting me know," said Jaywalker, who was genuinely appreciative. He'd long had mixed feelings about what sort of prosecutor he liked going up against at trial. There were the sneaky ones, and there were the open ones, of which Burke was a perfect example. But the thing was, with the sneaky ones, Jaywalker could feel free to fight fire with fire. With someone like Burke, he was compelled to return decency with decency. Not as much fun sometimes, but in the long run, probably better for everyone. "By the way," he asked Burke, "how'd you get my home number?" It was unlisted, and although Jaywalker gave it out freely enough, he didn't remember Burke's ever having asked for it.

"Ve haff our vays," said Burke.

They shared a laugh, and said they'd see each other in the morning. Jaywalker poured himself a cup of coffee, his third of the evening, all *sans* Kahlúa, and retrieved the files he now knew he would have to review for Friday, thanks to Burke's sense of fair play.

A week or so before the trial had begun, Burke had confided to Jaywalker that he was putting in an application for a Criminal Court judgeship and might ask Jaywalker for a written letter of recommendation.

"I'd be delighted," Jaywalker had said. "But me? I mean, you do know what they think of me, don't you? I could be the kiss of death."

"Nonsense. Just because they can't figure out how to control you, it doesn't stop them from knowing you're the best there is."

"Cut the bullshit. I said I'd write the letter. You want it now?"

"No," Burke had said. "Wait till after the trial. You may hate my guts by then."

"I'm *sure* I'll hate your guts by then. But you can still count on the letter."

"Thanks," said Burke. "And when you write it, make sure you use my middle name, Francis. I understand there's an A.D.A. on Staten Island named Tom Burke who's thinking of putting his name in, too. Guy's supposed to be a total loser."

"Right, like you're not?"

Jaywalker smiled now, remembering the exchange. Robert Morgenthau, the octogenarian Manhattan D.A., had long enjoyed enough clout to get just about any of his assistants onto the bench, and he'd used that clout often, with generally good results. Contrary to popular wisdom, former prosecutors didn't always turn out to be tough judges, any more than former defense lawyers turned out to be lenient ones. Defense lawyers, after all, knew that their clients lied. Prosecutors, on the other hand, knew that cops lied, and a few prosecutors even had the balls to say so. Tom Burke was such a prosecutor, and he would make a terrific judge someday. The problem was that Bob Morgenthau, whether he knew it or not, couldn't afford to lose the Burkes in his office; there was a whole new generation of non-Burkes working their way up the ladder.

As he'd told Jaywalker he would, Burke led off Friday with the second of the two police officers who'd responded to Barry Tannenbaum's apartment and found him murdered. Burke's purpose was a limited one, to show that the body in the apartment was the same one the officer had seen the following day at the morgue, waiting to be autopsied. The officer confirmed that it was, and Jaywalker had no reason to question him.

Next Burke called Charles Hirsch, the Chief Medical Examiner. Jaywalker knew Dr. Hirsch well from having cross-examined him on two previous murder cases. Thin and just slightly gawky-looking, Hirsch was an extraordinary witness. He had a résumé that ran to fifteen pages of advanced degrees, hands-on research, teaching fellowships, academic positions and awards. He'd been qualified as an expert in forensic pathology in more courts than most lawyers set foot in during a lifetime. Jaywalker quickly rose and offered to stipulate to that expertise. This time, Burke accepted the offer, but he still spent a solid five minutes having Hirsch summarize his credentials. Without the stipulation, he could have gone on for hours.

MR. BURKE: Would you explain to the jury what you mean by the term "forensic pathologist."

DR. HIRSCH: Certainly. In its most basic meaning, a pathologist is a physician who specializes in learning the cause or causes of death. A forensic pathologist is a pathologist who brings that training and knowledge to the courtroom, where the disciplines of medicine and the law intersect.

Already, the jurors were ready to take this guy home and make him part of their families.

MR. BURKE: What is the primary tool employed by the forensic pathologist?

DR. HIRSCH: That would be the autopsy.

MR. BURKE: And what is an autopsy?

DR. HIRSCH: An autopsy is a full postmortem examination of a body, both external and internal, aided by microscopic and other types of studies of various organs, chiefly the blood, brain and liver.

MR. BURKE: Over the course of your career, how many autopsies have you conducted?

DR. HIRSCH: I would say that I've personally conducted upwards of ten thousand, and been present at and observed another five thousand.

MR. BURKE: I offer the witness as an expert in forensic pathology.

THE COURT: I believe Mr. Jaywalker has already stipulated that he is.

MR. BURKE: Did there come a time, Doctor, when you were called upon to perform an autopsy on

the body of one Barrington Tannenbaum, also known
as Barry Tannenbaum?

DR. HIRSCH: Yes, there did.

Burke had the witness recount the date, time, and condition in which he'd first seen the body. It had been fully
clothed, the upper half covered by a white cashmere sweater
with a large dark-red stain covering the chest and upper ab-
dominal area. Removal of the sweater had revealed a camel-
colored cotton turtleneck pullover, with a corresponding
stain even larger than that on the sweater. Beneath the
pullover, Dr. Hirsch had observed a large amount of what
appeared to be dried blood, covering the chest area. He'd
proceeded to wash the blood away with a saline solution
and had observed a wound. He described the location of the
wound, first in reference to the midline of the body, then in
terms of its distance from the soles of the body's feet.

MR. BURKE: Would you describe the wound
               itself for us.

DR. HIRSCH: Yes. It was a laceration, specifi-
               cally—

MR. BURKE: Let me stop you. What's a lacera-
               tion?

DR. HIRSCH: A laceration is a cut in or through
the skin, as opposed to an abrasion, which is a rub-
bing away of the skin, or a contusion, which is a
bruising of the skin.

MR. BURKE: Thank you. I believe I inter-
               rupted you midsentence.

DR. HIRSCH: There are several types of lacerations. There are elongated lacerations, in which the skin has been sliced open. There are punctures, in which the skin has been torn by an object coming into contact with it at more or less a right angle, in other words perpendicular. And there are combinations of the two, where the angle is significantly shallower. In this particular case, I was able to determine that the wound was a puncture, just about perpendicular to the surface of the chest.

MR. BURKE: How large was the wound?

DR. HIRSCH: Superficially, that is, on the surface, it was about three quarters of an inch in length, from left to right, by about one sixteenth of an inch in width. In terms of penetration, it was approximately five inches deep.

MR. BURKE: Were you able to determine where it led to?

DR. HIRSCH: Yes. By inserting a metal probe and following the path of least resistance, I was able to track the wound from its point of entry at the skin, and from there through the various layers of fat and muscle tissue. Whether by luck or design, it passed between two of the victim's ribs. From there it entered the chest cavity and proceeded through the wall of the pericardium. The pericardium is a sac that surrounds and contains the heart. Once inside the pericardium, the track continued and entered the left ventricle of the heart, rupturing it.

MR. BURKE: What happens when the left ventricle of the heart is ruptured?

DR. HIRSCH: Unless there's immediate medical intervention, massive bleeding occurs. That bleeding can be into the chest cavity, into the lungs, or out of the entrance wound itself.

MR. BURKE: And in this particular case?

DR. HIRSCH: In this particular case, it was all three. The individual bled into his chest cavity and his lungs, as well as out through the entrance wound. Hence the blood we see on the upper body garments he was wearing. Furthermore, the amount of blood on those garments, which was fairly significant, suggests that the instrument that had caused the wound was removed relatively quickly, probably before death. Otherwise, given the narrowness of the wound, the continued presence of the instrument would likely have acted something like a cork or stopper, limiting the volume of blood that could have escaped through the wound.

MR. BURKE: Can you tell us, to a degree of medical certainty, what the cause of death was?

DR. HIRSCH: Yes. The victim's heart stopped because of a massive loss of blood. That massive loss of blood was the direct result of the rupture to the left ventricle of his heart.

MR. BURKE: From examining the wound, can you tell us anything about the instrument that caused it?

DR. HIRSCH: Yes. I can tell you that it was a thin blade of some sort, no more than three-quarters of an inch wide, and no more than a sixteenth of an inch in thickness. It was sharply pointed at the tip. It was at least partly serrated on the cutting edge.

MR. BURKE: How do you know that?

DR. HIRSCH: I know that because I was able to observe a jagged tearing pattern in the tissue along one edge of the wound track, as opposed to a smooth pattern along the opposite edge.

MR. BURKE: Can you tell us anything about the length of the instrument that produced the wound?

DR. HIRSCH: I can say with certainty that the blade was at least five inches in length. Otherwise, the tip would not have reached as far as it did. I am less certain about its maximum length, but my belief is—

Jaywalker put one hand on the table in front of him, preparing to rise. The witness was about to speculate, and an objection might well be sustained. But the last thing Jaywalker wanted to do was give the jury the impression that he was trying to keep things out. Besides, from studying the autopsy report, he knew where this was going and didn't see how it would hurt. He decided to let the witness continue. Trials were like that. You had a split second in which to consider and weigh seven or eight variables before making a decision that might well determine the outcome of the entire trial. You learned to do it. After a while, you learned to do it without even thinking about it on a conscious level. There was no room for the hesitant at trial, no place for the second-guesser.

—that the blade was just about five inches, and no longer.

MR. BURKE: Upon what do you base that belief?

DR. HIRSCH: I base it upon my observation of a small depressed area surrounding the skin at the very beginning of the wound track. That depression suggests to me that the instrument used to inflict the wound was a knife with a handle, and the hilt, the perpendicular part that separates the blade from the handle and serves as a safety device of sorts, struck the skin with sufficient force to create a stamp, if you will. It's my belief that it was the presence of that hilt that stopped the knife from penetrating even deeper. Furthermore, it very probably tells us the overall length of the blade, though certainly not that of the handle, or therefore the total length of the knife itself.

At that point Burke withdrew from underneath the lectern an item wrapped in brown paper. He identified it as People's Exhibit 5, for identification and subject to connection. As before, he had a court officer hand it to the witness. Unwrapped, it appeared to be a silver-colored steak knife with a thin pointed blade and a serrated cutting edge. The blade looked to be about five inches long, by perhaps three-quarters of an inch wide. Separating the blade from the handle was a hilt.

MR. BURKE: Doctor, please take a look at that knife. First, have you ever seen it before?

DR. HIRSCH: Yes, you showed it to me several weeks ago, and again earlier this morning.

MR. BURKE: Are the properties of that knife

consistent with the wound you observed during your postmortem examination of Barry Tannenbaum?

DR. HIRSCH: Yes, they are.

MR. BURKE: In every way?

DR. HIRSCH: In every way.

Finally Burke did what good prosecutors do. He anticipated the areas ripe for cross-examination and tried to limit any gains Jaywalker might be able to make in exploring them. Hirsch had identified some general health concerns during his autopsy of Barry Tannenbaum and addressed them in his report. Specifically, there had been evidence of fairly advanced prostate cancer, with infiltration into the colon and bladder. There had also been a tumor, about the size of a golf ball, in Tannenbaum's large intestine. Finally, the heart itself had been enlarged, and there was some evidence of old scarring. Taken together, according to Hirsch, these last two findings were indicative of chronic heart disease. More specifically, they suggested that at some time in the past, perhaps as far back as a decade or more, Tannenbaum had survived a heart attack.

MR. BURKE: Did any of those things, either separately or in combination with each other, contribute in any way to the death of Mr. Tannenbaum?

DR. HIRSCH: No, absolutely not. This death was clearly a homicide, caused by bleeding due to the rupture of the left ventricle of the heart. Nothing more, nothing less.

During the autopsy, Hirsch had removed samples of blood, brain tissue and liver, and submitted those samples for laboratory study. The results had come back in the form of serology and toxicology reports. A small level of ethanol had been detected, as well as a moderate amount of Seconal, a barbiturate.

MR. BURKE: First of all, what is ethanol?

DR. HIRSCH: Ethanol is ethyl alcohol. It's the kind we ingest when we drink a beer, a glass of wine or a mixed drink.

MR. BURKE: How about a straight drink?

DR. HIRSCH: That, too.

Which brought a couple of laughs from the jury box, perhaps at the expense of Burke's Irish ancestry.

MR. BURKE: Are you able to tell us how much Mr. Tannenbaum had had to drink?

DR. HIRSCH: Yes. He'd had perhaps a single drink, no more than one and a half, during the six hours preceding his death.

MR. BURKE: And the Seconal?

DR. HIRSCH: That's a bit harder to quantify. Two pills, three or four at most. In other words, the amount an individual would take in order to sleep, assuming he'd experienced difficulty doing so, and had built up a bit of tolerance to the medication over time.

MR. BURKE: And did either the alcohol or the

Seconal, alone or in combination, contribute in any
way to Mr. Tannenbaum's death?

DR. HIRSCH: Absolutely not.

Jaywalker knew better than to attack Hirsch, and the truth
was, he had no reason to. The case wasn't about whether
Barry Tannenbaum had been stabbed to death or not. He had,
and everyone knew it. Still, there were a few points to be
made. Cross-examination doesn't necessarily mean beating
up a witness, Jaywalker knew. Often you could accomplish
much more by adopting the witness as your own.

MR. JAYWALKER: Doctor, I'm interested in the
expression Mr. Burke used when he showed you the
knife and asked you if its properties are *consistent with*
the wound sustained by Mr. Tannenbaum.

DR. HIRSCH: Yes.

MR. JAYWALKER: By agreeing, did you mean
                        to say that this knife *in fact*
                        caused the wound?

DR. HIRSCH: No. Only that it could have.

MR. JAYWALKER: I see. Might you care to estimate how many other knives in the city could have
caused the wound, just as easily?

MR. BURKE: Objection.

THE COURT: Overruled.

MR. JAYWALKER: Dozens?

DR. HIRSCH: Sure.

MR. JAYWALKER: Hundreds?

DR. HIRSCH: Yes.

MR. JAYWALKER: Thousands?

DR. HIRSCH: I'd say so.

MR. JAYWALKER: And this depression you described, this stamp you believe was created by the hilt of whatever knife was used. Would I be right in concluding that if you're correct about its origin, it tells us that considerable force was used in plunging the knife into the body?

MR. BURKE: Objection to "considerable."

THE COURT: Overruled. You may answer.

DR. HIRSCH: I would agree with "considerable force." We would have had a better idea of just how much if the blade had struck a rib. Then something would have had to give. Either the rib would have fractured or splintered, or the blade would have bent, broken or stopped moving forward. But as I said earlier, the blade missed the ribs.

MR. JAYWALKER: So we'll never know for sure.

DR. HIRSCH: Exactly.

MR. JAYWALKER: And we'll have to settle for "considerable force."

DR. HIRSCH: Right.

MR. JAYWALKER: Suggesting that a rather powerful person was responsible for the thrust of that knife, and that he plunged it home with an awful lot of muscle behind it.

This time, Burke's objection was sustained. But Jaywalker had made his point. And he knew that when it came time for summations, he would be allowed to argue it, and to ask the jurors to take a good look at Samara and ask themselves if she seemed capable of wielding a weapon with such brutal strength.

It wasn't much, but it was enough to send the jury out to lunch on.

By two o'clock Burke's detective was still unavailable, and rather than scurry around trying to find other witnesses to call out of turn, Burke asked to go over to Monday. That sort of thing occurs in just about every case that gets tried, and is a good reason never to believe a judge when he tells prospective jurors how long he expects a trial to last. To paraphrase a not-so-old expression, stuff happens.

"All right," said Judge Sobel, "we'll give the jury a long weekend. But make sure you have your detective here first thing Monday morning, or—"

"Or you'll dismiss the case?" suggested Jaywalker.

"In your dreams," said the judge. "In your dreams." Apparently he'd been taking a peek at the rest of the evidence.

"You'll probably get to testify sometime around the middle of next week," Jaywalker told Samara, once they'd walked up to Canal Street and were safely out of earshot of the jurors. "We'll need to spend some time getting you ready."

Spend some time. Not spend some *more* time, given the fact that they'd already had a dozen such sessions, spanning twice that number of hours. Though Jaywalker lived in dread that his witnesses might come off as rehearsed and memorized, he clung to his belief that there was no such thing as overpreparation. He would continue to work with Samara right up until the day she took the stand. The day? More like the minute.

"Want to come over this evening?" she asked. "I'd say now, but I'm going to enjoy my afternoon off, right up to curfew time. After that, though, I could be all yours."

Jaywalker looked at her, trying to figure out if she'd intended the double entendre, or if it existed only in his mind. "Let's make it nine o'clock tomorrow morning," he said. "At my office. There'll be fewer distractions there."

The way she somehow managed to pout and smile simultaneously told him no, it hadn't been just in his mind. And once again, as he turned from her and headed for the entrance to the subway, the words that came to mind were, *You moron.*

21

THE EYE-TALIAN DETECTIVE

By Monday morning Tom Burke had his detective ready to testify. He also had some additional paperwork for Jaywalker, in the form of a two-page typewritten report. In the Age of the Computer, with three-year-olds routinely exchanging e-mails with their octogenarian grandparents, and second graders being encouraged to hand in assignments created on word processors, the NYPD had apparently bought up the entire stock of the world's discarded typewriters, the old manual ones with misaligned keystrikers and dried-out ribbons, and taught its personnel how to use them with their thumbs, perhaps, or their elbows, with the additional requirement that they misspell every third word and ignore the rules of grammar at every conceivable opportunity.

Still, it took Jaywalker only a glance to see that the detective's *unavailability* on Friday had been the result of neither a conflicting court appearance nor a family emergency. He'd been busy working, working in connection with the trial. More specifically, he'd been running around collecting fingerprints, in some cases by retrieving existing cards from BCI files, in others by actually going out, locating individuals and, with their consent, taking inked impressions of their hands. Now Jaywalker all but groaned as he read the names of the individuals. Anthony Mazzini.

Alan Manheim. William Smythe. Kenneth Redding. Burke had handed his detective a list of the people whose names Jaywalker had proposed to Roger Ramseyer, the CID detective who'd testified on Thursday, as additional suspects whose prints should have been checked against the unknown ones found in Barry Tannenbaum's apartment. Now the jurors were going to hear that none of their prints—not even Mazzini's, who'd hung around the apartment for a good half an hour—matched any of the unknown ones. Jaywalker looked over at Burke, just in time to catch him trying to suppress a grin. "Nice work," he said.

"Hey," said Burke, "didn't anyone ever tell you how to catch red herrings?"

Jaywalker answered with a blank expression.

"You *spear* 'em."

Anthony Bonfiglio was a New Yorker through and through. He was a caricature right out of Little Italy, or maybe Pleasant Avenue. He could have played a wise guy on *The Sopranos,* or a mobbed-up cousin from one of *The Godfather* movies. He could have been a bookie or a loanshark or an enforcer, the kind of guy who keeps a baseball bat within arm's reach on the car seat next to him, not for hitting fungoes, but for busting kneecaps.

Instead, Bonfiglio had become a cop. And now, twenty years later, he was a detective, first grade, working homicides. Jaywalker knew him, having had to cross-examine him a couple of times over the years, and had little use for him. He strongly suspected that Bonfiglio was on the take, though he couldn't prove it. But jurors loved the tough cop image and positively ate the guy up.

Burke had Bonfiglio describe how he'd "caught" the homicide of Barry Tannenbaum just about a year and a half ago.

MR. BURKE: Was that because of some spe-

cial expertise on your part, or
some particular familiarity
with the victim?

DET. BONFIGLIO: Nah. It was my toin, was all.

The jurors laughed. They were in love with him already.

MR. BURKE: Can you tell us what you did
after being assigned to the
case?

DET. BONFIGLIO: Me and my partner, Eddie
Torres, we went to the apartment where the body got
found. The first officers were there. They'd established a crime scene. CSU was there, dustin' an'
liftin' prints, takin' photos, an' doin' some other stuff.

Bonfiglio had examined the body and satisfied himself that
he was looking at a murder victim, stabbed in the chest and,
judging from the amount of blood, through the heart. He'd
conferred with the various other officers and detectives on the
scene, who told him they'd recovered no weapon. He proceeded to conduct his own search, being careful to not touch
or disturb anything unnecessarily. He found no knife or other
implement that he believed had been used in the crime.

Generally, the apartment was neat and orderly. There
were some Chinese food containers on the kitchen counter,
with leftovers that were cold, but not yet spoiled. There
were no signs of a forced break-in, a ransacking, or any
kind of a struggle.

MR. BURKE: What did you do next?

DET. BONFIGLIO: I conducted a canvass of the
surrounding apartments. Specifickly, I interviewed a

Mrs. Benita Gristede, in Penthouse B, a Mr. Charles Robbins, in Penthouse C, and two occupants of the apartment directly beneath Mr. Tannenbaum. Lemme see, yeah. Mr. and Mrs. Goodwin, Chester and Lois.

MR. BURKE: Were any of those individuals able to tell you anything you considered significant?

Jaywalker resisted the urge to object, even though the question called for hearsay testimony. He knew from the detective's reports that only Benita Gristede had had anything to offer, and she was on Burke's witness list, anyway. So he let it go.

DET. BONFIGLIO: Yeah. Ms. Gristede did.

MR. BURKE: What did you do once you'd completed your canvass of the neighboring apartments?

DET. BONFIGLIO: Me an' my partner, we went back downstairs to the lobby, and we conversed with the doorman and the super. And I ast them to call the doorman who'd been on duty the night before an' have him come in. An' they did that.

MR. BURKE: And did there come a time when he arrived?

DET. BONFIGLIO: Yeah.

MR. BURKE: Do you recall his name?

DET. BONFIGLIO: Jussaminit. *(Reviews notes)* Yeah, José Lugo.

MR. BURKE:	And did you have a conversation with Mr. Lugo?
DET. BONFIGLIO:	Yeah.
MR. BURKE:	Your Honor, may we approach?
THE COURT:	Yes, come up.

Up at the bench, Burke explained that at this point he wanted to interrupt the witness's testimony in order to take that of the two individuals who'd supplied him with information, first Ms. Gristede, and then Mr. Lugo. Jaywalker objected but gave no reason. If pressed, he would have had to say that anything that was good for Burke had to be bad for him and his client, and that, furthermore, he was still pissed off at Burke for having lied about Detective Bonfiglio's unavailability on Friday.

"Your objection is overruled," said Judge Sobel. "I'll give you the option of cross-examining the witness now on what he's said so far, or reserving it all for later."

"Later," said Jaywalker, still in sulk mode.

The judge explained to the jurors what they were going to do, excused the witness and declared a fifteen-minute recess. Once the jurors had been escorted out of the room, he called the lawyers back up to the bench.

"Has there been an offer in this case?" he asked.

So it was starting. Matthew Sobel wasn't a meddler. Unlike some judges, he allowed lawyers to try their cases and pretty much refrained from attempting to bludgeon plea bargains out of them. But his question now, as gentle and as deferential as it was, spoke volumes compared to what others might have said—and had.

Why are we trying this case?

Can't you guys work something out here?

Doesn't your client know she's looking at twenty-five to life?

And Jaywalker's personal favorite, the impartial, *And you can tell her I said she's going to get every last day of it after the jury convicts her.*

Now, even Matthew Sobel was beginning to wonder. Jaywalker might have succeeded in throwing some sand in the jurors' eyes with his *This-case-is-so-strong-my-client-must-be-innocent* opening statement, but he hadn't fooled the judge, not for a minute. And the worst part was that the truly damaging evidence was yet to come. Wait until Sobel heard the testimony about Samara's lies, the stuff found in her apartment, and the timing and the amount of that little life insurance policy.

"My client is innocent," said Jaywalker. Not only did his words sound foolish even to himself, they also violated one of his cardinal principles. It was okay to say that his client *says* she's innocent, or *maintains* her innocence, or even *insists* she's innocent. But as soon as you said that she was innocent, stating it as a fact, you were vouching for her. And not having been in Barry Tannenbaum's apartment that evening a year and a half ago, Jaywalker was certainly in no position to be vouching for Samara.

Burke raised his palms upward, his way of explaining that Jaywalker's comment had said it all. Even if he'd considered offering Samara something less than murder, how could he, given her continuing claim of innocence?

Unpersuaded by such logic, Judge Sobel pressed on. "Would you consider a Man One," he asked Burke, "with a substantial sentence? I mean, I'd have a range of up to twenty-five years."

Jaywalker spoke up before Burke could answer. "My client is innocent," he said again, trying to make it sound a little more convincing this time.

But it didn't.

* * *

Benita Gristede was a small woman in her seventies or eighties, who looked as though she might have come over on the *Mayflower.* Having outlived her husband, she was the sole occupant of Penthouse B, the apartment that shared a common wall with Penthouse A, Barry Tannenbaum's apartment. On the evening of Barry's death, Mrs. Gristede had heard the sounds of an argument between a man and a woman in the adjoining apartment. She'd recognized the man's voice as that of her neighbor, Mr. Tannenbaum. The woman's voice, she was every bit as certain, had been that of his wife, known to Mrs. Gristede as Sam. The argument had occurred shortly before eight o'clock, toward the very end of that evening's episode of the game show *Wheel of Fortune.*

MR. BURKE: How is it that you recall that?

MRS. GRISTEDE: I recall that because the arguing was so loud, I had to turn the volume up in order to hear the TV.

MR. BURKE: Were you able to hear what the argument was about?

MRS. GRISTEDE: You mean the words?

MR. BURKE: Yes, the words.

MRS. GRISTEDE: No. Just that they were very loud.

MR. BURKE: The following day, did a detective come by and ask you some questions?

MRS. GRISTEDE: You mean the eye-talian one?

MR. BURKE: Yes.

MRS. GRISTEDE: Yes, he did. And I told him
                      exactly what I'm telling you.

On cross-examination, Jaywalker purposefully mumbled his first question to Mrs. Gristede, so she'd have to say
she couldn't hear him. Burke objected, and Judge Sobel had
to make a record of it, adding that he'd had trouble hearing
it, as well. He asked the court reporter to read it back.

COURT REPORTER: Sorry, I didn't get it, either.

It had been stunts like that that had landed Jaywalker in
front of the disciplinary committee. Well, like that and a lot
worse. Still, he wasn't quite ready to let the hearing thing go.

MR. JAYWALKER: You do wear a hearing aid,
                      though?

MRS. GRISTEDE: I most certainly do not.

MR. JAYWALKER: Would you say your hearing's
                      quite good, in fact?

MRS. GRISTEDE: I certainly would. Probably
                      better than yours.

Laughter from the jury box, at his expense. Never a
good omen.

MR. JAYWALKER: Yet you never heard a scream
                      that evening, did you?

MRS. GRISTEDE: No, I did not.

MR. JAYWALKER: Or a *thud?*

MRS. GRISTEDE: A thud?

MR. JAYWALKER: Yes, as though someone had just fallen to the floor.

MRS. GRISTEDE: I don't recall that.

MR. JAYWALKER: Now, you say you had to turn the volume up in order to hear the TV?

MRS. GRISTEDE: That's correct.

MR. JAYWALKER: Don't they show you everything in great big capital letters?

MRS. GRISTEDE: Yes.

MR. JAYWALKER: But you still turned the volume up to hear it?

MRS. GRISTEDE: I like to hear them say it. Besides…

MR. JAYWALKER: Besides what?

MRS. GRISTEDE: Besides, my eyes aren't so good.

Great, thought Jaywalker. He finally gets the old bat to admit that while her hearing may be perfect, she's half blind. The only problem was that she'd never claimed to have seen anything, only to have heard his client arguing with the victim right around the time he was stabbed to death.

* * *

José Lugo took the stand. Lugo was a short man in his forties, with a dark mustache that accentuated the serious expression he wore. He sat on the edge of his seat and answered Tom Burke's questions as though his own freedom hung in the balance.

Yes, he said, he'd been the doorman on duty during the four-to-midnight shift on the day before he'd received a call from his boss, Tony Mazzini, to come in and talk to the detectives. Lugo knew Barry Tannenbaum, the occupant of Penthouse A, and his wife, Samara. Asked by Burke if he could identify Samara, he hesitated for a split second, then pointed directly at her. Jaywalker couldn't be sure, but he thought he heard Lugo mumble an apology as he did so.

Lugo recalled that Mrs. Tannenbaum had arrived at the building early that evening, though he couldn't recall the exact time. But Burke was ready to help him out.

MR. BURKE: I show you what's been marked as People's Exhibit Seven for identification, and ask you if you recognize it.

MR. LUGO: Yes. It's the sign-in book, the log we keep at the doorman's station.

MR. BURKE: I offer it into evidence.

MR. JAYWALKER: No objection.

THE COURT: Received.

MR. BURKE: Will looking through that book help you remember what time Mrs. Tannenbaum arrived that evening?

MR. LUGO: It should.

MR. BURKE: Please take a look.

MR. LUGO: Yes, here it is. She arrived at
                   six-fifty. Ten minutes to seven.

MR. BURKE: Did she sign the book herself?

MR. LUGO: No, I signed in for her. I'm
allowed to do that, so long as I know the person.
Besides, she's Mr. Tannenbaum's wife. Was.

MR. BURKE: Did Mrs. Tannenbaum leave
                   while you were still on duty?

MR. LUGO: Yes.

MR. BURKE: Do you recall what time that
was?

MR. LUGO: It says here—

MR. BURKE: You're not allowed to read.
                   Just—

MR. JAYWALKER: No objection to his reading. It's
                   in evidence.

MR. BURKE: Thank you. Mr. Lugo, you may
                   read.

MR. LUGO: Eight-oh-five.

MR. BURKE: That's what time she left?

MR. LUGO: Didn't I just say that?

MR. BURKE: I guess you did. Now, how late did you work that night?

MR. LUGO: Till midnight.

MR. BURKE: Were you at the front door the entire time?

MR. LUGO: The entire time. Except when I had to— *(To the Court)* Your Honor, can I say "pee"?

Laughter.

THE COURT: You just did.

MR. LUGO: Except when I had to pee. But then I locked the door, so nobody could come in or go out.

MR. BURKE: And from the time Mrs. Tannenbaum left at eight-oh-five, until the time you went off duty at midnight, did anyone else come in to visit Mr. Tannenbaum, or leave after visiting him?

MR. LUGO: No.

MR. BURKE: Do you want to check the log-book to make sure?

MR. LUGO: I already did. The answer is no.

On cross, Jaywalker asked the witness if he'd noticed

anything strange about Samara, either when she'd arrived or when she'd left.

MR. LUGO: Strange?

MR. JAYWALKER: Yes. Like, was she covered with blood?

MR. LUGO: Blood?

MR. JAYWALKER: Blood.

MR. LUGO: I didn't see no blood.

MR. JAYWALKER: Not on her clothes?

MR. LUGO: No.

MR. JAYWALKER: Her face?

MR. LUGO: No.

MR. JAYWALKER: Her hands?

MR. LUGO: I didn't notice her hands.

MR. JAYWALKER: But you would have, if they'd been covered with blood, wouldn't—

MR. BURKE: Objection.

THE COURT: Sustained.

MR. JAYWALKER: Do you recall what she was wearing?

MR. LUGO: Clothes.

MR. JAYWALKER: I was hoping for a bit more de-
                     tail. Other than clothes, do you
                     remember anything specific?

MR. LUGO: No, I don't remember. It was a
                     long time ago.

MR. JAYWALKER: It was. But there was nothing
                     unusual about her clothes that
                     you remember?

MR. LUGO: No.

MR. JAYWALKER: This was August, August in
                     New York City, right?

MR. LUGO: Right.

MR. JAYWALKER: You don't remember, for example, that Samara was wearing a long coat, for example, or a jacket that seemed too warm for that time
of year, do you?

MR. LUGO: No, I don't remember anything
                     like that.

MR. JAYWALKER: When she left, was she carrying
                     anything?

MR. LUGO: Like what?

MR. JAYWALKER: Oh, like a knife, or a bloody
                     towel.

MR. LUGO: No, I don't remember anything
                   like that.

MR. JAYWALKER: And did she seem upset when
                   she left? Or in a hurry?

MR. LUGO: No, she seemed regular.

On redirect, Burke got Lugo to admit that Samara might
have been carrying a handbag, and might have been
wearing a lightweight jacket, although he really couldn't
say one way or the other.

They broke for lunch.

"How's it going?" Samara asked, on the way downstairs.

Jaywalker put a finger to his lips. He didn't think there
were any jurors in the elevator, but he didn't want to take
a chance. Once, years ago, he'd gotten into trouble by
mentioning to a colleague that he was on trial and "shov-
eling shit against the tide." A juror had overheard him and
reported it to the judge. Luckily, the juror had been only
an alternate.

"I don't know," Jaywalker lied, once they were safely
out on Centre Street. "Things could be worse, I guess." He
refrained from adding, *And soon enough, they will be.*

"But you don't think we're dead yet, do you?"

"What you mean *we,* white woman?"

It was an old joke, probably older than Samara. Which
might have had something to do with why it didn't seem
to strike her as particularly funny.

In the afternoon session, Burke called a young woman
employed as a programming assistant at ABC. Armed with
a thick binder, she testified that on the evening of the
murder, a year and a half ago, *Wheel of Fortune* had aired

at seven-thirty Eastern Standard Time, and had ended at eight.

Jaywalker asked her no questions.

Detective Bonfiglio was recalled and told that he was still under oath. Burke reminded him that when he'd been excused that morning, he'd just described how he'd had conversations with Mrs. Gristede of Penthouse B, and Mr. Lugo, the doorman who'd been called in.

MR. BURKE: Following those conversations, did you do something?

DET. BONFIGLIO: Yeah. By that time, CSU was finished and the morgue guys had come and taken the body. I ordered the crime scene sealed.

MR. BURKE: Meaning what?

DET. BONFIGLIO: Meaning the apartment was locked from the outside, crime scene tape was used, a notice was put on the door, and a seal was applied to it, so if anyone was to try to enter, they'd have to break the seal.

MR. BURKE: What did you do after that?

DET. BONFIGLIO: Me and my partner, we exited the premises, and we did thereafter proceed to the home of Samara Tannenbaum, to pay her a visit.

And in his best copspeak, Bonfiglio recounted their visit to Samara's. He described her initial claim that she hadn't seen her husband in about a week, followed by her admission that she'd been at his apartment the previous evening. Also her denial that the two of them had argued, similarly retreated from as soon as she'd been told that they had a witness who said otherwise.

MR. BURKE:	Can you describe her general demeanor?
DET. BONFIGLIO:	She was real nervous like, she—
MR. JAYWALKER:	Objection.
THE COURT:	Sustained.
MR. JAYWALKER:	Move to strike.
THE COURT:	Yes, the answer is stricken, and the jury will disregard it.

Fat chance, Jaywalker knew. Still, even though he couldn't expect the jurors to unhear it, he'd had to keep it out; otherwise Burke would be permitted to refer to it in his summation. But Burke was determined to get it in.

MR. BURKE:	Detective, did you have a chance to observe Mrs. Tannenbaum while you questioned her?
DET. BONFIGLIO:	Yes, I did.
MR. BURKE:	Tell us some of the things you observed.
DET. BONFIGLIO:	Observed? I dunno, I observed her face, her arms, her legs, her—
MR. BURKE:	I mean regarding her demeanor.

DET. BONFIGLIO: Oh. She was pespirin' a lot. You know, sweating. And her hands was like shaking. And she'd look away from me, every time I tried to make eye contack wid her.

MR. BURKE: Did there eventually come a time when you took some police action with respect to her?

Jaywalker, who'd been about to rise, eased back in his chair. Burke, to his credit, had skipped the part about Samara's saying she wanted to call her lawyer, as well as her refusal to consent to a search of her apartment without a warrant. Eliciting either of those facts would have been improper, since they represented nothing but Samara's invocation of her constitutional rights—in this case her right to counsel, her right to silence and her right to be free from unreasonable searches—and no inferences adverse to her could properly have been drawn by the jury. Still, there were plenty of prosecutors who would have tried, whether out of ignorance or arrogance. Jaywalker was only half sorry Burke hadn't; if he had, at least Samara would have had something to argue on appeal.

DET. BONFIGLIO: 'Scuse me? I don't unnastand.

Burke shot a look over at Jaywalker, who gave him a nod, meaning, *Go ahead, lead the witness; I won't object.* Although the two of them had never gotten far enough to try a case against each other before this one, they were unfailingly on the same page.

MR. BURKE: Did there come a time when you placed Mrs. Tannenbaum under arrest?

DET. BONFIGLIO: Yeah.

MR. BURKE: And what did you arrest her for?

DET. BONFIGLIO: For the murder of her husband.

MR. BURKE: Thank you. Detective, I now draw your attention to later that same day. Did there come a time when you and other members of the department executed a search warrant in connection with this investigation?

DET. BONFIGLIO: Yeah.

MR. BURKE: Where did that take place?

DET. BONFIGLIO: At Mrs. Tannenbaum's town house.

MR. BURKE: When did that take place?

DET. BONFIGLIO: That same night, at twenty-two-hunnerd hours. Ten o'clock, to youse.

MR. BURKE: Would you tell the jurors what you found, and where you found it?

DET. BONFIGLIO: There was a buncha stuff found. But me, personally, what I found was wedged in between a toilet tank and the wall in a upstairs bathroom. It was three things, ackshully. First, a blue bathroom towel, with some dark red stains on it. Inside it was a lady's shirt, same kinda stains. An' inside that was a knife, like a steak knife. It had stains, too.

One by one, Burke had a court officer hand the items to the witness, so that he could identify them. Although the stains on them were small—far smaller, for example, than the stain on the sweater the jurors had seen in the photograph of Barry Tannenbaum's body—they were nonetheless visible. With no objection from Jaywalker, the items were received in evidence. Burke asked permission to publish them to the jury, and Judge Sobel agreed.

This time the procedure was a little different. Before handing the items to the jurors, a court officer supplied each of them with a pair of latex gloves. The handling of bloodstained items had changed drastically since the dawning of the age of AIDS.

Jaywalker watched the jurors out of the corner of his eye as they passed the exhibits among them. As far as he could tell, neither the towel nor the blouse caused too much of a reaction. But when it came to the knife, there were jurors who recoiled from it and refused to touch it, even through gloves, and others who took the opportunity to stare at Samara with cold, hard looks. Even from where Jaywalker sat, a good twenty feet from the jury box, there was no missing the serrated edge, the sharply-tipped point and the pronounced hilt.

For Jaywalker and his client, this was an exceedingly uncomfortable moment, the kind of moment that made him want to crawl underneath the defense table and out of sight. But being a defense lawyer meant he couldn't do that. So instead he just sat there, pretending to review some notes and trying to look as nonchalant as possible, despite the fact that he felt as though he'd just been hit with a sledgehammer. Even when the jurors had finally completed their inspection of the knife, a process that had seemed to take hours, Jaywalker's agony wasn't over. Burke wanted more out of Bonfiglio.

He asked the detective if he'd conducted some further investigation on the case the previous Friday, just three days ago. Bonfiglio replied that he had. He'd located Anthony Mazzini, the super at Barry Tannenbaum's building; Alan Manheim, until recently one of Mr. Tannenbaum's lawyers; and William Smythe, Mr. Tannenbaum's personal accountant. With the consent of each of them, he'd taken a full set of their fingerprints. Kenneth Redding, the president of the building's co-op board, had been out of town. But because Redding was a former navy SEAL and had once gone through a security clearance investigation, his prints were on file with the Pentagon, and Bonfiglio had been able to obtain a copy of them. He'd then delivered all four sets of prints to Roger Ramseyer, the CID detective who'd testified on Thursday.

At that point Jaywalker managed to get Burke's attention, and the two of them huddled for a moment off to the side.

"You want a stipulation?" Jaywalker asked.

"No, thanks."

Burke's reply was quick enough—and decisive enough—to tell Jaywalker that it was more than a matter of prosecutorial stubbornness. Burke intended to bring Detective Ramseyer back to the stand, so he could squeeze a bit of drama out of the fact that in spite of Jaywalker's earlier insinuations, there'd been no matches between any of the "suspects" Jaywalker had asked Ramseyer about, once their known prints had been compared with the remaining unknowns found at the crime scene.

He who opens doors sometimes gets his fingers slammed.

Jaywalker didn't really have much to cross-examine Bonfiglio about, and with the wind pretty much gone out of the defense's sails, he barely felt up to the task. But the detective had hurt Samara too much to be ignored. Besides which, his testimony had been so central to the case that there was a good chance the jury might want all or part of it read back to them during their deliberations. There was no way Jaywalker could let such a read-back contain nothing but direct examination. With that in mind, he decided to begin where Burke had left off.

MR. JAYWALKER: Tell me, detective. Does the failure to find an individual's fingerprints at a crime scene rule him out as a suspect?

DET. BONFIGLIO: Not necessarily.

MR. JAYWALKER: Is that the same as *"No"*?

DET. BONFIGLIO: Yeah, I guess so.

MR. JAYWALKER: So it *doesn't* rule him out. Correct?

DET. BONFIGLIO: Correct.

MR. JAYWALKER: Can you tell us some of the reasons why it doesn't?

DET. BONFIGLIO: He mighta been wearin' gloves. He mighta not touched nothin'. He mighta wiped his prints off whaddeva he did touch.

MR. JAYWALKER: Or Crime Scene might have missed his prints?

DET. BONFIGLIO: Maybe.

MR. JAYWALKER: Or he might have touched only surfaces that prints don't adhere to?

DET. BONFIGLIO: Maybe.

MR. JAYWALKER: So right there, in about a minute's time, we've come up with, let's see, five possibilities to explain why someone might have been at the crime scene the evening of the murder, yet his prints weren't found the following day. Correct?

DET. BONFIGLIO: If you say so.

MR. JAYWALKER: I just did say so. My question is, do you agree?

DET. BONFIGLIO: I dunno. I forget the question.

THE COURT: Please read the question back.

(Court reporter rereads previous question)

MR. JAYWALKER: Correct, or not correct?

DET. BONFIGLIO: Correct.

It wasn't much, but it did accomplish at least two things. It brought back Jaywalker's "suspects" from the dead, even if they were now no better than on life support. And it cast the detective in the light of a partisan who was only grudgingly willing to make the most minuscule concession to the defense.

But with his halting responses and *I-forget-the-question* interruption, Bonfiglio had succeeded, whether intentionally or inadvertently, in depriving Jaywalker of any flow in his cross-examination. Already the jurors were beginning to squirm in their seats, look around the courtroom and roll their eyes.

Jaywalker spent a few minutes, but only a few, on

Samara's initial lies to Bonfiglio and his partner. No, at that point they hadn't yet told her that her husband had been murdered. Couldn't her response that she'd last seen him about a week ago be nothing but the equivalent of "It's none of your business"? Bonfiglio replied that he hadn't seen it that way. And hadn't Samara denied *fighting,* as opposed to *arguing?* Perhaps. And once she'd realized the seriousness of the detectives' inquiry, hadn't she almost immediately told the truth, both in terms of her presence at Barry's apartment the previous evening, and that they'd had an argument? Yes, agreed Bonfiglio, though it hadn't been until they'd confronted her with evidence that she was lying.

Not much headway there.

Jaywalker moved on to the execution of the search warrant, and the discovery of the knife, the blouse and the towel.

MR. JAYWALKER: That was a large town house you and your fellow officers had to search, wouldn't you say?

DET. BONFIGLIO: Depends on whatcha mean by large.

MR. JAYWALKER: Well, how many officers and detectives took part in the search, in total?

DET. BONFIGLIO: Countin' me?

MR. JAYWALKER: Yes.

DET. BONFIGLIO: Lemme see. Six, eight, ten. About ten.

MR. JAYWALKER: And how long were you there?

DET. BONFIGLIO: Searchin' the place?

MR. JAYWALKER: Well, were you doing anything else while you were there?

DET. BONFIGLIO: No.

MR. JAYWALKER: So how long did it take?

DET. BONFIGLIO: Uh, from twenty-two-hunnerd to oh-one-one-five the next mornin'. Adds up to three hours an' fifteen minutes.

MR. JAYWALKER: Pretty large town house?

DET. BONFIGLIO: Yeah, pretty large.

MR. JAYWALKER: Fourteen rooms?

DET. BONFIGLIO: I dunno, sumpin' like that.

MR. JAYWALKER: Lots of hiding places?

DET. BONFIGLIO: I'd say so.

MR. JAYWALKER: Yet the things you found, the towel, the blouse and the knife, they were almost in plain view, weren't they?

DET. BONFIGLIO: No. They was behind the toilet tank.

MR. JAYWALKER: Well, did you have to move anything to see them?

DET. BONFIGLIO: No.

MR. JAYWALKER: Lift anything?

DET. BONFIGLIO: No.

MR. JAYWALKER: They weren't, for example, hidden *inside* the toilet tank, were they?

DET. BONFIGLIO: Inside it? No.

MR. JAYWALKER: If they had been, you'd have had to lift off the top of the tank in order to see them, right?

DET. BONFIGLIO: Right.

MR. JAYWALKER: And you might have missed them.

DET. BONFIGLIO: I don't think so.

MR. JAYWALKER: Then again, if they'd been inside the tank, instead of behind it, they'd have gotten wet, right?

DET. BONFIGLIO: Right.

MR. JAYWALKER: And some or all of the blood might have washed off, right?

DET. BONFIGLIO: I s'pose so.

MR. JAYWALKER: Making it harder, if not altogether impossible, to identify Barry Tannenbaum's blood on them?

MR. BURKE: Objection.

THE COURT: Sustained. He's not qualified
                    to answer that.

MR. JAYWALKER: Well, would you agree, detective, that if the items had been unwrapped and
dropped into the toilet tank itself, any blood on them
would have at least become diluted by the water in
the tank?

DET. BONFIGLIO: Diluted? Yeah, I guess so.

MR. JAYWALKER: But in any event, they weren't
                 inside the tank at all, were they?

DET. BONFIGLIO: No.

MR. JAYWALKER: They were behind it.

DET. BONFIGLIO: Right.

MR. JAYWALKER: Nice and dry.

DET. BONFIGLIO: Right.

MR. JAYWALKER: Neatly wrapped up.

DET. BONFIGLIO: They was wrapped up.

MR. JAYWALKER: Almost as though somebody
had put them there, nice and neat, nice and dry, confident that they'd be found.

MR. BURKE: Objection.

THE COURT: Sustained.

Figuring that he wasn't going to get much more out of the detective, Jaywalker decided it was as good a place as any to quit.

Burke had one more thing he wanted to do before the judge broke for the day, and that was, as Jaywalker had anticipated, to recall Roger Ramseyer, the CID detective. Ramseyer testified that the previous Friday evening he'd been provided by Detective Bonfiglio with four known sets of prints, belonging to Anthony Mazzini, Alan Manheim, William Smythe and Kenneth Redding. Ramseyer had gone in to work on Saturday, his R.D.O., to compare the prints to those lifted from Barry Tannenbaum's apartment, but still classified as unknown.

MR. BURKE: What's an R.D.O., by the way?

DET. RAMSEYER: A regular day off.

MR. BURKE: I see. And did any of the prints on the four new cards match any of the remaining unknown prints?

DET. RAMSEYER: No, they did not.

As tempted as Jaywalker was to ask Ramseyer if he got paid for working on his day off—chances were he not only got paid, but got paid at overtime rates—he refrained from doing so. There was nothing significant to be gained by making the point, while the risk was that by showing off his knowledge, Jaywalker might come off as a wiseass. Samara was already in enough trouble with the jurors, he figured. She didn't need them disliking her lawyer on top of everything else.

With Jaywalker's "No questions," they broke for the day. As always, Judge Sobel cautioned the jurors not to discuss the case among themselves, not to come to any conclusions before the evidence was in, and to avoid going to any of the places mentioned in the testimony. Just in case any of them were planning on sneaking past the doorman that night, cutting the crime scene tape, breaking the seal and kicking in the door to Barry Tannenbaum's apartment.

But rules were rules.

Even Jaywalker, who'd quietly or not so quietly broken just about all of them at one time or another, knew that. But the knowledge did little to soothe him right now. In a trial that suddenly seemed to have as much to do with toilets and toilet tanks as anything else, it was by now pretty clear exactly where his client was headed. And as much as he hated the thought of losing his last trial, he knew that to think of defeat in personal terms was absurdly selfish. Sure, he'd be bummed out for six months or a year. But he'd deal. He'd buy himself a case of Kahlúa, and he'd get over it. But for Samara, defeat wouldn't be about a batting average or a wounded ego. It would be about spending fifteen years to life in state prison. And that was the *minimum*.

He wondered what he could do, what rule he could break, what stunt he could pull off, to change that outcome. What had he missed? What hadn't he thought of ? Or was this trial, as he'd suspected for so long, simply that one case in ten that, try as he might, there was nothing he could do about?

It certainly seemed so.

22

THANK YOU, JESUS

Tom Burke devoted Tuesday morning's session to preempting Jaywalker's *some-other-dude-did-it* defense. First he recalled the superintendent of Barry Tannenbaum's building, Anthony Mazzini, and asked him point-blank if it had been he who had killed Tannenbaum. Mazzini's astonished *"Me?"* came out so heartfelt and unrehearsed that Jaywalker realized immediately what Burke had done. He'd put the super back on the stand without ever telling him that he was going to pop that question to him. It was a brilliant tactic, and it worked. The jurors' reaction to Mazzini's genuineness was evident from their own smiles and nods, and even one or two hard glares in Jaywalker's direction.

On cross, Jaywalker could do little but get Mazzini to admit he'd had, and still had access to, a key to Tannenbaum's apartment, and that he'd been vaguely aware of a disagreement between Tannenbaum and the president of the co-op, Kenneth Redding. When Mazzini denied that he'd sided with Redding in the dispute, there was little Jaywalker could do. On redirect examination, Burke asked his witness if he was sure he hadn't had some reason to want to kill Tannenbaum.

MR. MAZZINI: *Kill him?* The man used to tip
                      me two grand at Christmastime.
                      Why would I want to kill him?

Even Jaywalker had to admit it was a pretty good
question. He toyed with the idea of asking Mazzini if he knew
what the asking price for Penthouse A was, and how much
there might have been in it for him if he could have gotten
Tannenbaum thrown out of the building for causing water
damage to Redding's apartment. But all he had to go on was
Samara's suggestion that Mazzini and Redding had shared
a common interest, and faced with the witness's denials, his
pursuit of that line of questioning would only have led him
into a dead end and further antagonized the jurors.

So Jaywalker settled for getting the super to admit that
he'd remained in the apartment for half an hour after the
discovery of the body, that he'd walked around some, and
that sure, he'd probably touched some things.

Not much, certainly, but—coupled with the fact that his
fingerprints hadn't been found there—at least something
for Jaywalker to talk about on summation.

Next Burke called Kenneth Redding, who'd flown in
from Aruba the night before, cutting short a vacation, a fact
that he seemed none too happy about. Yes, he'd had a
dispute with Tannenbaum, Redding admitted, but that
came with the job of being president of the co-op board.
It was a tightly run building, and at one time or another he'd
had issues with just about every one of its owners and
tenants. The point of contention between Redding and Tannenbaum had involved an unpaid bill of about thirteen
thousand dollars, representing the cost of damage to Redding's apartment not covered by Tannenbaum's insurance.
Redding had demanded payment, and Tannenbaum had
refused, claiming that Redding had taken advantage by

upgrading his kitchen at Tannenbaum's expense. Redding denied that he'd done so.

MR. BURKE: In any event, given your finances and those of Mr. Tannenbaum, as you understand them to have been, would you call the amount in dispute a lot of money?

MR. REDDING: Personally, I'd call it chump change.

MR. BURKE: Enough to kill someone over?

MR. REDDING: *(Laughing)* It'd take a helluva lot more than that to get me to kill someone.

The jurors' chuckles made it clear that they were in full agreement.

Again, about all Jaywalker could do on cross was to establish that Redding, like Mazzini, had a passkey that opened the door to every apartment in the building, though Redding was initially a little less forthcoming about admitting the fact. Apparently the bylaws of the co-op didn't provide for the arrangement, but he'd gotten Mazzini to make him a key anyway.

MR. REDDING: You know, for emergency use.

MR. JAYWALKER: Like a fire, or a similar disaster?

MR. REDDING: Yeah, that sort of thing. Exactly.

MR. JAYWALKER: So in the event of a nuclear

attack, say, you could go from floor to floor, unlocking everyone's apartment?

MR. BURKE: Objection.

MR. JAYWALKER: I'll withdraw the question.

Burke followed up by calling Alan Manheim. The very first question out of Burke's mouth was whether Manheim currently had, or had ever had, a key to either Barry Tannenbaum's apartment or Samara's town house. Manheim replied emphatically that he didn't, and never had.

Manheim testified that he'd been employed on a full-time basis as Barry Tannenbaum's personal lawyer for eleven years. During that time, he'd been involved in, among other things, the purchase and sale of several homes and other properties, the negotiation of a divorce settlement with Tannenbaum's third wife, and the drawing up of a prenuptial agreement between Barry and Samara, the terms of which fully protected Barry in the event of yet another divorce, and ensured that Samara would walk away with precisely what she'd brought to the marriage—which, in round numbers, had been nothing.

Manheim had continued to work for Tannenbaum in a variety of capacities, as significant as securing a non-refundable ten-million-dollar advance to write an autobiography, never even begun, and as mundane as paying overdue parking tickets. Then, about six months before Tannenbaum's death, he and Manheim had abruptly parted company.

MR. BURKE: And why was that?

MR. MANHEIM: We had a disagreement.

MR. BURKE: Would you describe the nature
                    of the disagreement.

MR. MANHEIM: There were two issues, really. For one thing, there was Mr. Tannenbaum's health. He'd been diagnosed with cancer, and he wanted to update his will. Specifically, he wanted to know if there was any way he could disinherit his wife, and leave his estate entirely to his foundations, his endowments, his university and various charities he'd set up.

MR. BURKE: What did you tell him?

MR. MANHEIM: I told him that even were he to write Samara out of his will, it wouldn't work. The law would step in and give her half of his assets.

MR. BURKE: Was that an accurate statement of the law?

MR. MANHEIM: Yes. It's so fundamental, they teach it to you in the first year of law school.

MR. BURKE: Is it fair to say that your response didn't particularly endear yourself with Mr. Tannenbaum?

MR. MANHEIM: Yes, that's accurate. He wasn't happy about it.

MR. BURKE: You said there was another issue.

MR. MANHEIM: Yes.

MR. BURKE: Tell us about that.

MR. MANHEIM: Barry—how shall I say this?—

had a bit of a paranoid streak. He accused me of stealing, of embezzling funds from him.

MR. BURKE: Was there any merit to that accusation?

MR. MANHEIM: No, absolutely not. None whatsoever.

MR. BURKE: And how was the matter resolved, if indeed it was?

MR. MANHEIM: I became more and more incensed at his repeated accusations. Finally I offered my resignation.

MR. BURKE: And?

MR. MANHEIM: And Mr. Tannenbaum accepted it.

MR. BURKE: And six months later, did you get even by plunging a steak knife into his heart?

MR. MANHEIM: Absolutely not. I got even by securing an even better-paying job, and by continuing to be the very best attorney I can possibly be.

If it was a crude way of eliciting a denial, it was also effective. What interested Jaywalker, however, wasn't what Burke had asked his witness; it was what he had refrained from asking. Which meant one of two things, as far as Jaywalker was concerned. Either Burke didn't want to go there for some reason, or he was setting a trap for Jaywalker.

There's a rule of thumb employed by just about all

lawyers who try cases, and it goes like this: "Never ask a question unless you already know the answer."

As he did with most rules, Jaywalker chose to ignore it, but only selectively. His modification altered it to read, "If you're ahead on points, never ask a question unless you know the answer. If you're in trouble already, fuck it." Early in the second week of Samara Tannenbaum's trial, Jaywalker was a lot of things, but one thing he wasn't was ahead on points. It was definitely time to fuck it.

MR. JAYWALKER: Mr. Manheim, you say you landed an even better-paying job after leaving Mr. Tannenbaum's employ. Is that correct?

MR. MANHEIM: Yes.

MR. JAYWALKER: Would you say Mr. Tannenbaum was underpaying you?

MR. MANHEIM: Considering everything I was doing, yes I would.

MR. JAYWALKER: I see. And what was he paying you?

MR. MANHEIM: *(To the Court)* Do I have to answer that?

THE COURT: I'm afraid so.

MR. MANHEIM: *(Inaudible)*

MR. JAYWALKER: Can't hear you.

MR. MANHEIM: Two point seven.

MR. JAYWALKER: Two point seven what?

MR. MANHEIM: Million.

MR. JAYWALKER: Wow.

MR. BURKE: Objection.

THE COURT: Sustained.

MR. JAYWALKER: Sorry. Two million, seven hundred thousand. That was your total annual compensation?

MR. MANHEIM: Yes.

MR. JAYWALKER: No bonus at the end of the year?

MR. MANHEIM: Well, yes, but that varied from year to year.

MR. JAYWALKER: I see. Well, why don't you tell us how much it was for the last full year of your employment?

MR. MANHEIM: *(To the Court)* Do I really—

THE COURT: Yes.

MR. MANHEIM: One point five.

MR. JAYWALKER: Help me with the math here, if you would. Two point seven plus one point five comes to?

MR. MANHEIM: Four point two.

MR. JAYWALKER: Million.

MR. MANHEIM: Yes.

Okay, thought Jaywalker, here comes the trap Burke had
set for him. But why quit now? The jurors seemed absolutely stunned by the numbers, enough so that they appeared
to be having real trouble with Manheim. Perhaps some of
their distaste would rub off on Tannenbaum, as well. Jaywalker had won his share of cases for no better reason than
that the jurors ended up hating the victim more than they
did the defendant. Besides, he was having too much fun with
the witness to quit now. He shot one last look in Burke's direction, to see if he could pick up a poker player's "tell." But
if Burke was setting Jaywalker up, he gave no sign of it.

MR. JAYWALKER: And this embezzlement, or
                 alleged embezzlement, I should say. What was the
                 total amount in controversy, including end-of-the-
                 year bonuses, if there were any?

MR. MANHEIM: There were no bonuses in-
                 volved.

MR. JAYWALKER: So?

MR. MANHEIM: *(Looks at the Court)*

THE COURT: Please answer the question.

MR. MANHEIM: Two hundred and twenty-seven.

MR. JAYWALKER: Two hundred and twenty-
                 seven what?

MR. MANHEIM: Million.

MR. JAYWALKER: Two hundred and twenty-seven million dollars. And did Mr. Tannenbaum ever threaten to go to the police or the federal authorities, or to sue you civilly, or to go public with his claim? Any of those things?

MR. MANHEIM: He never threatened. He hinted, I guess you could say. I told him go ahead, I had nothing to hide.

MR. JAYWALKER: You weren't worried?

MR. MANHEIM: No. Why should I have been?

Just as there are ups and downs to any trial, so, too, are there special moments. Alan Manheim had delivered such a special moment in the midst of his answer to Jaywalker's question. Not with what he said, but how he said it. He got the "No" out all right. But two words later, on *should,* his voice cracked, and the word came out in falsetto. No one missed it. No one *could* have missed it. So Jaywalker let it hang there for a good fifteen seconds, staring at the witness, not saying a word.

If you don't think fifteen seconds can be an eternity, try doing absolutely nothing for that long, right now.

Finally, Jaywalker broke his own silence just long enough to ask one final question.

MR. JAYWALKER: Tell me, Mr. Manheim. That two hundred and twenty-seven million dollars. Would you call that chump change?

MR. MANHEIM: No.

They broke for lunch.

* * *

"You shredded him," said Samara, once she and Jay-walker were safely out of earshot of the jurors. "You were sensational."

She was right, at least about the shredding part. For a prosecution witness, Alan Manheim had come off quite poorly. His multimillion-dollar compensation, along with the distinct possibility that he'd stolen many times that amount from his employer, had to have had a negative impact on jurors who worked hard just to make ends meet at the end of the month. Still, it was quite a stretch to ask those same jurors to conclude that because Manheim was overpaid and perhaps even a thief, he was therefore also a murderer. And even if they wanted to make that leap and consider a scenario in which Manheim had murdered Barry Tannenbaum before Tannenbaum could expose the embezzlement, then made it look as though Samara had done it, there remained the little problem of access. How could Manheim have sneaked into the building past José Lugo, gotten into Tannenbaum's apartment, stabbed him to death, locked the door on his way out without a key and slipped out of the building past Lugo? And even if he'd managed to do all those things, that was the easy part. The hard part would have been getting into Samara's town house without a key, hiding the towel, the blouse (*her* blouse) and the knife, and then sneaking back out—all while Samara had been there.

"Don't get cocky," he cautioned Samara. "We had a good moment, but in the long run, it probably doesn't mean anything."

"If I feel like getting cocky," she smiled, "I'll get cocky." And then she did the one-raised-eyebrow thing.

That from a woman who was an odds-on favorite to end up with twenty-five years to life from this trial. How she was able to joke about it, Jaywalker had no idea. Not only joke about it, but actually squeeze a laugh out of him.

"Go get something to eat," he told her. "I'll see you back in the courtroom." And before she could turn that into a joke, too, he turned and walked away.

That afternoon Burke called the fourth and last of Jaywalker's "suspects," William Smythe. Smythe, a CPA with an English accent and a tweedy three-piece suit, was Barry Tannenbaum's full-time personal accountant. At least he had been, up until the time of Tannenbaum's death.

As he had with Alan Manheim, Burke began by having Smythe make it clear that he'd never had a key to either Barry's apartment or Samara's town house. Then he asked him if he'd ever had a dispute with Tannenbaum, or if Tannenbaum had ever accused him of any wrongdoing.

MR. SMYTHE: Absolutely not. I mean, as would be the case with any two people who worked together on financial matters for sixteen years, we had our occasional differences of opinion as to how to do certain things. But it was never more than that. I loved Barry like a brother, and I'd like to think he felt the same way about me.

Pardon me while I vomit, thought Jaywalker. But from the look Judge Sobel shot his way, he realized he must have done more than just think it. Jaywalker's wife used to accuse him of snorting out loud whenever he wanted to register his disapproval of something but didn't want to come right out and say so. Perhaps he'd snorted just now, though he hadn't been aware of doing so. Evidently it was becoming an unconscious habit, like a tremor or a facial tic. Maybe it was the first sign of dementia, of early-onset Alzheimer's disease.

God, how he needed to get out of this racket.

Burke had Smythe describe his duties as Tannenbaum's accountant, and they were extensive—not only in their breadth, but in the depth of trust they revealed. Smythe ran his employer's personal finances far more than Manheim had. He kept track of receipts and expenditures, balanced the books and juggled half a dozen bank accounts. He enjoyed full power of attorney to sign his employer's name to leases and other contracts. When a check went out over Barry Tannenbaum's name, chances were William Smythe had actually signed it, a fact well known and condoned by all of Tannenbaum's many bankers.

Aside from his *I-loved-him-like-a-brother* speech, Smythe came off as a genuinely likeable witness. Unlike Manheim, he'd had no reason to fear retaliation at the hand of Barry Tannenbaum. And had he been inclined to steal any of Barry's riches, he could have done so easily enough, with the simple stroke of a pen.

On cross-examination, Jaywalker decided against attacking Smythe and in favor of adopting him as his own witness. There remained only two names on Tom Burke's witness list, one of which Jaywalker recognized as a handwriting expert. He figured that the other one had to be someone from the company who had written the insurance policy on Barry Tannenbaum's life. It made sense that Burke would wind up his case with his evidence of motive—in other words, leaving best for last. Samara had assured Jaywalker over and over again that while she recognized her signature on the application and conceded that the funds for the premium appeared to have come out of her checking account, she'd known nothing of the policy until Jaywalker himself had broken the news to her.

Maybe Smythe knew something about it.

MR. JAYWALKER: Mr. Smythe, you've described how you enjoyed complete access to Barry Tannenbaum's books and bank accounts. Did you have similar access to Samara's account?

MR. SMYTHE: In a way, albeit indirectly.

Albeit? In all his years of practice, Jaywalker had never before heard a witness utter the word. It struck him as so bizarre, in fact, that he wondered if it might not have some hidden significance. In a lesser trial, he would have chosen to play around with it a little, to see if he couldn't at very least make the witness seem patrician, removed from the real world inhabited by the jurors. But he decided to let it pass and focused instead on the other interesting word Smythe had used in his answer.

MR. JAYWALKER: What do you mean by *indirectly?*

MR. SMYTHE: In a technical sense, Mrs. Tannenbaum's account was held jointly with her husband. Either of them could make deposits or write checks. Although the way it turned out in practice, Mr. Tannenbaum made all the deposits, and Mrs. Tannenbaum wrote all the checks.

A ripple of knowing laughter from the jury box. Samara the freeloader, the sponger. Not a good image.

MR. JAYWALKER: So did you occasionally sign checks for Samara?

MR. SMYTHE: Yes, if you choose to look at it that way. I prefer to think that I was signing them on behalf of Mr. Tannenbaum, in order to cover some of his wife's expenses.

MR. JAYWALKER: And in the same vein, did you from time to time present Samara with documents for her to sign?

MR. SMYTHE: I did.

MR. JAYWALKER: What sorts of documents?

MR. SMYTHE: Oh, tax returns, driver's license renewals, health insurance claims, credit card contracts. That sort of thing.

MR. JAYWALKER: In other words, when there were agencies or entities involved who wouldn't be expected to be comfortable accepting your signature in place of hers?

MR. SMYTHE: That's a good way of looking at it.

MR. JAYWALKER: And would you characterize Samara as having been extremely diligent in reading through each of the items you presented for her signature, or somewhat less than extremely diligent?

MR. SMYTHE: Somewhat less.

A couple of chuckles from the jury box. Samara the airhead, the bubble-brain. Fine with Jaywalker.

MR. JAYWALKER: In fact, there were lots of times when she'd indicate in one way or another that she didn't want to be bothered and left the reading of the fine print to you. Is that fair to say?

MR. SMYTHE: Yes.

MR. JAYWALKER: And even a lot of the large print?

MR. SMYTHE: Yes, again. Except in the case

of tax returns. Those I always made her read before
I permitted her to sign.

MR. JAYWALKER: Because the law compels you
                   to, right?

MR. SMYTHE: And because it's the right
                   thing to do.

   Jaywalker walked over to the prosecution table and
asked for the original of the life insurance policy application. It had a tag on it indicating that Burke had had it pre-
marked as People's Exhibit 9. Jaywalker removed the tag
and handed the document to the court reporter, asking her
to re-mark it as a defense exhibit.
   Prosecutors hate it when you do that.

MR. JAYWALKER: Mr. Smythe, I show you
what's been marked Defendant's A for identification
and ask you if you recognize it.

MR. SMYTHE: Yes. Mr. Burke showed it to
                   me some time ago.

MR. JAYWALKER: And what do you recognize it
                   as?

MR. SMYTHE: It's an application for an insurance policy on Mr. Tannenbaum's life. And it appears to have been signed by Mrs. Tannenbaum.

MR. JAYWALKER: And the defense stipulates
                   that in fact it was.

THE COURT: Mr. Burke?

MR. BURKE: So stipulated.

What else could Burke do? Jaywalker had not only co-opted his second-best exhibit, a runner-up to the murder weapon itself, now he was stealing Burke's thunder by conceding that the exhibit bore Samara's signature. Out of the corner of his eye, Jaywalker could see Burke scratching a name off his witness list, no doubt that of the handwriting expert. Now, completing his trifecta, Jaywalker offered the document into evidence as Defendant's A. Burke could do nothing but mutter, "No objection."

MR. JAYWALKER: Isn't it a fact, Mr. Smythe, that Samara signed this document only because you placed it in front of her and asked her to?

MR. SMYTHE: That is absolutely not the fact.

MR. JAYWALKER: Yet you've told us that that exact thing happened routinely, didn't you?

MR. SMYTHE: It happened.

MR. JAYWALKER: Routinely?

MR. BURKE: Objection.

THE COURT: Perhaps you'd like to re-phrase the question.

MR. JAYWALKER: Sure. Would you say it happened more than once over the years since Barry and Samara married?

MR. SMYTHE: More than once? Yes.

MR. JAYWALKER: More than half a dozen times?

MR. SMYTHE: Yes.

MR. JAYWALKER: More than a dozen?

MR. SMYTHE: Yes.

MR. JAYWALKER: More than two dozen?

MR. SMYTHE: Most likely.

MR. JAYWALKER: Routinely?

MR. BURKE: Objection.

THE COURT: Sustained.

Again Jaywalker walked over to the prosecution table and huddled with Burke.

"What is it you want this time?" Burke asked. "My undershorts?"

"Not yet," said Jaywalker. "But I'll take that check over there, the one that paid for the premium."

Burke coughed it up and sat helplessly by as Jaywalker had the exhibit re-marked, identified by the witness and received in evidence as Defendant's B.

MR. JAYWALKER: Do you recognize the signa-
                   ture on that check?

MR. SMYTHE: Yes, I do.

MR. JAYWALKER: Would you read us the name
                   that was signed.

MR. SMYTHE:	"Samara M. Tannenbaum."
MR. JAYWALKER:	Did Samara in fact sign that check?
MR. SMYTHE:	No.
MR. JAYWALKER:	Sorry, I couldn't hear your answer.
MR. SMYTHE:	No, she didn't sign it.
MR. JAYWALKER:	Who did sign it?
MR. SMYTHE:	I did.
MR. JAYWALKER:	You signed Samara's name?
MR. SMYTHE:	Yes.

Jaywalker had a few more questions written down for Smythe, but anything else was going to be severely anti-climactic. He knew the accountant would no doubt have a logical explanation for having done what he did. But why give him the chance to rehabilitate himself? Better to leave that to Burke on redirect examination and then come back on recross.

A lot of lawyers never know enough to quit while they're ahead. Jaywalker, who'd been ahead precious little in this trial, was going to be damned if he made that mistake.

"No further questions," he said.

Burke was on his feet before Jaywalker was off his.

MR. BURKE:	A few minutes ago Mr. Jaywalker asked you about this document, Defendant's A in evidence. Specifically, after conceding that it

bears his client's signature, he asked you if she signed it only because you told her to. Do you recall his asking you that?

MR. SMYTHE: Yes, I do.

MR. BURKE: And you replied, rather emphatically—

MR. JAYWALKER: Objection.

THE COURT: Sustained. Leave out the characterization, please.

MR. BURKE: And you replied with the words "absolutely not."

MR. SMYTHE: Yes.

MR. BURKE: Can you tell us why you said, "absolutely not"?

MR. SMYTHE: Yes. I never gave Mrs. Tannenbaum that document to sign. In fact, I'd never even seen it until you showed it to me, several weeks after Mr. Tannenbaum's death.

MR. BURKE: How can you be certain that you never gave it to Mrs. Tannenbaum to sign?

MR. SMYTHE: Because unlike Mrs. Tannenbaum, I read every word of everything I ever gave her.

Nicely done, thought Jaywalker. But how was Smythe

going to explain away his signature on the check? It turned out it wouldn't take long for him to find out, and he didn't like the explanation any better than he'd liked the previous one.

MR. BURKE: What about Defendant's B in evidence, the check that paid for the premium? You say you signed that yourself. Is that correct?

MR. SMYTHE: Yes, it is.

MR. BURKE: How do you explain that?

MR. SMYTHE: Just as I used to collect Mr. Tannenbaum's bills as they came in, so did I collect Mrs. Tannenbaum's. When a bill showed up from a life insurance company in the amount of some twenty-seven-thousand dollars, I made it a point to question Mr. Tannenbaum about it.

MR. BURKE: Not *Mrs.* Tannenbaum?

MR. SMYTHE: No, I figured that wouldn't have done me much good.

MR. BURKE: Why not?

MR. SMYTHE: Let's just say that Mrs. Tannenbaum doesn't have much of a head for business.

More laughter, again at the expense of the bubble-brain.

MR. BURKE: And what was Mr. Tannenbaum's response?

MR. SMYTHE: I don't recall his exact words. But as was his habit with just about all of his wife's bills, he told me to go ahead and pay it.

MR. BURKE: You say, "just about all." Were there exceptions?

MR. SMYTHE: I do recall that on one occasion he declined to cover a twelve-thousand-dollar charge for a bathroom mat in the shape of an elephant. He felt that was a wee bit extravagant, and he made her return it.

MR. BURKE: I see. In any event, when Mr. Tannenbaum told you to go ahead and pay the bill for the insurance premium, what did you do?

MR. SMYTHE: I paid it.

MR. BURKE: And how did you do that?

MR. SMYTHE: I wrote out a check, signed Mrs. Tannenbaum's name and sent it off.

MR. BURKE: And the check you wrote out and signed. Is that Defendant's B in evidence?

MR. SMYTHE: It is.

And just like that, the last of Jaywalker's "suspects" was, for all intents and purposes, crossed off the list.

Burke had one remaining witness, and following a recess, he called her. Miranda Thomas was a dark-skinned woman in her thirties or forties, with a slight singsong lilt to her voice that suggested to Jaywalker that she might have been born in Jamaica. The Caribbean version, not the Queens one. She was employed as a custodian of records by the Equitable Life Insurance Company. Burke had her identify Defendant's A as an application for a term life insurance policy, submitted by Samara Tannenbaum on the life of her husband, Barrington Tannenbaum, in the amount of twenty-five million dollars. Next he had her identify Defendant's B as the twenty-seven-thousand-dollar check that represented the initial—and, as it turned out, the only—premium paid toward the policy. Then he handed her an original of the policy itself and had it introduced as People's 10 in evidence. It seemed to Jaywalker that Burke derived great satisfaction from finally being allowed to get one of his own documents received as a prosecution exhibit.

MR. BURKE: You used the phrase "term" a moment ago. What is a term life insurance policy?

MS. THOMAS: A term policy continues in effect for a stated period of time. During that period, or term, as well as during any subsequent renewal periods, a term policy pays off in case of death. But unlike a whole life policy, a term policy builds no equity. Hence, it has no cash value or value that can be borrowed against. At the end of the term, unless renewed, it has no worth.

MR. BURKE: What was the term of this particular policy?

MS. THOMAS: Six months.

MR. BURKE: Is that a normal period for a life
                    insurance policy?

MS. THOMAS: No. A year is much more common. But we'll issue a six-month policy if asked to,
under certain conditions.

MR. BURKE: What sorts of conditions?

MS. THOMAS: People occasionally take out a
short-term policy when they're going to be traveling
abroad or engaging in some dangerous occupation.
If you were going up in a space shuttle, for example,
you might want a policy of that sort.

MR. BURKE: As far as you know, was Mr.
Tannenbaum planning on going into space?

MS. THOMAS: Not so far as I know.

MR. BURKE: Are you by any chance familiar
                    with the date of Mr. Tannen-
                    baum's death?

MS. THOMAS: Yes, I have it right here in my
notes.

MR. BURKE: How long before Mr. Tannen-
                    baum's death was this policy
                    first applied for?

MS. THOMAS: Let me see. Thirty-three days.

MR. BURKE: And paid for?

MS. THOMAS: Twenty-seven days.

MR. BURKE: And issued?

MS. THOMAS: Twenty-two days. Though by regulation, it would have related back to the date the check was put in the mail and postmarked. So in that respect, twenty-seven days, again.

MR. BURKE: Do you know if Mr. Tannen-baum was required to undergo a medical examination before this policy was issued?

MS. THOMAS: No, he would not have been.

MR. BURKE: Why not?

MS. THOMAS: Because the policy was written with certain exclusions, so as to exempt death from any specified pre-existing medical conditions. As you can see from the application, several of those are typed in under the medical history section. Specifically, had Mr. Tannenbaum died from either cancer or heart disease, the policy would not have paid off.

MR. BURKE: Wouldn't you consider those pretty major exclusions?

MR. JAYWALKER: Objection.

THE COURT: Sustained.

MR. BURKE: Had Mr. Tannenbaum not died during the term of the policy, and had Mrs. Tannenbaum elected to renew it for succeeding terms, would the premium have remained the same?

MS. THOMAS: No. As Mr. Tannenbaum got

older, the premium would have increased with each renewal, eventually becoming prohibitively expensive.

MR. BURKE: So as a long-term investment, how much sense does this sort of policy make?

MS. THOMAS: No sense at all, really. It only makes sense if you're afraid the individual is likely to die very soon.

MR. BURKE: But not of cancer.

MS. THOMAS: Correct.

MR. BURKE: And not of heart disease.

MS. THOMAS: Correct again.

MR. BURKE: Did there come a time when Equitable learned of Mr. Tannenbaum's death?

MS. THOMAS: Yes.

MR. BURKE: Was that because a claim was made under the policy?

MS. THOMAS: No, no claim has yet been made, so far as I can ascertain.

MR. BURKE: How long does one have to make a claim?

MS. THOMAS: The policy says seven years. But the courts seem to say a claim can always be made.

MR. BURKE: So how did the folks at Equitable learn of Mr. Tannen-
baum's death?

MS. THOMAS: Like everyone else, I imagine.
Someone at Equitable saw it on the news or read
about it in the paper.

MR. BURKE: And did there come a time
when either that someone or another someone at
Equitable put two and two together and realized,
"Hey, we've got a twenty-five-million-dollar policy
on that guy"?

MS. THOMAS: Yes, something like that. According to our records, the issuing agent, a Mr. Garibaldi, realized that.

MR. BURKE: And what, if anything, did Mr.
Garibaldi do at that point?

MS. THOMAS: He informed his supervisor.

MR. BURKE: And what did his supervisor
do?

MS. THOMAS: He phoned your supervisor. He
thought it looked pretty fish—

MR. JAYWALKER: Objection.

THE COURT: Sustained, as to anything after,
"He phoned your supervisor." The rest is stricken,
and the jury will disregard it.

But there it was, hanging in midair, just waiting for the

jurors to fill in the final syllable for themselves. No open-book exam, with the answers typed in bold at the end of each chapter, could ever have been easier.

Burke sat down, barely able to suppress a triumphant smirk. Jaywalker had labored hard and long to prepare the jury for just this testimony. He'd brought up the life insurance business as early as jury selection and hammered away at it repeatedly. He'd talked about it again in his opening statement. He'd even tried to defuse it in his cross-examination of the previous witness, the accountant, Mr. Smythe. But none of those efforts had come close to preparing the jury for just how devastating the evidence would prove to Samara. Talk about motive? Here she'd bet twenty-seven thousand dollars of her own money, hoping to rake in a pot of twenty-five million on the possibility that within six months' time her husband would be dead. Not from cancer or heart disease, the things he was known to have had, and the things that just about everybody died from. What did that leave? Drag racing? Lightning? Snakebite? Spontaneous human combustion?

What it left was murder.

Still, Jaywalker couldn't very well leave Miranda Thomas alone. She'd hurt Samara far too much for that. He rose slowly from his seat, gathered his notes and worked his way over to the lectern, all the while giving the witness his most dangerous gunfighter squint, as though he knew he had something on her.

Though Lord knew he didn't.

MR. JAYWALKER: Ms. Thomas, you'd have us believe that policies such as this, where the payout is huge but so are the premiums, make no sense except for risk takers. Yet that's not quite true, is it?

MS. THOMAS: Excuse me?

MR. JAYWALKER: Isn't it true that there's an entirely separate category of individuals who take out precisely this sort of life insurance with very little regard to risky endeavors?

MS. THOMAS: I'm not sure what you're getting at.

MR. JAYWALKER: By any chance, does the term "estate taxes" help you remember?

MS. THOMAS: I don't know.

MR. JAYWALKER: You do know what estate taxes are, don't you?

MS. THOMAS: Yes.

MR. JAYWALKER: What are they?

MS. THOMAS: They're the percentage the government takes out of an estate before it gets distributed.

MR. JAYWALKER: Do all estates get taxed?

MS. THOMAS: No.

MR. JAYWALKER: Only those up in the millions, right?

MS. THOMAS: Right.

MR. JAYWALKER: Only those of the rich?

MS. THOMAS: Right.

MR. JAYWALKER: Was Barry Tannenbaum rich?

MS. THOMAS: I wouldn't know.

MR. JAYWALKER: Really?

MS. THOMAS: Really.

MR. JAYWALKER: Had you ever heard of him? Before his death, I mean.

MS. THOMAS: Yes.

MR. JAYWALKER: What had you heard about him?

MS. THOMAS: I don't know.

MR. JAYWALKER: Let me help you. Had you heard that he was one of the oldest men in the world?

MS. THOMAS: No.

MR. JAYWALKER: One of the tallest?

MS. THOMAS: No.

MR. JAYWALKER: One of the best looking?

MS. THOMAS: No.

MR. JAYWALKER: What *had* you heard?

MS. THOMAS: That he was rich.

MR. JAYWALKER: One of the richest in the entire world?

MS. THOMAS: Supposedly.

MR. JAYWALKER: Ms. Thomas, isn't it a fact, a dirty little fact, that policies of this sort are frequently used by the very, very rich as a strategy to avoid paying estate taxes?

MS. THOMAS: I suppose that's possible.

MR. JAYWALKER: They can afford the huge premiums, after all. And the payouts, when they're made, aren't counted as part of their estates. So they're distributed tax-free. Right?

MS. THOMAS: I guess.

MR. JAYWALKER: You guess? Or am I right?

MS. THOMAS: You're right.

MR. JAYWALKER: So really, companies like yours engage in this game. They collect these huge premiums, which are calculated by actuaries to more than cover the huge payouts. Everybody wins, don't they?

MS. THOMAS: You could say so.

MR. JAYWALKER: Except the government, which gets cheated out of its revenue. And who do you think gets taxed in order to make up that lost revenue?

MS. THOMAS: I wouldn't know.

MR. JAYWALKER: Of course you would. You get taxed, and I get taxed, and Mr. Burke gets taxed. And Stanley Merkel here, and Leona Sturdivant, and Vito—

MR. BURKE: Objection!

THE COURT: Sustained.

MR. JAYWALKER: —Todesco, and Shirley Johnson, and—

MR. BURKE: Objection! Objection!

THE COURT: The objection is sustained. Sit down, Mr. Jaywalker. *(Mr. Jaywalker sits)* Thank you. The jury is instructed to disregard the references made to individual jurors. Mr. Jaywalker, do you have any further questions of the witness?

MR. JAYWALKER: No.

Burke did, though. He had Ms. Thomas insist that by writing such policies, her company was acting perfectly legally. The insurance industry was highly regulated, she explained, and couldn't get away with breaking the law. Furthermore, even with its tax advantages, the six-month premium continued to make the Tannenbaum policy highly unusual as an investment strategy, because of the exclusion clause.

On recross, Jaywalker tried to get her to say that the six-month term of the policy might represent nothing more sinister than a simple shortage of funds on the part of the premium payer. When she hedged, Jaywalker abruptly changed course, something he'd earned a well-deserved reputation for doing over the years.

MR. JAYWALKER: Personally, you don't see this as a tax-avoidance strategy at all, do you, Ms. Thomas?

MS. THOMAS: No, I don't.

MR. JAYWALKER: You see it as a transparent, high-stakes bet that Mr. Tannenbaum was going to be dead within six months, don't you?

MS. THOMAS: Exactly.

MR. JAYWALKER: And not dead from cancer or heart disease, right?

MS. THOMAS: Right.

MR. JAYWALKER: As you tried to say earlier, before I so rudely interrupted you, the whole thing looks pretty damn fishy to you, doesn't it?

MS. THOMAS: *(To the Court)* Am I allowed to answer that?

THE COURT: Yes.

MS. THOMAS: I'd say it looks more than fishy.

MR. JAYWALKER: What does it look like to you?

MS. THOMAS:	*(Looks at the Court)*

THE COURT:	Go ahead.

MS. THOMAS: You're not going to like this, but it looks to me like your client took out the policy because she planned on killing her husband.

There are courtrooms, and there are quiet courtrooms. Right then, that one was as quiet as any that Jaywalker had ever been in. It was as though the judge, the staff, the jurors and the spectators were witnessing the complete and utter self-destruction of a lawyer and his client, right before their very eyes. Talk about spontaneous human combustion. It was as though it wouldn't have surprised anyone if, at that very moment, Jaywalker had burst into flames, or vaporized. Instead, he plunged right on, as though totally oblivious.

MR. JAYWALKER:	Now, you're not a detective, are you, Ms. Thomas?

MS. THOMAS:	No, of course not.

MR. JAYWALKER:	Or a federal agent?

MS. THOMAS:	No.

MR. JAYWALKER:	If you don't mind my asking, how far did you go in school?

MS. THOMAS:	I have a high school equivalency diploma.

MR. JAYWALKER:	And yet you can see clear through this little scheme of Samara's, can't you?

MS. THOMAS: Yes, I can.

MR. JAYWALKER: It's that obvious, isn't it?

MS. THOMAS: I sure think so.

MR. JAYWALKER: Tell me, Ms. Thomas. Has it ever occurred to you that's it's a little bit *too* obvious?

MS. THOMAS: What do you mean by that?

And all Jaywalker—born a Jew, raised a Unitarian and long ago converted to atheism—could think was, *Thank you, Jesus!*

MR. JAYWALKER: *What I mean is that it's so Goddamned obvious that it's got to be a frame! That no one in their right mind could possibly believe they could get away with—*

His speech was drowned out by Tom Burke's shouts of objection, and by the repeated banging of the judge's gavel. When finally some semblance of quiet was restored, which took a minute, Jaywalker took advantage of it to say, "No more questions." And Burke, red-faced and livid, announced that The People's case had concluded.

23

TUNA FISH AND PROMISES

With the conclusion of The People's case, Judge Sobel sent the jurors home for the day, with his usual admonitions. Then he denied Jaywalker's motion to dismiss the case. Next he offered Samara the option of leaving, explaining that he needed to confer with the lawyers. She took him up on it, explaining to Jaywalker that she needed to do some shopping. Ice, he decided, pure ice in her veins.

Only when the courtroom was completely empty of media and spectators did the judge return his attention to Jaywalker.

"I hereby find you in summary contempt for that speech of yours. It was improper, prejudicial and uncalled for."

"She asked—"

The judge silenced Jaywalker with his gavel. In an otherwise quiet courtroom, it only took one bang this time.

"However, because I'm aware of your situation with the disciplinary committee, I'm not going to add to your troubles with jail time or a fine. This time. But please consider this your one and only warning. Things could get a lot worse for you, believe me."

"I can't imagine how."

"Off the record," said the judge, signaling the court reporter to give her fingers a rest. "Come on," he told Jaywalker, his voice softening now. "Three years may seem like a long time, but it isn't exactly the end of the world."

"*Three years?* Is *that* what you think I'm worried about? Listen, three years away from this business is going to feel like paradise. Chances are, I'll like it so much I'll re-up for another three. Believe me, it's not the three years that's turning me into a lunatic. It's the twenty-five to life you're going to end up giving my client for something I'm not at all sure she did."

"Why don't we leave that for the jury to decide?" the judge suggested.

"Who?" asked Jaywalker, gesturing to the empty jury box. "*The MENSA Twelve?* How can I blame them? Shit, *I'd* convict her on this record."

"So talk to Mr. Burke, work something out."

Jaywalker swung around to Burke, who'd been packing his notes and exhibits into his briefcase. "Want to give her an A.C.D.?" Jaywalker asked. "With two days community service?"

Burke laughed in spite of himself. The letters A.C.D. stood for an Adjournment in Contemplation of a Dismissal. It was what they gave turnstile-hoppers or loiterers, people with no prior arrests who'd committed minor infractions and said they were sorry for what they'd done.

Murderers need not apply.

Despite her stated intent of going shopping, Samara was waiting for Jaywalker out on Centre Street, shifting her weight from one foot to the other, trying to ward off the cold.

"We have to talk," he told her.

"I'm not going to plead guilty."

For a bubble-brain, she made a pretty good mind reader.

"It's too cold to go shopping," she said. "Come to my place. I promise I won't rape you."

Jaywalker managed a thin smile. Rape was about the last thing on his mind. He was tired, tired and cold. Not

eating breakfast or lunch while he was on trial kept him
mentally sharp, but it also produced a throbbing headache
by midafternoon and left him unable to fight off the early
evening chill.

"Sure," he said. "Why not?"

Samara had promised not to rape Jaywalker, but she'd
said nothing about not force-feeding him. She made him
eat a tuna fish sandwich that she actually made herself,
without a recipe, and drink two cups of sweet, hot tea with
lemon. Gradually, he could feel the chill inside him begin
to subside and the headache taper off to a more or less manageable level.

They spent two solid hours going over her testimony one
last time, but the truth was, they needn't have bothered.
Either Jaywalker had already fully prepared her for all of
his questions and the worst Burke could throw at her, or she
was truly innocent. Somewhere along the way, it occurred
to Jaywalker that he might never know. She might get convicted—hell, she was *going* to get convicted—and he might
still never know. She would be one of those forgotten
inmates who live out the rest of their lives with their noses
stuck in law books, composing long letters and rambling
writs of habeas corpus, protesting their innocence to anyone still willing to listen, until death finally catches up to
them at seventy, lying on a cot in some wretched prison in-
firmary, hooked up to a bunch of plastic tubes.

And even then, he wouldn't know.

When she reappeared in her bathrobe, he realized he
hadn't been aware that she'd left.

"You promised," he reminded her.

"And I won't," she assured him, settling onto the sofa
across from his chair. "But why haven't we? I mean, I heard
about that *stairwell* thing. Is it me? Do I turn you off?"

"*God,* no."

"What, then?"

"First of all, that stairwell thing was overblown."

They laughed as one, Samara because she thought it was a clever joke, Jaywalker because it hadn't been. "Let me try that again," he said. "No, you don't turn me off. You turn me on more than you can possibly imagine. Even if I am old enough to be your father."

"Barry was old enough to be my grandfather."

The devil on Jaywalker's left shoulder wanted to say, *Yeah, and look what you did to him.* But the angel on his right shoulder quickly slapped a hand over his mouth and changed it into a more relevant, "Yeah, but Barry didn't happen to be defending you on a murder charge."

"So?"

"So it would be like the worst kind of conflict of interest. Don't you see? Here I am, knocking my brains out, trying to keep you from spending the rest of your life in prison. I don't sleep. I don't eat. I can't afford to be taking time out to worry about whether I've got bad breath or my dick's not big enough, or if I'm not being attentive enough to your, um, needs."

"Your breath's fine. I don't care how big your dick is. And I'm an adult. I can worry about my needs enough for both of us."

"Sorry," said Jaywalker. "I just can't do it."

Samara pouted. He'd forgotten that pout, forgotten the effect it always had on him, since the very first day he'd set eyes on her.

"How about after?" she was asking him.

"After what?"

"After the trial."

"Sure," he said. "After will be just fine."

"Promise?"

And, so help him, he promised her. How could he not have? How could he have told her, fifteen hours before she was about to take the witness stand, that the moment the jury convicted her, the judge would exonerate her bail and remand her on the spot? Maybe the two of them would get a chance to hug before the court officers slipped the cuffs on her and dragged her off. If they were lucky.

So he promised her. And they even shook pinkies on it, like a couple of ten-year-olds. And then he said good-night to her and took a cab home.

24

FINDING HER FATHER

"The defense calls Samara Tannenbaum."

With those words, Jaywalker began the day by breaking at least two of his own rules. First, he much preferred to call his client as his final witness. Not only would doing that have allowed him to build up the drama surrounding her appearance, it also would have permitted Samara to hear the testimony of any other defense witnesses before having to take the stand herself. The rule that requires witnesses to remain outside the courtroom before testifying doesn't apply to defendants, for obvious reasons. Second, Jaywalker liked to let the jury know when they should expect no additional witnesses. It was an easy enough thing to do: all he had to do was say, "The defense calls its only witness, Samara Tannenbaum," or "its final witness, Samara Tannenbaum."

But the truth was, Jaywalker still wasn't sure whether or not he was going to put on anyone besides Samara. And that was because he hadn't yet decided whether to ask Samara about the discovery of the Seconal in her spice cabinet. He thought he believed her about that, but he couldn't be sure. And if the jurors were skeptical, the story would backfire and do more harm than good. Jaywalker had his investigator, Nicolo LeGrosso, standing by. Nicky had subpoenaed the records from the pharmacy that had filled the prescription. The order had been called in by a physician who, it turned out, didn't appear to exist. It had been picked up by someone who'd simply scrawled Samara's initials on the registry. The pharmacy was very nervous about having anyone testify, since under federal law they shouldn't have honored a phoned-in prescription for a controlled substance in the first place, let alone one from a nonexistent physician. And there was always the chance that if they sent the employee who'd collected the money and handed over the drugs, he or she might identify Samara as the recipient, rightly or wrongly. Were that to happen, there wouldn't be a hole in the floor big enough for Samara and Jaywalker to disappear into. So he was still on the fence about the whole Seconal thing and had been forced to break his own rule this time.

Even without a gradual buildup or an announcement that there will be nothing more to follow, the moment when a defendant rises and walks to the witness stand is a dramatic one. And if the charge happens to be murder, and the victim the husband of the accused, the word *dramatic* falls short of adequately describing it. Awesome comes closer; *pivotal* is no overstatement. Because this is the moment everyone's been waiting for. The lawyers, the judge, the court personnel, the media, the spectators and the jurors. *Especially* the jurors. Something about human nature leads ordinary people who are fully capable of making a wide variety and staggering number of errors on the simplest of assignments to believe with iron-clad certainty that all they'll have to do is look at and listen to a defendant, and they'll know in a heartbeat if they're hearing the truth or not.

What *these* jurors saw, as Samara raised her right hand and dutifully swore to tell the truth, the whole truth and nothing but the truth, was a woman who looked small, nervous and alone. A stunningly pretty woman, to be sure, but Jaywalker's own mental jury was still very much out on the question of whether that prettiness, in the end, would contribute to her salvation or prove to be her undoing.

She took her seat, not quite on the edge of the chair, but not so far back as to look relaxed. Just as Jaywalker had had her practice. She put her hands in her lap, out of sight and away from her face.

THE CLERK:	Would you give your first name and last, and spell them for the record.
MS. TANNENBAUM:	My name is Samara M. Tannenbaum. S-A-M-A-R-A T-A-N-N-E-N-B-A-U-M.
THE CLERK:	What is your county of residence?
MS. TANNENBAUM:	Manhattan.
THE COURT:	You may inquire, Mr. Jaywalker.
MR. JAYWALKER:	Thank you. How old are you, Samara?
MS. TANNENBAUM:	I'm twenty-eight.
MR. JAYWALKER:	Are you currently employed?
MS. TANNENBAUM:	No.
MR. JAYWALKER:	Have you been employed in the past?

MS. TANNENBAUM: Yes, starting when I was fourteen.

These were softballs, grounders. They were only
partly aimed to elicit information. Their real purpose was
to warm Samara up, to give her a chance to find her
voice and develop something of a rhythm. Jaywalker
himself had been on the witness stand a fair amount back
in his DEA days, and even a couple of times since. He
knew it wasn't a particularly comfortable chair to sit in,
as chairs went.

He also wanted the jurors to get to know Samara. Not just
the Samara they'd read about, the dark-haired tabloid beauty
with the checkered past, the Las Vegas gold digger who'd
hit the jackpot, the spoiled trophy wife. He wanted them to
know her as he knew her, and—if she could somehow work
her magic with them the same way she'd worked it with
him—to come to like her as he liked her. If a jury likes a
defendant, especially a female defendant, they may end up
convicting her, but they're going to have an awfully hard
time doing so. On the other hand, if they take a dislike to
her, it'll be easy, particularly for the women on the jury. Find
that hard to believe? Ask Martha Stewart, why don't you?

So he went back to the beginning, Jaywalker did, back
to when Samara Moss had been a child growing up outside
of Prairie Creek, Indiana. Back to a time before she'd had
a penny to her name. Back to before she'd ever dreamed
that there was a world beyond the Midwest, a world without cornfields and trailer parks and rusted-out pickup
trucks. Back to before she'd ever even heard of Las Vegas
or Barry Tannenbaum or New York City.

MR. JAYWALKER: Who raised you, Samara?

MS. TANNENBAUM: My mother, sort of.

MR. JAYWALKER: Did you know your father?

MS. TANNENBAUM: No, I never met him.

MR. JAYWALKER: What was your home like?

MS. TANNENBAUM: It was a half trailer that somebody had abandoned. It had no water or electric hookup. And it was missing the half with the bedroom and bathroom.

MR. JAYWALKER: What did you use for a bathroom?

MS. TANNENBAUM: In nice weather, we used the field out back. When it was too cold, a stove pot. It was my job to empty it each morning.

MR. JAYWALKER: What did you and your mother do for food?

MS. TANNENBAUM: When there was money, we bought it, like everyone else. When there wasn't, my mother used to have me beg for groceries outside the Kroger's, the nearest supermarket. Sometimes she'd give me a boost so I could climb up into the Dumpster they kept out back, see what I could find. Sometimes neighbors left food by the door of our trailer. There was a black family that lived up the road and did that whenever they could, even though they were dirt-poor themselves. Then, after a while, they moved away, and my mother started taking in men, overnight guests. And they would give her money, five or ten dollars at a time.

MR. JAYWALKER: Where did they sleep?

MS. TANNENBAUM: On the sofa, with my mother.

MR. JAYWALKER: In the same room as you?

MS. TANNENBAUM: There was only one room. If
the weather was okay, my mother would send me out
in the field. If it was cold or rainy or snowy, she'd
put me to bed on the floor, in the corner. Cover me
up with a blanket and make me face the other way,
so I couldn't see.

MR. JAYWALKER: Did you know what was
                              going on?

MS. TANNENBAUM: I had ears. I could hear.

MR. JAYWALKER: How old were you?

MS. TANNENBAUM: Ten, eleven.

MR. JAYWALKER: How did these men treat you?

MS. TANNENBAUM: Some of them were nice to
                              me. Some of them weren't.

MR. JAYWALKER: Tell us about some of the
                              ones who weren't.

MS. TANNENBAUM: They…they did things to
                              me.

MR. JAYWALKER: What kinds of things?

MS. TANNENBAUM: You know.

MR. JAYWALKER: No, we don't know. Not unless you tell us.

MS. TANNENBAUM: They'd kiss me, touch me under my clothes, in places where they weren't supposed to. Make me touch them. Put their thing in my mouth, or on my front, or between my legs.

MR. JAYWALKER: Their thing?

MS. TANNENBAUM: Their penis.

MR. JAYWALKER: Did you ever tell your mother?

MS. TANNENBAUM: Yes.

MR. JAYWALKER: And?

MS. TANNENBAUM: She'd slap me, say she didn't believe me. But I know she did. She knew.

MR. BURKE: Objection.

THE COURT: Sustained. Strike the part about what her mother knew. The jury will disregard it.

MR. JAYWALKER: What else, if anything, did she do or say?

MS. TANNENBAUM: She'd tell me not to lie, not to complain, that we needed the money for food. If I cried, she'd hit me.

| MR. JAYWALKER: | So what did you do? |

MS. TANNENBAUM: I'd close my eyes and pretend I wasn't there, that I was someplace else altogether. I put up with it as long as I could. And when I couldn't put up with it anymore, I ran away.

| MR. JAYWALKER: | How old were you when you ran away? |

| MS. TANNENBAUM: | Fourteen years and one day. |

| MR. JAYWALKER: | How is it that you remember that? |

| MS. TANNENBAUM: | I remember that because I waited to see what I'd get for my birthday. |

| MR. JAYWALKER: | And what did you get? |

| MS. TANNENBAUM: | Nothing. |

| MR. JAYWALKER: | Did you ever see your mother again? |

| MS. TANNENBAUM: | No. |

It wasn't just the squalor and the sexual abuse and the separation Jaywalker wanted the jurors to hear, although their transfixed silence spoke loudly enough about the impact those things were having upon them. But beyond that, he was laying out a pattern for them, a template of a mother not only willing to barter sex for food, but equally willing to enlist her only child as an accomplice to the practice. How surprising would it be that within a year or two of her flight from home, Samara herself would be imitating her mother's survival strategy and adopting it as her own? Would the jurors excuse her behavior? Perhaps not. But at least they'd be able to understand her actions, and hopefully empathize with her. And empathy, Jaywalker firmly believed, lay at the doorstep to forgiveness.

He had Samara talk about how she'd hitchhiked her way west, careful to catch rides at truck stops, lest the police pick her up and send her back home. She described reaching Nevada, and finally Las Vegas itself, with high hopes of becoming a model or a showgirl.

MR. JAYWALKER: What happened to those hopes?

MS. TANNENBAUM: They didn't last very long.

MR. JAYWALKER: Why not?

MS. TANNENBAUM: I couldn't sing or dance. I was too young and too short. My legs weren't long enough. My breasts weren't big enough, and I didn't have any money to have them made bigger.

MR. JAYWALKER: So what did you do?

MS. TANNENBAUM: I tried lying about my age, but they check a lot out there. I'd bus tables, wash dishes, whatever I could. Usually I'd get fired after a week or two, when they'd find out that the Social Security number I'd given them didn't match up.

MR. JAYWALKER: Where did you live?

MS. TANNENBAUM: There are some very bad

boardinghouses off the strip, places none of the tourists ever get to see.

MR. JAYWALKER: How did you pay the rent?

MS. TANNENBAUM: With whatever money I could make working. And when that ran out—

Her voice broke off, midsentence. They hadn't rehearsed it that way, or planned it. It just happened. Which was how the best stuff almost always came from the witness stand. You didn't script it. Instead, you tried to impart to the witness just what it was you were seeking to accomplish, the feeling you were striving to create. And every once in a while a witness would get it, and the result would be pure magic. Samara, by doing nothing more than stopping midsentence, showed Jaywalker that she'd gotten it, at least this one time, and worked a little bit of magic.

MR. JAYWALKER: And when the money ran out?

MS. TANNENBAUM: And when the money ran out, I did what my mother had done. I took men home, or let them take me home. And when they offered me gifts or money afterwards, I kept it.

MR. JAYWALKER: Did you consider yourself a prostitute?

MS. TANNENBAUM: Not at the time, I didn't.

MR. JAYWALKER: And now that you look back on it?

MS. TANNENBAUM: Yes, I'd have to say I was a prostitute.

MR. JAYWALKER: How do you feel about that?

MS. TANNENBAUM: I certainly don't feel good about it. I mean, I'm not going to brag about it or anything like that. But I'm not ashamed of it, either, and I'm certainly not going to lie about it. It's what I did. It's part of my life. It's how I survived.

She'd been telling her story for nearly an hour now, and Jaywalker sensed that it had been long enough. As receptive as the jurors had seemed throughout it, he didn't want to risk overstaying his welcome. The same was true of Judge Sobel. To abuse the considerable leeway he'd shown would be a mistake. The last thing Jaywalker wanted to hear was, "Let's move along, counselor." So with a single question, he yanked Samara, and with her the trial itself, back to the business at hand.

MR. JAYWALKER: Did there come a time, Samara, when you met an individual named Barry Tannenbaum?

MS. TANNENBAUM: Yes, there did.

THE COURT: Forgive me, Mr. Jaywalker, but perhaps this would be as good a time as any to take our mid-morning recess.

MR. JAYWALKER: That would be fine, Your Honor.

* * *

There's a rule, which may be invoked by either side, that once a witness has begun testifying, there may be no discussion between the witness and the lawyer who's put the witness on the stand. When the witness happens to be the defendant, however, that rule gets trumped by a higher constitutional rule: the right to consult with counsel. At the moment the conflict provided something of a conundrum for Jaywalker, who'd never met a rule he didn't want to break. So in Samara's case, he ended up breaking both rules, first by telling her how well she was doing, and then by turning his back and walking away from her. Just in case Burke took the chance of asking Samara on cross-examination if she'd discussed her answers with her lawyer during recess, Jaywalker wanted her to be able to answer truthfully that she hadn't.

And there was another reason for his caution. Just as jurors watch the defendant like hawks in the courtroom, looking for some telltale sign of guilt or innocence, so do they continue to look for clues out in the corridor, in the elevator and down on the street. As grateful as Jaywalker was for having Samara out on bail, rather than locked up on Rikers Island, he was aware of the risks. The well-known defense attorney F. Lee Bailey, after winning a murder acquittal for Carl Coppalino in New Jersey, had made the mistake of allowing his client to be photographed cavorting on the beach with his lover in Florida, while he awaited a second murder trial. To Jaywalker's thinking, Bailey had lost the second case right then and there, before the trial had even begun.

So he would let the jurors see Samara heading to the ladies' room, talking with the court officers or standing alone with her thoughts by the elevator bank. What they weren't going to see, or think they were seeing, was her lawyer whispering in her ear and coaching her, telling her what to say and how to say it, when to smile demurely, and when to allow a tear to well up and roll down her cheek.

Besides, there was no need for him to tell her any of those things. He'd already done so, a hundred times over.

After the recess, Jaywalker picked up precisely where he'd left off.

MR. JAYWALKER: Did there come a time when you met a man named Barry Tannenbaum?

MS. TANNENBAUM: Yes, there did.

MR. JAYWALKER: When and where was that?

MS. TANNENBAUM: I was eighteen, so it would have been in 1997, I think. I'd just become legal, so I could work at the hotels. You didn't have to be twenty-one back then. So I was working in one of the cocktail lounges at Caesars Palace. That's where I first saw Barry.

MR. JAYWALKER: Tell us about that first meeting.

MS. TANNENBAUM: I saw this man sitting alone at a table in the corner. He was smallish, not too much bigger than I am. He was already sixty-one, old enough to have been my grandfather, as a lot of people have pointed out since. He was pale, and his hair was thinning, though I didn't know that right away, because he was wearing a wig, a wig and sunglasses. So nobody would recognize him, he told me later.

MR. JAYWALKER: Would you have recognized him?

MS. TANNENBAUM: Me? I'd never heard of him. In fact, I figured he had to be gay. You know, the wig, the shades. I figured he was scoping out guys.

MR. JAYWALKER: So it wasn't your intention to hit on him?

MS. TANNENBAUM: No. I was legit by then. I didn't have to do that anymore.

Gay or straight, the man had looked so alone and so sad that Samara had walked over to his table, even though it wasn't part of her station, and asked him if he was okay. He'd replied that he wasn't sure. She could see that he was drinking Diet Coke—she knew from the lemon slice he'd removed from the rim of the glass but hadn't used—so on her next trip by, she'd brought him another one, no charge. He'd seemed terribly grateful for the gesture, she recalled. And when she got off her shift, at three in the morning, he was waiting for her, just outside the door. At his invitation, they'd gone to his room upstairs, where he'd taken off the wig and the sunglasses, but no more. And for the next five hours, they'd talked.

MS. TANNENBAUM: *Talked.* I couldn't believe it. I mean, I'd never talked to anyone in my whole life, not for more than a minute or two. And then it would be about the weather, or to say, "Please pass the salt," or "Do you know what time it is?" or "Your place or mine?"

MR. JAYWALKER: What did you talk about?

MS. TANNENBAUM: All sorts of stuff. Where we'd grown up, what we liked, what we hated, whether we cried when we were sad or when we were happy—

MR. JAYWALKER: How did that come up?

MS. TANNENBAUM: It's going to sound silly.

MR. JAYWALKER: Try us.

MS. TANNENBAUM: At some point, I started crying, just like that. And Barry asked me what was the matter. And I told him nothing was the matter. When he asked me again, I felt I had to tell him the truth. So I told him I was crying because I'd never been so happy in my life.

MR. JAYWALKER: Did you go to bed with Barry that night? Did you have sex with him?

MS. TANNENBAUM: No, not that night. Not for a month, maybe two. I still thought he was gay. Anyway, it wasn't about sex. I'd had enough sex by then to last me a lifetime. Two or three lifetimes.

MR. JAYWALKER: Was it about money?

MS. TANNENBAUM: *(Laughs)* I'd bought him Diet Cokes all night, out of my own paycheck, because I figured he couldn't afford to spring for a real drink. I didn't think he had a dollar to his name, to be honest.

MR. JAYWALKER: But he had a room at Caesars Palace, didn't he?

MS. TANNENBAUM: Back then, the big hotels would comp just about anybody, at least once. I don't know if they still do it. But in those days, all you had to do was ask. You have no idea how many flat broke guys there were back then, hanging on by their teeth, waiting for their luck to turn.

MR. JAYWALKER: So if it wasn't about sex and it wasn't about money, what *was* it about?

MS. TANNENBAUM: To tell you the truth, I had absolutely no idea. Love, I probably would have said at the time. Now that I'm older, and maybe just a tiny bit smarter, I guess maybe it was about finding my father. You know, the father I never had.

And right there, she lost it. No solitary tear welled up and trickled slowly down her cheek. No practiced feminine sob begged for the audience's attention. Without warning, Samara doubled over as though shot through the gut with a cannonball, her face contorted in pain, her hands knotted into fists, her shoulders shaking uncontrollably, her body heaving for breath. Strange, low animal noises rose from somewhere deep inside her. There was nothing in the least bit attractive about it, nothing charming, nothing to make some Hollywood director envious. But it was *real*.

For a full minute she stayed contorted like that, showing no sign that she was the least bit capable of reclaiming herself from whatever demons had so suddenly and so unexpectedly seized possession of her. Jaywalker stood by helplessly, hugging the sides of the lectern with both hands to hold himself back from rushing to her. They hadn't rehearsed this. They hadn't talked about it. They had contingency plans for just about anything that might happen while she was on the stand, right down to sneezing fits and bladder issues. But they had no plan in place for a total meltdown. There was no adjustment for something like this in Jaywalker's mental playbook. All he knew was that his client was in a place way beyond where the offering of a tissue or the extending of a glass of water made any sense, light-years past the point of asking her if she could use a few minutes to compose herself before continuing.

"I think," said Judge Sobel, "that we're going to take our lunch break a little early today."

And all Jaywalker could do was to say thank-you, walk to the defense table and take his seat, and do what everyone else in the courtroom was doing: watch and listen, and try to *not* watch and listen, as Samara continued to writhe in the agonizing memory of her lost childhood. Only when the jurors had been led out, the judge had left the bench and the last of the spectators had filed out of the room in silence, could he then make his way to her and collect her from where she crouched, by then on one knee, on the bare floor of the witness stand. Only then could he take her in his arms and hold her and rock her, until finally he felt the first subtle signals that her body was beginning to unclench and soften, and he could at last allow himself to believe that she was on her way back from whatever long-ago and far-away place her story had carried her off to.

25

FROZEN IN TIME

Samara had pretty much regained control of herself by the time the afternoon session began, but from Jaywalker's perspective, her doing so proved a mixed blessing. While she was able to respond to his questions without outburst or interruption, there was something missing from her answers. Gone was her willingness to elaborate, to speculate into her own motives and to question her own actions in retrospect. Gone, too, was her vulnerability, which, even as it had been her undoing in the morning session, had also stamped her testimony with the unmistakable imprimatur of genuineness. Jaywalker strongly suspected that she was not only aware that she was closing up, but that she'd even made a conscious choice to do so. It was as though she'd resolved to make a tradeoff, so determined was she to keep hold of her emotional equilibrium, even if doing so came at the expense of her credibility with the jury. And while Jaywalker could understand and even appreciate her decision, he didn't let it stop him from trying to draw her out whenever an opportunity presented itself, even as she dug her heels in and resisted.

MR. JAYWALKER: Did the relationship continue, after that first morning?

MS. TANNENBAUM: Yes, it did.

MR. JAYWALKER: Would you describe its progress for us, please.

MS. TANNENBAUM: The only way I can describe it is to say that Barry courted me. I know that's kind of a foolish, old-fashioned word, but that's what he did, he courted me.

MR. JAYWALKER: Tell us what you mean by that.

MS. TANNENBAUM: I mean that we dated. We went to movies. He bought me flowers. We held hands. We talked for hours on end. Again, nothing like that had ever happened to me before.

MR. JAYWALKER: Was there a sexual component to the relationship?

MS. TANNENBAUM: Not at first, no. The truth was, I never found Barry terribly attractive. Not only was he a lot older than I was, but, well, he wasn't the best looking guy in the world. So there was an attraction, but it wasn't a sexual one. It was more like holding hands, kissing, saying nice things to each other. It was about tenderness, I guess.

MR. JAYWALKER: Did you like that?

MS. TANNENBAUM: Like it? I absolutely *loved* it. I'd never known there *was* such a thing.

She described how the relationship had progressed from

those first days. Barry had been called back to New York
on business, but he phoned her each day, sent her cards,
had flowers delivered. Not gaudy displays, but small,
tasteful bouquets. She remembered a half dozen yellow
roses, for example, arriving on the sixth day after they'd
met. Still, she never suspected he had money, not until a
fellow cocktail waitress made a comment about her sugar
daddy. When Samara looked puzzled by the reference, the
other waitress dismissed her with a "Yeah, right." But the
next day the waitress showed up with a recent issue of
People magazine, featuring a story about the ten richest
bachelors in America. Barry was number one. Samara had
stared at his photograph for a full five minutes, trying to
make the connection between the man she was falling in
love with and the one staring out from the pages.

Whatever lingering doubts she had disappeared a few
weeks later, when Barry, forced to cancel a return trip to
Vegas for business reasons, asked Samara to come to New
York instead. She explained that even were she willing to
risk almost certainly losing her job by doing so, she didn't
have enough money to buy a bus ticket. He told her that
wouldn't be necessary, he'd send one of his planes for her.

One of his planes.

For Samara, being in New York City was like being
Cinderella at the ball. Barry bought her clothes and jewelry,
wined and dined her, took her to the theater, a concert, the
ballet and the opera. She hadn't even known there was
such a thing as the opera. They went to bed, finally, but
even that was nothing like she'd ever experienced. They did
it on silk sheets in his penthouse apartment, overlooking
the twinkling lights of Manhattan. And instead of it being
all about his satisfaction, it was all about hers. Instead of
seeking to possess her, all he seemed to want was to please
her. Unlike all of her prior *Wham-bam-thank-you-ma'am*
experiences, with Barry it wasn't over just because he was
done. It wasn't over until they lay in each other's arms,

marveling over their good fortune at having met. In a word, it was love, something that Samara had never come close to tasting in all of her eighteen years. Not as an infant, not as an adolescent, not as a teenager, not as the adult she'd become long before she should have.

MR. JAYWALKER: What was your reaction to all this?

MS. TANNENBAUM: I was overwhelmed. Who wouldn't be? I was in heaven. And yet—

MR. JAYWALKER: And yet?

MS. TANNENBAUM: And yet I kept waiting for the clock to strike midnight. I kept waiting to wake up and find out it was over. Every time Barry would open his mouth, I'd hold my breath, figuring he was about to ask me to take my things and leave.

MR. JAYWALKER: Did he ever ask you to leave?

MS. TANNENBAUM: No. He asked me to marry him.

They were married six months later, in a small civil ceremony in Scarsdale, where Barry had a home, or, as Samara put it, a mansion straight out of *Gone with the Wind*. She'd signed a bunch of papers beforehand, which Barry's lawyers and accountants had put in front of her, including a prenuptial agreement that, as it was explained to her, would leave her out on the street were she ever to file for divorce. She couldn't have cared less. She'd been out on the street for eighteen years, one way or another, and had had her fill of it. And the thought of her ever divorcing Barry seemed about as likely as her walking on the moon.

Outside of storybooks, of course, nothing lasts forever, all things come to an end, and it's rare indeed that the prince and princess ride off into the sunset to live happily ever after. It was certainly no accident that Barry had left a trail of three failed marriages in his wake prior to meeting Samara, no small thing that he was forty-four years older than she, and not to be overlooked that they came from backgrounds so divergent that they might as well have been from different planets altogether. The two-week honeymoon in Paris was interrupted hourly by mergers and acquisitions, by IPOs and CFOs, by board meetings and boards of inquiry. A month into the marriage, Samara woke up to the reality that for Barry, business came first, second and third. There was a good reason why he'd risen through the ranks of the wealthiest bachelors in America to the top spot, an honor relinquished now only on something of a mere technicality, at least to Barry's way of thinking. And that reason was his single-minded, almost pathological dedication to maintaining his financial empire. It was as though, on the heels of his third divorce, Barry had flown out to Las Vegas to re-up, to find himself a replacement wife. He'd found her, taken a brief sabbatical, just long enough to consolidate her (what Samara had described as courting) and marry her. Once that had been checked off the agenda, it was back to business as usual.

With Barry's attention turned from the lines of his wife's bottom to the bottom line, the marriage never had a chance. Samara found herself alone in a city so alien to her that she was literally afraid to go out. She had no friends; there were no clubs for gold diggers, no meetings of Former Trailer Trash Anonymous, no chapter of Prairie Creek, Indiana, junior-high-school dropouts. She begged Barry to find her a job, any kind of job. But he refused, insisting that no wife of his would ever embarrass him by working. A family was out of the question: Barry already had five children and twelve grandchildren from his previous marriages, and though his alimony and support payments cost him only a negligible fraction of his wealth, he was pretty much estranged from all his progeny, and infuriated by the idea of paying them anything or potentially increasing their numbers. Even lovemaking became an extremely rare event.

MR. JAYWALKER: Tell us about that.

MS. TANNENBAUM: At first I thought Barry's being so gentle in bed was all about tenderness. Soon I realized that wasn't it at all. He was a hypochondriac, one of those people who are convinced they're dying but are afraid to go the doctor because they might find out that they're right. Or that they're wrong and are just flat-out crazy. He'd had a heart attack some years back and was afraid that exerting himself during sex with someone much younger than him might give him another one and kill him. And he'd read somewhere on his computer—that's where he got all his medical advice from—that there'd been this experiment that showed that producing sperm takes a lot out of mice, and they live shorter lives as a result. Barry figured the same had to be true with humans. So he tried not to come—you know, to ejaculate—because he was afraid that every time he did, it meant there went another month off his life span.

With no friends, no social life, no sex life, no job and no hope of raising a family, it didn't take long for Samara to become resentful of Barry and rebel against him. Her rebellion took the form of overcoming her fears and venturing outside. But not during the day, to shop or sightsee or pamper herself, as Barry encouraged her to. Instead, she waited for cover of darkness, and sought out clubs that opened late and stayed open later. She'd worked the night owl shift in Las Vegas, after all, and the sight of the sun coming up as she emerged from some smoke-filled sub-terranean lounge was nothing new to her. And as far as gaining entree to some of the city's more trendy spots, that proved no problem at all. Barry had already provided Samara with identification asserting that she was twenty-two, not so much to get her into places or served drinks as to protect himself from charges of cradle robbing. And on the rare occasion when Samara's fake ID or good looks alone failed to get her through the door, her last name more than sufficed.

But Manhattan proved to be no Vegas, where what happened there stayed there. It wasn't long before the tabloids picked up on Samara's late-night outings, and word got back to Barry. At first he put up with it, figuring she would get it out of her system. But soon the rumors got uglier, linking Samara to men, and backing up words with photos.

MR. JAYWALKER: Were the rumors true?

MS. TANNENBAUM: Do you mean, was I seeing other men?

MR. JAYWALKER: Yes.

MS. TANNENBAUM: Yes, I was.

MR. JAYWALKER: And were you sleeping with them?

MS. TANNENBAUM: Some of them.

MR. JAYWALKER: How did that come about?

MS. TANNENBAUM: I allowed it to. I was bored, I had no life. It was like Barry had turned this switch on in me, showed me what lovemaking was, and what intimacy was about. And then he'd tried to turn the switch off, just like that. I was eighteen, nineteen by then, I guess. I'd had sex, but I'd never made love before. I wanted more of it.

MR. JAYWALKER: What was Barry's reaction?

MS. TANNENBAUM: I'm sure he was embarrassed, horrified, whatever. I guess the word I'm looking for is humiliated. It was very important for Barry to be in control of absolutely everything. And here I was, six months into our marriage, running around like a tramp. I'm sure it was very hard on him, to suddenly feel out of control, like a victim.

MR. JAYWALKER: You used the word tramp. Were you taking money from these men, or gifts, as you'd done back in Las Vegas?

MS. TANNENBAUM: No, it was nothing like that. Barry gave me all the money I needed. I didn't want his money, I wanted a life.

It didn't take too long for things to come to a head. Within months, Samara's photo had made the front page of every tabloid, many times over, as often as not with a generous helping of leg or cleavage, as she dodged the cameras on the arm of some minor celebrity. It didn't help matters that the men were uniformly young and good-looking. Barry cornered her one afternoon, literally cornered her, in the living room of his Scarsdale mansion, grabbing her by the arms and demanding an end to her behavior.

MR. JAYWALKER: And?

MS. TANNENBAUM: And I threatened to call the
                   police.

MR. JAYWALKER: Did you agree to his de-
                   mands?

MS. TANNENBAUM: No, not unless he'd let me
get a job or get pregnant. And he wouldn't. So I told
him I was moving out, that I had friends with money
who'd take care of me. In order to stop me from
doing that and humiliating him even more, he agreed
to get me my own place in the city. All he asked was
that I be more discreet about what I did and who I
did it with, and that I continue to act like his wife in
public, when he needed me to. Appearance was very
important to Barry.

MR. JAYWALKER: And how did that work out?

MS. TANNENBAUM: It worked out okay, for a
while. He bought me a town house in Midtown and
set up a joint bank account so I could furnish it. It
gave me something to do, something I found out I
was good at. At least I think I was. It also gave me
space. I know that's a dumb California word, but it's
how I felt.

MR. JAYWALKER: You say it worked out okay
                   for a while.

MS. TANNENBAUM: Yes. But the tabloids and the
gossip columns are like sharks. They get a taste of
blood, and they keep coming around for more. I know
it was my own fault, for having started it all in the first
place. But they'd stake out my home, follow me
whenever I went out, snap my picture on the street

corner, in the supermarket, wherever they could. If I squatted down to pick up a tissue, the next day there'd be a shot up my skirt. If I bent over instead, it would be of my butt. One time, they got me coming out of a women's health clinic, where I'd gone to have a breast exam, 'cause I thought I'd felt a lump. The photo made all the front pages, and the headlines made it sound like I had AIDS or herpes, or had just gotten an abortion. Somebody sent copies to Barry, and he went absolutely nuts. I don't blame him, really. I would've, too, if I'd been in his shoes.

Samara had tried to rein in her behavior, spending less time at her place and more at Barry's penthouse apartment, or their home in Scarsdale. But with Barry consumed by work and often absent for days at a time, she would eventually gravitate back to her own place, her own life and her own friends. Even as she could see the humiliation her behavior brought him, she felt powerless to change her behavior.

Occasionally there would be flare-ups, intense shouting arguments filled with threats and ultimatums. Never was there physical force, yet never was there resolution, either. Instead a stalemate of sorts set in, with Samara able to continue defying Barry because by that time she had too much on him. Even as he held firm to the purse strings to her life, she would threaten to go public with his fears, his foibles, his anxieties and his sexual neuroses. If theirs was a love-hate relationship, it was sorely out of balance, with precious little love and more than enough anger to go around. Barry hated Samara for continually humiliating him and victimizing him, while Samara hated Barry for keeping her trapped in a prison without walls.

MR. JAYWALKER: How long did this stalemate continue?

MS. TANNENBAUM: Forever. I mean, we made some adjustments, some accommodations over the years. We continued to see each other and appear together in public when some occasion called for it. But privately, we led our own lives. I stayed at my place, and Barry at either of his. He hated it, but that's the way it was.

MR. JAYWALKER: How about your finances? Who looked after them?

MS. TANNENBAUM: Barry had lawyers and accountants who pretty much took care of everything. If something needed to be signed, one of them would call and come over, have me sign. But mostly they took care of things without me. Barry had met me when I was eighteen and didn't know anything. By the time he…he died, I was twenty-six and had learned some stuff. But to Barry, it was like I was frozen in time. I'd always be the eighteen-year-old cocktail waitress who couldn't be trusted to write a check. That was a big part of the problem right there.

MR. JAYWALKER: Let's go forward to August, August of a year and a half ago, the month Barry died. How did things stand between the two of you by that time?

MS. TANNENBAUM: They were pretty much the same, I guess. I was no longer a favorite of the tabloids, but every once in a while I'd do something stupid, and there would be my photo, with my hair messed up or a nipple showing, or something like that. And Barry would get humiliated all over again and go ballistic, and we'd have a good scream over it.

At which point Judge Sobel interrupted, politely as always, and asked if it might be a good time for the mid-afternoon break. Some judges fall asleep during testimony; others try to take down every word on a laptop; still others work on shopping lists, bill paying, checkbook balancing and Little League lineups. Matthew Sobel listened. And from listening, he knew that Jaywalker had reached the moment when he was about to have Samara describe the evening of the murder, and he decided that the jurors should be as fresh and alert as possible for her account.

"It would be a perfect time," said Jaywalker.

The day had gone reasonably well, he felt. If, in the afternoon session, Samara had been guarded emotionally, and surely she had been, at least she hadn't allowed her reticence to cut her answers short. Perhaps the biggest challenge faced by a lawyer in examining his own client is that the defendant will invariably try to summarize the facts instead of elaborating on them. Good lawyers will therefore devote hours of practice sessions to drawing out the minute details of events, repeatedly explaining to the witness the need to convey those details to the jury. Jaywalker, as he did with most things, took it a step further.

"You're going to get nervous on the witness stand," he'd told Samara more than once. "You're going to look out from where you're sitting and see hundreds of strangers. You're going to see reporters and sketch artists and gawkers. It's going to freak you out, trust me. And when that happens, your natural impulse is going to be to summarize, to cut things short. Everybody does it. What I need is for you to fight that impulse as hard as you possibly can. And the best way to fight it is to slow down and give me as much detail as you can come up with."

It had worked.

Had Samara testified simply that Barry had been a hypochondriac preoccupied with his health, the jurors would have heard her, but it would have been only her intellectual conclusion that they heard. When she went on to describe how, having come across an item about mice on the Internet, Barry had become afraid to ejaculate, lest it shorten his life span by a month, they *got* it. So, too, when she'd complained about how the tabloid photographers wouldn't let her alone. Words. Only when she described the health clinic episode and the headline suggesting she had AIDS or herpes or was coming from an abortion, or when she talked about the photo revealing her nipple, did she give them something to truly picture and remember and take home with them that night. The difference lay in the fact that they hadn't been forced to accept her conclusions. Instead they'd taken her details and drawn their own conclusions from them.

What Jaywalker was less happy about was the way Samara had been so ready to acknowledge the depth of her anger at Barry. Where had that come from? He couldn't remember her bringing it up in any of their sessions. Had she done so, he almost certainly would have worked with her to tone it down. As it stood, that anger, especially when coupled with the life insurance policy, could have provided her with enough motivation to kill Barry a dozen times over. And Tom Burke certainly hadn't missed it. Jaywalker had noticed him out of the corner of his eye, scribbling away on his notepad, as soon as the words were out of Samara's mouth.

Not that Jaywalker himself wouldn't do his best to patch things up before Burke got a chance to exploit them. Still, the anger was there, and it didn't help matters.

With the jurors settled back in their seats following the recess, Jaywalker wasted no time in getting to the part of Samara's testimony that they'd been waiting for all day. Waiting for, as a matter of fact, for a week and a half now.

MR. JAYWALKER: Do you recall the very last time you saw Barry?

MS. TANNENBAUM: Yes, I do.

MR. JAYWALKER: When was that?

MS. TANNENBAUM: The evening everyone says he was murdered.

MR. JAYWALKER: And where was it you saw him?

MS. TANNENBAUM: At his apartment.

She described how she'd gone there at Barry's invitation to discuss something he'd said was important but which she could no longer remember. It had been around dinnertime when she'd arrived, and he'd ordered Chinese food, which they'd eaten straight from the takeout cartons. Barry hadn't eaten much, she recalled. He'd complained he had a cold, or the flu, or something like that. Typical Barry.

Within twenty minutes they'd found themselves arguing over whatever it was Barry had wanted to talk about. Perhaps it had been his humiliation over her latest antic, or perhaps she was just saying that to fill in the blank in her memory, she couldn't be sure. In any event, the argument quickly turned nasty and loud, and ended when Samara called Barry a name she knew he hated and stormed out.

MR. JAYWALKER: Do you remember the name
                        you called him?

MS. TANNENBAUM: I do.

MR. JAYWALKER: What name?

MS. TANNENBAUM: I called him an asshole. I'd
called him lots of things at one time or another, but
that was the only one he really hated. He'd told me
it made me sound like a slut, like the trailer trash I
was. I'd told him I didn't care. If I was trailer trash,
I was trailer trash. Whatever. Anyway, that's what I
called him that night, just to push his button. That's
how angry I was.

MR. JAYWALKER: And yet you don't remem-
                        ber what it was you were
                        angry about?

MS. TANNENBAUM: Exactly. I mean, how stupid
                        is that? But that's how it
                        was with the two of us.

From Barry's, she'd caught a cab and gone straight
home. She hadn't bathed or showered, washed her hair
or her clothes, or done anything else out of the ordinary.
She no longer recalled what time she'd gone to bed or
fallen asleep. Only that sometime the next afternoon two
detectives had come and rung her doorbell, asking to talk
with her, and she'd let them in. When she'd asked them
what it was about, they'd refused to tell her, which had
annoyed her.

MR. JAYWALKER: What did they ask you?

MS. TANNENBAUM: They wanted to know when was the last time I'd seen my husband.

MR. JAYWALKER: What did you answer?

MS. TANNENBAUM: I asked them why, or what business it was of theirs. Something like that. They still wouldn't answer me. So I said about a week ago.

MR. JAYWALKER: Was that the truth?

MS. TANNENBAUM: No, it was a lie.

MR. JAYWALKER: Why did you lie to them?

MS. TANNENBAUM: I don't know. Like I said, they were piss—they were annoying me, telling me I had to answer their questions but refusing to answer any of mine. Maybe that's why I lied, to get even. I'm honestly not sure.

MR. JAYWALKER: What happened next?

MS. TANNENBAUM: They told me I was lying. They told me they had a witness who could put me in Barry's apartment the night before. So I said yes, I'd been there, so what?

MR. JAYWALKER: What happened then?

MS. TANNENBAUM: They asked me if we'd had a fight, Barry and me. I didn't think it was any of their business, what went on between my husband and me, and I think I told them that.

MR. JAYWALKER: Did you ever say yes or no about having had a fight the previous evening?

MS. TANNENBAUM: I said no. We hadn't had a fight. To me, a fight is when two people hit each other, throw things, stuff like that. What we'd had was an argument.

MR. JAYWALKER: Did you volunteer that?

MS. TANNENBAUM: I wasn't volunteering anything. As far as I was concerned, I'd let these guys into my home, and they didn't have the decency to tell me why they were there and what it was all about. I was just supposed to listen up and answer whatever they asked me, like some five-year-old.

MR. JAYWALKER: What happened next?

MS. TANNENBAUM: They told me I was lying again, that they had another witness who'd heard us fighting. I told them again that we hadn't been fighting. They said how about arguing? And that's when I said sure, we argued, we argued all the time.

MR. JAYWALKER: What's the next thing you recall happening?

MS. TANNENBAUM: One of them, the one who testified here the other day—

MR. JAYWALKER: Detective Bonfiglio?

MS. TANNENBAUM: Yeah, Bonfiglio, the nasty
one. He told me my husband was dead, that somebody
had killed him. He said it just like that, to hurt me.

Jaywalker knew he had to tiptoe here, in order to avoid
revealing that at that point Samara had asked to call her
lawyer, triggering an end to the questioning.

MR. JAYWALKER: Did there come a time, a
                      minute or so later, when
                      something happened?

MS. TANNENBAUM: Yes.

MR. JAYWALKER: What happened?

MS. TANNENBAUM: They put handcuffs on me,
behind my back, real tight. And they told me I was
under arrest for murdering my husband.

MR. JAYWALKER: Did you murder your hus-
                      band, Samara?

MS. TANNENBAUM: Absolutely not.

MR. JAYWALKER: Did you do anything to him
                      physically that evening?

MS. TANNENBAUM: No.

MR. JAYWALKER: At any time while you were
                      in Barry's apartment, did you
                      have a knife in your hand?

MS. TANNENBAUM: Never.

MR. JAYWALKER: Did you stab him in the
                 chest with a knife or any
                 other sharp instrument?

MS. TANNENBAUM: No, absolutely not.

MR. JAYWALKER: Have you told us everything
                 about that evening that you
                 can recall?

MS. TANNENBAUM: Yes, except for what the
fight—the argument was about. I still can't remember that.

Jaywalker was aware of the salty taste before realizing
he'd bitten the inside of his cheek hard enough to draw
blood. Had she really said *fight,* instead of *argument,*
before correcting herself? *Shit,* he thought. *Shit, shit, shit.*
Burke would have a field day with that slip, he knew. Even
a couple of the jurors could be heard mumbling over it. So
into the breach he went.

MR. JAYWALKER: I noticed you used the word
                 fight.

MS. TANNENBAUM: Fight, argument, whatever
you want to call it. I've heard those two words so
many times since that day that I'm dizzy. All I know
is, I didn't touch Barry that night. And I certainly
didn't stick a knife into him or anything like that.
That I'd remember, I'm pretty damn sure.

For an impromptu recovery, it wasn't bad, and Jaywalker left it at that. He walked over to Burke then and

asked to borrow several of his exhibits. The first one he showed Samara was the towel.

MR. JAYWALKER: Do you recognize this?

MS. TANNENBAUM: I'm not sure. It looks like the towels I have, but there's no way for me to know for sure if it's mine or not. It might be. That's the best I can say.

MR. JAYWALKER: Did you ever wrap a blouse and a knife in it, and stick it behind the toilet tank in your upstairs guest bathroom?

MS. TANNENBAUM: Absolutely not.

MR. JAYWALKER: How about this blouse?

MS. TANNENBAUM: It's mine.

MR. JAYWALKER: How do you know?

MS. TANNENBAUM: I just do.

MR. JAYWALKER: Did you wear it to Barry's apartment that last evening you saw him? Or have it with you?

MS. TANNENBAUM: No, definitely not.

MR. JAYWALKER: You say definitely not. How can you be so certain?

MS. TANNENBAUM: It's part of a set I own, a blouse and a pair of slacks Barry bought me. Same pattern, same colors. I only wore them as an ensemble. You know, together. Also, look at the material. It's silk, too heavy to wear in the summer.

MR. JAYWALKER: Did you ever wrap this blouse, along with a knife, in the towel I just showed you and hide it behind a toilet tank?

MS. TANNENBAUM: No, never.

MR. JAYWALKER: And this knife? Do you recognize it?

MS. TANNENBAUM: I do.

MR. JAYWALKER: How do you recognize it?

MS. TANNENBAUM: It's identical to a set of steak knives I own. It's the same size and shape and everything else, as the others in my kitchen drawer.

MR. JAYWALKER: Did you have it with you at Barry's apartment the last time you were there?

MS. TANNENBAUM: I did not.

MR. JAYWALKER: Did you hide it behind your toilet tank?

MS. TANNENBAUM: I did not.

Jaywalker asked her if she could explain the dark stains on each of the three items. Samara replied that she had no idea how they'd gotten there. Yes, she'd heard Detective Ramseyer testify that they were bloodstains, specifically

Barry Tannenbaum's. No, she hadn't stabbed Barry or cut him with that knife, any other knife, or anything else. Nor could she explain how the three items had ended up behind the toilet tank. Obviously someone had put them there, she said, but it definitely hadn't been her.

From his own exhibits, Jaywalker showed Samara the life insurance application and had her identify her signature. She had absolutely no recollection of having signed it, however, and she'd never sought to take out a policy on Barry's life or anyone else's. She often signed papers that were presented to her by Barry's accountant or lawyer, and rarely took the trouble to read them, instead trusting their assurances that it was in her interest to sign them. Shown the cancelled check that had paid for the six-month premium, she agreed with the testimony of William Smythe that it didn't bear her signature and denied that she'd ever seen it, either before or after it had been deposited by the insurance company. Nor had she noticed the significant dent it made in her account. She rarely if ever opened her bank statements or balanced her checkbook, leaving those tasks to others.

Jaywalker took a deep breath. It was four-thirty, and he was down to one or two remaining topics on his notes. The first of those involved Samara's discovery of the Seconal. Even though she adamantly denied any prior knowledge of it and claimed never to have heard of the phantom prescribing physician, Jaywalker was afraid the whole thing looked too suspicious. Asking the jurors to believe that whoever had murdered Barry and framed Samara had also been diabolical enough to plant the Seconal in her spice cabinet, hoping the police would find it, was a stretch of immense proportions. Even to Jaywalker, it seemed much more likely that Samara herself had phoned in the prescription, posing as someone from a doctor's office, had been surprised when the pharmacy had asked for the doctor's name, and in her haste had made up a name on the spot, a name that just happened to have the same initials as her own. What were the odds of that? He tried multiplying twenty-six by twenty-six in his head, but couldn't. But he was able to remember that twenty-five squared was six hundred and something. He took his pen and crossed the word Seconal off his list.

It was time to wrap it up.

MR. JAYWALKER: Samara, you've told us there were times you got angry at Barry, very angry. Is that correct?

MS. TANNENBAUM: Yes, I did.

MR. JAYWALKER: Did you ever, in all of your eight years of marriage, get angry enough to want to harm him physically?

MS. TANNENBAUM: No, never.

MR. JAYWALKER: Did you ever strike him, either with part of your body or with something else?

MS. TANNENBAUM: Only once. One time, about five years ago, I threw a soda bottle at him. It hit him on the shoulder, I think.

MR. JAYWALKER: Did it break?

MS. TANNENBAUM: Break? It was one of those plastic ones that you can't break even if you try.

MR. JAYWALKER: Did it appear to injure him?

MS. TANNENBAUM: No, it just bounced off him. It was empty. It wouldn't have injured a mouse. We had a good laugh over it.

MR. JAYWALKER: Other than that incident, did you ever physically harm your husband, or attempt to?

MS. TANNENBAUM: No, never.

MR. JAYWALKER: Did you love him?

MS. TANNENBAUM: I'm honestly not sure. I know I thought I did, at first. But Barry was hard to love, the way he was obsessed with his businesses. And I've never been good at loving. I think I learned early on in my life to close up, to not give of myself. So maybe love was hard for both of us.

MR. JAYWALKER: Did you want to get out of the relationship?

MS. TANNENBAUM: Only when we were arguing, or fighting, as some people call it. Other than those times, no. I was Mrs. Barry Tannenbaum. Plus I had my own place, my own friends, my own life. As they say in Vegas, it might not have been blackjack, but it was good enough to stick with.

MR. JAYWALKER: Did you murder Barry?

MS. TANNENBAUM: No, I did not.

MR. JAYWALKER: Did you take this knife, or

anything else, and plunge it through his chest and into his heart?

MS. TANNENBAUM: God, no.

With her denial, Jaywalker walked back to the defense table and took his seat. On a scale of one to ten, he would have given her a solid nine, deducting half a point for too much emotional control down the home stretch and another half for the *argument-fight* slip. Though he had to give her credit for patching that up a second time, entirely un-prompted, near the very end of her testimony.

The only problem was that, given the sheer weight of the evidence against her, he knew a nine wasn't going to be good enough. Hell, a perfect ten might not even do it.

Then again, there was still cross-examination. Jaywalker had learned over the years that jurors subconsciously deducted points on their own during a witness's direct examination. The reason was simple. Direct examination, they intuitively understood, was spoon-fed. It could be re-hearsed, re-rehearsed and re-re-rehearsed until it flowed from the witness's mouth with something approaching per-fection. Cross-examination was different. On cross, the witness was suddenly confronted with unexpected ques-tions and forced to come up with unrehearsed answers.

Most lawyers, if they were aware of the difference at all, regarded it as nothing more than an accepted fact of the trial process. To Jaywalker, it was an opportunity. If he spent twenty hours preparing a defendant for his own questions, and he did, he spent forty preparing that same witness for the prosecutor's questions. What they might include, how to pause reflectively before answering, what the absolute best answer was, and precisely how that answer should be delivered. The result was that, unlike most witnesses, who tend to come off well enough on direct but not so well on cross, Jaywalker's witnesses—and especially Jaywalker's defendants—did even better on cross than they did on direct. And the same jurors who'd deducted points during direct without ever realizing they were doing so were equally prone to give extra credit on cross. So it was entirely conceivable that Samara's best might still be yet to come.

But not now.

Even before Tom Burke rose and asked to approach the bench, Jaywalker knew he would. Rather than start his cross-examination now, at quarter of five, he asked Judge Sobel's permission to go over to the morning.

"Not the morning," said the judge. "I've got my calendar call then. But, yes, you can begin with her tomorrow afternoon." Then he proceeded to explain to the jurors that they wouldn't have to show up until two o'clock the following day. To those who had jobs, children, parents or even pets to look after, the five-hour respite seemed to come as the best news in the world. Press people into involuntary servitude for a couple of weeks, and they'll rejoice over a slice of stale bread.

"Great job," Burke said to Jaywalker, once the jurors had filed out of the courtroom.

"I'm sure you'll blow her away in the first five minutes," said Jaywalker.

If the exchange represented mind games played by opponents, and surely it did, at the same time it reflected hard-earned respect and genuine affection between two men who were not only among the very best at what they did for a living, but who also might have been the best of friends, had only Jaywalker allowed himself that sort of indulgence.

Jaywalker walked Samara up to Canal Street. "You did great," he told her. "Do half as well tomorrow, and I'll take care of the rest."

"Do you want to go over cross-examination?" she asked. "One last time?"

"No," he said, "you're ready." Which was his way of

saying, *If you're not now, you never will be.* He hailed her a cab and opened the door for her to get in.

"You sure?" she asked. "I mean, we have until tomorrow afternoon. To get me even readier, I mean."

He smiled at the transparency of her invitation. "Remember what we said," he reminded her.

"After," she said.

"After," he echoed.

At home that evening, Jaywalker pondered the trial schedule. Tomorrow was Thursday. Burke could easily take all afternoon cross-examining Samara. Add on redirect and recross, and she might even be back on the stand Friday morning. Having steered clear of the Seconal issue, Jaywalker had no other witnesses to call, and he doubted that Burke would feel the need to put on a rebuttal case. But even if Samara were to finish up tomorrow, that still left the charge conference with the judge, which would take an hour, and the two summations, figure a couple of hours each. Judge Sobel wouldn't charge the jury and give them the case on Friday afternoon, not with the weekend coming. It was one thing to bring a deliberating jury back on a Saturday and then waste Sunday when you had no choice, but quite another to do it deliberately. Particularly in winter, when it meant having to heat the courtroom and the jury room.

So whenever Samara finished, whether it was tomorrow afternoon or sometime Friday, summations wouldn't take place until Monday, at the earliest. Which meant that Tom Burke was the only one who had to stay up late tonight, working on his cross-examination of Samara. Well, too bad for him. For once in his life, Jaywalker could afford to relax and forget about a case he was in the midst of trying.

As if.

26

POUNDING THE TABLE

There's a general rule that prosecutors make poor cross-examiners. Not that there's anything innate about this particular characteristic, at least not in the sense that the job somehow attracts underqualified questioners or corrupts qualified ones. Rather, it's more likely a simple matter of insufficient practice. Many trials, if not most, consist of a series of prosecution witnesses and few, if any, defense witnesses. As a result, the assistant district attorney typically gets all sorts of opportunities to conduct direct examinations of various sizes, shapes and varieties, but only rarely does he get a chance to cross-examine. And when he does, that lack of practice tends to show.

Not so with Tom Burke.

Because a handful of cases from Judge Sobel's calendar call were still left over from the morning session, Burke didn't begin with Samara until just after three o'clock. When he did, he took her back to her very first encounter with Barry, back to when she was eighteen and working as a cocktail waitress at Caesars Palace.

MR. BURKE: That was a very short time after you had, as you put it, been accepting money and other gifts for sexual favors. Isn't that so?

MS. TANNENBAUM: I'm not sure I said "sexual favors," but yes, it was a short time after that.

MR. BURKE: So whatever you want to call it, you'd stopped doing it.

MS. TANNENBAUM: That's right. I'd turned eighteen, finally, and I was getting a paycheck.

MR. BURKE: And then one night you spied Barry Tannenbaum.

MS. TANNENBAUM: Right. Although I didn't know he was Barry Tannenbaum, or who Barry Tannenbaum was.

MR. BURKE: I see. Tell us, did he initiate contact with you, or did you initiate contact with him?

MS. TANNENBAUM: I'm not sure what you mean by initiate contact.

MR. BURKE: Did he approach you first, or did you approach him?

MS. TANNENBAUM: I approached him.

MR. BURKE: In fact, you began bringing him drinks.

MS. TANNENBAUM: Diet Cokes.

| MR. BURKE: | Those are drinks, aren't they? |

| MS. TANNENBAUM: | Not in Vegas, they're not. |

A ripple of laughter from the jury box signaled that Samara had scored a point. More importantly, it suggested that they were still willing to like her. But Jaywalker also detected a danger sign in Samara's answers. She was sparring with Burke, trying to get the better of him whenever she could, even in little ways. Jaywalker had warned her against that, but now he was seeing how hard it was for her to suppress her natural feistiness. *Chill out,* he told her subliminally, *and just answer the questions.* But even as he sent her the message, he doubted that she was fully capable of hearing it.

| MR. BURKE: | And isn't it a fact, Mrs. Tannenbaum, that when your shift ended that night, you and Barry went out? |

| MS. TANNENBAUM: | Went out? No, that's not a fact. |

| MR. BURKE: | Where did you go? |

| MS. TANNENBAUM: | To his apartment, upstairs in the hotel. |

| MR. BURKE: | Ah. That's not going out, is it? |

| MS. TANNENBAUM: | Here's the problem I'm having, Mr. Burke. |

Jaywalker cringed in his seat. The last thing he wanted
from Samara was combativeness. Sixty seconds into her
cross-examination, she was about to deliver a lecture to
Burke, to tell him what was wrong with his questions. Jaywalker tried to think of a basis on which to object, but
couldn't. Besides, the jury would only see it for what it
was, an attempt to shut up his own client. He slid down in
his seat, gritted his teeth and waited for the worst.

> MS. TANNENBAUM: *(Continuing)* Where I come
> from, and especially in Las Vegas, some of these
> terms you're using have special meanings. *Drinks*
> have alcohol in them. *Partying* means doing cocaine.
> *Dating* means having sex. And *going out* means hav-
> ing sex on a regular basis.

There was actually an audible clap from somewhere in
the jury box. Jaywalker felt his teeth unclench ever so
slightly, and his body began to relax a bit. He allowed
himself to straighten up in his chair and exhale a breath he
suddenly realized he'd been holding so long he could feel
his pulse pounding in his temples. Maybe, just maybe,
Samara had what it took to pull this off, after all.

But Burke had a nice way of rolling with the punch.
Instead of taking issue with Samara's speech and trying to
pick it apart, he genuinely seemed to get a kick out of it.
He quickly established that whatever one wanted to call it,
she had indeed spent a number of hours in Barry's hotel
room that first night. He left it to the jurors to decide precisely what they were doing. Then he took Samara to the
point where she'd learned who Barry was, and how much
money he was reported to have.

> MR. BURKE: When did you learn about
>   that?

MS. TANNENBAUM: I'm not sure. Maybe two weeks after we'd met. Something like that.

MR. BURKE: From an article in a magazine, right?

MS. TANNENBAUM: Right.

MR. BURKE: And how soon after that did you fly to New York to be with him?

MS. TANNENBAUM: You're doing it again.

MR. BURKE: Excuse me?

MS. TANNENBAUM: I need to know what you mean by "be with him."

MR. BURKE: *Touché.* To visit him. Is that better?

MS. TANNENBAUM: Much better. I came to New York about two weeks after I found out.

MR. BURKE: And within six months, you were married.

MS. TANNENBAUM: That's right.

Burke left it there. The timing of the events made the implication clear enough. Jaywalker had spent hours preparing Samara for a barrage of questions about how much

Barry's wealth had to do with her marrying him. It was a factor, she was readily prepared to admit, but so were his tenderness, his gentleness and his interest in the things she had to say, which were all novel concepts to her. But Burke was smart enough to know that Jaywalker would have primed Samara with just that sort of response, and he wasn't about to give her an opening.

He showed her a copy of the prenuptial agreement, which bore a date one week before the wedding, and asked her if the signature at the bottom was hers.

MS. TANNENBAUM: Yes, it is.

MR. BURKE: Do you remember signing it?

MS. TANNENBAUM: Not specifically, but I can see that I did. It's my handwriting.

MR. BURKE: I'll offer it as People's Eleven.

MR. JAYWALKER: No objection.

THE COURT: Received.

MR. BURKE: Do you recall who presented it to you for your signature?

MS. TANNENBAUM: I really don't. It might have been Barry, it might have been Bill Smythe.

MR. BURKE:	Did you read it before signing it?
MS. TANNENBAUM:	I'm sure I didn't. It's, let me see, twenty-two pages long.
MR. BURKE:	Did you understand what you were agreeing to?
MS. TANNENBAUM:	Basically, yes.
MR. BURKE:	And what was that?
MS. TANNENBAUM:	That if I ever divorced Barry, I would get absolutely nothing.
MR. BURKE:	Did you believe that to be true?
MS. TANNENBAUM:	Sure. I didn't think they'd go and waste twenty-two pages on it if it wasn't.
MR. BURKE:	Over the years since, did you ever come to rethink the subject and decide it wasn't true?
MS. TANNENBAUM:	No, I've always assumed it was true.
MR. BURKE:	Even after eight years of marriage?

MS. TANNENBAUM: Yes. I figured "ever" meant
                    exactly that.

Nice job, Jaywalker had to admit. Question by question,
Burke had painted Samara into a corner. Even though no
judge in the world would have strictly enforced a prenuptial agreement after eight years of marriage, Burke had
gotten Samara to say that she didn't know that. So as far as
she was concerned, divorce wasn't an option, not unless she
wanted to be out on the street again. From there, Burke
shifted gears and moved on to other avenues by which
Samara might hope to end up with a chunk of Barry's money.

MR. BURKE: Did you know anything
                    about your husband's will?

MS. TANNENBAUM: No, I didn't.

MR. BURKE: Do you know anything
                    about wills in general?

MS. TANNENBAUM: I know what a will is.

MR. BURKE: Was it your understanding
                    that if Barry were to die,
                    you'd inherit a fortune?

MS. TANNENBAUM: I didn't know. I mean, I
                    didn't know if that was the
                    case or not.

MR. BURKE: Had you ever heard that
under the law, an individual can't disinherit his or her
spouse? That even if the individual should try to do that,
the spouse would still be entitled to half of the estate?

MS. TANNENBAUM: No, I hadn't heard that.

MR. BURKE: So as far as you knew, not only would you have gotten nothing if you divorced Barry, but the same might have been true if he'd died?

MS. TANNENBAUM: I suppose so. I really didn't spend a lot of time trying to figure out stuff like that.

MR. BURKE: It didn't interest you?

MS. TANNENBAUM: Not really.

MR. BURKE: You married one of the richest men on the planet, yet you weren't really interested in his money?

MS. TANNENBAUM: I don't think I said that. I loved the fact that Barry was rich, and that I had a nice place to live and all sorts of other nice things, and that I didn't have to worry about money anymore. But did I wake up in the morning thinking about his will, or how much I'd get if he died? No.

MR. BURKE: Yesterday you told us that Barry was convinced he was going to die.

MS. TANNENBAUM: That's right, he was.

MR. BURKE: In fact, he was convinced you were going to kill him, wasn't he?

MS. TANNENBAUM: If he was, he was very good at keeping it secret.

MR. BURKE: Let's talk about life insurance for a minute, okay?

MS. TANNENBAUM: Okay.

MR. BURKE: Disregarding for the moment the twenty-five-million-dollar policy that you signed the application for, did your husband have any other life insurance?

MS. TANNENBAUM: I have no idea.

MR. BURKE: Did Barry ever mention it?

MS. TANNENBAUM: Not that I recall.

MR. BURKE: Did you ever ask?

MS. TANNENBAUM: No.

MR. BURKE: In eight years of marriage, the subject never even came up in conversation?

MS. TANNENBAUM: I don't think you have a very clear understanding of our marriage, Mr. Burke. I was Barry's wife, not his business partner.

MR. BURKE: So you had absolutely no idea if he had any life insurance or not. Is that what you're telling us? Again, we're not counting that twenty-five-million-dollar policy.

MS. TANNENBAUM: I had no idea about that, either.

Score one for Samara.

MR. BURKE: So just to review for a moment. So far as you knew, you'd have gotten absolutely nothing if you'd divorced Barry. Correct?

MR. JAYWALKER: Objection. Asked and answered.

THE COURT: I'll permit it.

MR. BURKE: Was that your understanding?

MS. TANNENBAUM: Yes.

MR. BURKE: And for all you knew, you might have gotten absolutely nothing under Barry's will if he were to die. Right?

MS. TANNENBAUM: Right.

MR. BURKE: And finally, you might have gotten absolutely nothing in the way of life insurance, because again, there might not have been any? Right?

MS. TANNENBAUM: Right.

MR. BURKE: You were sitting in a pretty precarious position, wouldn't you say?

MR. JAYWALKER: Objection. Argumentative.

Even as the judge sustained the objection, Jaywalker knew that Burke had not only wiped out Samara's previous point, but had scored heavily on his own. The jury didn't need to hear Samara's answer in order to understand that, at least so far as she knew, her fortunes were in serious jeopardy of turning full circle, from trailer trash to princess, and then back again to trailer trash.

Still, Burke wasn't quite ready to take his foot off Samara's throat. He got her to admit that the relationship had gradually disintegrated over the years, as she felt increasingly trapped in a marriage to a man who constantly put his business affairs ahead of her, even as he grew more and more bitter about the various ways in which she humiliated him.

MR. BURKE: Now, shortly before your husband was murdered, you were aware that his health was bad, weren't you?

MS. TANNENBAUM: I knew that he had a cold that last night I saw him, or the flu. Something like that.

MR. BURKE: Something like that. Anything else?

MS. TANNENBAUM: Like I said, he was always complaining about something or other, always afraid he was sick or dying.

MR. BURKE: How about coronary disease, heart disease? Did you know anything about that?

MS. TANNENBAUM:	I knew he'd had a heart attack, back before I knew him.
MR. BURKE:	How about cancer? Did you know he was suffering from cancer?
MS. TANNENBAUM:	No.
MR. BURKE:	You never knew that?
MS. TANNENBAUM:	No, not until after his death.

MR. BURKE: You're telling us that this eccentric hypochondriac, who was constantly complaining he was sick and continually expressing his fears that he was dying, never once told you he had cancer?

Jaywalker's objection and Samara's feeble "That's right" were completely beside the point. Burke's implication was crystal clear: Samara was lying. Not only had she believed she was financially vulnerable in a marriage that was rapidly disintegrating, but even were the marriage to somehow survive, she'd known full well that her husband might not. Desperate to protect herself in one way or another, she'd gambled on insuring Barry's life for a huge sum, and then murdered him during the brief six-month window afforded by the policy. Or so Tom Burke would argue in his summation, with logic that was pretty irresistible.

And just as Jaywalker knew it would, that brought Burke to the insurance policy. He pulled out the application now, folded it so that the last page was on top, and had a court officer place it in front of Samara.

MR. BURKE: Tell us again whose signa-
                        ture that is, please.

MS. TANNENBAUM: Mine.

MR. BURKE: In your own handwriting?

MS. TANNENBAUM: It's my own handwriting,
                        yes.

MR. BURKE: No one put a gun to your
                        head and ordered you to
                        sign it, did they?

MS. TANNENBAUM: No.

MR. BURKE: No one tricked you or de-
                        ceived you into signing it,
                        did they?

MS. TANNENBAUM: I have no idea. I don't remember signing it, so I can't really tell you the specific circumstances.

MR. BURKE: No one blindfolded you?

MS. TANNENBAUM: No one blindfolded me. I'm
                        pretty sure I'd remember
                        that.

MR. BURKE: Would you turn the page,
                        please, so that the cover
                        page is on top. Have you
                        done that?

MS. TANNENBAUM: Yes.

MR. BURKE:	Do you see some capital letters in bold print at the very top of that cover page?
MS. TANNENBAUM:	Yes.
MR. BURKE:	Would you read that portion to the jurors, please.
MS. TANNENBAUM:	Out loud?
MR. BURKE:	Yes, out loud.
MS. TANNENBAUM:	*(Reading)* "Application for term life insurance policy."

MR. BURKE: Look halfway down the page, if you would, to the words, "Summary of contents." Would you read the print, also in capitals and also in bold, immediately following those words.

MS. TANNENBAUM: *(Pointing)* Here?

MR. BURKE: Yes, there.

MS. TANNENBAUM: *(Reading)* "Name of insured, Barrington Tannenbaum. Amount of policy, twenty-five million dollars. Term of policy, six months. Name of beneficiary, Samara M. Tannenbaum."

MR. BURKE: Thank you.

Burke put the application away and moved to the items found in Samara's town house. As Jaywalker had on direct examination, he had her identify the towel as one that looked like hers, the blouse as definitely hers, and the knife as identical to a set in her kitchen. And as Jaywalker had, he gave her an opportunity to explain who, other than she, might have hidden the items behind the toilet tank of her upstairs bathroom. Samara had no answer. She'd been home alone the entire time, from her arrival after visiting Barry until the detectives showed up the following day. Did she think someone had sneaked in and hidden the things there without her noticing, or put them there after she'd been taken away in handcuffs? Or perhaps the detectives had planted the items, out of some inexplicable desire to frame her?

Again, Samara had no answers.

Had she perhaps hidden them there only temporarily, figuring to get rid of them as soon as she could, only to be surprised by the speed with which the police had shown up? No, she insisted, that wasn't the case; she'd never put them there in the first place, though she couldn't say who had, or how they'd managed to accomplish it.

There comes a time in cross-examination when jurors have heard enough, when their eyes begin to glaze over out of skepticism, and they slide back in their chairs with something that looks very much like outright disbelief. As often as not, that time comes without a clear line of demarcation. In Hollywood, or on the TV screen, there was always a dramatic *Gotcha!* instant, followed by either loud music or a fade to a commercial break. In real life, there's generally nothing to accompany the moment but sadness.

Samara was no longer being believed. And if Samara was no longer being believed, this trial was as good as over. Jaywalker knew that as surely as he knew his own last name.

It was nearly five o'clock. Burke asked to approach the bench. There he requested permission to go over to the following morning to complete his cross-examination. Judge

Sobel agreed. Jaywalker was too beaten to object, and aware that even if he did, it would do no good. At that point, in fact, he'd pretty much decided that nothing would do any good.

Trials are a little like sporting events, at least in the sense that both are contests that develop rhythms of their own after a while. Almost invariably, there's a series of momentum shifts, a pattern of highs and lows that could almost be charted on graph paper. An hour ago, the defense had been riding a crest of sorts. Samara's feistiness had earned her points in the early sparring. But Burke had weathered it, and bit by bit he'd succeeded in surrounding her with the evidence and trapping her with the facts. It reminded Jaywalker of the unsolicited advice he'd once heard an old-time trial lawyer dispensing in the hallway to anyone willing to stop long enough to listen. "When you've got the facts," he'd been saying, "pound the facts. When you've got the law, pound the law. When you don't have either one, pound the table."

From the outset, the trouble with this case had been that the prosecution had both the facts and the law on its side. At one or two minor high points in the trial, Jaywalker had deluded himself into believing that in spite of that imbalance, he might somehow figure out a way to walk Samara out of court. Now, he realized, he was going to be pretty much reduced to pounding the table. And while that might produce some noise, it was facts and law that generally produced victories.

That night, in spite of knowing better, Jaywalker poured himself a generous measure of Kahlúa, placed it on his kitchen countertop and pulled up a stool. For a good twenty minutes he sat in front of it in near darkness, doing nothing but staring at the tumbler and the almost-black liquid that filled the lower half of it. Even without putting his nose over it, he could smell the thick coffee aroma drifting his way, all but taste the syrupy sweetness as it magically kissed away the harsh bite of the alcohol. Only when he'd told himself for the twentieth time that he couldn't do it—not to himself, not to his profession and most of all not to his client—did he dare to shift his weight slightly, first to one side, then to the other, in order to remove his hands from underneath him, where they'd grown numb from his weight.

Slowly, carefully, he poured the liquid back into the bottle from which it had come. He didn't want to spill any, after all, not with a verdict likely by early next week. He would be needing it then, it and a lot more.

He rinsed out the glass and opened the dishwasher, then saw that it was full, not of dirty dishes and glasses, but of clean ones he hadn't bothered putting away earlier in the week. So he set the glass in the sink. His wife would've scolded him for that act of laziness, he knew. But his wife was dead, and he lived alone now. And suddenly the full impact of that terrible aloneness hit him head-on and knocked the wind right out of him, and he found himself gripping the counter with both hands in order to steady himself. *Thank God for that suspension,* he told himself. *Thank God I won't have to keep doing this anymore.*

27

ROCK BOTTOM

If Jaywalker thought he and Samara had hit bottom the previous afternoon, he was about to learn a whole new definition of the phrase. Before the jury was led in Friday morning, Tom Burke asked for a conference in the judge's robing room. Jaywalker told Samara to relax and wait in the courtroom, then followed the judge, the clerk, the court reporter and Burke through the side door.

"What gives?" he asked Burke.

"I'm afraid you're not going to like it," was all Burke would say. And from the grim look on his face, it was clear he meant it.

Once the reporter was seated and ready, Burke wasted no time in getting to the point. "I learned this morning," he said, "less than an hour ago, in fact, what I'm about to place on the record. It concerns the defendant, and an incident that dates back to when she was fourteen years old and living in Vigo County, Indiana, under the name Samantha Musgrove."

The name actually sounded vaguely familiar, but Jaywalker was already too busy feigning righteous indignation to pursue that tangent. He'd donned his most exaggerated stage frown, making sure Sobel didn't miss it. No matter what it was that Burke had dug up, it was ancient history, too remote in time to allow into evidence. More-over, Samara had been a child at the time. And what if she'd chosen to condense her name? So had Jaywalker, for that matter. Big deal. What mattered was that Samara was twenty-eight now. There was no way in hell Judge Sobel was going to permit Burke to question her about something she'd done when she'd been fourteen.

"It seems," said Burke, "that contrary to the defendant's earlier testimony that she left home because she didn't get any birthday presents, the facts are actually a little differ-ent. The real reason seems to have been that she was molested by one of her mother's boyfriends, a man by the name of Roger McBride. The defendant appears to have gotten even with Mr. McBride by assaulting him and then fleeing the state immediately afterward. And incidentally, according to my atlas, at least, Vigo County includes Prai-rie Creek."

"Assuming for the moment that this is all true," said the judge, "you're going to have a very hard time convincing me that it bears directly on her credibility. First, she was fourteen at the time. Second, it was a long time ago. Third, for all we know, her act may have been justified. And fourth, assault isn't one of those crimes, such as perjury or forgery, for example, that have much to do with truth-telling."

Jaywalker smiled. He couldn't have said it better himself.

"All true," said Burke. "Which is why The People con-cede we'd have no right to go into it on the issue of the de-fendant's credibility."

"And how else would you be entitled to bring it up?"

"As a prior similar act."

By that, Burke meant some previous act that could shed light not just on the defendant's credibility but on her having committed the crime itself. For example, proof that a defendant had robbed banks in the past with a unique *modus operandi*—say by presenting a demand note written in red crayon and illustrated with five happy faces—would be admissible to show that he'd robbed one more in precisely the same fashion.

"You've convinced me it was prior," said the judge. "But that it was an assault, and this case is, in effect, an assault causing death? That hardly meets the *similar* test."

"With all due respect," said Burke, "you're going to change your mind when you hear how she assaulted Mr. McBride. It seems she took a knife and plunged it into his chest, up to the hilt. It happened to miss his heart by an eighth of an inch. Apparently the blade wasn't quite long enough."

Jaywalker felt his knees go weak and almost buckle. All he could do was watch helplessly as Burke produced copies of four pages of material he said he'd received by fax that morning. There was an incident report, a follow-up report, a wanted notice and a copy of a photograph. Though it was grainy, black-and-white and of poor quality, there was no mistaking Samara's dark eyes peering out from the page, or her pouty lower lip.

Burke had been dead-on when he'd predicted that Judge Sobel would change his mind. And though Jaywalker argued long and hard, claiming remoteness, surprise, lack of adequate notice and denial of due process, he got nowhere. The one thing he couldn't argue was ambush, that Burke had known about the incident all along and had sat on it, waiting to spring it at the perfect moment. Jaywalker knew prosecutors who pulled stunts like that, and he wouldn't have been the least bit shy about accusing them of doing so. But he knew Tom Burke too well to even suggest it. Besides which, there was a perfect rebuttal to any claim of ambush. Had she chosen to, Samara could have told her lawyer about the incident herself, instead of waiting for the prosecutor to discover it, or fail to. If anyone had ambushed Jaywalker, it hadn't been Burke, it had been Samara.

"Mr. Jaywalker," said the judge, "I'm prepared to let Mr. Burke question the defendant about this, both the incident itself and the flight, including the name change. At the appropriate time, I'll instruct the jurors about how they may use the evidence and how they may not. That said, I suggest, as strongly as I possibly can, that you spend the next fifteen minutes talking to your client about taking a plea. We'll be in recess until ten-fifteen."

So first there'd been bottom, and now there was rock bottom.

He took Samara into one of the stairwells, where they wouldn't be in danger of being overheard by any of the jurors milling about.

"Is this where you ask me for a blow job?" she joked.

"You wish," he said. Then he looked her hard in the eye and asked her, "Does the name Samantha Musgrove mean anything to you?"

He expected her to say no, to deny it was her. In a way, he hoped she would. He had no idea how Burke had come up with the stuff, but it seemed unlikely it had been based upon fingerprint records. Samara—or Samantha, or whoever she was—had been fourteen at the time of the incident. That, plus the fact that it didn't appear she'd ever been arrested in connection with it, made it highly unlikely that she'd been fingerprinted. Had she been, it wouldn't have taken all this time to surface. Sure, the names were suspiciously similar and the locations virtually identical. And the photo certainly looked like a younger version of Samara. But suppose she were to insist that it wasn't her? What could Burke do about it, really, other than ask her the same questions over and over, only to hear her repeated denials?

"I'm Samantha Musgrove," Samara said instead. "Or at least I was, until I ran away from home."

So much for denial.

Jaywalker proceeded to tell Samara everything that had occurred in the robing room, right up to and including the judge's strong suggestion to work out a guilty plea. He even showed her copies of the documents Burke had supplied him with.

"Yeah, I stabbed that guy McGuire, or whatever his name was," she said. "I'm only sorry I didn't kill the bastard. Want to know what he did to me?"

Jaywalker nodded.

"He came up behind me, put a knife to my throat, pulled down my jeans and raped me, but I mean *hard*. And not even where you're supposed to rape someone, if you know what I mean."

Jaywalker nodded again, by way of acknowledging that he had a pretty good idea of what she meant by that.

"Afterwards, he was so damn drunk he fell asleep and started snoring, right there on the floor. So yeah, I rolled him over, took his knife out of his hand and tried to kill him with it. And I'd do it again today, if I got the chance. But Barry? I never touched him. I swear on my life. So you tell me. Am I supposed to plead guilty to something I didn't do because of something I did do fourteen years ago?"

"Maybe," said Jaywalker. "If it saves you ten years of your life, or something like that."

"Well, *fuck* it, I'm not going to do it. They can give me a hundred years, for all I care. I don't give a fuck."

Her bravado was matched only by her tears. Yet in the face of all the facts and all the evidence, and now with this prior similar act piled on as the icing on top of the prosecution's case, Samara still wasn't budging. And so help him, Jaywalker couldn't quite bring himself to the point of calling her a liar to her face. Because some tiny part of him still wasn't fully convinced she was lying about Barry's stabbing. In spite of how damning everything looked, his own internal jury was still out on the question of whether history had in fact repeated itself.

"Okay," he said, once she'd calmed down enough to listen to him. "I need you to do me a favor."

"What's that?"

"You can admit what you did to McBride, and you can deny that you stabbed Barry, any way you like. But try to go easy on the language. I mean personally, I've got no problem with it. But you use the word *fuck* more often in one sentence than a lot of those jurors have heard over a lifetime. Think you can manage that?"

"I'll try," said Samara, breaking into something more or less resembling a smile.

"And answer me one other thing, if you don't mind."

"What?"

"Why didn't you tell me about it?"

Samara's only answer was a shrug.

"After all this time, didn't you think you could trust me?"

"No," she said, "it wasn't that."

"What, then?"

"I almost told you the night we…the night I found the Seconal in my spice cabinet. Don't you remember?"

Jaywalker remembered the night. He nodded, though he wasn't quite sure what the connection was.

"I guess I was afraid that if I told you about the old stabbing, you'd never believe I was innocent, not in a million years…."

As guesses go, it was a pretty reasonable one.

"And as a result, you wouldn't have fought for me as hard."

The words stung him. In a single sentence, she'd knocked Jaywalker down to the level of every other lawyer in the world, the last place he wanted to be. But who could blame her? What it meant was that he'd failed her. In his egocentric concern over the prospect of losing his last trial, he had failed to convince Samara that he was different from all the rest of them. Who could possibly have expected her to understand that while the knowledge of the earlier stabbing might have been too much for every other defense lawyer in the world to have overcome, it wouldn't have mattered to him? That when it came time to go to war, Jaywalker fought for those he believed to be guilty no less than he fought for those he believed to be innocent?

Long ago, he'd heard that Abraham Lincoln had once boasted that he would never represent a guilty defendant. Lincoln might have been a great man, but in Jaywalker's book that one remark, if accurately quoted, branded him as an absolutely worthless criminal defense lawyer. Who was he to decide that help should be extended only to the virtuous and withheld from the sinners? To Jaywalker, it smacked of tax relief for only the wealthy. Luckily, and in spite of his gross misunderstanding of the defender's role, Lincoln had somehow managed to find other work, though, perhaps tellingly, as a Republican.

Matthew Sobel, who Jaywalker considered as fair and temperate a judge as there was in the system, couldn't conceal his disappointment when Jaywalker reported to him that there would be no guilty plea. He shook his head in something between disbelief and frustration, and the look on his face turned absolutely grave. It was obvious to Jaywalker that Sobel wasn't looking forward to sentencing Samara to life in prison. Yet that was exactly what the law would require him to do in the event of a conviction—an eventuality that was rapidly becoming a certainty.

To be fair to Samara, she did about as well as she possibly could have on the remainder of Burke's cross-examination, looking him squarely in the eye and answering every question he threw her way. She readily confessed to the fourteen-year-old stabbing, admitting that she'd done it at a point when her attacker had been sound asleep and no longer a threat to her. And she didn't flinch before answering that, yes, she'd tried to kill the man and had even assumed she'd succeeded in doing so. Two weeks later, she'd happened to pick up a newspaper in Reno and had recognized Roger McBride in a photo buried near the back of the paper. McBride, described as the "random victim of a deranged teenager," was said to have miraculously survived a near-death experience and was shown leaving the hospital in a wheelchair, accompanied by his wife and two daughters. A warrant had been issued for the teenager's arrest.

As forthcoming as Samara was about the old assault, she wouldn't give an inch when Burke attempted to establish a link between the McBride assault and the murder of Barry Tannenbaum, with Samara's rage proposed as the common denominator. On five consecutive occasions, Burke began his questions with the phrase, "Isn't it a fact," trying to get her to admit that she'd stabbed both men. She listened patiently to each question before answering, "No, it isn't a fact," five times. Of course, the questions were never meant for her in the first place. Burke was much too smart to expect her to suddenly find religion at this late stage of the game and confess her guilt, too smart even to hope that she might commit some Freudian slip of the tongue and give herself away, however slightly. No, his questions were for the jurors; he was giving them a sneak preview of his summation, only in question form. And their faces, every one of them as grave as the judge's had been earlier, told Jaywalker everything he needed to know.

Bottom?

Rock bottom?

Right now they were beneath the ocean floor itself. They were miles down, down where the molten iron core of the planet lay. Down where life as we know it cannot exist.

Whatever other cross-examination Burke had saved for Samara from the previous afternoon, he decided to leave it on his notepad, choosing instead to end with his devastating series of *Isn't-it-a-fact* questions.

Jaywalker managed to pry himself up from his seat and spend fifteen minutes on redirect. He had no real hope of rehabilitating Samara; she was way beyond rehabilitation by that point. But he couldn't let Burke have the last word, not with the jurors about to depart for the weekend. So he picked and chose from his notes, pretending it still mattered. He asked Samara when she'd first learned her husband had cancer; she replied that it hadn't been until Jaywalker himself had read Barry's autopsy report to her. Did she understand the meaning of the phrase, *a spouse's right to take against the will?* No, she'd never heard it and had no idea what the words meant.

Lame stuff like that.

When Burke avoided the temptation of overkill and declined to recross Samara, Jaywalker stood up and announced that the defense was resting. He tried to do it in his firmest, most confident voice, but he knew full well that he wasn't fooling anyone. Not the jurors, not the spectators, not his client, not the judge. Not even himself.

"And The People rest, as well," echoed Burke.

Judge Sobel read the jurors his usual admonitions. He instructed them to report back Monday morning for the lawyers' summations, the court's charge and their deliberations. He told them the court officers would be giving them additional instruction regarding bringing an overnight bag with toilet articles and a change of clothes, in the event that their deliberations were to go over to a second day. Jaywalker noticed that the judge seemed to go out of his way to avoid mentioning the term *sequestration,* much the way doctors of an earlier generation used to refrain from uttering the word *cancer.* But this being a murder trial, once the jurors were given the case to decide, they wouldn't be permitted to return to their homes, families and jobs until such time as they reached either a verdict or an intractable impasse. Jaywalker could have waived the sequestration rule, had he chosen to. But he actually liked the idea of jurors being locked up, even if only overnight and in some motel out by LaGuardia Airport. Let them get a taste of what it was like to sleep in a strange bed, doubled up with a roommate not of their own choosing, having been told what TV programs they could or couldn't watch and what newspapers they could or couldn't read. Maybe they would think twice before sending someone off to prison for years of infinitely tighter restrictions.

With the jurors excused, the judge spent the next forty-five minutes explaining what he intended to include in his charge to the jury. Jaywalker had a few additional requests and a couple of objections, but it was all pretty standard stuff. About the only point of contention was the stabbing of Roger McBride, the prior similar act, and the way in which the jury could and could not use it.

Then, just before one o'clock, Burke rose to make a request. Jaywalker had in fact been expecting it for some time now, dreading it. He'd even dared to think that Burke might somehow forget to do it, or decide not to. No such luck.

"Based on this morning's developments," Burke said in an even, untheatrical voice, "which reveal not only a prior stabbing to the chest of another victim, but also an admitted history of flight, complete with a name change, The People ask that the defendant's bail be exonerated at this time, and that she be remanded."

Jaywalker stood up, feigning shock and surprise. "My client has made herself available to the court without fail," he pointed out. "She wears a bracelet around her ankle. It contains a GPS transponder that tells the corrections department and the district attorney's office where she is at any given moment, within sixteen feet, I believe it is. Should she cut it off, an electronic signal would go out in a fraction of a second, allowing law enforcement to literally beat her to the airport by an hour. Considering all—"

Judge Sobel held up one hand. *Here it comes,* thought Jaywalker, *the extreme likelihood of a conviction, coupled with the Indiana warrant, when weighed against the relatively minimal inconvenience to the defendant of a weekend spent on Rikers Island.*

"I'm satisfied that the present bail conditions are sufficient to insure the defendant's return to court," said the judge. "Should she be so foolish as to prove me wrong, the law gives me extremely wide latitude at the time of sentencing. Do I make myself clear, Mrs. Tannenbaum?"

"Yes, Your Honor."

"Have a good weekend, everyone."

Jaywalker found himself standing there like an idiot, realizing for the first time that he'd been on the verge of tears. He managed to nod in the judge's direction and silently mouth the words, "Thank you." He didn't dare try to say anything out loud.

28

PROCRASTINATION AND PANIC

Jaywalker was by nature a procrastinator. He'd realized it early on in school, when he'd found it all but impossible to tackle a homework assignment, however mundane and simple, until the last conceivable moment. "Don't worry, I'll do it," he'd explained on one occasion to his father, a stickler for advance preparation. "It's just that I work better under pressure."

He'd been five at the time.

That said, Jaywalker had been working on summing up in Samara's case, in one way or another, for a year and a half now. If that sounds like an exaggeration, it isn't. As soon as Jaywalker got a case—and he'd gotten Samara's a year ago August—he began to think of it in terms of an argument, a debate. What facts were beyond contesting? What others were less certain, but still worth conceding in the name of gaining credibility with the jury? And what one or two issues did that leave to go to war over? Then he would print the word SUMMATION at the top of a sheet of paper, jot down some preliminary thoughts and place the page in a folder bearing the same title. As his investigation of the case progressed over time, he would add to the folder, a word here, an idea there, even a bit of specific language that he felt might resonate with a jury someday.

Over the months that followed, the folder would gradually grow thick with additions, revisions and modifications, until it contained, in rough form, just about everything that would go into his summation. About all that remained was for the trial itself to unfold and reveal just how closely the actual testimony would track Jaywalker's expectations. Sometimes there were a few surprises, necessitating minor modifications. More often, there weren't. If you worked hard enough before a trial, not only were you ready for what took place, you actually *dictated* what took place, caused it to unfold precisely the way you'd planned.

Samara's case had been different.

Samara's case, from the very beginning, had defied all the rules. In one sense, the facts were barely in dispute. Someone who'd been at Barry Tannenbaum's apartment had taken a knife and plunged it into his chest, causing his death. Samara had been there at the time it had happened, or pretty close to it. The two of them had been heard arguing loudly, and she'd left minutes afterward. Confronted by detectives the following day, she'd lied about having been there, and about whether or not she'd argued with Barry. A search of her apartment had revealed a knife consistent in all ways with the murder weapon, a blouse she admitted owning and a towel. All three items had Barry's blood on them.

It only got worse from there.

Samara, who'd knowingly signed a prenuptial agreement leaving her with nothing were she to divorce Barry, also believed she could be disinherited by him under the terms of his will. And as far as she knew, her husband had no life insurance. Barry was in poor health, with cancer and heart disease. Although she denied knowing about the cancer, she acknowledged that Barry was obsessed with his health and fearful he was dying. A month before he actually did, she'd signed her name to an application for a twenty-five-million-dollar policy on his life. For it to pay off,

Barry would have had to die within six months, though not of heart disease or cancer.

Nobody other than Samara appeared to have been in Barry's apartment around the time he was murdered. No one but she had been in the home where the knife, the blouse and the towel were subsequently found.

And now, to top things off, it turned out that once before in her life, Samara had taken a knife and stabbed a man in the chest. Although, by the grace of God or the fortuitous intervention of a couple of millimeters of human tissue, the difference depending upon one's particular set of beliefs, that earlier victim had managed to survive.

The problem with Samara's case was that absolutely everything was beyond contesting. Everything, that was, except whether it had been Samara or somebody else who'd murdered Barry. Early on in the trial, Jaywalker had told the jurors that it had been somebody else. He'd even hinted at four possible suspects. But one by one, the testimony had cleared them. Anthony Mazzini, the super, might have milled around Barry's apartment after letting the detectives in, but other than that he was above suspicion. Kenneth Redding, the co-op board president, had had a minor disagreement with Barry but hardly a reason to kill him. Alan Manheim, the recently fired lawyer, might or might not have stolen a lot of money from Barry, but he was fully prepared to defend himself. And William Smythe, Barry's accountant, had come off on the witness stand as a straight shooter. More to the point, none of those individuals, not one of them, had had access to Samara's town house. Even if one of them, or all of them acting together, had murdered Barry, there was still no way they could have gotten the knife, the blouse and the towel into Samara's place.

So who did that leave? The detectives? At least they would have had the opportunity to plant the evidence, assuming they'd wanted to. But why? Well, it went something like this. A murder's been committed. Who do the police immediately suspect? The husband or wife, boy-friend or girlfriend, that's who. Why? Well, the police would have us think it's because statistics show that some-one close to the victim is most often the guilty party. But those statistics are fatally skewed from the outset. Once the authorities fix on a suspect, abuses immediately begin to creep into the process. Other possible suspects are allowed to disappear entirely or fade from consideration, to be re-membered only twelve or fifteen years later, when some newly tested piece of DNA evidence walks someone out of prison. But in the moment, all attention gets focused on the person closest to the victim. Careless statements made by that person, minor inconsistencies in his or her story, and anything short of an airtight alibi, soon turn the police's suspicion into certainty. A confession follows. Never mind whether it happens to be full or partial, consistent with the facts or at odds with them, true or false. An arrest is made, a favorite reporter is alerted, and a perp walk is arranged. That afternoon, just in time for the evening news, the police commissioner holds a triumphant press conference. The media eat it up and spit it out, and a public on the verge of panic is assured it can rest easy. The murder, it turns out, was nothing but a domestic squabble gone bad. No random killer remains at large, walking their streets and stalking their loved ones.

And why did the police focus on that spouse or lover or best friend in the first place? Because it was easy, that's why. They knew right off the bat who they were looking for and where to do the looking. Crime solved, killer ap-prehended, case closed, end of story.

But could Jaywalker really stand up in front of the jurors and tell them with a straight face that the detectives, having actually found the knife, the blouse and the towel at Barry's apartment, or inside some trash can or storm drain nearby, had decided to plant the items in Samara's town house out

of their own misplaced certainty of her guilt? And even if
they'd done that—already a leap of gigantic length—that
still didn't explain who'd murdered Barry in the first place.

That was Friday night.

By Saturday morning, Jaywalker had decided that the
best way to present his defense would be to come right out
and admit to the jury that he had no idea who'd murdered
Barry, except that it hadn't been Samara. And the genius
of the American court system, he would explain, was that
he didn't have to know, and neither did they. Remember,
he would tell them, the defendant has no burden of proof.
It wasn't the defense's job to convince you who actually
committed the murder. It was the prosecution's job to
convince you that Samara did it, and they had to convince
you beyond all reasonable doubt. So the jurors mustn't let
Tom Burke get away with an argument that went *If not
Samara, who?* That wasn't good enough. And if, during deliberations, a fellow juror were to try to make that argument, they should soundly reject it.

You'll be given a verdict sheet, he would tell them, *right
before you begin your deliberations. It's going to list the
crime that Samara's charged with: murder. Right after
that, it's going to ask you to check one of two boxes,
"Guilty" or "Not guilty." After "Not guilty," there's not
going to be a P.S., "Well, if 'Not guilty,' please explain who
did do it."*

In other words, he would tell them, *you're not being
asked to play detectives here, to solve the crime. We've got
plenty of detectives who get paid good taxpayer money to
do just that. Nor are you being called upon to play God,
to somehow transport yourselves back a year and a half
ago in order to try to divine what might have happened that
August night. You are jurors. Your job, as awesomely important as it is, is at the same time magnificently simple.*

He crossed off *magnificently* and substituted *majestically.*

Your job is to pass judgment, he would tell them, *to pass
judgment on the evidence that you heard in this courtroom. Does that evidence convince you that it was Samara
Tannenbaum who murdered her husband? And does it
convince you of that beyond all reasonable doubt? Your
answer must be a resounding* "No!"

Was *ringing* better than *resounding*? How about both?
Okay, *a ringing and resounding* "No!"

Not bad.

By Saturday night Jaywalker's kitchen floor was littered
with torn pieces of paper, all of them discarded arguments
that at one moment had sounded like possibilities but
twenty minutes later had struck him as totally worthless.

Maybe he needed to focus on a single suspect.

He went back to his List of Four. Anthony Mazzini, the
super, was a nonstarter. Among other things, the jurors
would never believe he had the intellect to pull off such an
elaborate frame. Kenneth Redding, the co-op board president, simply hadn't had enough at stake to do it. And
William Smythe, Barry's accountant, had come off too
squeaky-clean to seem capable of murder.

That left Alan Manheim, Barry's recently fired personal
lawyer. Jaywalker reviewed his notes from Manheim's testimony. On direct, Burke had had Manheim admit that he
and Barry had had a "falling-out." They'd parted company
over Barry's accusations of embezzlement six months
before Barry's murder. True, Manheim denied the charge,
even to the point of boasting that shortly after leaving
Barry's employ, he'd landed a better paying position.

Jaywalker had gotten Manheim to offer the opinion that
he'd been underpaid by Barry, even at the rate of over four
million dollars annually, counting his bonus. And the
amount of that little alleged embezzlement? Jaywalker
would remind the jurors of that. In Manheim's own words,
two hundred and twenty-seven million dollars. Jaywalker

would repeat the numbers, as though in absolute awe of them. There were people on the jury who felt lucky to make two hundred and twenty-seven *dollars* a week, including overtime. There were jurors who couldn't *count* to two hundred and twenty-seven million, let alone visualize the significance of that kind of wealth.

Manheim had had everything to lose. His money, his reputation, his new job, his law license. Not to mention his freedom. *That's grand larceny Barry Tannenbaum accused him of,* Jaywalker would tell the jurors. *That's about as grand as larceny can get, as a matter of fact.* Was that reason enough for Manheim to want Barry Tannenbaum out of the way? Here was how he would like them to think of it, Jaywalker would tell them. Alan Manheim, the alleged thief and embezzler, didn't just have a reason to kill Barry Tannenbaum, he had *two hundred and twenty-seven million* reasons.

Manheim had come off as a terrible witness, a fact only enhanced because it had been the prosecution who'd called him in the first place. He was sleazy, smug and self-serving. If Jaywalker were to end up deciding to point the jurors in the direction of one suspect to the exclusion of all others, Alan Manheim was certainly going to be his guy.

Jaywalker turned the lights off. It was past two in the morning, and he suspected he was no longer operating on all cylinders. He knew if he were to refocus and read back the last of the notes he'd written, the stuff about Alan Manheim, they, too, would end up in pieces on the kitchen floor. So he told himself his thinking was getting too fuzzy to continue. And then he told himself something else, the sacred creed of all procrastinators.

There was always tomorrow.

But as seductive a lover as she can be at first, procrastination makes a hideously cruel mistress. He who allows himself to be folded into her welcoming arms buys no true respite. The warmth and safe harbor she promises him are but an illusion, a simple projection of his own needs. All he ends up with is pure agony, drawn out, intensified and robbed of the tiniest measure of comfort or the least semblance of peace.

It would be hours before sleep would come to Jaywalker, and when it did, it came in fits and starts, punctuated by fragments of dreams that came and went, but refused to make sense. Alan Manheim appeared in one of them, laughing at Jaywalker from the witness stand, the pupils of his eyes dilated and transformed into dollar signs. "But how could I have gotten into her home," he taunted, "in order to hide the evidence?" Jaywalker's wife was in a second dream, gently scolding him for not emptying the dishwasher or being able to win the impossible case, the one out of ten nobody could win. In yet another, a serene Roger McBride was being wheeled from the hospital by his adoring wife and children, a knife still stuck in his chest. His hands were folded pontifically in his lap, clasped around something that at first glance looked like a large metal cross. Only when the wheelchair drew nearer was Jaywalker able to see that it wasn't a cross at all but an enormous jailer's key.

By Sunday morning Jaywalker was experiencing the first symptoms of panic. He wasn't talking to himself yet, or pacing the floor. In fact, he was still in what he considered his constructive mode, jotting ideas down on paper as they occurred to him, then discarding them as soon as it occurred to him that they were worthless. So it was a controlled panic still, but an incremental step along the way to full-blown, out-and-out hysteria.

It had happened before, in other cases, preparing for other summations. Arguments that had seemed airtight suddenly developed leaks and needed patching, reinforcing or restructuring. But there'd always been a solution; it had simply been a matter of holding the problem up to the light, identifying the weakness and addressing it.

Samara's case was, as it was in almost every other respect, different. It defied repair. It was almost as though it had taken on a life of its own at some point, a willfulness, and was intent on proving to Jaywalker that whatever he did and however he did it, it didn't matter; the evidence would change, mutate, morph and reinvent itself in order to defeat him. Look at how he'd proposed not one but four possible suspects for the jury to consider. Back comes Detective Roger Ramseyer to blow them all out of the water with new fingerprint checks. And Samara. Just when it had looked as though she'd survived the worst of Tom Burke's cross-examination, up pops the fourteen-year-old incident to make her look like a serial stabber.

It was even happening now with Jaywalker's summation. He'd promised the jurors in his opening that it would be the very strength of the prosecution's case that would point them to the realization that someone had to be framing Samara. Well, he'd been right about the first part of the equation. The evidence against Samara *was* overwhelming, more overwhelming than even Jaywalker could have imagined. But the second part was missing in action. Nowhere did the evidence break down of its own weight; nowhere did it reveal meaningful cracks or gaps that in any way suggested innocence on Samara's part or guilt on anyone else's.

So what did you do when you couldn't sum up?

It was a question Jaywalker had never been forced to answer before, not in more than twenty years of trying cases. And even as it occurred to him, he forced himself to ignore it. There had to be a way to win this case, there simply had to be. It was just a matter of his not having figured it out yet. It was just a matter of time.

Something he was rapidly running out of.

29

BUTTERFLIES

Jaywalker arrived at the courthouse neurotically early, as he always did on summation day. He showed up drawn, pale, gaunt and tired. But inside, he was pumped on adrenaline. Over the past two weeks, he'd slept an average of three hours a night and had lost a total of seventeen pounds. His good-luck suit hung loosely enough on him by now that, had he wanted to, he could have had the buttons moved and worn it double-breasted. His hair was combed, more or less, and he was clean-shaven, but even shaving had extracted its price. Jaywalker shaved two hundred and fifty times a year without incident. (He took weekends and holidays off.) He could shave with one eye closed. Hell, he could have shaved with both eyes closed, if he'd had to. But on summation day, he always managed to cut himself and then to bleed like a hemophiliac. Always. One time he'd had to sum up with tiny pieces of toilet tissue stuck to his chin and neck, in order to keep from bleeding onto his shirt and tie, his notes, or even the jurors in the front row of the box. They'd acquitted his client, they told him afterward, not so much because they'd doubted his guilt, but because they'd been afraid that a conviction might have pushed Jaywalker over the line, and made him go home and finish the job.

Chances were they'd only been kidding. Then again, did it really matter? An acquittal was an acquittal in Jaywalker's book, and he wasn't about to apologize for it.

The courtroom was packed by the time Jaywalker entered. More of the media were on hand than during the testimony itself. Summations were easy for the press; they produced ready-made sound bites, perfect for the evening news or the following morning's print columns. And from the beginning, this case had had everything. A beautiful young woman from an obscure, impoverished past. Dark hints of sex abuse, persistent rumors of prostitution, veiled accusations of gold digging. A much older man, eccentric, powerful, fabulously wealthy, three times married and three times divorced. Sprinkle in generous measures of infidelity, jealousy and humiliation. Take one fatal stabbing to the heart. Add a murder weapon, hidden and found in the wife's home, stained with the husband's blood. Stir until a perfect motive reveals itself. And, just before serving, finish it off with an old secret, newly unearthed, a dark secret of rape and revenge.

Even the lawyers, it seemed, had been perfectly cast for their parts. An earnest young prosecutor who'd worked his way up in one of the best offices in the country, without having checked his good nature or sense of proportion at the courtroom door. Against him, an iconoclastic, rule-breaking veteran with a reputation for being among the very best in the business, particularly when it came time to sum up. And there would be no two-day Johnnie Cochrane filibuster from him. Whatever he had to say, they knew, Jaywalker could be counted on to compact it into the morning session and then sit down. They knew it not because he'd confided in them that he would, but because he'd always kept it short. He was hardly one of their darlings, Jaywalker. He might be ten times the lawyer that some of them were, but he would never sit for an interview,

tip them off to his trial strategy, or say something clever
when a microphone was shoved in his face. Still, he was a
winner, and the public loved winners.

Yet this time there was even more.

The media had long ago learned of Jaywalker's difficul-
ties with the disciplinary committee. His suspension had
actually appeared in print, though only buried deep in the
pages of the *New York Law Journal,* a daily whose circu-
lation, beyond actual members of the bar, ranked it right
up there with such heralded publications as *Klezmer Music
Enthusiast, Tadpole Lovers' World* and *The Big Apple
Alternate-Side-of-the-Street-Parking Almanac.* As the beginning of Samara's trial had drawn near, Judge Sobel had
circulated a request among the media, asking them to
refrain from reporting on Jaywalker's suspension and the
facts underlying it, including one particular event said to
have occurred in a stairwell of the very courthouse where
the main drama was to be played out. The media had
grudgingly complied, on the proviso that the moment the
jurors were sequestered to begin their deliberations—and
presumably insulated from the news—the media could run
with the story in all its sordid details. So tonight's commen-
taries and tomorrow's articles would be assured of having
yet one more enticing garnish to top them off, a juicy bit
of dirt about one of the key players.

Nothing like a little human interest to give a lift to an
otherwise flaccid story.

The butterflies were back.

Even before he took his seat at the defense table, a good
twenty minutes before the judge took the bench, Jaywalker
could feel them beginning to stir. It was almost as though
they had ears and knew to begin beating their wings as soon
as the clerk said, "All rise!" or the judge announced, "Bring
in the jury." As if on cue, they would take flight then, hundreds of them, thousands of them. They absolutely tortured

Jaywalker, causing an excruciating sensation to his mid-section, filling his ears with a high-pitched ringing sound and pushing him to the very edge of nausea. But they fueled him, too, the butterflies did. And in a very real sense, they made him what he was.

Judge Sobel spent a few minutes telling the jurors what summations were. Mostly he told them what they weren't: evidence. Jaywalker wasn't overly fond of that particular instruction. Had it been up to him, he would have dispensed with the evidence altogether and had the jurors instead decide the case purely on the basis of the summations. Particularly Samara's case.

Now the judge turned from the jury box to the defense table. "Mr. Jaywalker," he said. Nothing more, nothing less.

By the time he would sit down again, Jaywalker would have spoken to the jurors for close to two and a half hours, without a break and without glancing at his notes more than once or twice, just to make sure he hadn't left anything out. He reminded them what they'd learned as far back as jury selection, that it wasn't their job to figure out whether or not Samara had killed her husband; it was their job to decide if the prosecution had proved that she had, and had proved it beyond all reasonable doubt. He pointed out how totally different those two jobs were.

He retold Samara's life story for them, from being raped in a trailer in Prairie Creek, Indiana, to her escape to Las Vegas, to becoming Mrs. Barry Tannenbaum in New York. He posed the extreme unlikelihood that a woman of her small size and strength, even if she'd wanted to, could have plunged a knife up to the hilt into someone's chest. He pointed out the total absurdity of the notion that she would have then saved the murder weapon, still caked with her husband's blood, as some sort of souvenir for the police to find. He warned them of the terrible danger of convicting someone on nothing but circumstantial evidence. He exalted the majesty of the presumption of innocence, the logic of placing the burden of proof upon the prosecution, and the special wisdom of a system that demanded proof beyond all reasonable doubt. He reminded them about Alan Manheim and his two hundred and twenty-seven million reasons for having wanted Barry Tannenbaum dead. But even as he did that, he cautioned them not to saddle the defense with the burden of proving Manheim's guilt, or anyone else's. The only burden of proof, he told them over and over again, was squarely upon the prosecution. The defense didn't have to prove or disprove anything.

He spoke from the lectern and moved around the courtroom, returning periodically to where Samara sat. He quoted from the testimony and used the exhibits. His voice rose and fell, and toward the very end he was reduced to a hoarse, gravelly whisper, which served only to accentuate his final words, which he used to beseech the jurors to find Samara not guilty.

Those who made it a habit to show up for Jaywalker summations—and there were literally scores who did exactly that—would afterward agree among themselves that his closing argument on behalf of Samara Tannenbaum had to rank among his very best ever, particularly if one were to consider what he'd been up against. It was crisp, dramatic, well modulated, emotional and extraordinary in every sense imaginable. In a word, it was everything it could possibly have been.

Everything, that is, but good enough.

Tom Burke delivered his summation early that same afternoon. He began by conceding that "Things aren't always what they seem to be. But," he quickly added, "sometimes they *are*." From there he led the jurors through an exhaustive and methodical review of the evidence that firmly linked Samara to the murder. Her presence at Barry's apartment right around the time of his death. Their heated argument. Her lies to the detectives the next day. The murder weapon and other items found in her town house, complete with Barry's blood. The life insurance policy, along with Samara's belief that it was the only way she would end up with anything from Barry. And, finally, the fourteen-year-old assault, which, Burke argued, placed Samara's unique signature on Barry Tannenbaum's murder.

Listening to the argument and looking at the jurors, Jaywalker found himself wondering how they could possibly reject Burke's analysis. There was simply no way that they could fail to convict Samara. He was reduced to fantasizing that there might be some closet weirdo on the jury, someone who would refuse to deliberate or might hold out irrationally, leading to an eleven-to-one hung jury and a mistrial. What a win that would be. He started bargaining with the god he didn't believe in, offering up small sacrifices in exchange for that lone holdout. He would stop drinking. He would start eating three meals a day. He would file his back taxes, visit his daughter, make a dentist appointment, go for that PSA test he kept putting off.

At one point, as quietly as he could, Jaywalker reached for his briefcase. He located his jury folder, slipped his chart out of it and scanned the notes he'd scribbled almost two weeks ago. Twelve names, twelve occupations, twelve sets of notations, ratings and question marks. But, so far as he could tell, no indication of a weirdo among them.

Burke sat down after an hour and a half. As Jaywalker had long ago learned, it generally takes less time to say something than it takes to say nothing.

Judge Sobel took just under an hour to charge the jury. It was quarter of four by the time he finished ruling on the lawyers' objections, exceptions and additional requests. Turning back to the jury box, he announced, "You may now retire to begin your deliberations."

And the butterflies came back.

They came back because that first hour of deliberations was always a dangerous time. If there was going to be an acquittal driven purely by emotion—and by now Jaywalker knew that was the only kind of an acquittal he had a right to hope for—it had to come quickly. It had to come before the jurors had a chance to settle back and begin to analyze the evidence. On the other hand, there were juries that began by taking a preliminary vote to see where everyone stood. Jaywalker could easily imagine this jury deciding to do just that, only to realize that all twelve of them had cast their ballots for conviction.

5:00.

An hour had gone by, and nothing had happened. No quick verdict, either guilty or not guilty. Bit by bit, the butterflies landed, folded their wings and sat still. But Jaywalker knew only too well how lightly they slept. The instant there was the slightest noise from the jury room, even if it turned out to be a single buzzer signifying nothing more than a desire for a fresh pitcher of water or a look at some mundane exhibit, the butterflies would take flight again.

5:45.

With six o'clock approaching, the question on all lips was, what was the judge going to do about dinner? Was he going to break for it soon and bring the jury back afterward for more deliberations? Or would he instead let them work for another couple of hours, with the jurors then taken to a hotel immediately following their dinner? Some judges even gave their deliberating juries the option of choosing. Whenever that happened, the jurors would huddle and answer through their foreperson, and Jaywalker would always try to read their response like tea leaves, searching for the tiniest indication that they were close to a verdict, or digging in for lengthy deliberations.

He read everything there was to read. He looked for

tips from the court officers, who liked him not only because he was a former DEA agent, but because he was a civil servant at heart, one of them. They hung out by the door to the jury room and usually had a pretty good idea of what was happening on the other side. Were the jurors arguing, fighting, shouting down a dissenting voice? Were they carefully working their way through the testimony, witness by witness? Or had they stopped talking to each other altogether? Jaywalker needed to know. He needed to know which way they were leaning, how they were split, and whether they were making progress or hopelessly divided. If he knew those things, or at least had a pretty good idea, he would know whether to urge the judge to declare a mistrial, or to argue that the jurors should be given more time. And knowing which position to take could make all the difference in the world.

He even read lunch orders, Jaywalker did. He'd get the clerk to give him a peek at the list of sandwiches and beverages the jurors submitted each morning of their sequestration. In one particular case he'd tried a few years back, Jaywalker had come across an order requesting eleven ham-and-Swiss sandwiches on hard rolls, and one peanut butter-and-bacon on light white toast with the crust cut off. Right then he'd known he had a hung jury, eleven to one.

6:10.

Judge Sobel told the lawyers that he intended to let the jury deliberate for another hour before sending them to dinner and a hotel. Jaywalker voiced no objection. As far as he was concerned, the window for a quick emotional acquittal had already slammed shut. The danger right now was of a *Don't-lock-us-up, we'll-reach-a-verdict-soon* conviction. He would sweat out every one of the next sixty minutes, he and his butterflies.

And Samara?

It was hard to tell. About the last thing she struck Jaywalker as being was a religious person. Yet looking at her
now, as she sat alone toward the very back of the courtroom, he had to marvel at her composure. Didn't she know
what was going on?

From time to time, he would wander over and sit down
next to her, though whether the gesture was made to offer
her comfort or to receive it from her, he couldn't have
answered with certainty. But each time he joined her, it
would only be for a few minutes. Soon it would become
clear that their metabolisms were totally out of synch, he
with his frenzied hordes of butterflies, she with her strange,
calm composure.

He was reminded of a young woman he'd once come
across in an emergency room. Jaywalker had been there
because he'd dislocated a shoulder in a Saturday morning
pickup basketball game and was waiting to have it popped
back into place. The woman, who wore a gauzy purple
shawl over her head and spoke only Spanish, was there on
much more serious business. Her three-year-old son had
fallen three stories from an unprotected window onto the
asphalt pavement below and was clinging to life. Yet she
sat there in the waiting area the entire time, her hands
clasped together, a beatific smile on her face. From time
to time, he could hear her speak the words, *"Si dios
quiere."* If it's God's will.

What a blessing, he'd thought back then.

What lunacy, he thought now.

Jaywalker found out a little later that the boy had
already been dead when he'd arrived at the hospital. He
learned that from the doctor who popped his shoulder
back into its socket. The boy had probably died right
there on the pavement, the doctor told him, or in the ambulance. They just hadn't gotten around to telling his
mother yet.

Samara, too, was already dead. But no one had gotten

around to telling *her,* either. So she sat there now, comforted by her faith or her innocence, or whatever else it was that allowed her to get through this.

6:33.

The buzzer sounded.

The butterflies erupted into flight, and Jaywalker could actually feel his heart begin to fibrillate. He held his breath, waiting for a second buzz. Two buzzes meant a verdict; one signified nothing but a question or request of some sort.

There had only been one.

He allowed himself to exhale and take a new breath. The fibrillation gradually subsided. This was how his heart would give out, Jaywalker felt quite certain. He would die waiting for the second buzzer to sound.

A court officer appeared with a note. He was a friend of Jaywalker's, and as the two of them made eye contact, the officer pursed his lips and shook his head from side to side, almost imperceptibly, but not quite.

Fuck.

Dear Judge Sobel:

We the jury are very close to reaching a unanimous verdict, but first we have a question. Are we allowed to find the defendant guilty, and recommend mercy at the time of her sentence, because of her past?

Stanley Merkel
Foreman

Fuck, fuck, fuck.

So this is how it ends, thought Jaywalker. For Samara,

for him, for the whole stupid business of having decided to be a criminal defense lawyer in the first place.

The judge was summoned to come down from his chambers. Even before he arrived, the media began appearing, filtering into the courtroom. So far as Jaywalker knew, nobody had told them there was a note, much less what it said. But they knew. The fuckers knew. A couple of them tried to talk to him. Those who knew him knew enough to steer clear.

He walked back to where Samara sat. The expression on her face told him that while she still might be composed, she wasn't stupid, and she wasn't oblivious.

"Not good, huh?"

"Not good."

He told her what the note said. He didn't have to tell her what it meant. She nodded. He decided she was probably in shock, and that was why she could remain so calm.

The judge appeared, and Jaywalker led Samara to the defense table and sat down next to her. Sobel informed the lawyers that he intended to bring the jurors in and tell them that while they were free to make any recommendation they wanted, they needed to understand that sentencing was the province of the court, and he would feel free to reject their recommendation or even ignore it altogether, should it come to that.

Jaywalker objected. He wanted the judge to forbid the jurors from making any recommendations. If they felt Samara deserved mercy, they should acquit her.

Sobel said he would stick to his answer.

6:51.

As the jurors file in, they seem to give the defense table a wider berth as they pass it on their way to the jury box. They studiously refuse every chance to make eye contact. They study their hands, their feet, the judge, each other. And Tom Burke. They look like they've come from a funeral or a wake, held for someone very young, someone who hadn't been expected to die.

Jaywalker stares at them, trying to make it even harder for them. The only thing he gets in return is a fleeting glance from Juror Number 8, Carmelita Rosado, the kindergarten teacher. Yet even in that fleeting glance, he can see that her eyes are glassy, suggesting that she's been crying.

He grabs that scrap of information and holds on to it for dear life. He drags Samara onto it with him, and together they cling to it as tightly as they can.

"Will the foreman please rise," says the clerk.

Mr. Merkel stands.

"In the case of The People of the State of New York versus Samara Tannenbaum, has the jury reached a verdict?"

More butterflies, more fibrillation.

"No."

"Thank you. Please be seated."

It has only been a formality, one of the many rituals that take place during any trial. Yet even knowing that, and knowing full well from their note that the jurors *haven't* reached a verdict, for Jaywalker the little charade has amounted to a near-death experience. As for Samara, who doesn't know the rules of the ritual, he can't even begin to imagine what it must have been like. But outwardly, at least, she refuses to crumble.

The judge reads the jurors' note aloud and responds to it as he earlier indicated he would. When Mr. Merkel raises his hand with a question, the judge politely refuses to hear it. Instead, he sends the jurors back to the jury room, with instructions to communicate through another note.

So five minutes later there's another buzz, another onset of fibrillation and another note.

Dear Judge Sobel:

We the jury are disappointed in your answer, but will abide by it. At this point, we are extremely close to reaching a unanimous verdict. We request that you allow us to continue our deliberations until 8:00 p.m., to give us a chance to resolve our differences. If we are unable to do it by then, we would like to stop for the evening.

Stanley Merkel
Foreman

With both lawyers in agreement, Judge Sobel composes a note of his own and has it delivered to the jury room. Essentially, it informs the jurors that their request will be granted.

7:00.

One hour to get through.

By now it's absolutely clear to Jaywalker that the jury stands eleven-to-one for conviction, or at best ten-to-two. From her glassy eyes, he guesses that Carmelita Rosado is his holdout. If there's another, he'll put his money on Juror Number 10, Angelina Olivetti, the actress waiting tables between casting calls. Two young women, both on the quiet side. Jaywalker thought about challenging both of them, but ended up having to save his peremptories for other jurors he feared more. While neither Rosado nor Olivetti struck him as particularly defense oriented, he was at least able to take comfort from the fact that they seemed weak. In other words, while they might go along with the majority, they weren't leaders. They weren't the kind of jurors likely to organize a stampede to convict Samara.

Now that same weakness has suddenly turned into a liability. Will the two of them, or one of them, if that's what it's already down to, have the strength to withstand the pressure now being applied by the rest of the jurors?

"Where were you during the testimony, on another planet or something?"

"Weren't you listening?"

"Are you saying the rest of us are all wrong?"

"What part of 'Guilty' don't you get?"

"You know you're the only thing that's standing between us and going home, don't you?"

"As long as you know you're the one who's locking us up in some godforsaken, flea-bag motel."

"I don't want to say anything, but I've got an eighty-six-year-old mother at home, waiting for me to give her her insulin shot and put her to bed. But I'm sure you couldn't care less."

7:30.

Halfway there.

According to one court officer, there have been a few raised voices in the jury room but no outright shouting. Shouting would be good, a suggestion that someone has dug in and is being stubborn. Raised voices are harder to read.

7:46.

The same court officer reports to Jaywalker that he's heard some crying from what sounds like a woman juror. Crying is bad. Crying can only mean despair at having to convict, coupled with frustration over not being able to force the judge to be lenient. Crying is very bad.

7:48.

Has the clock stopped moving? Has someone been tampering with it?

7:50.

Jaywalker can no longer sit still. His bladder has been calling to him for a half an hour now, but he's afraid to leave the courtroom, afraid that as soon as he does, the buzzer will sound twice, afraid that his leaving the court-room will *cause* that to happen. So he paces the floor, out of nervousness, and to keep from wetting his pants. If he can just hold out for another ten minutes, he figures, so can Carmelita Rosado or Angelina Olivetti.

Or so his magical thinking goes.

7:57.

Judge Sobel reappears and takes the bench. Jaywalker and Samara resume their places at the defense table, Burke at the prosecution's. Jaywalker's legs are crossed tightly, his knees knocking together almost audibly. *Let them think it's nerves,* he tells himself. He remembers his former client, the one who used to wet himself every time he had to stand before the judge unless Jaywalker was there to hold his hand and squeeze it tightly.

"It's not eight o'clock yet," says Burke.

"Bring in the jury," says the judge.

"Would the foreman please rise."

Mr. Merkel stands.

"Mr. Foreman, in the case of The People of the State of New York versus Samara Tannenbaum, has the jury reached a verdict?"

"No, not yet."

Jaywalker exhales.

As soon as the jurors had been led out to a late dinner and an even later overnight stay, Tom Burke rose and renewed his application to have Samara remanded. "It's obvious to all of us that the jury is on the verge of—"

"Excuse me," said Jaywalker, also rising, "but I'm on the verge of wetting my pants. I need a three-minute break. Then I'll be happy to come back and talk about this for as long as you like."

"There's nothing to talk about," said Judge Sobel. "Mr. Burke, if you're afraid the defendant is going to flee, station your detectives outside her building tonight, front and back. Mrs. Tannenbaum, I trust you'll be here promptly at nine-thirty tomorrow morning?"

"Yes, Your Honor."

"Mr. Jaywalker. Mr. Jaywalker?"

But Jaywalker was already halfway down the aisle. Magical thinking or not, his strategy seemed to have worked. Now if only the janitorial crew hadn't already locked the door to the men's room, it would be an unmitigated triumph.

To think about it, all that had really happened was that Samara wouldn't be convicted tonight. Tomorrow, of course, would be another story. Right now, that tiniest of victories felt like pure nirvana to Jaywalker. It felt almost as good, in fact, as it did when a turn of the knob succeeded in opening the men's room door.

30

Washing his hands in the men's room sink, Jaywalker happened to look up and catch his reflection in the mirror. Neither the full-length crack in the glass nor the accumulation of city grime and cigarette tar could diminish the breadth of the grin on his face. He closed his eyes, took a deep breath and silently thanked his *I-know-there's-no-God-but-just-in-case-I'm-wrong* for having granted the night's reprieve. Anyone who thought you spelled relief with the brand name of an antacid had it all wrong. Relief was making it to eight o'clock without a conviction. Relief was making it to the men's room without a catastrophe.

When Jaywalker opened his eyes, the grin was still there. It was still there as he checked the paper towel dispenser, with, as Detective Bonfiglio might have put it, *negative results*. It was still there as he shook his hands dry, or at least tried his best to. It was still there when he opened the door, stepped out into the hallway and found himself face-to-face with Samara.

"What's so funny?" she wanted to know.

"Nothing," he said. "Everything. We're alive. We're coming back tomorrow. Somebody in that jury room still believes in you."

"And you?" she asked, looking up into his eyes, cutting

off all escape routes, leaving him no place to hide. "Do you still believe in me?"

"Yes," he said, "I still believe in you."

"Do you mean that? I mean really, *really* mean it?"

"Of course I do."

Could there possibly have been another answer?

Still her eyes wouldn't let go of his. It was as though she was testing him, challenging his faith in her innocence. He readied himself for whatever might come next. Would she ask him to take an oath, perhaps, or to repeat *Samara didn't do it* twenty times over?

What she actually did say took him by surprise. "Then come home with me." And the way she said it, it wasn't quite a command, yet it wasn't simply a question, either. It was something halfway in between. It was a request, he decided, a request with the *please* left out, lest it sound too much like begging. And, as before, there could be only one possible answer.

"Yes," said Jaywalker, "I'll come home with you."

It was raining out on Centre Street, an icy rain that turned to sleet even as they stood there, waiting for a cab.

"C'mon," Jaywalker said to Samara, and they bent into the sleet and began walking uptown, arms locked together. At Canal Street, a little old Korean woman was huddled in a doorway, hawking umbrellas. "Faw dolla, faw dolla."

Jaywalker reached into his side pocket for four singles. It was a New York thing, knowing never to carry your money in your wallet. Walking up to the woman, he asked, "Is there any chance this one's going to last longer than the one you sold me two weeks ago?"

"Three dolla."

"Deal."

The sleet was coming down even harder, and by now the pavement had a coating of slush on it. Even huddled tightly together underneath their three-dolla special, Samara and

Jaywalker were getting pelted. And still there were no cabs in sight. Another New York thing.

So they ducked down into the subway and rode the Lexington Avenue local uptown, the about-to-be-convicted "billionheiress" and her about-to-be-suspended lawyer.

By the time they emerged at Sixty-eighth Street, the sleet had changed over again, this time to snow. It was a wet, heavy snow, lit up by the streetlamps like soggy corn flakes, but it was better than what had preceded it. Jaywalker wrapped one arm around Samara's shoulders, leaving the other to carry both his briefcase and the umbrella, an easy enough task if it had had two hands attached to it. He pondered the situation for a moment. The trial was all but over, he knew, and with one day left on his ticket, chances were he would have no more use for the briefcase. Then again, life could be funny, and one of the best parts about it was that you never knew for sure. So, at the next corner, he tossed the umbrella into a wire trash can.

"Hey," said Samara, "you paid good money for that thing. I could've carried it."

"No point," Jaywalker explained. "Once they get wet, they're no good anymore. That's the whole idea. That woman back there on Canal Street? She's their vice president in charge of market research. In two years she'll have enough money to buy Manhattan, dismantle it and ship it back home."

Samara laughed at the thought, a hearty laugh, totally free of self-consciousness. Like her tears on the witness stand, her frequent lapses into locker-room language and just about everything else about her, there was nothing restrained about her laughter, nothing contrived or controlled. The tabloid writers who'd been so quick to tag her as a gold digger had gotten it all wrong. The truth was, she operated without a plan, Samara did. If something struck her as funny, she laughed at it like a child. If it struck her as sad, she bawled. And if it struck her as absurd, she came right out and said so, without measuring her words or bothering to pretty them up.

Her laughter now was infectious, downright contagious. In spite of himself, or perhaps because of what the two of them had been through over the last couple of hours, Jaywalker found himself letting go and laughing right along with her. They laughed at his dumb remark, at the fact that they were laughing at it, at their dripping hair and their soaking clothes. They laughed because they were together. This time tomorrow she would be in jail and he'd no longer be a lawyer, but right now they were together, heading to her place for the night, and that was enough.

Or, as Samara would have so eloquently stated, *fuck tomorrow*.

When they reached her town house, Jaywalker noticed a gray Ford Crown Victoria idling across the street. There were two overfed white guys sitting in it, and the windshield was fogged up where coffee containers sat on the dashboard. Tom Burke had evidently taken to heart Judge Sobel's suggestion of stationing detectives outside Samara's building. If Samara noticed them, she said nothing. It took a cop to spot a cop, Jaywalker knew from his DEA days. Then again, Samara had done her share of flirting with the law, and not much got past her. Maybe she'd noticed them and just didn't care.

He let go of her just long enough for her to open the door to her town house. Once inside, they looked at each other in the light and began laughing all over again. They were completely covered with snow, both of them. Their clothing, their hair, their eyebrows, their eyelashes.

"You're going to look great when you're old and gray," said Jaywalker. He'd meant it as a compliment; he'd always loved the contrast of a young face, whether male or female,

against a shock of gray hair. But all it earned from Samara
was a sharp jab to the ribs. He caught her by the wrist, and
found the other one, as well. They were tiny, so tiny he
could completely circle his fingers around them. Drawing
them against his chest, he wrapped his arms around her. All
he'd meant to do was to immobilize her, to tie her hands up
and prevent them from inflicting further damage. Or maybe
not. But if he'd expected her to struggle, she surprised him
once again. He felt her body go soft in his arms, and his
reaction was to look down at her, at the precise moment
she'd chosen to look up at him. Their eyes locked, and Jaywalker found himself experiencing the same sensation he'd
felt the very first time he'd seen her, and then the first time
he'd seen her all over again, six years later. Only this time
they weren't sitting across a desk in his office or squinting
through wire-reinforced glass in a visiting room on Rikers
Island. This time she was in his arms.

They peeled off each other's snow-caked clothes, dropping them in a heap on the hallway floor. Almost as if
there'd been preset ground rules, Samara stopped when she
got to his boxer shorts, Jaywalker at her bra, her dental-
floss thong, and her electronic ankle bracelet. He didn't
actually *know* it was a thong until she turned away from
him and motioned him to follow as she began climbing the
stairs. *God*, he thought, looking upward at her, *whoever
invented those things deserves a Nobel prize.* And for the
first time in his life, he was prepared to forgive Bill for
having been rendered totally helpless in front of Monica.
Well, perhaps not exactly in front of her.

They ended up in the den, or perhaps it was the study;
Jaywalker couldn't remember. It was a modest-sized room,
dominated by a huge fireplace, which in turn was surrounded by an equally oversize U-shaped sectional sofa.
There were logs laid in the fireplace, and he looked around
for a book of matches. But she picked up what looked like
a TV remote, pointed and clicked, and just like that, fire

happened. It might not have been Jaywalker's weapon of choice, but it did the trick.

"So," she said, standing there in the firelight. "Is it *after* yet?"

"It's close enough," said Jaywalker.

Even as extended foreplay goes, seven and a half years is an awfully long time. With a buildup of that length, it would have been entirely understandable, indeed all but inevitable, that the reality would fall far short of the anticipation.

It didn't.

Finally going to bed with Samara turned out to exceed everything Jaywalker had imagined, hoped for and dreamed about in his wildest and most X-rated fantasies. If her bethonged backside had driven him crazy, so now did the rest of her. But there was more. Not only was she physically exquisite, she was, well, *talented*. So much so, in fact, that once or twice Jaywalker caught himself remembering the details of her past. But each time his hesitation proved to be only fleeting and soon evaporated. And if Samara didn't try to make him feel as though he were her first ever (a tall order if ever there'd been one), she somehow managed to succeed in making him feel that he was her best ever, smothering any self-doubts he might have had with an unending barrage of kisses, touches, caresses, moans and all sorts of other stuff that in the end would leave him breathlessly begging for less. Totally forgotten were any concerns over the freshness of his breath, the size of his personal endowment or the satisfaction of Samara's needs; all three of those areas seemed to work out just fine, thank you. Suffice it to say that in spite of however great the anticipation might have been, the experience itself proved to be anything but anticlimactic, both figuratively and literally. In fact, at one such moment, Samara was heard to remark, "That's three months off your life expectancy so far."

"Me?" Jaywalker gasped. "Then *you've* lost *years*."

"It's not the same, silly. Don't you know *anything?*"

This from a woman twenty years his junior, sitting astride him totally naked, her small breasts framing a pair of outrageously pointed nipples. And already she was busy at work trying to deprive him of yet another month of his life.

At some point, when they'd been forced to come up for air, Samara caught Jaywalker pinching the bridge of his nose. "Headache?" she asked.

He nodded.

"I'm sure Barry left some aspirin here," she said. "Or some ibuprofen. He was a regular walking pharmacy."

"I can't take any of that stuff," said Jaywalker, who'd developed an allergy late in life. "My head blows up, and I look like a manatee."

"So what can we do for you?" she asked.

"You've done more than you can imagine."

"Seriously."

"Seriously? I guess I should eat something," he said. "It's been about a day and a half."

"And by something, you probably don't mean ice cream."

The thought of brain-freeze caused him to reach for the bridge of his nose again. "Probably not."

"Pizza?"

"You've got pizza?"

"No," said Samara. "But I've got a phone. This is New York, remember?"

At his insistence, they ordered not one but two medium pies. When the pizzas arrived thirty minutes later, they kept the plain one for themselves. The pepperoni, meatball and extra cheese, Jaywalker had redelivered to the gray Crown Victoria across the street.

"So what's a manatee?" Samara asked. They were sitting on the rug in front of the fire, eating pizza. Collectively, they were down to an ankle bracelet.

"A manatee's a sea cow. And trust me, you wouldn't want me looking like one."

"I do trust you," she said. "And I'm sorry I didn't trust you enough to tell you about that other stabbing business, and about being Samantha Musgrove. I guess I thought that as long as I didn't tell anyone, it would be like the whole thing was just one long bad dream that had never really happened."

"Whatever made you pick *Samara?* I mean, *Moss* I can understand. Short and sweet, easy to remember. But *Samara?*"

"Do you know what a samara is?"

"No," he confessed.

It was her turn to teach. "A samara is the seedpod that grows on a maple tree. It has a pair of tiny little wings attached to it. When it leaves the tree, the wings catch the wind, and it flies far, far away, so it can begin a new life all on its own."

"Nice," said Jaywalker. "And you were only fourteen when you realized that was you?"

"I was a very old fourteen."

"So you were. Samara," he said, just to hear the sound of it. "Pretty name, Samara Moss."

"The Moss part was because I was hoping for a soft landing. It beat *Musgrove,* anyway."

Jaywalker nodded solemnly, or about as solemnly as a naked man eating pizza can nod. He couldn't be sure, but it felt like his headache was already beginning to melt away. Maybe it was a good idea to remember to eat something every day, he decided.

"Funny," said Samara, "in all these years, this is only the second time I've told anyone about it."

"About what?"

"The Samantha Musgrove stuff."

"I'm very honored," said Jaywalker, wiping a string of cheese off his chin with the back of his hand. "When was the first?"

"Eight years ago. Back when I believed in true love, sharing your innermost secrets, and all that *till-death-do-us-part* crap."

Jaywalker had just taken another bite, and when his lower jaw dropped, so did a mouthful of pizza, not something to be advised when one happens to be both sitting and naked. The thing was, his ears had heard the words Samara had just said, but his brain was still struggling to make sense of them. "You told—"

She nodded.

"—Barry?"

"We were getting married," Samara said with an explanatory shrug. "I thought I loved him. I figured he had a right to know."

"You told him about the whole thing?"

Another nod.

"The rape, the stabbing, even that your name had once been—"

"All of it."

"—Samantha Musgrove?"

"Yes."

"Musgrove, Musgrove," Jaywalker repeated. "Where have I heard that name before?"

"At the trial. It was my name, back in Indiana. That's what we've been talking about this whole time."

"I know, I know. But where else?"

"The Seconal," said Samara. "Remember the name of the doctor who prescribed it? The doctor who turned out not to exist? Samuel Musgrove. It's how as soon as I found the Seconal, I knew right away it had to be part of the frame-up. Only I couldn't tell you, not without going into the whole past—"

"Whoa."

"Whoa, what?"

"Who else besides Barry knew about the name Musgrove?"

She seemed to think for a minute, before saying, "Nobody."

"Are you sure?"

"Sure, I'm sure. Until Friday, when you told me Mr. Burke had found out about it, Barry was the only person I ever told."

Jaywalker jumped up and immediately began pacing the room, totally oblivious to his nakedness. The headache was back with a vengeance, pounding between his eyes and at his temples. Samara was staring at him as though he and his mind had suddenly parted company. But when she opened her mouth to say something, he held up a hand and shushed her.

Barry had known about the earlier stabbing, and about the name Samantha Musgrove. No one else had. Could Barry have ordered the Seconal, using the name Samuel Musgrove, to make it look as though Samara had done it? And if Barry had kept aspirin or ibuprofen at Samara's town house, as she said he had, that meant he'd spent time there. If he'd wanted to, he could have brought the Seconal there on one of his visits. He could have taken one of her knives, too.

"Tell me," Jaywalker said. "Did Barry have a key to this place?"

"He did once. So I guess so. Why?"

"What time is it?"

Samara got up, disappeared into another room and called out, "Two-fifteen."

"A phone," said Jaywalker. "I need a phone."

When she returned, she was wearing a robe. Apparently she preferred to have something on if he was going to flip out and she was going to have to take him to an emergency room. But she did have a cordless phone in one hand.

Jaywalker grabbed it and punched in a number. Funny, the old ones he could always remember. It was short-term memory he had a problem with, frequently forgetting his own number. Then again, he didn't call himself all that often.

"Unlisted subscriber information," a woman said.

"This is Detective Anthony Bonfiglio," said Jaywalker, "Twenty-first Squad Homicide, shield two-two-oh-five. I need an unlisted number for a Thomas Francis Burke. Stat."

He motioned Samara to bring him something to write with. She found a pen and a sheet of paper.

"I'm showing one Thomas F. Burke," said the woman, "five unlisted Thomas Burkes without middle names or initials, and three T. Burkes."

"I'll take them all."

She read him the listings. "I'll need a written confirmation by seventeen hundred today," she told him. She gave him a fax number.

"You got it," said Jaywalker, not bothering to write down the number.

He spoke briefly with two Tom Burkes and three nameless women, none of whom seemed too thrilled to have been woken at, as one of them so artfully put it, "three fucking o'clock in the fucking morning." But on the sixth try, he heard a familiar, if sleepy, voice.

"Tom, wake up, it's Jaywalker."

"Jesus. What time is it?"

"I don't know," Jaywalker lied. "A little after midnight."

"How did you get my number?"

"Ve haff our vays."

"What do you want?" Burke asked.

"I need you to get up and get dressed."

"Are you nuts?"

"Probably," Jaywalker conceded. "But I think I've just about got this case figured out."

"As I understand it," said Burke, "so does the jury."

"The jury doesn't have a clue. And neither have you or I, all this time. But when you meet me, I'm going to explain it to you."

"I'm sure you are," said Burke. "In court, at nine-thirty."

"Tom?"

There was silence on the other end, and for a moment Jaywalker was afraid he'd blown it. Then he heard a "What?" that sounded somewhere between exasperated and resigned.

"Tom, you know I'd never fuck with you, right?"

"What time is it really?"

"Two-thirty, quarter of three. Something like that."

"You who'd never fuck with me."

"I need you to trust me on this, Tom. I need you to meet me at Barry's building as soon as you can. And, Tom?"

"Yes?"

"Bring your shield."

"My shield?"

"You know," said Jaywalker, "that phony tin the old man gives you guys, in case you get stopped for speeding or hitting on a hooker."

Burke showed up wearing a leather bomber jacket, jeans and a Yankee cap. But at least he was dry. Jaywalker had been forced to retrieve his soaking clothes from the pile he and Samara had created earlier in the evening. His coat had been so wet, however, that she had forced him to put on one of Barry's, even though the sleeves came to just below Jaywalker's elbows and the shoulders were so narrow that they threatened to cut off his blood supply. The guy must've been an absolute shrimp, he decided.

Burke wasn't alone. He'd managed to track down Detective Bonfiglio and bring him along, perhaps as a bodyguard, perhaps as a witness to Jaywalker's need for civil commitment.

"Evening, counselor," said the detective.

"Evening, Tony. By the way, you owe the Unlisted Subscriber Operator a fax by seventeen hundred hours."

"Say what?"

"Never mind."

"Cut it out, girls," said Burke. Then, to Jaywalker, "This better be good."

"This is better than good," Jaywalker assured him. "This is absolutely unbelievable."

"That's exactly what I'm afraid of."

It turned out that José Lugo was working the midnight-to-eight shift on the door, so they didn't need their shields after all. Which was just as well, because Jaywalker had bought his at a Times Square novelty shop. Lugo got hold of Anthony Mazzini, who, though groggy-eyed and grumbling, produced a passkey and, once the POLICE DEPARTMENT DO NOT CROSS tape had been lifted away and the crime scene seal broken, let the three of them into Penthouse A.

Once inside, it took them a few minutes to locate the circuit breakers and turn on the lights. It was immediately apparent that the tape and the seal had done their job. Nothing appeared to have been touched since Jaywalker's earlier visit.

"Okay," said Burke to Jaywalker. "Make like Charlie Chan. Explain to us what you think you've figured out."

"Sure," said Jaywalker, "I can do that. But remember, I said *just about*. I now know who killed Barry, but I'm still trying to figure out exactly how he managed to pull it off."

"He?" said Bonfiglio. "You mean to tell us your girlfriend's a trannie?"

"Be nice, Tony," warned Jaywalker. "You can come off looking like a hero in this thing, or the genius who locked up an innocent woman and wouldn't let go. Your choice."

"I got a choice for you, dickhead."

"Hey," said Burke, "I said cut it out."

Jaywalker led them into the kitchen. The outline of Barry's body was still on the floor. A year and a half had passed, but he might just as well have died yesterday.

"Okay," said Jaywalker. "See this coat I'm wearing?" With some difficulty he raised his arms, to demonstrate how short the sleeves were on him.

"Yeah," said Bonfiglio, "it's a thing a beauty."

"It was Barry's," said Jaywalker. "He kept it at Samara's, along with a lot of other stuff. Clothes, medication, personal items. In other words, he stayed there from time to time. He had his own key. He had access."

Neither Burke nor Bonfiglio seemed overly impressed.

"Barry was dying from cancer," said Jaywalker. "He had an inoperable malignant tumor that was going to kill him in a matter of months, maybe even weeks. Samara thought Barry was a hypochondriac and bought his explanation that he had the flu. But Barry knew. And the thing is, he hated Samara. He hated the way she humiliated him by running around and seeing other men, and it drove him crazy to think that when he did die, she'd end up with half his estate. He even tried to get Alan Manheim to write her out of his will, but as Manheim explained to him, it wouldn't do any good, Samara would still get half, under equitable distribution."

"You sure that's the law?" asked Bonfiglio.

"That's the law," said Burke.

"So what does Barry do?" Jaywalker asked rhetorically. "He figures out a way to disinherit Samara. He takes out the life insurance policy himself. He tells Samara to sign the application, and like a good little girl, she does, without ever looking at it. A week or so later, when Bill Smythe gets the bill and asks Barry about it, Barry tells him to go ahead and pay the premium out of the joint account. Smythe does."

Jaywalker was pacing now, trying to put the pieces together. "Do you remember why Samara goes over to Barry's the evening of the murder?"

"To kill him?" was Bonfiglio's guess.

"He asked her to," said Burke.

"Right. And what happens?"

"They eat Chinks," said Bonfiglio.

"Forget what they ate. What happens next?"

"They get into a fight," said Bonfiglio.

"A shouting argument," said Burke.

"Exactly. Over some bullshit thing. Samara can't even recall what it was, only that Barry started it. That's important. Remember," said Jaywalker, "he knew how to push her buttons. And once they're arguing, Barry makes sure their voices are loud enough to be overheard and recognized."

Burke nodded, but only tentatively.

"Samara storms out, just like she said she did on the stand."

"And right about then," said Bonfiglio, "Spiderman crawls through the window an' offs Barry."

Jaywalker ignored the remark. It was actually working better this way, with the detective having cast himself as the sarcastic doubter and Burke forced to play the role of an impartial third person.

"Here's where it gets interesting," Jaywalker explained. "Barry downs a stiff drink and a couple of Seconals. Maybe he'd done that earlier, maybe he excuses himself for a moment and does it now. It doesn't matter. He takes a knife he swiped from Samara's some time ago."

"Bullshit," said Bonfiglio.

Jaywalker said nothing. Instead, he walked to a set of drawers and rummaged through them until he found a table knife with a rounded tip. He wasn't about to trust Bonfiglio with anything sharper. Handing it to the detective, he said, "Show us how you'd stab me in the heart, as many ways as you can. You know, from the front, the rear, the side, whatever."

"Fuck you."

"Do it," said Burke.

Bonfiglio scowled but did as he'd been told. He proceeded to mimic stabbing Jaywalker from the front, first with his right hand on the knife raised above him, then his left, and then both hands. He repeated the process underhanded. He walked around behind Jaywalker, grabbed him unnecessarily roughly around the neck and brought the knife to his chest that way. He tried a couple of other variations, as well.

"How many does that make?" Jaywalker asked.

"Ten, twelve," said Burke.

"What do they all have in common?"

Burke shrugged. Bonfiglio scowled, looking as though he wished he could play the game for real.

"Every single time you went to kill me," said Jaywalker, "you did it with the knife held so the blade was up and down. If Samara had stabbed Barry, that's how she would have done it, too. Anybody would have. That's how you knife someone. But if she'd done it that way, the blade would have gone in perpendicular to Barry's ribs and no doubt would have struck one of them, or even two. Only it didn't. How do we know that?"

"Hirsch," said Burke.

"Right. Hirsch was crystal-clear on that point. The blade went in flat. That's why it never hit a rib. Hard to do, unless…"

"Unless what?" It was actually Bonfiglio who asked the question.

"Unless," said Jaywalker, "you were feeling your ribs with the fingers of one hand to locate the soft spot, so you could get the blade in laterally, right between them."

There was an eerie silence in the room. Burke walked over to the chalk outline of the body on the floor, and looked down at it. "Interesting," he admitted. "But it doesn't begin to explain how he managed to get the knife to Samara's afterwards, hide it behind the toilet, come back here, collapse on the floor and die. Does it?"

"No," said Jaywalker, "but that's actually the easy part. Remember that word *access*. Barry had hidden those things days earlier. Weeks, maybe. He drew some of his own blood, or stuck a finger. Remember, the total amount on the knife, the blouse and the towel wasn't much at all. And the blood was dried. Those things could have been planted anytime. And he hid them where the blood would stay dry and intact. Sitting in the toilet tank, the logical place for Samara to hide them if she really wanted to be stupid enough to save them as souvenirs, the blood would have dissolved in the water. After a flush or two, it would have been history."

Burke was still far from being convinced. "So you concede the knife was Samara's?"

"Absolutely," said Jaywalker.

"Yet you claim it wasn't the murder weapon. Or, as you'd like us to believe, the suicide weapon."

"Right."

At that point Jaywalker reached into one pocket of Barry's coat and, with considerable difficulty, withdrew the six knives he'd taken before leaving Samara's. The coat might have fit horribly, but it came in handy for his rabbit-out-of-the-hat moment. Or, to be more precise, his steak-knives-out-of-the-pocket moment.

"Voila!" he announced.

Burke paid close attention, while Bonfiglio pretended his best not to. But even he was watching.

"These are Samara's steak knives," said Jaywalker. "They come in sets of six or eight. Never an odd number, right? One of them ended up behind Samara's toilet tank. That makes seven, which leaves one. And that's the one that Barry used to kill himself with."

"And then ate?" Bonfiglio wanted to know.

"No," said Jaywalker, playing the straight man. "If he'd swallowed it, Hirsch would have found it."

"So where is it?" asked Burke and Bonfiglio in perfect tandem.

"I don't know," said Jaywalker.

"Great," said Bonfiglio. "You got everything figgered out but the kicker."

Burke's wrinkled forehead indicated he pretty much agreed. "You get over that hump," he said, "and maybe we've got something to talk about. But without it, I'm afraid…"

"I know," said Jaywalker. "And for the life of me, I can't figure out how Barry got rid of it. I know this much. With the alcohol and Seconal in him, he could've handled the pain, could even have pulled the knife out. You know, the way that Crocodile Hunter guy pulled the stingray thing out of his heart before dying. I figure Barry had a minute left at that point, certainly a half a minute, before he would have passed out and collapsed. So it's got to be here somewhere."

"We gave this place a thorough toss," said Bonfiglio. "The crime scene guys did, too. If there was a knife here, we woulda found it."

"Like you found the Seconal Barry planted in Samara's kitchen cabinet?"

"What Seconal?" Burke asked.

"Somebody phoned in a phony prescription a week or so before Barry's death. It was supposed to be for Samara, but she never knew anything about it. She found it among her spices and called me to come see it. Think about that for a minute. If it was hers, and if she'd used it to drug Barry before stabbing him, why would she bring it to my attention? Why wouldn't she just throw it away? What's more, the doctor who prescribed it doesn't exist. I was going to ask her about it at trial, but like a jerk, I decided against it. I was afraid that the name of the phantom doctor sounded too much like Samara Moss, her maiden name.

"Now get this," Jaywalker continued. "When Samara fled Indiana, she left the rape and the stabbing behind her. In the fourteen years since, she's never told a soul about it, or that her true name was Samantha Musgrove. Not even I knew about it. Nobody did. With one exception."

"Barry," said the chorus.

"Right. Now see if you can guess what the name of the phantom doctor was on the Seconal bottle."

When there were no takers, Jaywalker produced the bottle from the other pocket of Barry's coat and handed it to Burke.

"Samuel Musgrove, M.D.," read Burke.

"Bingo," said Jaywalker.

"Okay," said Burke, "so Barry could have done that, planted the Seconal. I'll give you that much. But let's get back to the eighth knife. Want to tell us where it is?"

"My guess is it's got to be right here, in the kitchen." He proceeded to divide the room into three, assigning them each a section to search. Jaywalker took the third that included the refrigerator and freezer, and the microwave. He gave Burke most of the cabinets. Bonfiglio ended up with the sink, the trash can, and the dishwasher, grumbling that they'd already been done, "with negative results."

They searched in silence for fifteen minutes.

Jaywalker came up dry.

So did Burke.

But sometimes one out of three can be good enough. When it happened, it happened quietly, with no fanfare. When Bonfiglio went to open the dishwasher, he found it was in the locked position, as though ready to run a load of dishes. But when he lifted the handle and opened it, it became clear that that wasn't the case.

Bonfiglio looked carefully. What he saw was a fairly full load of dishes, all of them clean. And there, down on the lower rack, inside the utensil holder among the spoons, forks and table knives, was the eighth steak knife. Barry Tannenbaum had done just as Jaywalker had figured. Fortified on alcohol and Seconal, he'd found the soft spot between his ribs, plunged the knife into his chest and pulled it out. Then he'd placed it in the loaded, soaped and ready-to-run dishwasher. All he had to do at that point was to close it and push the start button. Then he collapsed on the floor and bled to death.

"Nice work, detective," said Jaywalker, taking care to keep his voice free of sarcasm or irony. In the end, he knew, he'd be needing Bonfiglio on his side.

"Thanks," said the detective, the first suggestion of a hero's smile beginning to spread across his face.

Joseph Teller

"Absofuckinglutely unbelievable," said Burke.

"Don't say I didn't warn you," said Jaywalker.

The best part, of course, had been leaving it to Bonfiglio to find the knife. Having tried cases for two decades now, Jaywalker had come to learn a valuable lesson. Sometimes the very smartest thing you could do was to let the jurors solve the final piece of the puzzle themselves. So once Jaywalker had put it all together—with a slight assist from his wife, returning to him in a dream to nag him about unloading the dishwasher—he'd tucked it away and saved the moment of triumph for the detective.

31

YES, NO, MAYBE SO

It was quite a morning in Part 51.

The jurors, having arrived earlier only to be told to suspend their deliberations, were led into the courtroom and seated in the jury box. The media filled the first three benches of the spectator section, on both sides of the center aisle. The rest of the rows were packed, leaving a good fifty people standing along the back and side walls.

Word gets around fast in a courthouse.

With Samara and Jaywalker sitting at the defense table, Tom Burke rose slowly to his feet. "Pursuant to our earlier conversation, with respect to the case of The People versus Samara Moss Tannenbaum, true name Samantha Musgrove, The People hereby move for a mistrial."

"You understand the full implications of that," said Judge Sobel. "As I'm sure you know, when the defense obtains a mistrial, the case can be retried in front of another jury. But when a mistrial is granted on the prosecution's motion, jeopardy attaches, and the case is over forever."

"Yes," said Burke.

"And I understand your office will be filing a written statement setting forth the reasons for your motion."

"That's correct."

"Mr. Jaywalker?"

"I don't believe we have any objection."

"The motion is granted," said Judge Sobel.

Just like that.

The media went absolutely nuts. Broadcasts were interrupted, specials were hastily put together, and headlines were reset. Before he could get out of the courthouse, Jaywalker was besieged for interviews with Oprah, Katie Couric, Larry King, *Court TV* and all the late-night hosts. Characteristically, he turned them all down, although he was thinking about Jon Stewart's offer when he caught somebody referring to him as the new "celebrity lawyer." At that point, he broke into a run and disappeared from view.

Samara was only a little less bashful. She faced the lights and microphones for about twelve seconds, just long enough to say how happy she was, and to thank Burke, Bonfiglio, the judge, the jury and Jaywalker. If there happened to be any future Oscar winners or Miss Americas within earshot, they might have learned a thing or two. Though probably not.

It turned out that the jurors had indeed stood at eleven-to-one for conviction. But the holdout had been neither Carmelita Rosado, the kindergarten teacher, nor Angelina Olivetti, the actress and waitress. It had been Juror Number 12, George Stetson, the ramrod-straight retired marine colonel Jaywalker had been unable to knock off because he'd run out of challenges. "They would have had to carry me out in a body bag," Stetson was quoted as saying later, "before I'd have surrendered." Several of his fellow jurors shared a somewhat different recollection, that Stetson had in fact been prepared to change his vote to guilty earlier that morning, which would have made it unanimous, when they'd suddenly been directed to cease their deliberations.

That Friday afternoon Jaywalker was officially suspended from the practice of law for three years, effective immediately. A petition started making the rounds, asking the disciplinary committee judges to reconsider their sentence in light of Jaywalker's latest success, but he quickly put an end to it. Three years was actually sounding pretty damn good to him at that point. Not too long ago, in fact, a client of his, a career burglar facing twelve-and-a-half to twenty-five, had heard about the suspension.

"Three years?" he'd said incredulously. "They wanna give you a *trey? Muthafucka,* I wish they'd offa that kinda time to me. *Sheeet,* I could do me a trey standin' on my dick."

After the previous night, Jaywalker wouldn't have been able to do much of anything standing on his dick. Still, he figured he could do the three years, one way or another.

Jaywalker's love affair with Samara lasted longer than he thought it would. They went out for the better part of six months, if you were willing to adopt Samara's trial-testimony definition of going out as having sex on a regular basis. Indeed, with a little luck, their relationship might have turned out to be one of those rarest things of all, a love affair complete with a storybook ending. Samara was getting her inheritance after all, and Jaywalker his long-anticipated sabbatical. In a word, they were both free.

But evidently it wasn't meant to be.

When it unraveled, it unraveled in a hurry. They were sitting in front of the fireplace one night, the same fireplace they'd first made love in front of. But it was July, and the only fire this time was at the far end of a generous joint Samara had expertly rolled for the two of them. They were talking about the trial. They did that infrequently, but they did it. It had been Jaywalker's last trial, after all, and Samara's first *and* last. A watershed event for both of them.

"How did you figure out there had to be another knife in the dishwasher?" she asked him, her eyes watery from the smoke but as arresting as ever.

"It had to be there somewhere," said Jaywalker. "The

dishwasher seemed a logical enough place. The refrigerator or the freezer would have destroyed any fingerprints, but the blood would have been preserved. So I figured the dishwasher was a good bet." For some reason, he realized, he'd shied away from telling her about the dream he'd had. That would remain his secret, his and his wife's.

"Pretty clever of us, huh?"

"Us?"

"Yeah," said Samara, with a mischievous grin. "You deserve credit for figuring it out."

"And you?"

"Is my case really over?"

"Yup."

"They can never try me again, no matter what?"

"No matter what. It'd be double jeopardy."

"And we're both adults?"

"I certainly am."

She smiled, and for a moment Jaywalker thought she was reacting to his clever reply. But her smile was just a bit too smug and stayed on her face just a moment too long for it to be simply that. It was a smile of satisfaction, a smile of triumph over having pulled something off despite overwhelming odds. But Jaywalker had absolutely no clue what it really meant.

So he asked her. "What?" he said.

"Nothing."

"C'mon," he said. "You can trust me."

She smiled again and took a long hit from the joint. "You don't really think it was Barry who put that knife in the dishwasher, do you?"

Jaywalker said nothing. He probably couldn't have if he'd wanted to. All he was aware of was a rushing noise in his ears, so deafening as to drown out everything else. Her words, his thoughts, everything.

And that was it, the end of the conversation. What was more, she would never, ever go there again, no matter how hard he pushed her. It was as though smoking the joint had loosened her tongue for a moment, but only for a moment.

So it was never as though he really knew one way or the other. But that was the problem, right there. It would have been okay if he'd known she was guilty. Hell, he'd represented enough guilty people in his day, and had gotten his share of them off and then some. He could have lived with knowing she was guilty.

It was the *not* knowing that proved to be intolerable, the notion that she might have been playing him all along. And every time he would confront her and ask her, she would deflect his questions and dodge his accusations. She'd say something meant to sound funny, like, "You always said it didn't matter to you one way or the other," or "You're not my lawyer anymore, so our conversations aren't privileged, are they?" Only her comments never sounded funny to Jaywalker.

So he was left to wonder.

He would fall asleep wondering, and he'd wake up wondering. He'd wonder while they were making love. Was the woman in his arms the innocent victim of a sinister frameup that had come perilously close to working? Or was she a serial stabber who emerged, locustlike, every twelve or fourteen years to strike again? And when he caught himself the third time—or perhaps it was even the fourth or fifth—counting the steak knives left in Samara's kitchen drawer before going upstairs and climbing into bed with her, just to make sure they were all present and accounted for, he decided it was just too much.

Tom Burke had begun his summation by saying, "Sometimes things aren't what they seem to be. But sometimes they are." When you came right down to it, maybe the reason why Samara had seemed so guilty for so long was because she was.

Years and years ago, when Jaywalker's daughter had

been a toddler of two, she'd picked up an expression, latched on to it, and used it whenever she was asked a yes-or-no question. *"Yes, no, maybe so,"* she would chant in a lilting, singsong voice. As cute as it was, it meant absolutely nothing, of course. All it did was list the possibilities. But in her two-year-old wisdom, his daughter had been smarter than Tom Burke, smarter than Anthony Bonfiglio, smarter by far than Jaywalker. Truth could be a slippery thing, far more elusive and hard to get your hands around than a simple black-or-white, up-or-down concept like guilty or not guilty.

Sometimes things aren't what they seem to be.

Sometimes they are.

And sometimes, you just don't know.

* * * * *

*Turn the page for
an excerpt from*

Bronx Justice,

*the next Jaywalker case from
Joseph Teller.*

*Coming in 2010,
only from
MIRA Books.*

Jaywalker is dreaming when the ringing of his phone jars him awake. Something about hiking with his wife in the Canadian Rockies. He understands right away that it has to have been a dream, because his wife has been dead for nearly ten years now, and he hasn't hiked the Rockies in twice that long.

Groping out in the darkness for the phone, his first fear is for his daughter. Is she out driving? Riding with some pimply-faced boyfriend who's had his learner's permit for two weeks now and thinks of driving as some sort of video game? Then he remembers. His daughter is in her early thirties. She has a husband with no pimples, a child of her own, a career and a house in New Jersey.

"Hello?" Jaywalker says into the phone, then holds his breath and readies himself for the worst. The clock radio next to the phone glows three-seventeen.

"Pete?" says an unfamiliar male voice.

"I think," says Jaywalker, "that you may have dialed the wrong number. What number were you trying to—"

The line goes dead. No "Sorry," no "Ooops." Just a click, followed by silence and eventually a dial tone.

Jaywalker recradles the phone. He lies on his back in the

dark, feeling his pulse pounding in his temples. Relief and annoyance duel for his attention, but only briefly. For already, Jaywalker is elsewhere. He's lying in bed in the dark, to be sure, but somehow his hair is brown instead of gray, his face less lined, his body more muscular. And his wife lies beside him, her warm body pressed against his back.

"Who was it?" she asks him.

"A mother," he says. "A mother whose son has just been arrested. A rape case. And it sounds like a bad one."

"For them," says Jaywalker's wife. "But that means a good one for you, right?"

"Right," agrees Jaywalker. He's not yet thirty, this younger version of him. He's been out of Legal Aid for a little over a year now, struggling to build a practice on his own. And *struggling* is definitely the operative word here. So he knows his wife is right: what's bad for the young man and his family is at the same time good for the lawyer and his. It's one of the strange paradoxes of criminal law that Jaywalker will never quite get comfortable with, that his earning a living is dependent upon the suffering of others.

What he doesn't know, what he has absolutely no way of knowing at this point, as he lies in the dark, is that this new case will be different, that it will mark a crossroads in his career and in his life. Should he live to be a hundred, no case that will ever come his way will end up affecting him as this one will. Before he's done with it, and it with him, it will change him in ways that will be as profound as they are unimaginable. It will transform him, molding him and pounding him and shaping him into the lawyer and the man he is today, almost thirty years later. So this is more than just the case he'll forever wake up to when the phone rings in the middle of the night. This is the case that he'll retry in his mind over and over again for the rest of his days, changing a phrase here, adding a word there, tweaking his summation for the hundredth—no, the thousandth—time. And long after he's grown old and senile and has forgotten the names and faces and details of other cases, this is the one that Jaywalker will remember on his deathbed, as clearly and as vividly as if it began yesterday.